Shashi Deshpande is the author of several novels, most notably *The Dark Holds No Terrors*; *That Long Silence*, which won the Sahitya Akademi award; *Small Remedies, Moving On* and *In the Country of Deceit*. She also has four books for children, a collection of essays and several volumes of short stories to her credit. In addition, Deshpande has translated the memoirs of her father, the renowned dramatist and scholar, Shriranga, from Kannada into English, and has just completed translating a contemporary Marathi novel.

Shashi Deshpande and her husband live in Bangalore.

———————

'[Shashi Deshpande's] novels are extraordinary attempts at exploring the essential aloneness of an individual while simultaneously celebrating the amorphous entity called family, which can, by turns be claustrophobic and supportive...her special value lies in an uncompromising toughness, in her attempts to do what has never been attempted in English, her insistence on being read on her own terms and a refusal to be packaged according to the demands of the market'—Meenakshi Mukherjee in *The Hindu*

PRAISE FOR *MOVING ON*

'Riveting ... does not shirk from the big questions ... forces us to accept life in all its stifling details and magnificent unpredictability' —*India Today*

'*Moving On* moves us in unexpected ways'—*The Hindu*

'Complex, turbulent, engrossing...a saga that traces the epic dimensions of the human mind'—*Hindustan Times*

Moving On

SHASHI DESHPANDE

PENGUIN BOOKS

PENGUIN BOOKS
Published by the Penguin Group
Penguin Books India Pvt. Ltd, 11 Community Centre, Panchsheel Park, New Delhi
110 017, India
Penguin Group (USA) Inc., 375 Hudson Street, New York, New York 10014, USA
Penguin Group (Canada), 90 Eglinton Avenue East, Suite 700, Toronto, Ontario,
M4P 2Y3, Canada (a division of Pearson Penguin Canada Inc.)
Penguin Books Ltd, 80 Strand, London WC2R 0RL, England
Penguin Ireland, 25 St Stephen's Green, Dublin 2, Ireland (a division of Penguin
Books Ltd)
Penguin Group (Australia), 250 Camberwell Road, Camberwell, Victoria 3124,
Australia (a division of Pearson Australia Group Pty Ltd)
Penguin Group (NZ), 67 Apollo Drive, Rosedale, North Shore 0632, New Zealand
(a division of Pearson New Zealand Ltd)
Penguin Group (South Africa) (Pty) Ltd, 24 Sturdee Avenue, Rosebank, Johannesburg
2196, South Africa

Penguin Books Ltd, Registered Offices: 80 Strand, London WC2R 0RL, England

First published in Viking by Penguin Books India 2004
Published in Penguin Books 2008

Copyright © Shashi Deshpande 2004

10 9 8 7 6 5 4 3 2 1

ISBN 9780143064251

This is a work of fiction Names, characters, places and incidents are either the
product of the author's imagination or are used fictiously, and any resemblance to
actual persons, living or dead, events, or locales is entirely coincidental.

While every effort has been made to trace copyright holders and obtain permission,
this has not been possible in all cases; any omissions brought to our attention will
be remedied in future editions.

Typeset in Sabon by Mantra Virtual Services, New Delhi
Printed at Repro India Ltd., Navi Mumbai

CONTENTS

PART I

All the stories that have ever been told
are the stories of families
from Adam and of Eve onward.

Erica Jong,
Inventing Mamory

baba's diary

1 January 1997

The first day of the year seems a good day to begin what I have had in my mind for some time. Yet, it is over half an hour since I sat down, pen in hand, notebook before me, and I have only written the date. What is it that inhibits me? I have written before, and with a fair amount of ease. Though, of course, the writing I have done until now has been different; it was always writing for a purpose—papers for journals, a chapter for a textbook, letters, official memos. And what is my purpose now? Merely a need to scribble my thoughts. No, it is more than a need, it is an *urge* to do something about the chaotic jumble of thoughts and memories that have been troubling me so greatly. Such a vague purpose—if it is a purpose at all. But a sense of limited time urges me on. The awareness that my life is coming to a close makes me want to speak, to share my thoughts with someone. I imagine that this is a normal human emotion, for even my father, an otherwise inarticulate man, made me a confidant in his last days. Unlike my father, I have no one I can talk to. Therefore this book. A poor substitute for a human ear, but then, was I any more responsive than a blank sheet of paper?

I paid little attention to what my father was saying, I let the things he was saying slide over me, leaving me untouched.

So I thought. Now the things he said are coming back to me, they throng my mind and compel me to see my father differently. I thought him a quiet, sedate man; no, let me be honest, I thought him rather dull. But when I recollect his words, when I connect them to other, almost forgotten aspects of him, I see a man who was something of a rebel. He was also, what is even more rare, a man whose actions scrupulously followed his convictions. He was one of the many children of an orthodox and wealthy landed man—wealthy, that is, according to the standards of the time and the place they lived in. His father, like many others of his kind, identified himself as a 'landlord', as if it was a profession, when what it really meant was living a life of lordly inactivity. The family had enough land to enable them to live a life of ease, to marry their daughters into well-to-do families and to bring home daughters-in-law who came from equally wealthy, if not wealthier families.

My father, however, never fitted in. Even as a boy he was different from his siblings and cousins. The fact that he was the first in the family—and the village—to venture out for his school and college education tells its own story. Perhaps my grandfather (it seems strange to use the word for a man I had never heard of until I was nearly eighteen) imagined that my father's degree, if and when he got one, would enhance the family's prestige and status; he may also have hoped that it would increase the amount of dowry they could expect from a future father-in-law. However, my father returned with not just a BA degree, but something else that threw all the family plans into complete disarray: he came back a Gandhian. Those were the early days of Gandhiji's new movement. Today, it is easy to imagine that its influence was immediate and all-pervasive. But an event—whether a war, a natural disaster, or a change of rulers—means nothing to people unless it touches their lives, even if only tangentially. And for my father's village, isolated like so many were then, Gandhiji and the freedom movement were, I now surmise, only strange and distant cries. Suddenly, here it came into the family, touching their lives, not tangentially, but head on. Impacting on them catastrophically. For, not only had this son of a Brahmin family joined the movement, he had even gone to jail. At that time, and in that place, going to jail was not considered a badge of honour of patriotism. And to his father, his son's going to jail was not only an ignominy, it was treachery. How could he, the son of a man who had been created a Rao Bahadur by the British, go against them! For his mother, there was the additional horror of her son having lived in jail in close contact with people of all castes; she heard there had even been some Muslims among his cell mates! And so, a puja was performed to purify him; in fact, to purify the entire family. My father went through it mainly so as not to displease his mother. Perhaps his acquiescence lulled the family into complacency; the little rebellion, they must have thought, was over. Time to go on to the next thing, the inevitable solution for wayward sons: marriage. Once married, a young man would settle down and forget about his youthful escapades. So would my father, they thought. His involvement with the freedom struggle was, they were sure, only a brief fling. Little did they know. It was not just the freedom struggle that my father had aligned himself with; he had imbibed the entire Gandhian philosophy. What this meant they had no idea until my father made his announcement: yes, he would get married, but it would be to a girl he had chosen himself. This was bad enough, but what came next was infinitely worse; to them it was like the end of the world. For the girl he had chosen was a Harijan girl, an orphan who had been brought up as a daughter by his guru, the man who had initiated him into Gandhism.

Harijan. When he spoke to me, my father used the word coined by Gandhiji. But *his* father, who had a foul tongue even at the best of times (my father said that abuses slid off his tongue as comfortably as the Vishnu stotra or the Gayatri mantra did), used other words for the girl. My father did not specify the words, but I imagine the angry old man used the most abusive and derogatory ones he could find. Which only strengthened my father's resolve. His father threatened, his mother wept, the family was in turmoil, but my father remained firm. He walked out on them and in a few days he got married. His father then did the only thing he could do—he disowned his son ritually, he disinherited him legally. There was a complete severance between my father and his family; not even his mother could find any excuse for what he had done. My father too excised his past. He not only gave up his family, he even cast off his family name.

When, much later, he spoke of this to me, he said that he gave me the name Badri Narayan, a double-barrelled first name, so that the second part could function as a surname. He had come to know the difficulty of not having one in a place like Bombay. Like I said, I did not pay much attention to the story of his past. I was young, intent on my studies, concentrating on getting admission to a medical college. The unusualness of my father talking to me of his past did not really strike me. To me it was a distant tale. But I remember very distinctly how animated he was when he spoke of his dislike of the life his family led. I remember the vehemence with which he spoke of his hatred of the presumption of superiority of the Brahmins; his abhorrence of the sloth, the preoccupation with rituals and feasts, the enormous importance given to food and the idea of purity that centred around exclusions. 'I was a misfit there,' he said to me; I remember that. But, never having known the kind of life he spoke of, I was not able to imagine how much of a misfit he must have been, how impossible it must have been for him to live like the rest of them.

To go back to my father's story: yes, he married the orphaned Harijan girl. I can't remember whether my father told me her name, or anything more about her. I think he did not; there would have been no need for him to use her name even when she was alive—men didn't address wives by their names. In fact, speaking to me, he referred to her as 'your mother'. Catching my look of incomprehension, he added, 'your *first* mother', as if that explained everything. It took me a moment to understand that he meant *his* first wife. In any case, her role in his life was very fleeting, for unfortunately she died soon after marriage—I don't know how or why. Perhaps in childbirth, or of typhoid or TB, or of a snake bite. There were a great many ways of dying then and women had more opportunities of dying young than men; I learnt this during the course of my medical studies. Whatever the cause, she died, leaving him desolate. I imagine this last from the fact that my father changed the course of his life after her death. His guru got him a job with a nationalist newspaper in Bombay, whose editor was also one of Gandhiji's disciples. And so my father moved to Bombay and started a new life. A new job, which in reality suited him better than his earlier activity in the movement. I know that he found his work at the desk both congenial and satisfying. In a while he had a new wife as well, a match that was arranged by his boss. Though this time the girl was, suitably, a Brahmin, my father still had the satisfaction of living up to his ideals, since she was fatherless and had the inauspicious Mangal in her horoscope. As her family could give only a very small dowry to compensate for this flaw, getting her married had become a problem for them. It must have seemed a miracle when my father not only disregarded the fearful Mangal, he rejected even the thought of taking a dowry. My mother was much younger than he was; I don't know whether he thought this an advantage or a handicap. In a short while they had a daughter, Gayatri, and two years later I was born.

My father's boss had given them two rooms out of his own very large flat for a peppercorn of a rent. Two rooms and a kitchen—and this within sight of the sea, for the house was almost within stone's throw of Chowpatty beach. A wife, two children, a good job—I suppose my father was settling down to enjoy these things when disaster struck again. My mother died. She woke up screaming in pain one night and my father, thinking, naturally enough, that it was some kind of a female problem— he must have thought she was pregnant—took her to a nearby maternity home. They had to wait until the doctor, who was conducting a delivery, could come to examine her. By the time he did, she had lapsed into unconsciousness. They moved her as swiftly as they could to another hospital for the emergency surgery she needed, but it was no use. She was dead. It was acute perforative appendicitis.

I don't think anyone told me this story, nor did I ever hear others speaking of it. But somehow, sometime, the knowledge came to me that she had died of a ruptured appendix. Later, as a medical student, when I was on duty one night, a patient came to the hospital in the same critical condition. As I watched the sequence of events, I had a strange feeling of witnessing my mother's death. When the patient died a day later of a massive infection, I was so upset that the nurse was surprised. She was a kind woman I think, because she crossed the barrier that is always there between nurses and doctors—yes, even fledgling doctors—and told me to control myself. She said that a doctor could not afford to break down before his patients, that I had to get used to patients suffering and dying. But it was not *this* patient's death that had brought on my grief; it was my mother's death that had come back to me. I saw it all: the perforated appendix, the septicaemia, the shock and the eventual death. I saw, too, my father trying to understand what had happened, returning home to his two motherless children.

But let me not get dramatic; melodrama has no place in my father's story. I see him quietly accepting his fate of having become a widower for the second time—this time with two children to look after. Two infants, really, for Gayatri was only three and I was scarcely a year old. I think it was then that a kind of melancholy settled on my father. Once again I am imagining this, because I have no idea what he was like before my mother died. I don't think he ever was a very cheerful or genial man. But the greyness that was part of his personality must have come upon him after he lost a young wife for the second time. I rarely saw him laughing; smiling, yes, but laughing? No, I never saw that, not once.

Yet, ours was not a sad or melancholy home. Gayatri and I led a very normal life, we never felt the shadow of tragedy or loss looming over us. There was a woman who cooked for us once a day, we had our school and friends, and our father was always there when we needed him. Above all, we had each other. Beyond this, there was a kind of freedom which I now know was unusual for young people then, a freedom which, again, I only now realize, meant a great deal to me. My father was not an interfering man, nor was he an authoritarian parent; Gayatri and I never felt the pressure of parental authority which most of our friends grumbled about. Gayatri, being older, had a greater share of responsibility, which she took on early and easily. She was the most important person in my life, far more important than my father, who was only an occasional presence in it. Her cheerfulness and affection shaped my world. We shared everything. When my father told me one day that I would have to sleep in his room henceforth, not in the room Gayatri and I had shared, she told me very simply what had happened to her, making no mystery of the fact of her menstruation. As a child I was often an object of pity to women, but I myself, never having known a mother, felt no sense of loss. Only sometimes at night when I was in bed, or when I was low, a kind of memory came to me, a memory that had no substance. It was like the shadow of a shadow, a vague sense of having been cuddled in a lap, the feel of the rough texture of a fabric against my skin, a smell, which I knew later was the scent of women. But this was rare and never gloom-inducing. Gayatri did not let me feel any sense of loss. Yet, she was never a mother figure to me; she was always a sister and a companion.

It was Gayatri's sunny nature and her vivacity that made our home a gathering place for our friends. I say 'our' friends, but only a few were mine; most of them were hers. The greater freedom our father permitted us made it possible for us to have a mixed group of boys and girls, something that was very uncommon then. Among them were two young men, related in some way to our father's patron. His brother's grandchildren, if I remember right. That they were part of the family was all that mattered; the exact relationship never needed to be spelt out. Since in a sense we shared the same house, our two rooms being part of their large home, the two brothers were in and out of our house like the rest of the family were. Their names, Ramakrishna and Balakrishna, were inevitably shortened by everyone to RK and BK, and RK and BK they remained to us after that. These two brothers lived in Bangalore and came to Bombay for their holidays once a year. Later, the younger brother joined a college in Bombay, by which time our friendship was firmly established. The other brother joined the Civil Service and being both older and more reserved was, to me at least, a distant figure. Which is why my father and I were so taken by surprise when he came with a proposal to marry Gayatri.

Gayatri, though not beautiful, was an attractive girl—slender, tall and vivacious. It should not have surprised us that she could attract a man, yet we were surprised. I remember coming home from school the day RK spoke to my father. My father's face immediately told me something had happened; he looked bewildered, no, confused. Gayatri only smiled and said, 'I'll tell you later.' Which she did, without any fuss or affectation. I was surprised by her behaviour, by the way she seemed to accept what had happened as perfectly natural. I didn't think of this then—a schoolboy of fifteen is not interested in the nuances of romantic love, but I think now that he had already spoken to her of his feelings, that she had told him she reciprocated. It took me some time to accept the fact that she was ready for RK's proposal, that she was just as eager as he was to be married. I, who had accepted easily the biological facts of Gayatri's womanhood, was disturbed by this. I could see an excitement and a happiness in her that I could not share; it troubled me that I could not. I envied BK, who moved easily into an acceptance of these new feelings that had entered our midst. He responded to the situation by behaving with Gayatri the way a man would with a prospective sister-in-law. It was like he had known this would happen, that he was prepared for it. But I had a sense of being lost. It didn't last long; I soon got over this faint reservation about what had happened.

It was a little more difficult for my father. He had given his consent, of course. There was absolutely no reason for him to be obstructive. RK was a very estimable young man, with a promising future; Gayatri would be both comfortable and happy as his wife. But my father was unhappy about the fact that Gayatri's education would be interrupted. She was a clever girl, she had passed her Matriculation with very good marks and my father had had hopes for her. RK assured my father that she could join a college in Bangalore, but it was Gayatri herself who opted out of further education. She could not possibly combine her studies with her responsibilities at home, she said. Not only did she not have a mother-in-law, there were two sisters-in-law and an old senile grand-aunt at home; no, she could not possibly think of going to college. My father said nothing. I, however, argued with her. But when Gayatri decided on something, she was firm. And in this case, she knew with an absolute clarity what she wanted to do: RK was going to be the centre of her life henceforth. And that was that. I envied my sister that clarity of vision. Very few of us have it. I don't know whether her decision was right or wrong. After RK's death she went back to reading; she read enormously, Kannada mostly. I've forgotten English, she said. When we talked of the books she read, when we sat together with our Sanskrit Master, I could see an intelligent and thinking mind. If she had gone on with her studies, she could have done much. But why do I say that? She *did* do much. She was a pillar for so many of us; without her, our family life would have lost its centre, its source of light. But perhaps this is being selfish. In any case, it is too late now to think of such things. And whatever she did, it was *her* decision. I respected that.

To go back to where I was: if I say (write?) that Gayatri was very happy after her marriage, it means nothing. Gayatri had the temperament for happiness, but her marriage to RK needs something more than the usual word 'happy'. The ease between them and their absolute intimacy was as if they had known each other for many lifetimes. A moment comes back to me as I write this, a moment that seems now to be a symbol of their entire life together: RK at his table working on something, Gayatri entering the room, RK, aware in some way of her presence, pausing in his work, pulling off his glasses and looking at her, putting out his hand as if to say, *come and sit by me*, Gayatri responding, then realizing there were others in the room, the two of them smiling …

I'm getting sentimental. Let me go back to the plain fact: it was a good marriage. The fact that they never felt, or at least, never showed that they felt the lack of children, is an indication of what they were to each other. Their relationship was complete even without children. Few marriages are like that.

My father had a heart attack a few months after Gayatri's wedding. He must have been thankful then that she was married, that he did not have to worry about her. I know this, because I never saw in his eyes the kind of disturbance, the agitation I have seen in the eyes of patients who are afraid they will die without completing all their responsibilities. It always surprises me, this quality of taking on responsibility that humans have, so different from the instincts of an animal. But my father, once the worst was over, was calm and unperturbed. It had been a fairly massive infarct, it was touch and go for a while. Gayatri came and stayed with us for two months. He went back to work as soon as he could, but now it was an easier job. He was put in charge of the library, which meant that he was at home for longer hours. I can't say we grew closer, but we were certainly comfortable with each other. In any case, I did not have too much spare time myself. I was working hard, entirely focussed on my exams. I had to make sure I did well enough to get into medical college. My father shared this ambition of mine. He once told me that even if he died, there was enough money for me to graduate. No luxuries, no extras, he said, but you'll get through. Thankfully, he lived to see me enter medical college. The day I got admission was a happy day for us—it was one of those rare occasions when I saw him openly show his happiness. Gayatri had come on a visit and the three of us went out to celebrate. We went for a movie—I can't remember now which one, I think Dilip Kumar was the hero, I remember his stubble—and then to dinner.

By the time I started classes, my father had retired from his job. My hours in college were long and he was alone all day. He read the newspaper from end to end—strangely, not the paper he had worked for, but its rival—and wrote letters to the editor which, to my surprise, he tore up at the end of the day. It was during this time that he spoke to me of his past; what little I know of his life comes from these conversations. Actually, he gave me only the bare bones of his story. And I realize that I am trying to do the same thing now that I wanted to do in my work: identify a human being through the bones. Have I succeeded? Do I know my father better now? I don't know. But there is great satisfaction in remembering him and our relationship, in seeing things I never did then. Yes, it is like piecing information together. But let me not stray from the facts, let me get back to them.

I did worry about my father, about his being alone all day. Gayatri was even more anxious when I told her that there were nights when I would not be able to come home and that I would, perhaps, have to live in the hostel during my clinical terms. She asked my father to go and live with her—something even she must have known he would never agree to. But he recognized her concern enough to have a phone installed at home. Now, he could ring me up if he wanted me. In the event, this was not necessary. He died when I was at home, on a Sunday morning just before lunch. It was certainly not unexpected, but Gayatri was distraught. I was surprised by her total breakdown; she was inconsolable. I thought it ironical that most of the condolences were offered to me, the son. I was uncomfortable about accepting them; it seemed faintly dishonest. Not that I did not mourn my father's death. It was just that, at the time, I did not seem to have time to grieve. With Gayatri unusually listless and inactive, most of the work that follows on a death had to be done by me. I realized then how protected I had been by my father and Gayatri. But, in a way, the things I had to do cushioned me from understanding the extent of my loss.

Gayatri and I decided we would give up the house. We didn't need it any more since I was to move into the hostel. It was foolish of us, I knew that later when I understood the value of our tiny two-room home in that part of Bombay. But we were our father's children, we knew that we had been given the place at a ridiculously low rent, that it had been a token of goodwill for our father and that we had no right, morally at least, to hold on to it. And so we left the place in which we had lived all our lives. Life went on. Gayatri went back to RK and her home in Bangalore, which would henceforth be my home as well during the vacations. I moved into the hostel and got caught in the endless round of studies and examinations which makes up the life of a medical student. It was a new beginning for me, like it had been for my father when he walked out of his home. And only then did the fact of my father's death hit me; it hit me hard. It came to me in the form of emptiness, a blankness that seemed to swallow me up. My father had been a quiet man, speaking rarely and, when he did, very softly. There was something muted about him, not just his voice, but his very presence. Now, after his death, in my hostel room where he had never been, his absence became a huge dark shadow, a loud scream. I was faced not just with the finality of death, but with its ability to make nothing of life. In a while the feeling passed and I resumed my life. I enjoyed my work, I made some friends, I visited Gayatri in the vacations. BK, as her brother-in-law, was now part of my family, which added another dimension of pleasure to my visits. But the emptiness, the ice cube within me remained, surfacing suddenly at times, taking me by surprise, angering me too, by its persistence. Thoughts of my father and his rather joyless life came back to me when I became a father myself. My joy in my children was unbounded. I felt a kind of pleasure in having changed things, in having moved on, in knowing the kind of happiness my father had not experienced.

Looking back now, that pleasure of mine seems a rather naïve emotion. I will soon be swallowed up by the same emptiness, the same blankness that obliterated my father, I will be blotted out of existence as completely as he was. Nothing remains—neither my happiness, nor his lack of it. It has taken me a long time to understand this, to accept it. I have thought much of our fumbling attempts to come to terms with the idea of mortality. Heaven, paradise, another life, children, work, goodness—so many drugs to counter that terrible disease. All mere placebos. And yet, we live as if our existence is endless, as if it matters, as if the 'I' is of infinite significance. We are filled with pride in this 'I', in its uniqueness. It is true we are unique; we are, more than any other living organism, differentiated and particular. I now realize that the words of the Upanishads, *nama-rupa*, mean this very differentiation. But is it not exactly because of this differentiation, because there is none exactly the same as us, that we cease to exist with a greater finality than any other creature in this universe? We can never be replaced. It seems to me that this is the price we pay for our more evolved state: we are the true ephemera of the universe.

I go back to the question that plagued me after my father's death: how do we live knowing the fact of total extinction? Knowing the randomness of our existence, of its finiteness, how do we convince ourselves of its significance? Does the solution lie in accepting the fact, in embracing it and making it then of no account? In knowing that there is no cure, no drug to alleviate the disease? I have had much time in these last years to think of these things and I have begun to get some glimpses of an answer. Or rather, of the fact that there can never be any answer to these questions. I think of the astronomers searching the skies, trying to understand the universe and our place in it. I think of them moving away from a picture in which we are the centre of the universe to an unbounded, infinite universe in which we are not even a speck—no, not even that. What a giant leap of imagination it was for humanity to see our place, not as central, but as peripheral! To understand how insignificant we are in the whole scheme. Not surprising that the thought was considered blasphemous! What I find more astonishing is the thought that perhaps these men had some idea of what was waiting for them at the end of the road they were travelling on, that they knew they were moving towards a picture of their own insignificance. Nevertheless, they struggled on towards their goal. And ultimately, the knowledge itself proved to be the goal. It is through knowledge that we grasp creation, it is through knowledge that we really possess it all, it is through our knowledge that we conquer our evanescence. To know, to understand, to comprehend, is to become the creator. Through your knowledge you create a thing; without your knowledge, it is not. I think of Galileo's words: *Eppur si muove*. Still it moves. First the knowledge, then the denial, the recanting, and then these words to reaffirm the knowledge. *Eppur si muove*. Still it moves. The truth remains.

We are the true ephemera of the universe—this truth remains. I accept it and write it down here. My gesture against complete extinction. My fist-raising gesture of defiance saying—I am. I will be.

mr bones

I had been confused about what to do with Baba's diary—
diaries, rather, for there are two books. Should I throw them
out? Burn them? Put them away for a while and deal with them
later? I'd been reluctant at first to read them. I knew I would get
nothing but pain from reading my father's words, from visiting
the past. But I was curious too, let me admit that; it was the
curiosity of a child who wants to know what her parents are
saying about her. Thinking, hopefully, that she will catch them
saying wonderful things like 'She's so beautiful, she's so clever, I
love her more than the others'. I remember how, after Malu left
home and went to Pune, I hoped to hear my parents say, 'But
thank god Jiji is here, thank god Jiji is with us.' It never happened;
if they said it, I never heard them. I felt aggrieved for a while, but
I got over it in time. Now of course, things are different; I am no
longer looking for the 'good girl' approving pat. When you are
nearly forty, unless you're a complete fool, you know that your
relationship with your parents has gone way beyond such
simplicities. No, it was not praise that I was looking for in the
diaries; on the contrary, I was afraid—afraid of what I would
find in them. And yet, something pushed me on. The way the
diaries had been kept on the table, prominently visible, like a

message to me, like Baba saying, 'This is for you'. The way he had left them, displaying them to me almost, I knew that reading them would not be an intrusion. Actually, the fact that he hadn't destroyed them was significant enough. Death didn't come to him unannounced; he was given notice, he had enough time to prepare for the event. Which he did, putting his affairs in order, writing his will, clearing the house of a lot of unnecessary stuff; the sparseness of objects in the house was evidence of this. I had not found any letters, no, not even Malu's scrawls written at the time when she lived away from home. I know how Mai treasured those letters; I remember her folding them and putting them away in her cupboard among her saris after we had all read them. If they meant so much to her then, would she have destroyed them after Malu's death? No, it must have been Baba who got rid of things he didn't want anyone to see. Yet, the diaries remained. Did that mean he wanted me to see them? I was puzzled, confused, unable to decide.

And then it came to me, my moment of enlightenment. Who says enlightenment is for the Mahatmas and Buddhas alone? The magic moment comes to all of us; the secret is to recognize it when it comes, to hold on to the revelation. Like I did with my moment of epiphany yesterday. I was sitting in front of the TV, dinner plate on my lap, feet propped on a stool, idly noting that my toenails needed cutting and using the remote all the while, thinking at the same time and in the same idle way, what a marvellous invention it was, how it gives us complete control over the world contained in the set. Channel surfing, I raced past beaming news readers, past dancing, prancing lovers. I cut off, with sadistic pleasure, entire families grinning to show their gleaming teeth and young women swirling their unreal, plastic-looking sheets of hair about their head. And then I paused, resting on two people who looked familiar. It could have been a dramatic moment in any serial, a crucial moment in any story: the man and the woman standing, as they always do during such moments, back to back, mouthing their emotional dialogues to the walls. But I knew this serial, I'd seen it before; only off and on, true, yet long enough to know who these two were and what they were talking about. I gathered the story hadn't moved much in the weeks since I'd last watched. The couple was still estranged, the wife, the spoilt daughter of a rich man, continuing to live with her parents, refusing to go back to her husband and his middle-class home where, if there was not much money, there was love and goodness. Eventually, of course, she would go back, she would become a good wife, a good bahu, a good bhabhi, etc. Yes, that was waiting for her, but it was yet to come. Right now she was still adamant, harshly rejecting her patient husband's overtures, denying him even a sight of his own son. And then he said it, that man in his badly cut, badly stitched suit, his face crudely powdered, a lock of oily hair carefully arranged over his forehead—he said, 'You are wronging our son. He must know his father. We need to know our parents. Without this knowledge we can't go on, we will always remain incomplete.'

I sat up with a jerk at that, clutching at my plate which had almost fallen off my lap. Say it again, I muttered. But it was too late, it was time for a commercial break. I switched off the TV and went back to what the man had said. And thought of Baba's diaries. Yes, of course. This was it. This was the answer. Read this, Baba was saying, know who I am, know what your parents are.

But I could be wrong. For Baba didn't know when he began writing, that I would come home. I had been so intransigent, so adamant all these years, coming in only at the death, so to say, for Mai and Gayatri—why should he even have imagined I would come back? Maybe, when he began this record, he was writing for himself, looking back as people do when they're coming to the end of the journey. Baba was a doctor, he knew what his symptoms portended, he knew that he didn't have much time.

Raja wrote to me about Baba's illness. He gave me the diagnosis and the doctor's prognosis, all of which, Raja said, was known to Baba. He said no more. Unlike the time when he had come to tell me Mai was dying, when he had come prepared to force me to go back, he left it to me to take my decision. In fact, he made it clear that he was not asking for help. And so I came with trepidation. I imagined Baba asking me, 'Why have you come?' Saying politely, as to a stranger, 'Since you're here, you can stay, but you don't have to. Not for me, anyway. I'm all right.' I had prepared my response. I've burnt my boats, I would say, I have nowhere to go, even if I want to. I've resigned from my job, I've given up my flat. (A job that I cared nothing about, two rooms that reeked of futility since Sachi had gone to the hostel!) In the event, I didn't have to say any of these things. He accepted my presence, he even seemed pleased to have me around. There may have been many reasons for this, I can only guess at them, and I may be wrong in my guesses. But I certainly know that my being with him and looking after the little details of daily living, things which he'd had to cope with after Gayatri's death, left him free to deal with his illness, to get on with the absorbing task of dying.

In the few months we were together, we got back to some kind of relationship. The knowledge of his impending death was always with us, like a third presence in the house. It was almost like my childhood days when Baba and I had formed a team. But now, there was no intimacy. In fact, he was easier and more intimate with Raja. It was not that he was uncommunicative with me, but he never spoke of himself, or of me, either—only of generalities and abstractions: politics; astronomy, in which he'd got so interested; his Sanskrit classes which came to an end only a month before his death. Most often, however, we spoke of mundane matters, of the petty details of keeping a house going. At times he reminded me of the teacher he had been, the teacher I had known so very briefly myself. Each time I'd attended his class, I had been uncomfortably aware of our relationship, hoping the other students didn't know it, because if they did, it would put me on the other side of the fence. But my discomfort soon vanished. The man lecturing to us was not my father, he was another man entirely. This was the way he was with me before his death, not letting our relationship obtrude on the scene, deliberately keeping his distance from me. So I thought, until I heard the joker on the small screen saying, 'We need to know our parents.'

At the end of his life, my father was a lonely man. It was a loneliness of his own choosing. He isolated himself as if, having lost his family, he wanted no other ties. It's easy to think that he wrote in his diary as a counter to his loneliness, that he was, in fact, communicating with himself. But I remember Baba's face when he was lecturing to his students; you could see his pleasure in communicating, in passing on knowledge. Yes, information mattered to my father and now, when I look at his writing, I know he is offering me that. I remember the time when he spoke to me, anger breaking through his patience, a patience which came out of compassion. I remember him saying, 'You can't turn your back on things, you've got to face them.'

But I had turned my back on him and on Mai.

You need to know your parents. I thought I knew them. Baba and Mai were a book I'd read a million times, I knew every word of it, I could visualize each page clearly. But it was not true. The Baba and Mai of my childhood were figures I had created for my own purposes, they were my childhood pacifiers, the comforters I hugged for security. Figures I had had to discard when I grew up.

And now Baba is bringing them back, offering me another picture. The truth. The truth remains, Baba says. But can there be any one truth about people? People are complex, undecipherable, protean—there is no absolute about them. How can there be *the* truth about Baba and Mai? Baba is only giving me *his* picture. Whatever it is, I can't turn my back on him once again, I can't wholly reject his words this time. The words of the dead matter much more than those of the living. It's the final closure of death which makes them so significant; there can never be anything else, never any more. No, I can't ignore his words. And there's something more too. I see a kind of bravado behind Baba's 'fist-raising gesture of defiance' as he calls it. Yes, there is the fear of dying, of ceasing to exist. He is making me a partner in his gesture against extinction. Without a partner, the gesture means nothing. If I do not read what he has written, the gesture is futile, it fails, the words are lost, falling into a bottomless abyss. It's I who have to catch them before that happens. I thought our partnership had been dissolved, but once again I have to be his partner, his *'bhidu'* as he called me, filling me with pride.

And then I think of Baba sitting alone in the house, writing, and his loneliness swells about me. I think of him, his wife dead, one child gone, the other estranged, and I put my head on the table and weep loudly and noisily, the way I had cried as a child, the sobs startling even me, the tears falling on Baba's writing, leaving inky trails down the page.

*

While other children grew up hearing stories of gods and heroes, of demons and miracles, we were brought up, so to say, on the miracle of the human body. 'What a piece of work is man': if Baba had read Shakespeare, he might have quoted this line to us. Instead, he would pick up my hand (or Malu's, but most often mine, for Malu was a little squeamish about the way he spoke of it, as if it was not *her* hand, but just any hand) and say, 'Look at this, look at the way it is put together, think of all the things it can do. Just see how it can hold and grasp. Why, between this and the brain, we've conquered the world, we've changed it to suit our purposes!'

'Thank god!' Raja once said, 'thank god the people we build houses for don't come back to confront us with our mistakes, with our small failures. If they did, I can't imagine what we would do, what we would say to them.' He had added, 'At first I thought it's because people are stupid. Now I know it's not that. It's a kind of conceit, really, a sort of smugness. By the time the house is ready, they have made it theirs. And they don't want to see any flaw in what's theirs. They close their eyes to the faults. We're lucky people are so in love with their own possessions that they see them as perfect. Almost perfect. That's what gets us architects off the hook.'

Moving On

Sometimes, remembering what Raja said, I imagine the creator of the human body saying, like Raja did, 'Thank god (God? God!) people don't come back to me with my mistakes, they don't confront me with the small flaws.' And then I imagine this creator pointing to Baba and saying, 'Look at this man, for example. He thinks the body is perfect. Yes, perfect! And he's an intelligent man. Just imagine that!'

Raja is right. People are in love with their own possessions, they refuse to see any imperfections in them. But Baba was neither stupid nor smug. His was a more detached view. And yet, the admiration was intense and fervent. He had absolute faith in the perfection of the human body. If fault lines showed up in the execution of the plan, that did not take away from the perfection of the plan itself. He sang praises, I remember, of the symmetry of the body. A symmetry that was not just aesthetic, but functional as well. He spoke of the efficiency of the organs, of the super-efficient back-up system. Look at the kidney and the liver, it's like having a huge chemical factory, a scrupulously selective waste disposal system inside us, he said. And the magnificence of the communication system, the network of nerves, the exquisitely minute signals sent and picked up with such rapidity. 'A marvellous piece of finely tuned mechanism': these were his words. For him the beauty of the human body had nothing to do with the luscious curves of the female form. (Would he have fallen in love with tiny Mai if that had been his ideal?) No, his ideal was the body of the athlete, the gymnast in action, the dancer when dancing, the swift, only-just coordinated movements of a child's body when playing. I once saw him watching the Olympics, enraptured by the almost completely fulfilled potential of the human body, of its grace in action. The fierce competitiveness of the men and women which the world watched with bated breath was irrelevant to him, the medals and victories passed him by.

'Haddi doctor'—that was my father's nickname in the hospital. When I first heard it, I thought it was insulting; I was furious. But Baba laughed. 'I *am* a bone man,' he said. 'It's the right name for me.'

'This remains when all is gone, this remains for centuries, for millenniums. It lasts, it survives, it carries our stories within it.'

This was the way he began his anatomy lectures for first-year students. When I was one of them and listened to these words, I had a sense of déjà vu, I knew I'd heard them before. Not these very words, and not on one occasion. It was a telescoping of various occasions, various conversations. As a child I was his disciple, a fascinated listener; from an early age I shared his interest. Unlike other children I was not frightened of human bones. To me, they were neither morbid nor gruesome. The bone which Baba held out to me was only an ulna, or a radius, or a phalanx. I knew the names, I learnt the geography of the human body early, in fact even before I studied the geography of the world. If Baba was the high priest, I was the acolyte. Standing on tiptoe before the chart of a skeleton which hung in the entrance passage of our home, I would intently follow the path traced by Baba's wooden pointer. I learnt about flat bones and long bones, small bones and big bones. In time it became a kind of parlour trick which Baba mischievously initiated when we had visitors. While the visitor watched (in admiration, I hoped), Baba would ask me, pointing to my body, 'What is this?'

'That's the supra sternal notch.'

'And this?'

'That's the clavicle.'

Soon I went on to more difficult words, more difficult questions like 'Why is the clavicle unusual?'

I had my answer pat. 'Because it is the only long bone placed horizontally.'

I must admit that I had to work hard at getting the names right. But I did, most of the time. And Baba's smile, when I negotiated the long and difficult words, was my reward.

Mai hated this performance. Showing off, she said irritably. Making a vain peacock of the child, she chided Baba.

She was right to dislike what we were doing, right to be angry with Baba for what he was making me do. It was too much like the sort of thing parents do to specially gifted children, making freaks of them. But Mai didn't understand that Baba was not showing me off. His sense of humour kept it from becoming too serious; it was a game in which the two of us were partners against the world, enjoying what we were doing. It was a tongue-in-cheek act, this performance of ours. Mai didn't understand this; nor did she understand what I now do, that Baba was sharing his passion for the human body with me, passing it on to me like a legacy.

'There has to be some passion in life, otherwise life becomes humdrum.'

I came across these words in a manuscript I was typing, the words, I gathered, of Max Müller. When I let the words roll back into my mind that evening, I thought of Baba. If this was true, I thought, Baba's life was certainly not humdrum. To the world, perhaps it was a dull life, for he was only a teacher in a medical college, a teacher of a non-clinical subject at that, not the more glamorous fields of surgery or medicine. Teaching anatomy—dry, factual and tedious. The student's bugbear. But Baba never found it dull. To see him setting off for work, a spring in his step, was to see a man whose work filled him with excitement. As a teacher, he had that small touch of eccentricity which makes for an unusual teacher whom students speak of and remember. I heard the stories about him, about how he went off on a tangent, speaking of things that were not in the text, bringing the subject suddenly to life. But this was much later, when I became, very briefly, a student myself. As a child, my only view of him as a professional was when I saw him conversing with colleagues, his face absorbed, his hands in the pockets of his white coat. This was a man different from the father I saw at home.

And then he would come home, shed his shoes in the passage, hang his white coat on the hook on the wall and call out, 'Vasu … ?' And in a moment, he would become the man I knew. Here, at home, was his other passion, his passion for Mai, which he revealed as openly, if in a different way, as his passion for his work. This passion was never expressed in words, I don't think I ever heard him say a word of endearment to Mai. Nothing but her name, 'Vasu'. But the way he said it, the way he waited for her reply, the eagerness with which he looked for her—all these proclaimed his love for Mai. It was as if his courtship of her never ceased; he was always wooing her, always trying to please her, to proclaim his love for her. Of the two of them, he was the admirer, she the one who let him admire her; she was the one in control, he was the one who gave in to her wishes. Even as children, Malu and I knew that if we wanted something, it was Mai's permission we needed. But Baba had some power too, which we used to our advantage. If Mai's 'no' withstood even Malu's pleas and blandishments, we would ask Baba to intercede for us.

'I'll try,' Baba would say. 'But remember I can't promise anything,' he warned as he went off to speak to her, walking with an exaggerated dramatic caution, while we waited in quivering anticipation.

And then he would come out, chuckling at the thought of our pleasure, saying, 'It's all right.' And the way he spoke, it was like the three of us were equally subject to Mai's will, equally under her control.

'I am the master in my house and I have my wife's permission to say so.'

It was BK who gifted a small wooden plaque with these words to Baba. One of those meant-to-be-a-joke gifts BK had found in a recently opened gift shop. Baba, always ready to enjoy a joke, even if it was against himself, happy too to openly admit he was in thrall to his wife, enjoyed the gift. But Mai, who had no sense of humour, was angry. And there was something more than her inability to see a joke here: the words declared something that should be unspoken, they revealed something that should remain invisible—so she must have thought.

'Put it away, I don't want it here,' she said, taking it off the table on which BK had carefully placed it. Baba let her take it away; he had not argued about that, either.

I know my parents.

Here they are in this wedding picture, a picture which has somehow survived the years and emerged almost unscathed through the turbulence of our family life. Something that Baba, even in his frenzy to get rid of things, could not discard or throw away. Newly-weds, photographed in a studio in the style of those times. Bride and groom, the two of them presenting their profiles to the camera. Profiles like those on a coin or a stamp. Blank. Expressionless. Their remote gazes looking away, into some far distance. A picture that was put up on the wall just above the bed in Baba and Mai's bedroom, blending so well into the dingy unpainted wall that it was scarcely noticed. Except by Malu and me. We loved to look at it. We would take it off the wall and sit on the bed gazing at it, admiring our parents, making approving faces at each other.

Silly girls, Mai would say. Put it back.

But the picture fascinated us. This was prehistory. These were our parents *before* we were born. And it had the added distinction of having appeared in a magazine. In the *Illustrated Weekly of India*, on the page which featured pictures of newly-weds. We gazed in awe at our parents; to see them in a magazine made them public figures—almost. (We didn't know then that the pictures were sent in by the families, that they had even, perhaps, paid for the insertion.) Yes, public figures. And we knew them, they were our parents, they were right here with us. Imagine that!

I see them differently now. I see the Mai and Baba I knew peeping through the masks they wore, I see what we as children had missed. The hint of a smile at the corners of Baba's mouth, the smile of a man giving in to the photographer's demands (*look this way, no, a little more to the left, a little higher, yes, that's right*) with an amused detachment. And I am struck by the gravity, almost verging on sternness, on Mai's face. Unnatural, surely, in a girl just a little over eighteen! Unusual, too, the lack of bashfulness, either real or put-on, so mandatory in a bride on public view. A girl, I think now, in complete control of herself.

And then, when I think of Mr Bones, when I go back to him,

I see shades and tones in this picture that change everything. Mr Bones, whose presence in our house adds a little footnote to every account of our family life. Mr Bones was our name for the picture of a skeleton that hung in the passage, a passage so dark that there was never enough light to see clearly, unless you opened the front door, or switched on the light in the passage. Its presence on the wall was a familiar part of my childhood; I guess it was a relic of Baba's student days, part of the baggage he brought to his married home.

Why was it called Mr Bones? I don't know, I can't remember the genesis of the name. Though I think it must have been Baba who, in one of his facetious moments, named it Mr Bones. *Mr Bones.* Making it a male, though it had no obvious features that marked it out as being of either sex. Mai didn't like having it there. I know this, because I heard her grumbling about it whenever she remembered its existence. Imagine putting that up on the wall! she said. Better on the wall than in the cupboard, Baba joked. Since Mai didn't know the expression 'skeleton in the cupboard', she ignored this and went on, 'Issha! What a thing for people to see the moment they enter. Other people have Ganapatis at the entrance.'

Not that she was religious, or that she would have had a Ganapati herself. Far from it. But that was the conventional thing to do and Mai, even if she was not really conventional, would have preferred a Ganapati to this bordering-on-the-obscene picture. A skeleton maybe, but for Mai, the uncovered body without skin, muscle or fat, was obscene.

'Ganapati! That would be Mr Flesh. Mr Flesh instead of Mr Bones—what's the difference?'

The joke fell flat. Not even a quiver of a smile on Mai's face. She was a woman with a single-track mind. But her disapproval made no difference. Mr Bones remained where he was.

It had seemed to me, specially when I was growing up, that Baba was the one who always gave in to Mai's wishes. Now, looking back, it occurs to me that he gave in when it was something that didn't matter much to him. When it came to things he cared about, yes, he had his way. He was as good as Mai at getting his way, perhaps even better, because he never openly stated his wishes. So that you never knew he had got what he wanted. It sort of slid from your hands into his. Now, if I tote up Baba's and Mai's likes and dislikes, I see how few of his wishes Baba gave up. Almost nothing, really. Mr Bones, of course, stayed on in the passage because Baba liked him there. And there were the bones that came in his pockets and turned up in odd places at home, something that horrified Mai. But she learnt to accept it finally.

There were other things, too. Our Sunday evenings, for example, which were always spent with BK, Kamala and the kids, mostly in their house. These family evenings were fixed points in our lives that never changed unless there was a crisis. We couldn't imagine a Sunday evening when we didn't get together. But Mai? I wonder now whether she'd have liked to do something else. See a movie or a play perhaps, or visit someone, or even just stay at home and be on her own. I remember her saying once, 'Shall we go for a movie tomorrow?' And Baba, Malu and I turning on her in complete astonishment, thinking—*doesn't she know it is Sunday tomorrow? How can we go for a picture?*

'Vasu, tomorrow is Sunday.'

'I know,' Mai said, with a certain inflection in her voice I didn't understand. 'And we are going out with BK and Kamala.'

Once, deciding on a silent mutiny—I recognize it as one now—she was not dressed even when it came close to the time BK's car would give us its warning honk. I can remember Baba chivvying her. 'Come on, Vasu, get ready, they'll be here soon.'

Ultimately she was dressed and ready when the car appeared.

But sometimes her boredom became apparent even to me, at the end of the evening. I recall her yawns of boredom when Baba and BK went on talking, Baba as high on nimbupani and conversation as BK on his single glass of Scotch. When Mai's yawns and her pointed glances had no effect on Baba—he was oblivious to them, to her restiveness, thinking perhaps that she was as happy to be in Kamala's company as he was in BK's—Mai sent me to remind him that we'd miss the last bus if we didn't leave right away. And Baba, looking at his watch, would say, 'Arre, is it really so late? Come on, let's go.' But even then it would be some time before BK and he finished whatever it was they were talking about. Mai, Malu and I would be ready, footwear on, before Baba rushed out. While we waited at the bus stop, he would cheerfully go on with what he and BK had been discussing, equally unaware, it seemed, of Mai's silence, her boredom, her displeasure. Was he really so unaware of these things as he seemed to be? Or was it just a huge pretence?

However, when it came to our annual visit to Bangalore, to Gayatri and RK's house, they came out into the open. I heard them talking about it once. They must have had this argument every year, though it was only that once that I heard them—Mai saying she didn't want to go, Baba persuading her, telling her she would enjoy the change, that Gayatri would be deeply hurt if she didn't go, and yes, RK too, how they looked forward to our visits, didn't she know that? And Mai arguing, saying, 'Yes, you and the children are wanted. But I won't be missed.'

I listened, horrified. Did this mean our visit would be cancelled? Not to go in summer to Bangalore, not to stay there a whole month with Gayatri and RK, not to stay in that house which seemed like heaven! But Mai didn't want to prevent *us* from going. They can go with Kamala and the children, she was saying. A little later, she offered Baba a concession. I'll go later with you. Let the girls go earlier, she said. If this was a relief—we would have our holiday—in another way it was just as bad, because it meant Mai didn't want to be with us!

Eventually, we went as usual—Mai, Malu and I with Kamala, Raja, Premi and Hemi. Five children and two women. Mai had lost that battle. Now that I've opened up the records, the list of battles she lost seems endless; I could go on and on. What about the way Baba stopped visiting Laxman? Mai had to go along with Baba's family, but he cut himself off from her brother. And … but why go on?

We need to know our parents.

I thought I knew them. But when I came home after getting Raja's message, I saw a censorious, joyless man; a miserly man, the state of his clothes, frayed and shabby, showing me he had bought nothing new for years. And I thought of the Baba I knew, humorous, tolerant, ready to be happy, a man who enjoyed spending money.

So, do I really know my parents? I don't know. One never knows the truth about others. But that's a cliché, such a commonplace thought that it scarcely needs to be said. I mean, who doesn't know that people are not what they seem to be? When I see a character in a movie or in a TV serial looking away to wipe a tear and then turning back with a smile plastered on the face, I always think—for god's sake, even an idiot can see through that! Of course we know what's happening, we see through the pretences, we go past the defences. Yet, when we think of our parents, of our lovers and children, it's different. We would like to see them the way we have always imagined them to be. To give up our ideas of them, to see through the pretences, is to have the cherished rag we go to bed with snatched away from our hands. It's like someone saying, 'Come on, grow up.'

Baba and Mai—my parents and yet, individuals as well. Did Baba want me to see them as such?

family stories

Sunday after Sunday we've worked together, the silent man and I, pulling things out of cupboards, bringing them down from lofts, from the backyard, out of the garage. I always thought of Baba and Gayatri as simple people. And yes, of course they were simple; they didn't need much and they rarely bought a thing they didn't need. They never forgot the habits of austerity learnt in childhood from a father who, both because of his principles and necessity, lived a spartan life. Even Gayatri, who became the wife of a fairly well-off man, was always thrifty. But now, clearing up the house, I've begun to think in exasperation that if they didn't have much, they didn't throw away anything either. At the same time, I know this is unfair. It's not even true, for clearly, Gayatri and Baba did some kind of clearing up after Mai's death; I don't see too many of her things, nor RK's, either. Yet, much remains. The years themselves have added to the accumulation.

I've been ruthless in getting rid of most of it, refusing to pause, to think, to let sentiment overcome my practicality. Week after week Mouna has carted away the detritus on a borrowed handcart. I don't know where he takes it, nor have I asked him what he does with it. I know that even if I asked, he would give me no reply. At first, I'd thought him dumb, his name, Mounappa, suggesting this. But I've realized since then that silence is his choice. I couldn't have had a better companion for the job. Working without words or comments has made it both easier and swifter. The man has been totally impersonal, like someone getting rid of trash from the garden. Or a professional doing his job after an earthquake, clearing up the debris of human lives and hopes, these things no more to him than a day's work.

We work together steadily through the day, Mouna disappearing every half hour—to smoke, I guess, from the overpowering reek of cheap cigarettes that he brings back with him. Now, finally, we seem to have come to the end of it. Well, almost. I had imagined that the clothes would be the worst, the hardest to deal with. But clothes are easy to dispose of, specially saris, which have no size and don't date. It's the books that are a problem. They seem, oddly enough, so much more personal than the clothes, so much harder to throw away, so much more impossible to give away. Who wants books? And these books are so varied and so many, I can't think of any one person or institution I can give them to. And what about the piles of Marathi magazines Baba obviously couldn't bear to throw away because they carry Mai's stories—what shall I do with them? Twice I've put them out for Mouna to take away on his cart and both the times I've brought them back inside with a groan—groaning both because of their weight and my own weakness at being unable to discard them. It looks like we're doomed to be ancestor worshippers; relics of our parents' lives become suddenly precious after they're dead. And we think: *no, I can't do this, let someone else do it*. Does this mean that I am going to carry these things on my back all my life?

Some decisions have been easy. Raja and I have shared RK's books between us—the Dickenses, the Trollopes, the Galsworthys, the Hardys. Who else would want them? And I've kept Baba's collection for myself. Not that I see myself reading them, but they tell me a great deal about his last years. It's a strange collection. Apart from the usual books people turn to as they get older, like books on philosophy, the Upanishads, the Gita, there are other, odder subjects—spiritualism, the occult, astronomy, astrology (Baba and astrology!), the *Tibetan Book of the Dead*. At first I was puzzled; they seemed most unlikely books for Baba to have. But I soon got an idea of what they were about and began to glimpse the road that Baba had travelled these last years. Each book has his name on the flyleaf as well as the date on which it was bought and I notice that most were bought after Mai's death. Which told me what Baba was doing: he was searching for Mai. I think of Baba holding out a bone, saying, 'This is it, this is us, this lasts when everything else is gone.' And then Mai died and there was nothing left, the last of her bones too disappearing into the river where we'd immersed her ashes. So what was left then? I can see him asking himself this question, a puzzled look on his face, the same look he had when he was confronted by a flaw in the human body. With Mai's death he had to confront the biggest flaw of the body—its transience. And so, like the young man who'd once raced down the stairs and across the road to get to the young girl he'd glimpsed through the window of his room, he began to search for her once again. All these books speak to me of his despairing search for something beyond, for a hope that though the body has gone, something remains.

'Where do the dead go?'

I remember the question coming out with a startling abruptness in the course of a lazy, disjointed after-dinner conversation. All of us on the porch, we children silent, knowing that this was the adults' time, that we were here on sufferance, knowing that if we spoke we would be asked to go to bed. Even the adults' voices were muted by the silence of the night. I don't know who asked the question—BK, I should imagine, for he enjoyed inciting people on to arguments. I can't recollect any of the arguments, only the animated voices, Gayatri's hand on my neck gently caressing me as I lay on her lap, inhaling the sandalwood fragrance of her body, revelling in its cushiony softness. Feeling, too, the reverberations entering my body from hers when she spoke. I can remember how sleepy I was and how reluctant to leave everyone awake and go to bed. And yes, I remember how Raja butted into the conversation, his voice loud and triumphant, announcing, 'I know where dead people go. They come out of Gate Number Thirteen and then go to Harishchandra Ghat.'

It was not a joke, nor had Raja any intention of being impertinent. It was a statement of fact. Dead people *were* carried out of the hospital through Gate Thirteen; even we children knew this. We had seen the stretchers being readied, we had seen the dead bodies being taken away through the narrow gate. But BK was furious.

I remind Raja of this incident. He only grunts. To him, his morning walk is a sacred ritual. A man who's just woken up to the idea of physical activity and physical fitness, he makes a fetish of it and is annoyed by my refusal to see it the way he does. He disapproves of what he considers the spirit of levity with which I look at it. Right now he's doing his deep breathing exercises, which means he can't talk.

'What made you remember that?' he asks when he can speak.

'The clearing up I'm doing—it's made me think that the real problem is not where the dead go, but what they leave behind. You know, Raja, I think the ancient Egyptians got it right. We should bury the dead with their belongings, so that we're free of that burden, free of *agonizing*—yes, you can laugh, but I tell you it's real agony thinking of what to do with the things. It would be such a relief to get rid of them.'

'I guess you haven't seen people fighting over property, even little bits like spoons, after a death. Who do you think would bury the dead with their property? And anyway, where do you get these hideously morbid ideas from?'

'Desperation. What do I do with all the stuff at home? Papers, piles and piles of papers. You should never, no, never have parents who write. And those magazines in which Mai's stories appeared—why do you think she kept them? And what do I do with them?'

'Give them to a library.'

'Raja, they're Marathi magazines! And this is Bangalore. Who would want them here?'

'Give them to a university or something. They take writers' manuscripts, don't they?'

'Mai's manuscripts! Poor thing! No one took her seriously as a writer, she didn't take herself seriously. No, I don't have a choice. I'll just have to give them to the raddiwala.'

'What!'

I laugh. Raja never fails to rise to the bait. He realizes he's been had, glares at me and begins walking again, waving his arms around in an exercise he will carry on with until we get to the park. It's to improve the circulation, he says. Blood circulates quite well on its own, I've told him. But he goes on with his windmill exercise nevertheless.

'Anyway, why do you need to do anything at all? Leave it be, the stuff can lie about in some corner. It needn't bother you, it's a big house, there's enough room.'

'I have to clear up the house for Sachi.'

'Sachi can do her own clearing up if it's necessary. Don't pamper the brat.'

'It's not pampering. These are *my* dead, Raja, these things belonged to my parents, to my uncle and aunt. I have no right to burden someone else, I have to do this myself. And if Sachi's going to sell the house, as she says she will, I might as well be prepared for it.'

We've talked of this earlier, I know how Raja feels about Sachi's idea of selling the house. To him it is sacrilege. Raja is the most ardent ancestor-worshipper I know. He gets sentimental and emotional to a degree that's hard to believe of a man who's otherwise so practical. Gayatri told me how, as a boy of sixteen, he had insisted on being on the spot when the old family house was demolished. It was as if he wanted to be with it in its last hours, she said. He wouldn't listen to her, he went there every day, and so finally did she, to keep him company, the two of them returning home each evening covered with dust.

But Raja has practical arguments too against selling the house. It's the wrong time to sell, he says, prices are low right now, you won't get a good price.

The morning light has steadily improved since we left home, the grey gradually dissolving into a diffuse whiteness. Figures which were a vague blur are becoming clearer, faces taking on identities. Raja's own face takes on a rigid, mask-like appearance and he looks straight ahead, resolutely avoiding eye contact with anyone. Morning walks, he says, are not for socializing, he does not want to talk to anyone. In spite of his precautions, someone calls out to him. He raises his arm in the mute greeting of walkers and mutters angrily, 'Who's that? Never seen the guy before.'

'The price of popularity. Look at me. Do you see anyone greeting me?'

'You're a rolling stone. How could anyone know you?'

We squeeze through the stone barriers and get into the park. Once inside we separate, the two of us having separate routines. As always, I'm the first to finish and as always, the pain in my back which forces me to stop, brings on a moment of panic, followed by outrage. This can't be happening to me! My body can't do this to me!

'Out?' Raja asks, coming up briefly for air. And then dives back for his toes without waiting for my response.

On our way back, at a slower pace this time, I confess to Raja my anger at the suspicion that my body is betraying me.

'Be reasonable, Jiji. You can't not change. There's a world of difference between twenty and forty.'

'I'm *not* forty!'

'Well, nearly.'

'Two years is not nearly, it's a long time. And anyway, I was brought up on Baba's theory of the Body Beautiful, the Body Perfect, remember?'

'Mr Bones, eh? That reminds me—did you find him when you were clearing up?'

'No. They must have disposed of him before leaving Bombay.'

That takes him back to the house, to Sachi's plan of selling it.

'Don't let her,' he says earnestly.

'How can I stop her?'

'You're her mother.'

'But once she's eighteen—that's next year—she can do what she wants.'

'And what about you?'

'What about me?'

'Where will you go?'

'Somewhere. Anywhere. I didn't have the house all these years, did I? I managed then, I will now. The whole world is open to me.'

'Don't talk like a kid.'

'You called me a rolling stone, remember?'

'Yes, but why sell the house? I don't understand Sachi.'

'It's the unfairness of it she minds. That Baba left it to her alone and not to the three of us jointly. She wants to set that right.'

'By selling the house?'

'Yes. And then buying a flat in all our names—Anand's, hers and mine.'

'I can't think of anything more stupid. You'll just be losing a lot of money on the two deals, that's all.'

'Yes, but we can buy a small flat, stash away the difference in the bank and live a life of sloth and ease. At least I will. Those two poor things have their studies. I'll have nothing to do—just be a lotus-eater.'

'You wouldn't joke if you knew how much trouble Kaka took to get this plot of land for the house.'

'I know, but Sachi doesn't. Even if I tell her, she won't care. I wouldn't blame her. Why should she agonize over people she never knew?'

'It's all your fault. You should have told her about the family. Do it now. Tell her everything.'

'You don't know what you're saying, Raja. Just leave it alone and let Sachi do what she wants.'

'That's all very well, but what about you?'

'I told you. I was serious when I said that I've lived in all kinds of places, I can do that again.'

We've now got to my gate. On most days, he leaves me here and goes on. But today he closes the gate behind me and stands on the other side with a look on his face that tells me what is coming. I'm in no mood to listen to him, but I know there's no way I can stop him from speaking.

'If you marry me, all these problems will be solved.'

'Thank you, Raja, I don't have any problems. And I've told you, I've told you so many times—'my exasperation breaks through—'I don't want to get married. Period.'

'I'm not asking you to "get married period", I'm asking you to marry me.'

If Raja is courting me—and I guess when a man keeps asking a woman to marry him, he is doing just that—he has a strange way of going about it. The reasons he produces for his desire to marry me certainly don't make him out to be an ardent lover. I like being married, he says. I enjoyed being married to Rukku and I'm sure it will be just as good with you. We know each other so well, it should be easy, he says. He brings in the children as well; he tells me how good it will be for his Pavan and for my Anand and Sachi to have a family. Once he had even said, making me laugh, something I regretted immediately seeing the look on his face, that two households are so much cheaper to maintain than one! A very persistent wooer indeed, with many reasons, even if they are the most mundane ones, for marrying me. Whereas I can produce only one reason for my negative: I don't want to get married.

I'd tried another defence the first time he'd made his offer, after I'd got over my initial shock. 'We're like brother and sister,' I had reminded him. 'Almost.'

'Not even almost. Your father's sister married my father's brother—what does that make us?'

'Cousins?'

'Bullshit. If there's no blood tie, there's nothing.'

But we grew up together, I remind him. And for long his

parents were Appaji and Amma to me, while mine were Baba and Mai to him.

But Raja strenuously refutes all the arguments I produce. Once he's made up his mind, he doesn't give up easily. He conveniently forgets the fact that he had treated Malu and me like he did his own sisters, Premi and Hemi, he ignores the kind of relationship our two families had, the way we had behaved with each other. Sometimes I think his desire to marry me is itself a legacy of that early responsibility he had to bear as the only boy among four girls. Look after the girls, he was told and he did. Possibly, he's still trying to look after me.

'You're an obstinate woman, Jiji,' he says now, suddenly, irritably. And then he adds, 'You're so prickly. You were not always this way.'

'Do you expect me to be the same as I was at twelve?'

His face changes. He thinks I am reminding him of Shyam; it makes him feel guilty. Later, when he has gone, I think—but why do I blame him for refusing to see me as anything but the child Jiji? Don't I still see in Raja the same plump boy who tumbled out of their old Fiat with loud whoops of joy every Sunday? The boy who was scrupulous about looking after his two sisters and Malu and me? Naturally, for him I'm still the Jiji of those days, a girl who was docile, eager to please, wanting everyone to like her.

But that Jiji was part of the 'Baba-Mai-Malu-and-I' entity. Once that disappeared, the old Jiji vanished too.

How far back does memory go? For me, it begins with Malu's birth. I was a little less than three then, but I can distinctly remember someone saying to me, 'You have a baby sister.' And then the infant in the cradle, the tiny face framed in a lace-frilled cap, the slightly pouting lips that quivered into what I thought was a smile, a smile for me, and the two black dots, one between the eyebrows, the other on one soft rounded cheek. There is nothing before this memory, as if I had no existence before Malu's birth. Even my name, Jiji, came to me with Malu. I had been Baby until then, no one called me Manjari. When Malu was born, a neighbour, so Malu and I were told when we were still at the age to find stories of our own infancies entrancing—this neighbour said, 'But she's *this* baby's Jiji now. How can you call her Baby?' And so I became Jiji.

In a sense, Malu was the most important person in our family. I was the first-born, but I had to wait for Malu to come to find my own name, as well as my place. With her entrance, I became the foil to Malu. I was strong, while she was delicate; I was practical and she was dreamy and absent-minded. I was the son of the family, the tough one, while Malu was the daughter, gentle and to be protected. In fact, Baba and I were the protectors who looked after Malu and Mai; or so we thought. In the long run, we were proved wrong. We were the survivors, yes, but our lives were dictated to by the dead. It was they who, even after their death, shaped our lives. 'Your mother's tough,' Shyam used to say to me. And I always thought, with a tinge of sorrow, that he was being critical. He doesn't like Mai, I thought with regret. But he was speaking the truth, I know that now.

To go back to Malu—yes, she was the focus of our family. More than anything else, it was her birth that brought the 'Baba-Mai-Malu-and-I' entity into existence.

Baba-Mai-Malu-and-I are going out.

Baba-Mai-Malu-and-I are going to see a picture.

Baba-Mai-Malu-and-I are going to eat ice cream.

Baba picks up my chant and says, *Baba-Mai-Malu-and-I are going to the toilet* when, shedding my knickers, I am rushing to the toilet.

Issha, Mai says, her usual exclamation of indignation, annoyed with the reference to something she considers unmentionable.

Baba-Mai-Malu-and-I was my world, the womb I slipped into after coming out of Mai's. The first time I was pulled out of it, rent away from it and pushed into the world outside is a moment I still remember, a moment of sheer absolute terror.

We are walking on the crowded pavement outside the hospital,

Baba carrying Malu in his arms, I holding Mai's hand, holding on to it with a tight grip, grasping Baba's trousers with the other hand. But the trousers keep slipping out of my hand with each step Baba takes, with the pushing and shoving of people who won't let us walk together. I hold Mai's hand even more tightly, with the desperation of a drowning person. Someone comes between us, forcing us apart, making me let go of her hand. I put out my hand to catch hold of Mai's once again after the person has moved away. I get hold of a hand, but I know in an instant, from the feel of the hand, from the way it does not curl around mine, that this is not Mai. I look up. It is not Mai, it is someone else, a woman who gives me a smile and walks on. I stand where I am, trapped among saris and trousers I don't recognize. And then the tragedy of it hits me. I'm lost. I can't find my way to Baba and Mai, they will never find me, I will never find them again. I open my mouth and begin to howl. The crowd around me moves away, leaving me isolated in the centre of a circle. I can see faces looking at me, I can hear voices asking me questions, but none of the faces are of Baba and Mai, none of the voices are theirs. I cry louder. I want Baba, I want Mai, I'm saying, but no one seems to understand me.

Suddenly there is Baba, Malu still in his arms. He puts Malu down and picks me up, making soothing sounds. I can hear laughter, I know people are laughing at me. Ashamed, I hide my face on Baba's shoulder. He pats me and soon my sobs peter out. I raise my head slowly and see that the crowd has dissolved, people are moving away. And there's Malu, standing where Baba had put her down before he picked me up, patiently waiting for him to pick her up again. Malu, staggering a little as if Baba had put her down too quickly, rocking her, and she was still trying to regain her balance. Her face, bewildered and a little scared, hits me. I'm terrified she'll be lost too. I begin to sob again, saying 'Malu', pointing to her, telling Baba to pick her up, not to leave her there. It takes him some time to understand what I'm saying. When he does, he picks Malu up and holds her on his other arm, so that the two of us are facing each other.

Okay? Baba asks me. Satisfied?

I nod. Yes, now I'm happy. Baba, Malu ... But where's Mai? Why is Mai not with us? Where is Mai?

Right then, down you go, he says and is putting me down, when I begin to cry again, calling for Mai. Baba laughs. Now, don't you start that all over again, he says. There she is, your Mai, right here, beside you.

Yes, there she is, perhaps there she had been all this while. How was it I hadn't seen her? And why hadn't she come to me when I was crying?

But it is all right, we are together once again, Baba, Mai, Malu and I.

This became a family joke, one which stayed with us for years. Baba pretending to be me, sobbing, his mouth open, his finger stabbing at the ground, saying some garbled incomprehensible words, words supposed to be 'Malu, pick Malu up'. Everyone laughed at Baba's little piece of acting, I joined the laughter too. I laughed with them, I laughed at myself, the frightened child who seemed to be so far away when I was cocooned in the cosiness of the world in which we were together. Yet sometimes, very rarely, the moment of absolute terror when I felt I'd been abandoned, came back. And sometimes, reliving the moment, it seemed to me that Mai had let go of my hand, that she had *wanted* me to be lost. The sense of betrayal brought back the fear, the sense of complete isolation. But these were rare moments, tiny dots on a huge canvas of a loving-and-wanting-me Mai. Nor did these dots make any impact on the fact of *my* loving and wanting Mai.

If Malu was the most important person in our family, Mai was the centre of it.

'Vasu,' Baba would call out the moment he entered, while he was still untying his shoelaces.

'Mai, Mai,' Malu and I would cry, hurtling towards her room when we returned from our rare outings without her, racing each other in our eagerness to get to her first, to be the first to tell her where we had gone and what we had done. The outing would become real only when we told her about it, more real than when we actually did the things we told her about.

Mai would be in her room, I can see her now at her table, looking up as we entered, her face blank as if she didn't see us, as if she didn't know us. A vacant, unfocussed look that stopped me in my tracks. But Malu ran on and climbed on to Mai's lap. And Mai's face changed, she came back from wherever she had been, she smiled—yes, she was glad to see us. Capping the pen in her hand, she carefully put it on the table, away from Malu's squirming body and my flailing hands.

'You're back. And what did you do?'

I try to get close to Mai, I butt her with my head, trying to find a place, not *between* her and Malu, but *with* them, *beside* them; I want to be part of the two of them.

'Aga, Jiji, aga, aga, what are you doing?' she says reprovingly. 'You're hurting me.'

But the other arm goes around me and now I am close, now I am part of Mai and Malu. I inhale with rapture the sandalwood fragrance of her body, feel the smoothness of the bare skin of her arm against my cheek. I am loved, I am wanted.

Yet, I always knew I had to work harder than Malu if I wanted to be loved. In fact, Malu didn't have to work at all, she just had to *be*. I understood this perfectly well, for that was how it had been for me too from the moment I saw her, a baby in the cradle, smiling at me. We loved her because she was Malu, not because of what she did. In our house, she came first, she mattered more than anyone else; I understood this too, for was I not part of the conspiracy to keep Malu always happy, always satisfied? And she was the little tyrant who knew her power, who used it to get what she wanted. It was her choice that dictated our Sunday special lunch, she who chose which movie we would see. She was the leader and I was her follower.

But outside the house, it was the other way round. There, I was the leader, the captain who got to choose her own team; whatever the game we played, I was the one who made the rules. I was also better known by the students, doctors and nurses in the hospital campus in which we lived. It was like a little kingdom, this campus, fenced in by long, spiked steel palings, with watchmen guarding the tall, heavy gates. A world in itself. Self-sufficient, with Pandu the barber who came home to cut Baba's hair, Tukaram who polished our shoes every Sunday, Gajanan who took away dirty clothes and brought them back clean and smooth, the tall, skinny plumber and his short, stout assistant who were really Mushtaq and Rafiq, but were always known as Don Quixote and Sancho Panza. We knew, both Malu and I, our place in this little kingdom, we knew we were specially privileged as a doctor's children. ('My father is an atomist,' Malu once said with proud dignity, a word Baba held on to gleefully for years, calling himself an atomist whenever he could.) But I was the one more at home in this world, inured to sights and sounds like Malu never was. The sight of sick patients, the moans we heard at night, the wailing of children, even the dead bodies and funeral processions, were part of our lives.

'What's there to be scared of?' I asked Premi when she ran away from the sight of a dead body being wheeled on a stretcher.

'It's a dead body,' she said.

'We don't call them dead bodies, we call them cadavers,' I said in lofty scorn, showing off my knowledge, boasting of my courage.

'What stink?' I would ask visiting children who turned up their noses at the various odours that permeated the campus. '*We* don't get any smell.'

And in a way it was true: the smell of formalin, of disinfectants and dressings, was so much a part of our lives that I was immune to it. Malu was different, but I had to include her in my bragging.

'We're not scared of dead bodies, are we, Malu?' I would ask.

'No,' she would quaver, feigning a nonchalance to match mine. Like the way she would pretend she didn't mind the smells, though I had seen her holding her nose when passing by the building that housed the mortuary and the autopsy room. 'No, we are not scared.'

But she *was* scared. She never went out in the evenings alone and at night, sometimes, she crept into my bed and held on to me tightly. I liked it, I liked it this way, I liked having her depend on me. That was my place—to look after her, to make her feel safe. It was my place too, I knew, to give in to her, to let her have what she wanted, never to cross her. Yet, I never doubted I was loved, I never felt unloved.

If I am so sure about this, why am I so hesitant about reading Baba's diaries, why does it disturb me so much, the idea that there will be something about me there? It's not Baba's privacy I am thinking of; no, I can't fool myself that it is *that* thought which makes me wary of reading what he has written. The dead have no right to privacy, they lose that right the moment they die. Then it becomes an open field. We are free to go through their lives, their cupboards, their drawers. We can unearth their little secrets: the sex manuals with the explicit pictures, the dirty underclothes, the unused condoms, the lubricating gels. No, it has nothing to do with privacy, this reluctance of mine.

The truth is, I'm scared. I'm scared of reading what Baba has said about me, I'm afraid of knowing that he judged me and found me wanting. I remember the time he said to me, 'Such a ramshackle way of living!' This was when I was leaving after Gayatri's death, going back, I told him, to a new job, a new place.

He said it in English, using the word 'ramshackle', a word I had never heard him use before, as if its use had been called for only now, as if this word and none other could describe my life.

It had hurt me. But his face told me that he had no intention of hurting me. Actually, he had spoken with the remote indifference of a stranger. Which rankled even more and made me angry too, so that I had retorted, 'What's ramshackle about it, Baba? I have a job, I earn money, I look after the children.'

'Yes, but look at the way you go about it—chopping and changing all the time, look at the way you keep moving about. Is that good for the children?'

I could have said it then, that we had had a stable enough life, Malu and I, that we grew up and lived in the same house for years, that our father had enough time for us, our mother was always there when we returned from school, we had uncles and aunts and cousins. But look at us! Look at what happened to us! So what difference does it make?

Of course I didn't say any of this. I was past arguing with Baba by then, I had no desire to get into arguments and recriminations. I said nothing. And in any case, there was nothing unusual in what had happened to our family. All families follow essentially the same path: a gradual distancing, a tapering off of bonds, hostility and rivalries between siblings, expectations and disappointments that distance parents and children. Things have to change; only a child can imagine that things remain the same forever, that families remain the way they were. And so our family changed too. After all, we were not unique.

And yet, in a way we were unique. What happened to us was not a gradual separation, it was not a slow distancing or a scarcely perceptible loosening of ties. We disintegrated in a moment. There we were, the four of us, a happy family tightly bonded together. And the next moment it was gone. Nothing left. Like a bubble at the touch of a finger.

'There's nothing as strong as a bone,' Baba would say. I had believed him implicitly. Which is why, when I fell off a bike and fractured my arm, what I felt after the pain had been dealt with and the arm put in a cast, was a sense of outrage. Of having been betrayed.

'But you said bones are strong,' I accused Baba. 'You said it.'

'Strong? Yes, they are strong—but only up to a point. Everything is strong up to a point. The only difference is where that point is. Nothing is so strong that it will never break.'

And then, to console me, he told me how easily bones heal and how quickly they unite again. 'Nothing heals faster than the bone,' he said. 'Give it some time and the ends will come together. It needs some time, that's all.'

That was the problem. Our family was given no time to heal; there was no time to pick up the pieces, to align them and put the thing in a cast. Perhaps we suffered, to use Baba's words, a comminuted fracture, the bones splintering into tiny, sharp, hurting pieces. Or was it something quite different, a cancer that had been growing inside, invisible and painless, until it announced itself ready for the kill? My old knowledge comes back to me and I remember that the very quality of regeneration of the bone makes it more vulnerable to cancer, the cells growing wildly, going berserk and out of control.

Tell her everything, Raja said. Did he mean these things too? How far back do I go to include 'everything'? How much do I need to tell Sachi to make her understand why her grandfather willed this house to her, bypassing me, his daughter and Anand, his grandson? What does she need this family history for? There was a time when it had seemed very important to her, when she wanted to know more, specially about her father and his family. She was suspicious of my silence about Shyam, of the total absence of his family from our lives. 'You haven't even kept a picture of him!' she hurled at me accusingly once, thinking perhaps of movies in which the dead father's picture hanging on the wall is the focus of the family's life. Sometimes I think it's the lack of drama she regretted, the complete absence of tragedy which came through my comfortable acceptance (as she saw it) of the lack of a husband, of the way I played down the fact of my widowhood.

But that was long ago. Her questions about her father, about his family, have ceased. She has only one question for me now: 'Why did my grandfather give me this house?' And to give her the answer I have to go back and tell her, as Raja says, everything. But to offer her even the bare facts is to open a Pandora's box, letting out a cloud of dark confusing events.

There is no need for me to do any such thing. Sachi is more equable now, no longer hostile to me, at least rarely openly. Why disturb this poise in our relationship? Why burden her or Anand with the past?

baba's diary

10 March 1997

It's over two months since I last wrote in this. I had thought I would write fairly regularly—if not every day, at least every few days; but it has not been possible. I can't complain about not having time (I have enough time, yet paradoxically, very little left), nor is it my health; I am doing better than I expected. I have now realized what the problem is: for me writing is an overflow, it is necessary for my mind to be so full of thoughts that I have no choice but to write. Is this what they call inspiration? No, I can't talk of inspiration for the kind of writing I'm doing; to say that I need inspiration to write my own meandering thoughts and ideas is to claim too much. And in any case, today it is neither my thoughts nor ideas that have propelled me into writing, but questions.

I have always been a questioning man; asking questions was the main tenet of my professional life. I tried to instil it in my students as well, telling them that to accept anything unquestioningly was to insult our capacity to think. The habit of asking questions, so deeply ingrained in me, still remains. But the questions I now find myself asking cannot be met by facts; or so it seems. Like the one I have been brooding over, the past few days. A very banal question, I admit; nevertheless, connected to individual lives, it becomes relevant and has all the freshness and crispness of a newly printed note. The question I ask myself is: do our lives hinge on happenings we have no control over? Are we wholly helpless? Or is it always some deliberate or unknowing choice of ours that is the turning point? I apply these questions to my father's life, to his first marriage and his wife's death—two events that changed the course of his life—and think: what if his wife had lived? Would he have gone on with his role in the freedom struggle? And where would that have taken him? I remember him telling me once that the governor of the State had been his colleague in those times and another, he had added, had become a cabinet minister at the Centre. Yes, definitely his life would have taken a different direction. Yet, the fact remains that the marriage was his own choice. And so was his decision to come to Bombay, to take up a new job and start a new life.

But when I think of my own life, it presents me with an entirely different picture and it seems that our lives hinge on happenings we have no control over, that they take turns we never anticipated. If I had ever thought of my end—and truth to tell, we never think of our death, the thought comes, if at all it does, in the shape of a fearful dark cloud looming on the horizon—I would have seen myself as being among my family, my wife and children, Gayatri and RK, BK possibly, and even, if I thought of living long enough, my grandchildren. But here I am at the fag end of my life, living alone in this house, with no company but a young man I hadn't heard of until he came to occupy the rooms on the first floor.

It was Gayatri's idea to rent out the two rooms on the first floor when I moved out of them after Vasu's death. We would rent them to single men, she said; they're not fussy, they're less trouble. And so the procession began—one young man after another, each getting another to take his place before moving out, all of them equally inconspicuous and silent, except for the noise of their two-wheelers. It never failed to amuse me, the way their vehicles, helmets and visors transformed these innocuous boys into swashbuckling heroes. Gayatri and I were happy with the arrangement. We had a sense of company, a semblance of company, rather. And the comforting thought of a young person around, 'in case ...' as Gayatri said, leaving the rest unsaid, superstitious about specifying the emergency. But Gayatri was fortunate; she died in an instant and at a time when Raja and I were both in the house, drinking the tea Gayatri had just got for us. It was the sound of a cup dropping that alerted us to the fact that something was wrong.

The tenant of the moment left soon after and Abhishek came in. I had to deal with him, something I had never had to do until then, having always left it to Gayatri to cope with the practical details. In the beginning, we had little to do with each other, our communication confined to a greeting, most often a wordless nod or a smile. And then he changed. I date the change to a time soon after my persistent problems were diagnosed as carcinoma colon. I don't know how he came to know about it. Raja may have spoken to him. Or, perhaps, there is no need to speak of these things; the body gives the truth away. Whatever it was, I guessed he knew, for instead of going briskly past me with a monosyllabic greeting, he lingered, sometimes reading his newspaper in the veranda with me instead of taking it upstairs. In the evenings too, if he came back early enough, he would chat with me for a while. I've learnt in the course of our conversations, stilted at first, but now easier, that he comes from a place quite close to the village my father came from. I was amused at myself when I realized how differently I saw him after this. What did the place mean to me, who had never even heard of it until I was nearly eighteen? Why should it mean anything to me? But it did. Some primitive instinct links us to our roots, even in this age of constant movement, of not belonging.

I never spoke to Abhishek of this matter. He is a man of his times, always ready to move on, each place a stepping stone to another, a rung on a ladder from which he climbs to another rung, the final destination being, of course, the US. He's preparing himself for the Great Leap; he told me that his job in a local software company was giving him just the work experience he required to make that final bid. But I'm sounding critical and I have no intention of being that; I would be a very ungrateful man were I to criticize him. He is a kind young man, going out of his way to help. Even before my illness, he had shown his readiness to help me. I remember the day he found me at a loss, unable to get an auto to go for a music performance. Raja, who was to have taken me to it, had called at the last minute to say that he was caught up in some work and couldn't come. Abhishek took me on his two-wheeler, he stayed on for the three hours of the performance; a great kindness, I knew, both because his time was precious to him and because, as he cheerfully admitted, he could not understand classical music at all.

When Raja came with his apologies the next day, he joked with Abhishek about having sat through the evening listening to my kind of music—'the toothless gharana', he called it. Old men singing through their dentures, he added in explanation. But behind his levity I could see that Raja was easier in his mind, knowing that if there was a crisis, Abhishek would be there for me. Raja takes his responsibilities seriously. It seems odd when I think of it, that BK's son has become my mainstay and prop while BK himself is left with a retarded daughter who is a burden. I sometimes wonder whether he thinks of it, whether he resents it that Raja, his son, is with me, instead of with him and Kamala.

This is not how it was meant to be. We had made our plans; we would live together in our old age, RK and Gayatri, BK and Kamala, Vasu and I. Our children would come and go, grandchildren would eventually be part of their visits, but otherwise, most of the time we would be there for one another. This was not just a dream. We were doing something more concrete than building castles in the air, we were working at translating the dream into a reality. Or rather, RK and BK were. They planned it well, the two brothers. RK bought two plots of land when the old house was sold, plots on which he and BK would build their future homes. RK was to build his right away, while BK would do so when he was ready to make the move from Bombay to Bangalore. And I ... yes, what about me?

I was part of the plan, of course, I knew that this was where I would eventually come. But I did not have the money to buy a plot of land. And I was not too sure about Vasu, either. Vasu was a real 'Mumbaikar' as I often teasingly called her. She was born and brought up in Bombay, it was her home, the place where she felt most comfortable, most herself, most alive. I saw the change in her when we returned to Bombay after our summer visits to Bangalore, the way she revived, like a wilting plant after it's been watered.

After Vasu's death, Gayatri began reading her stories. She admitted that she found it hard since she'd forgotten her Marathi in the years since she left Bombay. But she persisted; reading the stories gave her, I imagine, a sense of Vasu's presence. And brought her own childhood back, as she said to me, for all Vasu's stories were located in Bombay, a Bombay described in vivid and careful detail. Yes, Vasu loved Bombay. And there were her strong ties to her family as well—her mother and her brothers. Knowing all this, I had had my doubts about whether she would ever agree to leave Bombay. Nevertheless, when RK learnt that there was a narrow strip of land next to his plot, land left over due to a miscalculation and too small a piece to be sold on its own, I decided on the spur of the moment to buy it myself. We would merge the two plots into one and build a house together— RK's immediately, and ours, on the first floor, whenever we were ready to leave Bombay.

In the end, nothing worked out as planned. RK died before he could even begin building. Gayatri lost interest after that, but Raja built this house for her and moved in with her. I had thought BK would like to come back here, that he would be happy to get out of his small flat in a crowded area in Matunga, that he would build a large house for himself and live the life of a retired gentleman. BK, however, kept putting it off, until it became clear that he didn't really want to leave Bombay. When RK died, it was as if BK's ties to this place snapped. He made over his plot to Raja, who built a house for himself and lived in it with his wife and son. And Vasu, who I thought would never leave Bombay, was in such a hurry to get out that it was left to me to wind up our home and affairs in Bombay.

And so I go back to my question: what is it that controls our lives? I have never believed in Fate or Destiny, not in the sense of something that makes puppets of us. There's no Great Plan, no Creator with a Great Design. I believe that we are freak occurrences in a universe which in itself is a freak occurrence. Set in motion, it has no choice but to keep going. But when I look back and see how our plans were overturned, how nothing turned out as we'd expected it to, I have to rethink. And no, I still don't believe in Fate or Destiny. But I have begun to think that we come into this world with our lives mapped out for us. And that our actions, our struggles, are part of this map as well. We are not passive spectators of our own lives, we are not mute witnesses to the events in it. Yet, some of it remains beyond our control; at times, our own actions, our interactions with others, may work against our plans. We have to accept this.

Sometimes, sitting by myself, I go back to my college days, I remember my friends of those days, I try to recollect their names. So many lost, but those who were in the hostel with me remain. After all, we lived together for over five years. Gaitonde and Mistry, Patil and Dabholkar—I remember our conversations, the long sessions we had when, disgusted with exams, we put our books away and determinedly spent the night talking. We talked of so many things—of teachers and exams, of our future and of going abroad, of politics and families. And, of course, of girls, the devouring obsession of most young men. Mistry was the Romeo among us, forever falling in love, only to fall out after a while and move on with an incredible swiftness to the next girl about whom he would be just as passionate.

'It's his way of passing time,' I said in his defence once, when he was being targeted by the others. 'Some of us eat nuts and wafers, he goes for girls as a time pass.'

'Time pass? Okay, but it's such a magnificent time pass,

Narayan. Try it, I'm telling you, just try it.'

Magnificent time pass. I think of Mistry's words and they seem to me to be the right words for life itself. Life and time running parallel to each other, but time always the master, dictating the pace, setting the parameters of life. And life complying, trying to make the best of what there is between those parameters. And yes, how wonderful this best is. A magnificent time pass, indeed. Even now I can call it magnificent, for I have not forgotten all the excitement and happiness that my life held. Working, thinking, loving—yes, these have made my life wonderful for me. My children above all, my children specially, were a constant source of delight. I was surprised myself by the joy, by the amount of joy I got from my children. Sometimes I think it's not children, but childhood itself that creates happiness. I see childhood as a repeated happy motif in our lives: first our own, then our children's and finally our grandchildren's.

This is something I have been deprived of. It's been growing on me in these last few days, a desire to see Jiji and the children. I know it's a weakness, I try to conquer it. I tell myself that I will not let myself indulge in this 'just once before I die' kind of emotional blackmail with Jiji. I admit it: Jiji owes me nothing. When my father fell ill, I knew it was my duty to look after him, my responsibility to care for him. But there was something more than duty and responsibility that urged me on; it was a kind of tug, so that I was never free of thoughts of him, I felt a positive ache in me at the thought of his weakness and increasing helplessness. Perhaps Jiji may feel the same way about me; I don't know. But I do know that I can't expect anything from her—not because she is a daughter, but because I failed her in her time of need. If I had stood by her, if I had resisted Vasu … But I could not have done that, I could not have opposed Vasu. It was neither love nor loyalty, nor even, as Jiji charged me in her anger, blindness. 'You can't see what she is doing,' she said. But I could see it, I did see it. And yet, I could not go against Vasu. That would have been cruel, it would have been more cruel than what I did to Jiji. In retrospect, it seems to me that I did badly by everyone, that I let everyone down.

Gayatri tried to comfort me when I said this to her. 'You did what you thought was best at the time, Badri.'

But I didn't; I knew even then that I was wrong. And so, much as I want to see Jiji, I remain silent. The truth is that we have become strangers to each other, my daughter and I. But so were Vasu and I, in the days after we came here. So what did I achieve? I thought I knew Vasu well, I knew her inside out, every nuance of her being, every bone in her body. Yet, I had to accept that I knew nothing about her real self. It seems to me that we humans are fated to be strangers to one another.

I think of my excitement when I read in my first year in college of how much a bone can tell you on examination: race, gender, age, size, the kind of life lived, diseases suffered from, the cause of death and so on. All this information, the story of a human being, stored in the bone, waiting to be extracted by us. I was fascinated by the thought. I decided I would go into research, I would work in this area, unearth more knowledge on the subject. Now I know that even with the encyclopaedia of the DNA, our knowledge is doomed to remain incomplete. The fact is that our identities do not contain just us; by ourselves we mean nothing. An identity becomes active, positive and meaningful only in relation to others. The whole potential of who we are and what we are is realized only through our relationship with others.

'I'm a Gemini, what are you?' Louisa, my partner in dissection, asked me the moment we met.

What was I? I didn't know and it was not a thing I cared to know about either; I said so to her bluntly. I was ashamed of myself later, but let me offer some excuses for my behaviour: I was young, crude and shy with girls. And I must confess that I also had the arrogance of intelligence which made me call it stupid, the idea of any connection between us and the stars, the idea of there being any similarity between people merely because they happened to be born at the same time of the year. I scoffed loudly at her belief, I laughed scornfully at her ideas.

But Louisa didn't take offence. She was a guileless and friendly soul and, being a great believer in birth signs and forecasts, she set off on a crusade to change my ideas. She saw me as the great disbeliever, the kafir who had to be converted. 'Gemini and Aquarius,' she said, when she discovered my birth date. 'No wonder we quarrel so much. Now if you had been a Libra ...'

Later, despite our having, as she said, hostile birth signs, we became friends, a friendship that lasted until she got married to a senior, a Marwadi boy. Both the families opposed the marriage. I was her confidant at this time, I was her supporter and gave her a shoulder to sob on in her worst moments. By then we had learnt to leave our beliefs and disbeliefs alone. But now I think, perhaps there was something in her theory that some relationships work and some, inexplicably it seems, don't. It's not the birth signs, no Louisa, you were mistaken about that, but there is something that makes two people who come together have a relationship in which they bring out the best in each other. Like Gayatri and RK.

I remember Gayatri's wild weeping the evening after we immersed RK's ashes in the Ganga. It had been Gayatri's desire to go to Kashi with his ashes and at that time I had wondered where the desire came from. We'd grown up, the two of us, in a home in which there were no religious rituals. Our father positively hated them. But after her marriage, Gayatri, as the elder daughter-in-law of the family, had to perform all the rituals; she had quickly learned the drill. I remember a Navaratri when I happened to be in Bangalore. I saw her preparing for the festival, going through the ten days of a rigorous and hard schedule—the elaborate puja of the family deity with its million rules and restrictions, the festive meals, the constant visitors. I thought she coped remarkably well and told her so, admiring her for being able to adapt so well. 'It's like playing a role in a drama, isn't it?' I asked.

'I do it with faith,' she said reproachfully. And then added, Gayatri-like, tongue-in-cheek, 'Actually, Badri, it's easier to do things for God. If you do them the way you are supposed to, if you get them exactly right, God is pleased. At least, you can think so. But you can never please humans.'

In Kashi, after Raja had finished performing the rituals, we sat on the steps of the ghat, he and I a little away from Gayatri; we sensed that she wanted to be by herself. She sat in silence gazing at the river and Raja and I, apart from an occasional desultory remark, sat in silence as well, watching the chaotic, constantly moving crowds in which the only still centres were the ritual-performing Brahmins with families huddled around them. Looking at the spectacle before me—people bathing, women dressing behind saris held up as screens, some children hovering around a single lone pyre burning on the Harishchandra Ghat, waiting for the embers to cool so that they could collect them, I thought: whatever thought or instinct it was that brought Gayatri here, it was absolutely right. Here, the bleakness of death was absorbed by constant movement and activity, death itself was absorbed by life and life moved towards death—an endless cycle, nothing final, nothing ending.

In a while Gayatri got up, and Raja and I silently rose too. We went back to the hotel and spent the day quietly by ourselves, Gayatri, fairly composed now, no longer avoiding us. But at night, when I went to look in on her, I found her weeping, a wild weeping that went on and on. I sat quietly by her until she was calmer. When she returned after a wash, I gave her a glass of water. She drank it, put down her glass and spoke, as if to herself, 'I've left his body behind. Now I can go back to him.'

I didn't pay much attention to her words then; I was more concerned with her grief, which distressed me enormously. Later, after Vasu's death, I remembered both Gayatri's grief and her words. I envied her the simplicity, the completeness of her grief. Mine was like a bed of nails, it would never get easier, not even with time and use. Nothing could soften or blunt the sharpness of the nails. I understood, too, what she had said about going back to RK and I knew that it could never be that way for me. Vasu would never be a comforting presence for me. Our relationship was flawed.

Once again I think of Louisa's words. I don't know why I am

thinking so much of Louisa today. She gave up her career after her marriage and we lost touch after that. I never thought of her in all these years. And now she is back, her words returning to me.

'You're so proud of not believing,' she charged me in the early days of our friendship, when she still hoped to make a believer of me. 'What's so great about not believing?'

Decades later, I concede the truth of her words. To believe in something is what matters. Indeed, sometimes, believing is a miracle. Like Louisa looking at the disjunctive fragments of the human body and yet believing in the Resurrection. Yes, that is a miracle. That kind of faith was not given to me. I don't regret it, for I put my faith in knowledge, in reason and in the people I loved. If ultimately it didn't work out, it was not because these things failed me, it was because I failed them.

a happy utopia

When I came to be with Baba during his illness, I was a little uneasy. I thought it would be awkward, for we had forgotten what it was to live together as father and daughter. But Baba's illness was like a mutual friend, it formed a link between us. It helped us too, to find a routine, since his treatment demanded an adherence to a strict schedule. The chemo sessions were the points around which the cycle of our days revolved, they were the red marks on the calendar for both of us. We dreaded these times; well, I certainly did. Two days in the hospital and then back to a regular regime. In a day he would be moving around the house, in a week he would be taking short strolls in the front yard and going for a drive with Raja whenever Raja had the time. Unlike most doctors, Baba was a good patient; to my surprise, he was a good fighter as well. He wanted to live, I could see that clearly. Anand's and Sachi's visits did him much good. The one time they were here together, we lived a simulacrum of a normal family life: father, daughter and grandchildren. In spite of this, both Baba and I were aware of the huge gaps in our midst. The absence of Mai and Malu was not just the natural gap that death creates in families; their not being with us was like a presence, reminding us of things we wanted to forget, things which we thought we had forgotten. When Anand and Sachi were with us, it was easier; their ignorance seemed to keep unwanted memories away, their young voices warded off ghosts. I saw that Baba found much joy in his relationship with the grandchildren he scarcely knew. When Anand suddenly turned up after I'd spoken to him of a setback in Baba's condition, he cheered up enormously. He was almost like the man I knew, as easy and comfortable with Anand as he had been with me when I was a child. But after Anand left, it was a rapid slide downhill. Within a fortnight he was dead.

Anand and Sachi went away and, left alone in the house, I found myself inhabiting what I could only think of as a blank space. The routine that Baba and I had so carefully built between us had disappeared and there was nothing left: nothing I had to do, no dates to keep track of, no time of the day to wait for, no cooking; in fact, nothing. Yes, a blankness that carried a sense of anarchy. Not to have anyone making demands on you, not to have to meet others' demands, makes for a lack of order in life. It is others' demands that shape our lives; our own are so confused, so chaotic, so many, that they create nothing but disorder. *Man is a social animal*—I remember Sachi writing it out in neat letters in her social studies notebook. Alone in the house after Baba's death, free for the first time of the necessity of having to do anything for others, I understood the exact meaning of those words.

I took to going on long bus rides. Getting into any bus that went to the outskirts of the city, I would ride in it until it reached the terminus. I would linger there, sometimes joining the conductor and the driver at the little stalls that always seemed to be around, stalls that sold cigarettes, soft drinks and bananas. I'd sip my Limca or Mirinda until I saw the driver throw away his cigarette stub and grind it under his heel. I would get back into the bus then and ride back into town. The conductor and driver sometimes gave me odd looks. Once, a friendly conductor, seeing me doing this the third day in succession, asked me what I was doing, why I came all the way and went back. 'I'm passing the time,' I told him and he accepted it, sensing that I was speaking the truth. In a few days they got used to me, having decided, perhaps, that I was a harmless eccentric. I didn't mind. They ignored me and it was peaceful to sit in the bus and see the city go past me. It was a revelation to see it changing, to watch the process of change. I saw the farms and vacant bits of land being devoured by builders, the mushrooming of housing estates, the hills being slowly nibbled at to provide stone and granite. I watched the lorries filled with sand go past, looking as if they would break down under the weight of their load any moment. There was a sense of an unseen force wielding a whip, dictating a pace, and everyone frantically trying to keep up. These rides helped me to get through the early days, to cope with the long empty hours in an empty house.

Now I've got used to being alone. Living alone is an art that one learns finally to appreciate. To know that there is no need to look at the clock, that nothing is a must, is a pleasure. I can eat when I want, I can eat what I want, I can do things at times I find convenient. I think of Mai harrying us to have our baths early in the morning; she thought it indecent to sit about unbathed, in unwashed clothes. I gave up these early baths as soon as I left home, but the children's needs still kept me glued to the clock. Now I am free of that as well. The TV remote has become a symbol of my freedom; I'm mistress of all I survey, I decide what I want to see.

How long will this last? What will I do if Sachi insists on selling the house? Why is it that she has not once taken me into account, never imagined that I want a pause in my living after years of constant movement? I've written to her, telling her of Raja's objections to selling—the practical ones, that is. I don't want to bring in the emotional arguments, like saying that Raja's feelings matter—though I know that we need to take them into account. In fact, he has more right to take decisions than I, who stayed away all these years, who was never around when I was wanted. Raja was with Baba and Gayatri when Mai died, it was he who helped Baba after Gayatri's death. And much earlier, when Gayatri found it hard to move into her new home without RK, Raja stayed with her until Baba and Mai came. It was Raja, too, who planned and built the two rooms on the first floor so that Baba could have his own space.

All these things are part of the house. But to take them into account is to ignore the practicalities, one of which is that we don't really need such a large house. What we need is a small place to live in and some money in the bank for security.

'It makes sense. You of all people should approve of Sachi's pragmatism,' I tell Raja.

He refuses to be provoked into an argument. It's Saturday evening, his time of complete relaxation, something I've become part of since Baba's death. 'The Old Soaks' Club' Pavan called us when he was home the last time. There was, I thought, a slight touch of moral censoriousness in his tone, but Raja told me solemnly, with the touch of priggishness that comes over him when he speaks of his son, 'Pavan understands'. Raja, whose parenting involves a total frankness with his son, had told him that having a drink just once a week was his answer to the drinking problem he had got into after Rukku's death. Once a week and never alone. Baba, though not a drinker, had been his companion. And when I came home, I joined them, becoming part of the Saturday evening ritual.

'What will you have?' he asked me the first time.

'A gin? Gin and Limca, if you have it?'

He looked at Baba's deadpan face, then at mine and said, 'Sure.' But later, when we were getting things together in the kitchen, he hissed at me, 'How could you?'

'How could I what?'

'Ask for a drink with your father right there.'

'You mean I can drink out of his sight, but not when he's with me? Isn't that terrible hypocrisy, Raja?'

'It's not hypocrisy. It's just—why do you have to go out of your way to displease him? You're trying to prove what a rebel you are. You always were a show-off.'

I went out swiftly to Baba at that and asked him, 'Baba, do

you mind my having a drink?'

'Why should I?'

'This ... this ... orthodox Brahmin thinks I shouldn't be drinking. Not in your presence, he says.'

'Why, Raja, you're the son of a man whose weekly Scotch was a ritual, he drank it almost as if it was teertha. Didn't he drink in my company?'

'But he and you—you're friends.'

'What about Jiji, then?'

'She's—it's different.'

'How is it different?' I asked him, daring him to say it, daring him to say, *But you're a woman, you're a daughter.*'

'Oh, leave it alone. I'm sorry I said anything. Let's start all over again. Jiji, what will you have?'

'A gin and Limca, please. If you have it.'

'I don't have any Limca. Will a gin and tonic do?'

'Perfect.'

And Baba laughed.

Raja now accepts me as his drinking companion on Saturdays, he even enjoys it. Or so I think, though he never says so.

'The bank has released the money from Baba's account,' I tell Raja after he has started the music and we settle down for the evening.

'Good,' he says.

'And I've decided to get myself a car.'

'What!' He puts down his glass so suddenly the drink spills over. 'You said you were going to buy a computer.'

'That too.'

'Jiji, you're crazy. Squandering your money this way. It's going to vanish in no time.'

'There speaks the accountant's son!'

'No, I'm serious ...'

I try to reassure Raja. I tell him there's more money than I expected. Did he know that Baba had written a kind of basic guide on anatomy for first-year medical students? And did he know that it had been selling very well all these years?

'I found the correspondence and the accounts. He used to get quite a good sum every year, Raja. I think Baba got more out of his writing than Mai ever did from her stories. Good old Mr Bones,' I say. 'Still on our side.'

'But do you have any idea how much it costs to maintain a car?' Raja has a single-track mind. It's not easy to turn him away from whatever he's pursuing. 'And you don't even know how to drive.'

'I'll learn. It's not impossible. It's been done before. And let me fulfil at least one of my middle-class dreams, Raja. Having a car of my own—you privileged men who take these things for granted can't imagine what it means to people like me.'

'But why do you need a car?'

'What do you mean *why*? I bet if I were a man, you'd never have asked that question.'

'Not that argument again! It's stale and sick. Give it a rest, woman. What I'm trying to say is that you need to be careful with your money. What will you do when it's all gone?'

'You forget I've been supporting myself and two children all these years. I can still do that. I'll get a job.'

'At your age?'

'Thanks.'

'No, seriously, Jiji—the market is flooded with kids ready to work for peanuts. As long as they get enough for their fun times, they're happy. What chance do you have, competing with them?'

The drink makes me expansive—like it always does. Life is full of possibilities, I tell him. They stretch out before me, varied and never ending. These are the days of private enterprise, I tell him, in case he hasn't noticed. Of entrepreneurship. Of quickie millionaires. I can turn my car into a taxi, for instance.

'Who'd trust a woman driver?'

'Again! Really, Raja, haven't you noticed that the world has moved on? You don't say such things nowadays. And as for who'd trust a woman driver, the answer is—other women for a start. But I have another idea, an even better idea. Nirmala and I can start a proper yoga school. We have ten children coming to us now, we can have twenty—or why not thirty?'

'*We*?'

'For your information, I am now Nirmala's assistant. I've been helping her for the last three months.'

'And where would this school be?'

'In our garage, of course.'

'Your *garage*? I thought the classes were in Nirmala's house?'

'Yes, but there's not enough room. Anyway, that's not the point. We can always get a place. I'll get a loan. It's easier for a woman to get a bank loan, specially if you're starting a business.'

'Oh god,' Raja groans. 'You're talking rubbish. It's the drink. I'd better get us some food.'

The music comes to an end while he's gone and silence fills the room. I sit unmoving. As always, the euphoria has faded away and my confident plans evaporate like mist in sunshine. I can't escape the truth, which is that I don't want to do anything. It's an after-a-heavy-breakfast-on-a-summer-morning kind of lassitude that seems to have overtaken me. A lethargy that refuses to go away. When I remember the frantic pace of my life all these years, it seems to me that suddenly the driving force, whatever it was, I don't pretend to know what, has gone. No finger in my back prodding me to move on, no voice reminding me sternly that I should be up and doing. Doing a Beetle Bailey: Anand's phrase for this kind of a state—lying under a tree doing nothing, thinking of nothing. Unfortunately, as I reminded Anand, there's always Sarge appearing from round the corner, chivvying you, making you go back to work so that you start running all over again. But my 'Sarge' has disappeared. The need to survive, to keep the children fed and clothed, to pay for their schools—the things which kept me going are no longer there. Baba's money will look after the children. I can afford to relax, I don't need to struggle any longer. Raja is wrong, I'll never fall short of money. My needs are simple. I have enough clothes (and when they wear out, I can always wear Gayatri's and Mai's saris), I have a house to live in (provided Sachi doesn't sell it) and Raja to give me my weekly drink. I can live very happily this way. I can see myself going on like this (again, provided Sachi doesn't sell the house), living alone, becoming an eccentric old woman. Wearing Gayatri's magnificent silks (over tattered petticoats) even at home, eating what I like, when I like. Cream crackers and soup for lunch, pohe and sev for dinner and, when I want a change, masala dosas. And yes, talking to myself, something I've already begun doing. Yeah, a nutty old woman is what I'm going to end up as.

Raja, entering with parcels that spread the aroma of food through the room, asks, 'Who were you talking to?'

'Myself. I was telling myself my future, my fate.'

'Come and eat while the stuff is hot. And get the plates and spoons.'

It's from a new place he's discovered, Raja tells me, while he carefully unwraps the parcels. 'I heard it was very good. Though they always are when they're new.'

Raja's a great one for trying out new places. 'How is it?' he asks me anxiously the moment I begin, even before I've swallowed a morsel.

'Let me eat first.' He continues to look expectantly at me until I give my verdict. 'It's okay. Like any other place. The sagu is slightly more spicy than usual, though. You may not like it. It's just right for me.'

'I think this chutney is good, don't you?'

'Hmm—pudina! I hate pudina.'

'Really, Jiji, you have the oddest tastes!'

'What's odd about not liking pudina? Raja, do you realize this is loaded with cholesterol?'

'Who cares! I'm damned, anyway. All men are doomed to have heart problems. And you're a woman, you don't have to worry.'

'Yes, you do. I mean, we do. After menopause you're as vulnerable as a man. That gives me just a few years more.'

'Really, Jiji! Spare me the gory details of a woman's life.'

As we're clearing up, I notice that he carefully puts away the string that came with the parcels.

'That's what I was thinking of when you came back,' I tell

Raja. 'Of how one starts getting eccentric by living alone.'

'Eccentric? Who's eccentric?'

'Look at the way you're saving that string.'

'That's being sensible, not eccentric. But you're right. You will get eccentric living alone. So will I—eventually. Maybe. Which is why I say we should join forces.'

'You're not living alone. You have Pavan.'

'Only during the holidays. And he … Jiji, you've lived with adolescents—tell me honestly, does their being home make any difference?'

'All the difference. All the difference. You can't call your soul your own.'

This is the cue for starting on our children, the only time when we are on the same side. Both of us parents. And single parents at that.

'I must be one of the few unfortunate mothers whose children have higher standards than them,' I say to Raja, wallowing in self-pity. 'They're always looking down on me. And making their disapproval of me clear. Anand makes me feel sinful when I use a word he thinks mothers shouldn't use! And Sachi …'

Raja gets in with his story of Pavan's secretiveness. 'He never lets out anything. I have to literally squeeze it out of him—you know, like the last of the toothpaste.'

'That's normal, Raja. My children never tell me anything, either.'

'Yes, but what I can't bear is the way he makes me feel he's putting up with me, indulging a silly old man, you know.'

'Let's face it, Raja, we're a disappointment to our children.'

'And we disappoint our parents as well. You should listen to Amma speaking to me …'

'I'm past all that now.'

'I'm sorry, Jiji, I didn't mean to …'

'Oh, it's okay.'

The brief camaraderie was a mistake. It gets Raja back to his cause. And this time he adds, 'You haven't given me one solid reason for not marrying me.'

I have given him many reasons, enough reasons, even the fact that we can never agree on anything. But I know what he means when he says I have not given him a single 'solid' reason. Anyway, what is a solid reason? That I don't like Raja? That he's not good enough for me, or that I'm not good enough for him? None of these is true. What is true then? I don't know. That's the truth—I don't know.

'It will be good for our children,' he says earnestly. He is annoyed, on the verge of being furious, when I begin to laugh.

'It's not you, I'm not laughing at you,' I quickly reassure him before he begins sulking. Why are men so frightened of being laughed at? 'I was thinking of Sachi.'

I tell him about Sachi's behaviour towards a colleague who had shown interest in me. Her glowering presence during his visits and her deliberate rudeness which had finally made him retreat. It was quite a success for Sachi, I tell him.

'But were you serious?'

'I don't know. I think he was.'

'He wanted to marry you?'

'No. He wanted to sleep with me.'

He is about to speak, then stops. 'Say it, Raja, say it,' I urge him helpfully.

'You've changed, Jiji, you've changed enormously.'

He's thinking of the girl who gave up the window seat without protest to Malu, the girl who crouched at the feet of the others in the old Fiat to allow them to sit in greater comfort, the girl who was willing to do anything to please others. The girl who needed everybody's approval.

But what happens when all the people whose approval you wanted are no longer there?

'Yes, I've changed, Raja. I couldn't have survived if I hadn't changed.'

As always, Raja walks me home. Each time I tell him I don't need him, I can go back alone, it's just two streets away after all. But it makes no difference. The walk does me good, he says. I need the fresh air, he says. I know this is only partly true. Raja is still being the protecting male, the role our two families had thrust on him when we were children.

I have a strange dream at night. There are short dreams at first, little bits that I wake out of. And then I go back to sleep and there's another little snippet of a dream. Each time nothing remains, except the last one which I wake out of to find the daylight showing through the windows. In this dream, which I can remember, I'm in a place that looks like the set of a Hindi movie, a carpeted staircase branching into two after a broad landing. I go up the stairs and into a passage which has paintings on the panelled wall. I'm moving slowly along the passage, looking at the paintings as if I'm at a painting exhibition, when a door in the passage, which I haven't noticed until then, opens. A man looks out, then goes back in, leaving the door open. I go into the room and lie down on one of the twin beds. He comes to me and puts his arms around me. And almost immediately we start making love. I wake up at the moment of the climax, the dream still vivid in my mind. I try to erase it, but my body continues to retain the memory of that skin to skin contact, of its fierce and sudden arousal. I get out of bed in one angry movement and make myself a cup of tea, I get on with the chores of the day, but the dream lingers. A swift coupling which was so complete in the dream, but left me on the saw-edge of irritated frustration.

'I don't want to get married, Raja,' I told him. Which is true. But what if I add, 'I don't mind sex, though.' What will he do? What will he say? Will he call me a show-off again, or is that too innocent a word, inadequate for his purpose? And anyway, I can't think of sex with Raja, either. I know him so well that his body seems, somehow, taboo. I think of Shyam, such a stranger to me, a stranger in every way, and how his body could and did arouse me so much that I thought it was worth giving up the world for.

Later in the day, I suddenly identify the place in my dream, that place with the carpeted staircase and the panelled corridor: it was a government guest house we'd stayed in years ago during one of our summer visits to Bangalore. RK had arranged the overnight stay in the magnificent building, a relic of the past, of the times of the Maharaja and the British. Strange that a place of childhood joys and enjoyment should come back to me in such a dream. It's more than strange, it's incongruous, to associate a memory of childhood, a time when I had such an innocent relationship with my body, with my unexpressed sexual desires, my body's needs.

*

It's been a week since Abhishek's friend, Shridhar, installed the computer. I'm sitting in front of it when Abhishek rings the bell. 'Okay, ma'am?' he asks when I let him in, and I know he's referring to the computer.

After years of being a despised, looked-down-upon tenant, it's a strange experience to find myself on the other side of the fence, so to say. To be called 'ma'am' so respectfully, to be looked at as a landlady amuses me, yet makes me uncomfortable as well. I'm not used to such treatment. But since his friend has got me the computer, Abhishek and I seem to be on slightly different terms. He's less formal and more friendly, as if my ignorance and his expertise have levelled the ground and we are now on equal terms.

'The computer's okay, Abhishek. It's me you should be making anxious inquiries about.'

'Why, ma'am, are you still having trouble with it?'

'Well—not too much now. I'm slowly getting the hang of it. And I'm less scared of it.'

Abhishek laughs, remembering perhaps, my panic the first time I'd had trouble with it. After reassuring me, he'd asked a little hesitantly, 'Ma'am, didn't Shridhar give you any instructions?'

'He gave me a crash course. Really crash—it was at breakneck speed.' Saying 'no problem' with a maddening cheerfulness to all my queries, all my doubts. His hands had moved the mouse so swiftly that I was left totally clueless about what he was doing. His fingers moved rapidly over the keyboard, making me feel like a person who knows nothing about music, watching a pianist's hands.

'He's very busy, ma'am. He's only just started his own ...'

'I know that. I wasn't complaining. And anyway, he left me with an assistant.'

But the assistant, I realized as soon as we were on our own, wasn't really an assistant at all. He had seemed so knowledgeable until then, bringing out CDs from the bag with promptness, picking up the right wires for connections. But left to himself, he could say nothing but 'Yes, ma'am' very respectfully to everything that I said. He finally admitted that he was a novice, that he was on this job to learn and get some hands-on experience; his knowledge, he confessed, was severely limited.

So, I embarked on my own. After the initial nervousness, fear and even anger—no machine was going to make me feel stupid!— I began to learn. And faster when I decided mistakes didn't matter. Then I began to enjoy it—everything was so flexible, the words like nomads, free to move about, never fixed in a place. And the delete key fascinated me totally. Not only does nothing remain, it's as if it never was. Complete extinction. No rows of Xs, no ugly blobs, no lines drawn through the words, desperately hoping they won't make sense. History will henceforth go down without shadows, I thought, without any evidence of erasure, erasures which tell their own story. It's like thumbing your nose at Omar Khayyam. The moving finger is no longer the greatest force, for the delete key can erase everything. If only we could do this to our lives: press the delete key and wipe out what hurts us.

The telephone rings, startling me out of my thoughts. I leave the computer with reluctance, understanding why it can become an addiction.

'Yes?'

'Hello?' a strange voice cautiously asks. 'Has Ratna come today?'

I know who this is; it's Ratna's other employer, the woman who rings up each time Ratna stays away from work, making a major tragedy of her absence. Always asking the same questions: is she coming? Did she say anything about not coming today? As if I am specially privileged to have some information she doesn't. I guess this was true when Gayatri was alive, for I have seen Ratna's sense of loyalty to Gayatri; to her, this is still 'Gayatriamma's house'. Added to this was her compassion for Baba when he fell ill, which had made her more considerate towards us. Now I am in the same position as this anonymous anxious woman is, I'm no longer singled out for special consideration. But she doesn't believe that. Once again I have to go through my usual disclaimers of Ratna's intentions. I'm ready to put the phone down when the woman surprises me by saying, 'I hear you're selling the house.'

'I am?'

'My brother is looking for a house in this area. If you're selling, let me know. I'm interested.'

I make my denial and put down the phone, thinking—now who gave her that information?

'Was it you who told the other-house Amma I was selling the house?' I ask Ratna when she comes to work the next day.

'I? Why would I do such a thing?'

'I don't know. I'm asking you.'

'Of course I didn't. I don't have the time to gossip. I just do my work and go home.'

'But if you didn't, then who did?'

'How do I know? But the way you've been throwing out things, anyone would think you're going to sell it. Can't they see what's happening? Do they need to be told?'

She can't pinpoint who these people are, it remains the usual vague 'they'. Though I have to admit the truth of what she's saying, my uneasiness returns when in the afternoon I have another caller asking me the same question.

'Madam,' the man begins in English, 'this is regarding your house. I have got information that you are selling it?' he says, or asks rather, his voice rising interrogatively on the last words.

The abruptness of the question, coming from an unknown

person, angers me. 'Who are you?' I ask in Kannada, to emphasize that I'm no outsider, I belong here.

The man moves smoothly into Kannada himself, sounding more polite now, as if the familiar language propels him into the necessary courtesies.

'We are Adarsh Agency,' he says.

'An estate agent?'

'Yes, madam.'

They've heard—yes, again from the vague 'they'—that the house is for sale. Is that true? Can they come and see the place? And meet me?

No, I tell him, the house is not for sale. But neither my denial nor my refusal seems to affect his composure.

'All right,' he says. 'Take your time. But whenever you want to sell, call us.' He gives me a number, which I don't write down. As if he knows I haven't taken it down, he adds—and I realize, more from his tone than from the words, that it is a warning— 'And be careful, madam.'

'Take care', young people say these days to one another. It means nothing, the words are used carelessly, aping another culture, another way of life. But this man spoke in Kannada; in this language the words still carry their true meaning.

'What did you say?' I ask, as if I haven't heard him.

'I said, be careful, madam,' he repeats. 'It's for your own good that I'm telling you this.'

I'm disturbed when I put down the phone. What was that about? Was he warning me or threatening me? I must tell Raja about this, I think, and then remember that Raja is not in town. He's gone out on work. I put my anxiety in storage for the time being, but it returns when Abhishek brings up the topic again. He asks me, directly and abruptly, 'Ma'am, are you selling the house?'

I'm no longer surprised by the question. The 'Who told you?' is a mere formality, for of course I know the answer. This time it's a vague 'someone', a distant cousin, obviously, of 'they'.

'I may be going abroad for three months, so I thought I must find out. If you're selling, I may have to make other plans for when I return.'

No, I tell him, I'm not selling. Not right now, anyway. Possibly, not at all.

We have to scotch these rumours, specially since we've come to an agreement, Sachi, Anand and I. No, it's really just Sachi and I; Anand is agreeable to everything. Sachi has changed her mind. We won't do anything right now, she says. We'll talk about it when we meet. Raja was most relieved when I told him. Actually, this hasn't been a very happy house. I think of the many deaths it is associated with—Mai's, Gayatri's, Baba's. And RK's, too; though he didn't die here, the sadness of the fact that he died before he could come and live here is part of the house. I, who came in at the death all the three times, find the house full of memories. It must be worse for Raja, who went through these experiences with Gayatri and Baba. But then death, just as much as birth, knits us into the being of a house. Death *more* than birth, I think, because the finality of death keeps your memories chained to a place. With birth, there is a moving on, a going ahead, memories piling up, diluting the original ones.

This place means more to Raja than just a house; I have begun to understand that, to him, it is a symbol of the old family home. 'Our happy Utopia', he called the old house once. A tautology, surely, for why does Utopia need the prop of the adjective? Or maybe it does, for perfection does not necessarily include happiness, does it? And for us, for Raja and me certainly, the memories of the old house embrace perfection as well as happiness. Raja is right; it was a happy Utopia. I haven't thought of that house for a very long time. I've put it away, shut the door on memories, afraid to open it; memories of happiness can cause as much pain as sorrowful ones. And yet, once I open the door, it's all there, intact and dust-free, no cobwebs, either. Curiously, the first memory that rushes out at me is that of the snake, the snake we had all raced out to see when Venkoji, the driver, had announced its presence. We had run to the backyard, slowing down as we came closer, warned by Venkoji not to scare it. As if it was the snake that was endangered by us and not the other way round. And there it was, sunning itself, its long sleek length gleaming like a jewelled chain. We stood in silence and stared, unafraid and awed by its magnificence and beauty. Suddenly, sensing our presence perhaps, though we were absolutely quiet, scarcely even breathing, it slithered away into the grass, a kind of contempt in the way it ignored us, in its withdrawal.

Snake in the grass. When I hear the phrase I don't think of betrayal or treachery, but of the beauty and dignity of the snake we saw, of the silence and awe with which we watched it. The snake is, for me, a symbol of the perfection of those days, of the happiness of our holidays spent in that house. For us, coming to Bangalore from Bombay, the sense of unhurried time, of infinite space, was wonderful. Lying in bed, in the long open passage on the first floor overlooking the main hall, we could hear all the voices in the house, the early morning getting-ready-for-breakfast sounds a background to the voices, we could smell the coffee and the sambar which would accompany our idlis. It was heaven. Even better was the knowledge that I could continue to lie in bed, that there was no school bus to catch, no toast to be crammed down my throat, no milk to be gulped down. And then the thought that I was losing out on something would wake me up in an instant, the soft laziness suddenly erupting into frantic activity. I would rush down and RK would ask me, like he did every single day of the holidays: 'And what are your plans for today?'

It was RK and Gayatri who made the house what it was, they who made our holidays what they were. The days seemed disorganized and unstructured to us, something we relished after the monotony of our regulated-by-the-clock life in Bombay; but I know now that Gayatri's and RK's planning was the foundation on which these carefree days were built. It was more Gayatri than RK, actually. While RK wanted us to enjoy ourselves, Gayatri worked hard to see that we did. RK was a distant figure; he had a dignity that kept us a little away—a dignity, though not the pompousness that often goes with the position of a senior bureaucrat. There was, now that I think of it, a slight naivety about him which made him the endearing person he was. He wanted to communicate with us, to be with us, to meet us at our level, but he didn't quite know how to do it. Which made him a little awkward and uncomfortable when interacting with us— something rare in adults when they are with children. The fact is, RK was most at ease in his working life; he knew exactly his role and place there. For the rest, it was through Gayatri that he connected to the everyday world and to people; even his own sisters were more intimate with Gayatri than they were with him. The entire household revolved around RK—Gayatri arranged it that way—but he never seemed to be aware of it. He would occupy his chair at the head of the table with his special towel draped over its back as a matter of course, he would even sometimes offer us that special towel when we rushed in with wet hands, saying, 'Here, wipe your hands'. But aware of Gayatri's eyes which warned us not to take the towel, we would say, 'It's okay, Kaka', and go out to wipe our hands on the 'janata towel', as BK called it, which hung on the rod above the sink. And there was his special chair on the porch which we never dared to sit in, except when he was not at home. But *he* never thought of himself as anything special. 'And what are your plans for today?' he would ask. Then he would turn to Gayatri. 'What have you planned for them today, Gayatri? Do you need the car? What time shall I send Venkoji?'

And so it was a different outing each day: dosas at MTR, ice creams on MG Road, boating in Ulsoor Lake, roaming about in Lal Bagh and Cubbon Park. Yes, the lot. But there were also days when we did nothing but laze at home, playing interminable card games or carrom during the afternoons, or dark-room games in the large junk room, games which resulted in injuries which we concealed from the adults. And once, for a whole month we did nothing but ride our bikes.

If the days were our own, the evenings were spent with the

adults. In fact, the evenings belonged to the adults. We were on the sidelines; spectators, not participants. Sitting on the steps of the porch after dinner, exhausted but unable to tear myself away from everyone, not wanting to end the day, I would listen to the adults laughing and chatting, all of them relaxed and at ease, even RK a different man now, very clearly off duty. Mai's was the one voice rarely heard, until RK would turn to her and bring her into the conversation, calling her 'Vasundharabai', to show his enormous respect for her.

There was one summer when we children performed a play. BK was the unlikely force behind it, the initiator of this rather unusual activity. It began during our cycling mania, when our entire day was spent cycling in the front yard, going round and round in endless circles. Raja and I were quarrelling, I remember, about a puncture, Raja accusing me of having caused it.

'I told you to put blow,' he yelled at me.

'Why should I? You made the puncture, you put blow.'

BK, standing on the porch, cupped his hand round his ear as if he wanted to catch every word of our squabble. 'Translate that for me, if you please,' he said.

We stared blankly at him, Raja half on his bike, half off, our mouths open in astonishment.

'What language was that?' BK asked.

'English,' Raja said, his face and tone showing he was surprised by the question. Raja, as usual, unable to understand his father's sarcasm.

'English! You call that English! *Put blow!*' he repeated our words with a dramatic groan. 'I have to do something about this.'

The result was a play, a scene from Hamlet. I find it hard to believe it myself—Shakespeare and Hamlet for children who spoke of 'put blow', but yes, Hamlet it was. BK made us enact the grave diggers scene. I imagine now that BK thought of it, not only because Shakespeare was for him the epitome of exquisite language, but also because he had the brainwave of making it a special performance for Baba's birthday. It was another 'jokey' gift, like the 'I'm the boss in my house' plaque. A cheeky tribute to Baba's bone fixation. BK, who was as dignified as his brother, though more consciously so (both the brothers had an idea of their own importance as men, as heads of their families), loved practical jokes. His was a kind of verging-on-the-slapstick sense of humour—his only release, I guess, from the otherwise correct self that he presented to the world. And with Baba, he sometimes went back to their boyhood intimacy, behaving in a way that embarrassed Raja but delighted the rest of us.

But this time BK had taken on more than he could handle. Rehearsing us for the play—just fifteen minutes, really—was a nightmare for him. From the first day, he was more concerned that we should say the words right, with the correct accent, than that we should remember all of them. Raja, Premi and I who studied in English-medium schools were bad enough. But Pandu, BK's sister's son, who came from a Kannada school in Mysore and whose English sounded exactly like Kannada, defeated BK. He tried to bend Pandu's accent to a near-British one, something Pandu went along with cheerfully enough, accepting it, as we all did, as one of the queer vagaries of adults we had to endure. But his attempts produced such bizarre results that most of the time we were in fits of laughter and BK was tearing his hair out in despair. Actually, we understood Pandu's English, the way he spoke it naturally, better than we understood BK's when he put on an accent.

Our rehearsals were in secret, behind closed doors; BK wanted to spring a surprise on the family, specially on Baba. And we *did* surprise everyone. I can see Baba's face when we emerged as Shakespearan characters—Raja as Hamlet and Pandu as Horatio, with towels pinned to their shoulders and streaming down their backs, while Premi and I, the grave diggers, wore our usual T-shirts and shorts. Premi sulked at not getting the star role, but I enjoyed my role and played it with gusto, jumping about, asking for laughs, encouraged by the laughter, specially Gayatri's. I could see that she was enjoying what I was doing. But Raja was furious.

'Stop showing off,' he hissed at me and I was pleased to see his chagrin at my 'success'. But neither Raja nor I were the stars of our scene. The crowd-puller was the skull, which BK had got from god-knows-where and which, we were warned, we had to produce with a flourish. Baba got the point, he understood the joke, but Gayatri was horrified, shrieking at us not to touch it, asking someone to take it out of the house.

'And you a haddi doctor's sister!' BK said reprovingly, enjoying the effect of his joke. 'Surely you can't object to a bone!'

'Where did you get that from? Whose skull is it?'

'Ask your brother,' RK said, entering into BK's joke.

'I think it's a Hindu skull.'

'Can't be. Hindu skulls don't go wandering, not usually, anyway.'

All of them in it now, all of them pulling Gayatri's leg.

'Hindu, Muslim or Christian, I don't care. Just get it out of the house.'

And so Venkoji was asked to bury it in the backyard, as far away from the house as possible.

BK's love of all things British extended to music as well. He had brought home some records after his stay in England and the music provided the background to our evenings in their house. I said something derogatory about it once and Raja reproved me, saying knowledgeably, 'That's Bach.' Ignoramus that I was, I thought it was the Marathi word 'baak', so that the music was to me forever associated with a bench. But there were some records we could enjoy too. One of our special favourites was a song sung by a husky female voice, which began with the words 'Those were the days, my friend'. There was one summer when we played this record endlessly, over and over again. Premi, Malu and I never tired of listening to the sweet voice singing, 'Those were the days my friend, we thought they'd never end, we'd sing and dance forever and a day.'

Yes, we thought they'd never end, those days, we thought we'd sing and dance forever, we thought that things would go on in this way eternally, all of us together, enclosed in the laughter and love of adults. It was a magical world. I remember the evenings, everyone sitting on the porch after dinner, the smell of jasmine strong and powerful in the night, the adults talking. I can't remember what they talked about, just the voices, male and female, in three languages, weaving a soft comforting fabric. And the laughter, Baba's loud and hearty, BK's a sharp shout. Gayatri's girlish and happy. And the silences in between, when we heard the cries of the hawker who always came at this time of the night, crying out the name of the fruit which sounded to me like 'tattiningu'—the most tasteless fruit, I thought, but which Hemi wanted to have every day. Gayatri bargaining with the hawker, their soft murmurs—this was part of the magic of the evenings as well. And one evening we saw a procession go by, the flaring lights illuminating a god carried in a palanquin, which was preceded by the light bearers and followed by men and women who walked in utter silence, the only sound being the soft whisper of their bare feet on the ground. The women wore silks and diamonds which gleamed in the shifting light, while the men, in white zari-bordered dhotis, were bare-chested like the palanquin bearers. They stopped briefly before our gate in response to some invisible gesture from Gayatri, who silently offered a plate of puja things. Then the procession moved on, the shadows lengthening, wavering, the figures becoming dark silhouettes once more. A deeply satisfying spectacle which we absorbed in the same silence in which the men and women went past, a ghostly pageant that was clouded in mystery. I think of that moment now, of the utter silence in which we watched the procession go past, of the silence in which we then went to bed, finding release, when we had gone upstairs, in loud cries and horseplay.

'Those were the days my friend, we thought they'd never end …'

But they did end and I had a role to play in that ending. I didn't know it then, I put things together much later and realized what I had done. It was my discovery of the termites that was the beginning of the end. I was looking idly at the family pictures in the niche above the divan when I noticed that one of them looked odd. There was a kind of fuzzy cloud in a corner of it, a greyish white cloud that seemed to be moving, obscuring the faces of the children sitting on the floor at the feet of the adults. Horrified, I called out to Gayatri. She took down the picture, gave it one look and threw it away with a shriek of horror. I'd never seen her so disturbed. Even RK, who rarely entered into domestic life, came to comfort her, saying soothingly, 'We'll do something, we'll get rid of it.'

But Gayatri knew the propensity of termites to destroy better than he did. Workers came in after we left and attacked the niche on the wall where the picture had been. But it was of no use. The rot had gone too far; not much could be done. The solid, substantial structure that looked as if it would last forever, as if it would be there until eternity, was being slowly chewed up by termites. Soon after, the house was demolished and the site sold.

And so the end began with me. When I heard that the house had to be destroyed, I thought it was my fault. And later, when our family life in Bombay came to an end, that was my fault too. Mai said so to me. If she had said it in anger, I might have discounted it, I might have ignored it. But she said it in sorrow, such deep sorrow that I had to accept she meant it.

'Why didn't your father leave the house to you?' Sachi asked me, almost accusingly, as if guessing that it was because I'd done something wrong. Perhaps, I think now, in his eyes I *had* done wrong, perhaps he didn't trust me, perhaps he was afraid of my termite-like qualities.

*

It's the day of my driving test. I'm a little nervous, but I can see that my fellow victim is in an even worse condition. Considering her atrocious driving, she has every reason to be as terrified as she appears to be. Her daughter looks even more nervous than her. She'd been this way all through our lessons, drawing her breath in sharply each time her mother got close to another car, screaming 'Amma' when a two-wheeler shot across in front of us—something which had at first unnerved me too, until I'd realized that this was something all self-respecting scooter and auto drivers were bound to do. In fact, I think of them as suicide squads intent on harakiri. But the girl made a near-mishap of every small misjudgement of her mother's—of which there were plenty. Looking at her, hands clenched into fists, large eyes carrying a load of terror, obviously expecting a crash every moment, I'd wondered: why does the woman bring her along? It can't be for reassurance, this panic-stricken girl can't reassure anyone. Or is the girl a chaperone, protecting her mother from the possible lustful attentions of the instructor? But we'd been clearly told, on the very first day, that our instructor was good with 'ladies'. Which meant, I learnt, that not only was he guaranteed not to paw us, he would also be patient with us, making allowances for our dumbness. Assuming that women were bound to be slow, to make stupid mistakes and panic, taking these things into account when he dealt with them. Which is why, perhaps, he didn't bat an eyelid at the woman's mistakes, he rarely reproved her. The only reprimand he had was for the daughter when she screamed, the time her mother missed a van by a whisker at a traffic junction.

'You have to be silent, child,' he said. 'Otherwise, don't come from tomorrow.'

I could feel her sulking beside me after that, whether for the scolding or because he called her a child, I don't know. Fortunately, it did silence her and I, who had felt her terror infecting me, had relaxed too, no longer clenching my hands, or stretching my legs as if to push down the brakes even though I knew the instructor was using the brakes on her behalf. It was, no doubt, because of this knowledge that the instructor was so composed. It gave the woman, too, an illusion of safety which I thought was misleading; it was dangerous, in fact, to have this kind of dual control.

'Please don't use the brakes,' I told him early on.

'You don't worry about me, madam. You just do what you have to.'

But I did worry. How would I learn if I didn't have to cope with the risks myself? However, he soon understood that I was better on my own; he let me manage and I learnt to control the car. With that, the fear that once I switched on the ignition, the car would move on its own, mow people down and crash into walls and buildings, suddenly ceased. The instructor shook himself out of his condescension to say with a note of surprise, 'Madam, you are not like other women.'

This was qualified praise. I read him clearly: for a woman (those timid, dumb creatures), for a woman of *my age* (even more timid and dumb), I was not bad.

Today the instructor asks me to drive first. Presenting, as I had often done myself, the good student first. The daughter is not with us, since there is no room in the car for her. I see her long anxious face staring after us when I start the car. After one false start, I move smoothly away from the curb and join the stream of traffic. It gets easier once we go past the shopping complex. The official who's going to test us before giving us our licenses is by my side, arms folded across chest, face expressionless. Except for telling me once to 'go left', he says nothing, letting me choose the road. But I want to earn my license and so, quaking a little, I choose the busy ones. I goof up only twice, the first time when a scooterist and I narrowly miss each other. The man is ready to explode with anger when he notices the official by my side and the fact that the car belongs to a driving school. Understanding that I'm being tested, he stops, gives me a smile and drives off.

'Take a U-turn,' the man says a little later, coming out of his studied silence. I don't turn the steering wheel enough and go right. The instructor says something from the back, but the official holds up his hand to stop him. I move to a side and wait for a chance to take a U-turn so that I can go back to the road I am supposed to be on.

In a few moments, the instructor stops me. 'You come now, madam,' he tells my companion.

I get in at the back, shaky but triumphant, sure I'll get my license. My companion is a total disaster. She starts the car without locking the door, which flies open the moment the car starts moving. Flustered, she lets go the steering wheel to close the door. 'Amma,' the instructor instinctively shouts. She gets back to the wheel, by which time we've climbed up the curb. Luckily the car stops, parked drunkenly now, half on the road, half on the pavement. There is complete silence. A few curious passers-by peer into the car and seeing nothing dramatic is likely to happen, move on. My heart slows down.

'All right, close the door, reverse and go back to the road,' the instructor tells her. Somehow, after failing to start a dozen times, she manages to do that.

When we get back to the point we'd started off from, the girl is still there, as if she has not moved from the spot in all that time, her hands still twisting her dupatta. The instructor follows the official who walks away, so briskly that the instructor has to run to catch up with him. No amount of palm greasing will get this woman her license, I think. But I'm wrong. The instructor comes back to say, 'You've both passed, you're getting your licenses. But Amma,' he turns to the woman, 'please don't go anywhere alone. Take someone who knows driving with you. And,' he adds sternly, 'don't take your daughter, for god's sake.'

He gives the girl a glare as if he holds her responsible for all that has happened. To my surprise, the girl giggles. Both mother and daughter are euphoric, they hug each other, they smile at me. The woman begins talking to me, suddenly garrulous and intimate. And triumphant, as if she's come through with flying colours. 'I'll take you out tomorrow for a drive,' she says to her daughter. I blench, wondering whether I'll see them on the city page tomorrow. I imagine the headline: 'Mother and daughter die'—no, not that, please, not that. 'Mother and daughter injured in car crash.' I only hope there's someone at home with more sense. I watch them move away, huddled together in excited conversation, and have a momentary pang of regret. Why have Sachi and I never been able to have this kind of intimacy? Then I laugh at myself, imagining Sachi accompanying me every day

as this girl had, waiting for me to return from my driving test ...
No, impossible. Nevertheless, the regret returns when I get home
and become conscious of the fact that there's no one with whom
I can share my pleasure. I can't even ring Raja. Apart from the
fact that he's out of town, I haven't told him that I've joined a
driving school.

I put the key in the latch, eager to have a cup of tea and relax.
The door closes behind me with a click. And then I hear a sound.
I stand utterly still. Nothing. I move softly, certain that I have
heard a sound from the back, a sound that tells me there is
someone in the house. I go into my room—it's the way it was
when I left home. I leave my bag on the bed and go past the
central hall, the dining room and the kitchen. No, there is no
one, I was mistaken. And then it happens. There's a sound, a
figure flashes past me, so fast that it's just a blur. It takes me a
moment to recover, to move. By the time I go to the front door,
there's no one. The door is open and the person, whoever it was,
has gone out. I go to the gate and wonder whether to follow, to
give chase. But there is no one on the road, either. I go back and
carefully closing the door behind me fall into a chair, my legs
giving way under me, my body breaking out into a sweat. It
takes me a while to gather enough courage to go through the
house. There's nothing to indicate that there was an intruder
inside. Everything is as it was, except for a wicker basket which
has been overturned. Mechanically, I collect the pictures that
have fallen out and are scattered all around and then become
conscious of a smell, the smell of a strange human, the sweaty
odour of a young male. Putting the pictures back into the basket,
I wonder whether I should call the police. But nothing has been
taken; my little bit of money is intact. To involve the police is to
get caught up in their regime of paper work, it will mean going
to the police station whenever they want me to. No, there's no
point in bringing the police into this very minor break-in.

It's only much later that I begin to think: how did he get in?
The front door was locked, I opened it myself. So how did he ...?
I go to the back again and up the stairs that lead to the little yard

behind Abhishek's rooms. And then I see that the door at the head of the stairs is wide open. So this is how …! The door, not a very strong one, has been forced upon, the bolt twisted out of shape. I can't close it, so I drag an old trunk, put it across and then, descending the stairs, lock the door that leads from the back passage into my house. When finally I sit down to drink a cup of tea, I notice my hands are trembling. What did he want? What made him so desperate as to break in during the day?

At night I switch the TV on loud, increasing the sound to give an illusion of having company. Then I turn it down; it drowns all other sounds, I won't be able to hear anyone forcing a door open. I'm so nervous I almost jump out of my skin when the telephone rings. It's Nirmala, wanting to discuss our Saturday yoga class. Only when I put the phone down do I wonder why I didn't tell her what happened, why I didn't ask her to come and give me company. She's alone too, she would have come. It's too late now. I choose a book and try to sleep. But I keep waking up often, imagining sounds, voices. I turn from side to side, finding comfort for only a brief while in each new position. *The body has three sides*—the sentence keeps running through my mind. It's nearly three when I finally fall asleep. I wake up with a start to Ratna's peremptory bell in the morning.

In the light of the morning, my fears seem grossly exaggerated, though when I tell Ratna about the incident, she blows them up again. I get a man to come and fix the door for me, but Ratna says I need a steel bar to put across the door. And one for the front door as well, she adds.

'It's the construction workers,' she says. 'I'm sure it's them. Only they can know you've gone out. It's so easy for them to come from the scaffolding to the terrace.'

Ratna is biased; she has an ongoing feud with the men working on the renovation of the house behind ours. She's convinced they fling the debris deliberately into our yard, that they wait for her to put the clothes out to dry before they announce they're going to plaster the walls and therefore will she remove the clothes? Yet, what she says does make some sense. How would anyone know I was out?

'You'd better tell Raja-anna about it,' she says. 'Remember how they shut up when he came and shouted at them?'

A husband who lies about all day, only occasionally condescending to go to work, a brother-in-law who fell off a ladder and became her responsibility, a son who plays truant from school more often than he attends it—and yet, Ratna has this astounding faith in the efficacy of the male, in his authority. It was she who brought Raja into the picture last time when, in response to her remonstrations and arguments, the workers began making rude remarks each time they saw her. I'd tried to talk to them, but though I'd put on an act of confidence, bravado really, even I had felt in them a kind of insolent awareness of me as a woman. But when Raja came and yelled at them, they took it from him. They argued, they defended themselves, but they left us alone after that.

'Tell him,' she urges me now.

But I don't want to do that. I want the brakes under my feet, not someone else's. I don't want a dual control, the control should be mine, mine alone. And I'm not sure it was the workers, anyway. I don't see them as criminals. The figure I saw so fleetingly didn't give the impression of being one of them, though, again, I'm not sure I would recognize the workers out of their working clothes.

In a few days my fears recede, the incident becomes one of those inexplicable events best left alone. But the intruder's presence seems to linger in the house. There's a faint whiff of cigarettes in the closed-in space of the staircase. I think of him sitting there, smoking, waiting—for what? For me to return? He could have attacked me, strangled me, raped me, but he did none of these things. On the contrary, he ran away. And it's not just the cigarettes, there's another smell that seems to haunt me, the smell of a strange animal that makes my hackles rise in fear and hostility. I open the doors and windows wide in the daytime, but the moment I close them in the evening, the smells return.

I can't stay here alone, I think each night. And each morning when I wake up, the fears seem to shrink, they appear ridiculous. And yet, the thought of someone in the house gives me the creeps.

I feel a sense of desecration. And uneasiness, thinking of someone keeping a watch on me. We think we are invisible, but there are eyes watching us, keeping track of our movements; I feel queasy at the thought.

We must sell this house, I think. It's ridiculous, we're never going to live here, Anand and Sachi almost certainly never. As for me, I can go anywhere. No, it makes no sense keeping it; whatever Raja says, we must sell it. And then it occurs to me: is this what the intruder had come for? Was that his purpose—to scare me into selling the house?

following our destinies

I am glad I haven't said anything to Raja about The Intruder (so he has become in my mind), for Raja is in a bad mood. Depressed, I would have said, if it had been anyone but Raja. It was the same thing the last time he returned from visiting his parents.

'I wonder why I go,' he says, but both of us know it is a rhetorical question. The answer is clear: he visits his parents because he is a responsible son. It's a duty he cannot get out of, however little the pleasure he gets out of it; in fact, listening to him, it seems to me he gets no pleasure at all. He needn't go so often, because Premi is in Bombay. But Premi, he grumbles, doesn't bother to visit them even once a month. She's too busy, she says. She rings them up every day, but this is not enough for Raja, whose standards of filial duty are very high. And yet, it was Raja who escaped home early, leaving as soon as he had graduated, using the pretext of wanting to work with a firm of architects in Bangalore to get away. That RK had died and Gayatri was alone was an additional excuse, but the truth was that Raja and his father could not get on with each other. A classic father-son relationship Baba called it, laughing with the easy comfort of a man who had only daughters. When he was in his teens,

Raja used to often complain about his father—his constant disapproval of everything Raja did, his sarcasm, his pompous lecturing (Raja's words, not mine). By the time Raja left home, I was out of the family circle myself. However, my occasional visits to BK's house, usually for a festival or a ritual, gave me a glimpse of what was happening. I also saw Kamala's desperate attempts to bridge the growing gap between father and son.

I lost touch with all of them for a while, then met Raja once again when I came to be with Baba. I saw that there was an easy, intimate relationship between the two of them, something Raja had never had with his own father, not even with his uncle RK, though RK was fond of Raja; to him, Raja was the son he didn't have, he was the heir of the family. And Raja's response to RK was a stark contrast to the sulking, rebellious face he showed his own father. Now, to my surprise, Raja has become sympathetic towards his father, protective of him. It is his mother he has problems with.

'She's okay with me,' he says. 'It's what she does to Appa that I mind.'

She nags at him all day, she won't stop once she gets going, she just won't stop, Raja says. 'And she makes me the audience, I have to listen to her long list of complaints against Appa. She speaks in a loud voice, deliberately, so that Appa will hear her. I know he's listening, I know he knows I'm listening. It makes me feel ... Shit!' he says disgustedly. 'I can't bear to see what she's doing to him.'

BK, Raja tells me, has made a kind of retreat for himself in the grilled gallery where the children had once kept the toys they'd outgrown. He sits there all day, assaulted by the sound of the cars in the courtyard, the petrol fumes, the loud voices of people calling out to one another.

'I don't know how he stands it. Maybe the sounds help to drown out Amma's voice.'

I think of Kamala, gentle and smiling, never arguing, never dissenting. I think of her absorbed in her children, of the soft whispers in which she spoke to them. I think of her giving BK his place as father and husband, as head of the family. I remember how his comforts were looked after, scrupulously, almost religiously. I never saw BK doing any chore in the house; even his Scotch, soda and ice were placed before him by Kamala, her face, I remember now, a little turned away, her nose slightly wrinkled. BK was a great contrast to Baba, who was willing to do anything, whether it was taking us to the bathroom, tying or untying our drawstrings, or setting the table. It's hard for me to connect the soft gentle woman I knew with this strident unhappy one Raja is speaking of. In fact, if I hadn't seen it myself, I would have thought Raja was exaggerating. But I saw this new avatar of Kamala myself when I visited her and BK a year ago, a visit I was making after years. The shady lane in Matunga where they lived seemed unchanged, the building the same, if a little shabbier, but the house inside was unrecognizable. It was a total contrast to the one that had welcomed us so hospitably on Sundays after our visits to the beach. An air of ease and comfort combined with the aroma of food, of BK's pipe and the smell of his whiskey. And Kamala's soft voice, the musical jingle of her bangles mingling harmoniously with BK's and Baba's voices conversing, arguing, laughing.

It's a sad house now, the smell of stale food hitting you as soon as you enter, the dining table, so spotless then, littered with nearly-empty bottles of pickles and chutney. Wet towels on chair backs, unfolded clothes strewn on beds, dust everywhere—all this a mute witness to the fact that Kamala, once a perfect housewife, had given up coping. Everything faded, nothing replaced, the glass top of the centre table cracked years ago, as the dirt accumulated in the crack showed. But it was the tension in the house that shocked me, the hostility among the three who lived in it and the angry silence that hovered over it which frightened me.

It's Hemi who's the cause of it all, Hemi, the sweet-faced docile baby of the family, who always sat on her mother's lap and played with her sari. Hemi, who rarely had anything to say. So protected by her mother that she never played with us, was never part of our games. We accepted her as she was; her slowness, her silences, her blank face were as much part of her as Premi's quarrelsome nature was hers, or Raja's bossiness was part of him; it was just the 'Hemi'ness of her. But now, when I think of it, I have to wonder—didn't her parents see there was a problem? I can understand Kamala's ignorance, her refusal to see the unpleasant facts about Hemi; she was a mother and she was not a very bright woman. But BK was an intelligent man, he was well read and knowledgeable—didn't he realize she was not normal? And Baba, a doctor, didn't *he* see that Hemi was retarded? Or did they think that to be soft, docile and silent was the right way for a girl to be? For there was Kamala, soft, docile and silent too, and yet (or is it therefore?), such an excellent wife and mother. Premi and I were different. Premi, aggressive and loud (I remember her mutinous disobedience, her loud arguments with her father when he asked her to give me her bike to ride) and I, exuberant and tomboyish. Maybe they hoped we would grow out of such behaviour and become, hopefully, if not like Kamala, at least like Gayatri and Mai. Hoped that Hemi too would follow suit and we would all of us finally take the right path, leading us to our final destinies of becoming good wives and mothers.

It's quite clear now that Hemi is not normal. The sweet-faced girl has become a tall gaunt woman, dressed all day in cheap shapeless cotton kaftans which she buys from the little stalls on the road. She's prematurely grey and her face is no longer blank, but set in an angry glare that makes her look frightening. Self-willed, totally self-absorbed, Hemi stays in her room all day, coming out only at mealtimes. The day I visited them, she ignored both me and Kamala when she emerged from her room, though Kamala tried to make it seem normal, saying, 'Hemi, Jiji is here.' She went straight to her place and ate with a furious voracity that would have been embarrassing if it hadn't been so frightening. But Kamala's behaviour, the placating, almost servile way in which she spoke to her, the anxious fawning looks she kept giving her, made me more uncomfortable. And Hemi, ignoring everything, stalked out the moment she was done. BK, who had been steadily eating until then, suddenly said, 'She's a monster.' The words erupting out of him as if he had suppressed them for a long time and could no longer hold them within himself. 'She's a monster,' he said between clenched teeth and to my horror, began to sob. Above his muffled sobs I could hear the loud thuds of Hemi washing her clothes. This was the main activity of her day—washing her clothes and hanging them out to dry. Later, she would fold the dry clothes, throwing away any other clothes she'd plucked off the line by mistake.

Monster. I think of the five of us who grew up together, all of us following our destinies, if one believes in such a thing. Raja and I decided early what we were to be: he was to be an architect, I a doctor. Raja pursued his goal with a steady persistence; it was a straight road for him, no diversions, no sudden hazards threatening him, either. Whereas I strayed away and found it hard, no, impossible, to come back to the road I'd chalked out for myself. It was Premi who became a doctor instead, surprising everyone by her grit and determination. And Malu ... But her story remains incomplete. How do I know what she would have become? And wasn't Malu's fate better than Hemi's? What can be worse than being called a monster by one's own father?

But that was BK's grief speaking, his pain at what his daughter is. He's finally accepted the fact that Hemi is not normal, something that Kamala still hasn't. To Kamala, all Hemi's problems stem from the fact that she is not married, for which she blames BK. She thinks it's still not too late, that they can, even now, get Hemi married and all will be well. Overnight Hemi will be transformed from eccentric woman to happy wife and mother. Does Kamala really believe this? Or is it just a charade she's playing out, trying hard to convince herself that her child is all right, that there's nothing wrong with her, that the fault is their own? I don't know, but getting Hemi married is a theme she pursues unrelentingly, harrying BK all day. Her voice goes on and on, Raja tells me, blaming BK, telling him about 'suitable boys', urging him to do something 'at least now', sobbing finally, calling him a cruel, unfeeling father who's failed in his duty towards his daughter.

I can see Raja is confused, hating the situation, hating Hemi for creating the situation, pitying her, pitying his parents, angry with them, angry with Premi, though he knows she's doing all she can.

'You're lucky,' he says, as if he's envying me for having parents who are dead. And then, conscious of how he sounds, he corrects himself. 'No, no, I didn't mean it that way. I mean you're lucky you never had to see your parents become what mine have. Pathetic.'

Perhaps he's right. I remember Kamala in her pastel saris, her glossy hair neatly knotted, the diamonds gleaming in her ears, gold bangles jingling on her arms. And BK, elegant, dignified, well dressed. And the man I saw last year, staring blankly at the pages of an open book—such a shabby man, his shirt unironed and stained with food.

Now, Raja tells me, Kamala has started on him. Since your father hasn't been able to get Hemi married, it's your duty to look for a groom for her, she tells him. What will happen to her when both of us are gone?

'Think of that, she kept saying. Damn it, can't she see what Hemi is!'

It's frightening to think of what her parents expected of Hemi and what she has become. But isn't this true of all of us? Raja too, so exemplary a son now, so much a son to be proud of in the way he's succeeded in his profession—why, he too almost broke Kamala's heart; or so she said when he married Rukku, a Tamil girl older than him, instead of the girl Kamala had chosen for him. And Malu and I—when I think of the dreams Baba and Mai had for us ...! I may not be a Hemi, but I disappointed my parents just the same. 'I didn't mind your marriage so much,' Baba said to me, 'it made me angry that you gave up your studies. I thought you were giving up your life. It was like committing suicide.' Strong words from Baba who never expressed his disapproval so clearly.

'When I see Appa, I get the feeling that he's just waiting to die,' Raja says and the two of us fall silent. I remember BK's practical jokes, so surprising, astonishing really, in a man of his dignity. I remember him once singing a funny song. It was during our summer holidays and the singing was part of a game, a forfeit perhaps. BK sang, or rather chanted, something from a Lucille Ball serial. I knew even then that it was his way of pulling Baba's leg, for it was something about bones. It began, now let me see, yes, it began with the 'head bone' and went all the way down to the 'foot bone'. BK sang it with gestures, pointing to the bone mentioned, capering and dancing the while, Baba hysterical with laughter, Gayatri and Mai laughing too. Kamala wasn't laughing. I don't know whether she was embarrassed or puzzled. Puzzled, most likely, from the expression on her face, not understanding the song, the allusions or the jokes. BK and Kamala—such different people. Sharing nothing but a house and three children. Kamala, interested only in her home and children. And BK at the other end of the spectrum, scarcely noticing anything in his own home, his gaze moving in a remote way even over his own children, but interested in the world, in public and national events, in books and music. Sophisticated in his tastes and intellect, widely read. Nonetheless, the marriage worked; or rather, it seemed to. Until suddenly, the whole facade collapsed because of Hemi. But perhaps it could just as well have been something else.

Earlier, before BK and Kamala were married, Gayatri had earmarked Kamala for Baba. She was worried about her brother's continuing bachelorhood. He'd got his postgraduate degree, he had a job, he was earning a fair amount and he was nearly thirty; what was he waiting for? Truth was, Gayatri said later, he was waiting for Mai. Once she appeared, all his objections to marriage vanished. But at the time, Gayatri was anxious. She kept offering him suitable girls. Kamala, she thought, was a wonderful choice: a family they knew and were distantly linked to, a girl she knew well. But when Baba—so the story was told to us by Gayatri— came to know she was only sixteen, he said, 'Let her play with her dolls for some more time'. And then Gayatri added, laughing, 'Your Mai was only eighteen but he didn't ask *her* to go and play with her dolls.'

Gayatri didn't hold it against Baba that he refused Kamala. In any case, she was able to get Kamala into the family after all, arranging her marriage to BK when he returned from England a little later. And Baba, who'd so steadily rejected girls, met Mai soon after and married her. So we were two families instead of the one we would have been if Baba had married Kamala. Two couples with five children—just the ingredients for a happy togetherness.

'What if,' I'd asked Raja once, after hearing this story from Gayatri, 'what if Baba had married your mother? Would we have been we? I mean, would we have been born? Would there have been us?'

But Raja wasn't interested in the hypothetical question. I've yet to meet a man who finds the what-might-have-been of individual lives fascinating. Take the hypothesis up a notch, make it abstract, and they'll jump into the argument with pleasure. But individual lives? Your mother? My father? No way.

And in a way, Raja was right in ignoring my question. It's ridiculous to think of Baba marrying anyone but Mai. Not many children are witness to their parents' love affair, but Malu and I were, though we didn't know then that it was a love story. To us, they were just our parents. Baba and Mai.

*

The stories in which we play a role are the ones that fascinate us the most. Malu and I found the story of Baba's and Mai's coming together more enthralling than any fairy tale, because this was where *we* began. Not that we ever heard the story in its entirety; it came to us in bits and pieces, a pastiche we put together, though there were many gaps and pieces that didn't fit. This didn't matter, for the essence of the story, its truth, leapt out at us even through the blanks, the silences and the discrepancies. Gayatri gave us some bits of the story, Baba's tangential allusions some others and BK, through his jokes and digs at Baba, provided tiny bits that filled some of the blank spaces. And there was Laxman,

Mai's brother, who gifted us with the beginning of the story, the 'once upon a time' of it, boasting that it was he who was responsible for their coming together. Which was true, because they met when Laxman was brought to the hospital after he had been stabbed in a fracas. Laxman's version presented a melodramatic picture of a dying, almost dead man, though Baba said that Laxman had never been in any real danger. Whatever that may be, this was how and when Baba saw Mai for the first time. His eyes picked her out of the large milling crowd in Casualty, a crowd that was, unusually, not made up of family alone. The fact that Laxman had been involved in a public brawl and that he had already gathered a group of young men around himself, gave a hint of the future course of his life. But at that moment, Baba's eyes were riveted by the young girl in a plain cotton sari, her hair in two plaits, her silence and stillness marking her out from the others in that chaotic group. With the duty doctor still working on the patient, Baba had to move on. But he saw her again in the evening from the window of his room in the residents' quarters, waiting at the bus stop across the road. Instantly, impetuously, he ran out of his room, hurtled down the worn wooden stairs, out of the gate and across the road to the bus stop. The girl, thank god, was still there. After one curious look, she turned away, imagining he was, perhaps, rushing to catch a bus, such frantic haste a fairly common sight in Bombay after all.

I don't know what happened after that. I have no idea what he said to her and what she said to him. I once heard BK joking that Baba must have said to her, 'You have such beautiful bones.' Baba only laughed and Mai was silent. Man and woman—who knows what goes on between them, who ever knows the whole story? If they had been other people, I could have imagined things, I could have taken things out of my own experience and thought—*this* was what happened between them. But they are my parents. My imagination baulks at seeing them as lovers. Years later, I read a story of Mai's, 'Chandrika'. (Almost all of Mai's stories had the heroine's name for the title—Manasi, Annapoorna,

Madhavi and so on). In this story, a couple meets at a bus stop. They are there at the same time every day, waiting for the same bus. They soon begin to be aware of each other, sometimes they smile, specially on Mondays, as if to show their gladness at seeing each other after the one-day gap, they begin to wait for each other. If one misses the usual bus, the other lets the queue go past as well. Once, getting on to the bus, he steps on her foot and says, 'Sorry.' He looks anguished and she wonders why a stranger should feel her pain so much, why she should feel the need to comfort him. This word, 'sorry', is the only word they exchange, her reassuring smile the only positive communication between them. And then one day she comes to the bus stop with a card for him. It's a wedding invitation card. Her wedding. He takes it from her in silence. There's a lot of agonizing after that, I don't remember that part very well, but I remember vaguely that there is a happy ending, the silent lovers getting married after all.

I read the story when I was in college; I'd borrowed the magazine from a girl, something to read during the long hours of the afternoon and the evening. I had no idea Mai's story was in it until I opened it. When I read it, I thought: she writes of love, of deep unspoken love, but she did not understand my love for Shyam. And again I thought: she knows nothing of love. How can you love and not speak of it, how can you love and not crave to be together, how can you not touch each other? This inchoate, incomplete, unfulfilled thing—was this Mai's idea of love?

I didn't pursue the idea then. If I was angry with Mai for her opposition to my marriage with Shyam, I was homesick too at the time, just a month after our marriage. I was longing for her presence, for Baba and Malu, for our life at home. Yet, I wanted Shyam too, Shyam above all things, Shyam more than anyone else. My body was already tingling at the thought of his return, of him coming in, closing the door and holding me in his arms.

Such confusion, such terrible confusion ...

Anyway, whatever happened that day at the bus stop between Baba and Mai, or rather, whatever didn't happen, Baba didn't let her go out of his life. Soon after, or maybe not so soon after, he made his way to Mai's home and told them he wanted to marry her. Mai's family was deeply suspicious at first. Baba must have remembered that moment when Shyam said he wanted to marry me and Mai said, 'But he's a Sindhi!' So must Mai's family have said about Baba: 'But he's a South Indian!' And with more justification for their prejudice and ignorance. Mai's family had never moved beyond Bombay and Pune; their world was limited to people who spoke Marathi. They knew, of course, that there were people who spoke other languages, but they were not real people, they could never be part of your family or social circle. Besides, Baba was a Brahmin, a South Indian Brahmin which, to Mai's family, who saw people in terms of movie stereotypes, meant Tamil-speaking, *aiyayo*-exclaiming comedians. Also, for a man to make an offer for a girl was weird. Nevertheless, they saw that he was a simple, straightforward man. It reassured them, too, that he knew Marathi and that he was a doctor. This made a huge difference. (They didn't know then that he was only a medical teacher, and teaching a non-clinical subject at that; they thought all doctors made money—Baba said this once, joking, teasing Mai about her family.) And so they agreed. But their consent was not enough for Baba. He wanted Mai's 'yes'. I would like to meet her and talk to her, he said. He took her to an Irani restaurant opposite the hospital's main gate, a place which entered the history of our lives. Malu and I never passed it without a second look, without underlining it, so to say, after Baba told us that this was the place where Mai and he had met before they got married. He told her all about himself—that he was almost an orphan (the 'almost' was because of RK and Gayatri), that he had nothing besides what he earned from his job, that he intended to go on with teaching, that it was what he really wanted to do and so, perhaps, he would never be a rich man.

When Mai's agreement was conveyed to him, Baba thought she'd agreed *because* of what he'd said, no, *in spite* of what he'd said. He thought that she understood what he'd been trying to tell her—which meant, he thought, that to her, only he mattered. But one day, sitting in the same restaurant, while we were waiting for our 'butter brun' to arrive, Mai confessed that she hadn't heard a word of what he'd said to her that day. We were surrounded by the usual sounds of the restaurant—the clatter of plates and spoons, the loud voices of people talking, the screeching of the buses outside. True, how could Mai have heard Baba's soft voice above the din? But Baba's face fell when Mai made this revelation, I remember that. He soon recovered, he joked at himself and the moment passed. But he was hurt. Strange that Mai's only contribution to the jigsaw puzzle I'm now putting together should be this one, a bit that seems to have no place in the theme of the puzzle.

Whatever her intentions, Mai said 'yes', at which point Gayatri entered the scene. Gayatri, happy that her brother's defences were finally down, was dubious, however, about his sudden infatuation for a strange girl. She wondered about the girl, she wondered what kind of a family she came from. Baba had told her they were not Brahmins; this was not the real problem for Gayatri. Her doubts came out of the fact that they were petty shopkeepers with a ready-made garments shop. Were they uneducated? Rough and crude business people? But Gayatri had her share of surprises, for Bharat, Mai's older brother, was an engineer working in an automobile company in Pune. And Mai herself was dignified and poised. True, she hadn't studied beyond school, but then, neither had Gayatri. Gayatri approved. After meeting Mai and spending some time with her, she more than approved; she was pleased with Mai, charmed by her. All her life, all Mai's life rather, she gave Mai both her love and friendship. And Mai? One never knew about Mai, but I think she reciprocated. I know how she looked forward to the one fortnight in a year that Gayatri spent with us in Bombay, I saw how comfortable she was with her. At the end, when Mai turned away from everyone, Gayatri was the one person she turned to, the one person who knew everything.

To go back to my parents' marriage: they got married and Baba brought her to an apartment he had managed to get within the hospital campus. One of four apartments in an old building, with thick walls and huge windows that had to be kept closed all day against the smell of human shit that came from the pavements outside. In the mornings, before it was light, the pavements were lined by rows of squatting children, each with an old tin or a plastic mug; by afternoon the stink was at its strongest. It was to this place that Baba brought his bride, this was where Malu and I were born, this was home for us—the smell, the patients, the hospital crowds, were part of our world. At the centre were our parents. I can remember now the way his arm went round her waist, protectively encircling it, when crossing the road. I can remember us in the bus, returning from our once-a-month-treat of a movie and dinner, Malu sleeping, while I listen to the murmurs coming from Baba and Mai seated behind us. When the murmurs cease, I kneel on the seat and turn round to make sure they are still there. Yes, they are, but Mai has fallen asleep, her head resting on Baba's shoulder. Baba gives me a conspiratorial smile, his lips pursed, as if saying, *Sshh, she's sleeping.* And another day I see, though I know somehow I am not supposed to, his hand brushing her cheek gently, his voice saying 'rose petals'. And the colour coming up in Mai's delicate, creamy skin.

I know now that Baba was a passionate lover. I couldn't possibly have known this as a child, but after I met Shyam, I learnt the language and discovered the words, I travelled that country and became familiar with its topography. And then I understood the truth: yes, Baba was a passionate lover. And Mai? Again I have to go back to her writing, because when I think of Mai, I always come up against a blank wall, an enigmatic silence. Reading her stories in these last few months, I've thought—she's brought in a million small details of living, but of herself nothing, nothing at all. There's her first novel, *Manasi*, the one in which she broke out of the rigid formula of 'boy-meets-girl, boy-marries-girl' she'd perfected so well. In *Manasi*, the story does not end but begins with a wedding, a young man marrying a girl he had fallen in love with and ardently pursued. The usual clichéd situation of rich man and poor girl. The lover showers her with all the things he thinks she hasn't had until then—expensive saris, jewels, a chauffeur-driven car, etc. The girl sees this as arrogance, a patronizing that showcases her earlier poverty. And so she walks out on him after a fierce quarrel, she lives alone for years. It is in these years when they live apart that love begins to flower between them, it is then that the young man learns to meet her on equal ground. Finally, there is a reconciliation.

I saw the movie first and read the novel later. I thought the movie unreal, unnatural. How could people in love live apart that way? I was watching the movie with Shyam, his body beside mine, his arm about me, his hand holding mine, his breath on my face as he whispered in my ear. How then could I believe in the truth of Mai's story? Years later, when I came to be with Mai when she was dying, I saw their two rooms, Baba's and Mai's, each with a single bed, both celibate, ascetic almost, Mai's a little cluttered, Baba's as neat and tidy as if no one lived in it. I saw these two rooms and remembered their bedroom in Bombay, their things mingling into a harmonious whole, so that the room was Baba-and-Mai's, the bed was Baba-and-Mai's. In these two rooms I saw a reflection of the life they had led since coming here, I glimpsed the estrangement between them, the rooms making a loud statement that love had ended. Or had it? His agony when she was dying, his words, 'I can't bear it, I can't bear to see her', his agonized sobbing—did these things mean that love had survived? That, like in *Manasi*, the physical separation had renewed their love, removed the dross from it?

Baba was reading *Bleak House* in the months before his death. I found the book by his bed after he died and began reading it, mainly to fill the emptiness of my days. When I came to Ada's words about Richard, 'But if I had not had that hope I would have married him just the same, Esther, just the same', I thought—was this how it was for Baba? I had seen his anger against Mai, his anguish at what he thought she had done. But in the end, did he come to thinking that, whatever it was she had done, he loved her 'just the same, just the same'? I don't know, I really don't know.

If I'm thinking of telling Sachi 'everything', as Raja said, this is not the right way. All these surmises, these uncertainties, these doubts—what can they mean to her? A straightforward narration is better. *This is how it was.* No questions, no doubts. But I'm doing it the other way, I'm saying: *This is who we were, these are the things that happened to us.* And nothing comes clear. Who were we? And the things that happened to us—can I see them clearly enough to speak of them? Do I really know what happened? I'm beginning to think Shyam was right. His obsession with pictures, with images and perspectives, was part of his conviction that a picture tells a story better. The eye never sees a thing whole, I told Shyam once, still close then to my medical knowledge. It sees tiny bits which the brain puts together to make a picture. He found this a fascinating thought. 'In which case,' he said, 'my camera is the eye plus the brain.'

I thought of his words when I watched an old Hindi movie on TV last night. I sat through the entire movie, getting up only once to make myself some coffee. A movie about a couple who've been married for some years. The man, now in love with another woman, is trying to tell his wife about it. Dreading it, frightened of what the knowledge will do to her. Her innocence, which makes her so vulnerable, is the biggest obstacle for him. But finally he speaks. The scene lingers in my mind: the two of them in bed, she almost asleep and he, after a miserable hesitation, finally taking the plunge. *I don't love you,* he says. How strange, I thought, to say this, instead of *I love another.* And equally strange, his wife, who until then has seemed the stereotypical housewife, replies, *I don't love you either.* Their tones calm and reasonable, flat and dull almost. But the camera, catching the truth, shows shifting fractured images, the fragments like shards of grief, the pictures entirely deprived of colour, of whiteness even. Everything dark. As if all the agony that does not come through the words is here, in these pictures. Saying it better than words ever can.

I thought I could compress our entire story into a few words: *We were a happy family. And then it all came to an end.* What can those words mean? How much can they convey? Used so often and in such varying situations, they can have either a million meanings or none at all. And yet, there's this picture of Malu and me taken by Laxman, who in his early days went through a phase of toting his camera with him, taking pictures on all occasions. Malu and I, the first kids in the family, were his most wanted and willing subjects. Young enough to obey, to pose the way he wanted us to. And so we had these piles of 'cute' pictures, which could be captioned 'sisters'. Here's this one now, our heads leaning towards each other's, our cheeks supported on our palms, I beaming, clearly obeying Laxman's command of 'Smile, baby'. And Malu, grave in spite of all Laxman's coaxing (*Smile for me, Malu, smile for your Laxman-mama, baby?*), leaning so far towards me that her head is almost resting on my shoulder. Sisters. I saw a painting years later, a painting by Gainsborough of two girls, sisters obviously, in almost the same pose. And looking at the picture, I thought—who knows what happened to them later? This picture shows just the one moment. When I see our pictures, Malu's and mine, I see our entire history in it. But others will see only what the picture shows, that one moment. Only the surface. So pictures can fail too. Whereas words ...

Mai knew the potency of words, which is why she stopped speaking, stopped writing. If to speak, to write, is to be free of a burden, it is clear she did not want to be free; she wanted to bear her burden. 'Enough,' she said before she died. Enough. Just one word, saying more than all the words she had written until then. Enough of suffering. Enough of living. Enough.

I think of the printer's devil which converted fusion into fission in Anand's exam paper and Sachi's retort to Anand's indignation. 'So what's the difference?' she asked.

'What's the difference between fission and fusion? Everything, you stupid, everything,' Anand said.

Yes, everything. It's the difference between harmony and chaos, between creation and destruction. Only one letter less, only one letter different, but ...

What's the difference? Everything, Sachi, everything.

baba's diary

27 April 1997

It is difficult, almost impossible for me, at this stage in my life to remember at what point of time I decided to become a doctor. As far as I can remember, the thought was always with me; I knew very clearly what I wanted to do with my life. I was fortunate that I was able to achieve what I wanted and that I was not disappointed when I finally got to the place where I'd aspired to be. Anatomy and physiology, the subjects which most students found dry, tedious and fearfully voluminous to remember, a nightmare in fact when preparing for an examination, fascinated me; the structure and functioning of the human body filled me with awe. I was lucky, too, that we had a teacher who went beyond the syllabus and mere facts to seemingly irrelevant but fascinating ideas. It was from Dr Kapadia, our anatomy teacher, that I learnt how the human body can give us glimpses of the mystery of existence itself. He spoke with passion of the superiority of the human to all else in creation. We possess not merely the capacity to acquire knowledge, he said, but also the desire to pursue it for its own sake. What marks us out as specially privileged, he added, is the fact that we aspire for even such knowledge as is not absolutely necessary for survival. Above all, we have language and memory; he called them the two wonderful gifts of a fairy godmother. What, he asked, as if challenging us, is knowledge without language and memory? Language and memory, he said, are the tools which have enabled us to scale the ladder of creation and reach the heights we now occupy. I listened spellbound, completely enraptured, excited by these ideas; they filled the huge gaps in my life caused by my father's death, by Gayatri's distance.

The more I studied the body, the more I saw how everything in it was ordered to a purpose; I saw in it a perfection, an exquisite balance, a harmony. I knew, of course, that this was not the entire truth. In my clinical terms I learnt about the innumerable aberrations that are part of the human body. But this never affected my initial sense of awe and deep admiration for the perfection that was meant to be. It was this continuing awe and admiration which took me back to teaching anatomy, even after I had post-graduated in surgery. I remembered Dr Kapadia— who was dead by then—and how his lectures had crackled with excitement; with him, even the medical terminology became wonderfully evocative. 'The mitral valve,' he would say, his fingers coming together, tapering in a cone, 'like a bishop's mitre.' And again, 'The antagonist muscles,' he said, punching the air as he spoke, making the function he was describing come alive. I wanted to follow in his footsteps, to convey to my students the miracle of the human body, to give them a glimpse of the perfection Dr Kapadia had helped me to see. On a more practical level, a teaching job suited me better than surgery. I could not afford the long waiting period that surgery entailed. I had come to the end of the little money my father had left for me and I needed to start earning as soon as possible.

And then I met Vasu. I must admit that it was the perfection of her tiny dainty body, her exquisite face, that drew me to her so immediately. But I knew even then that this was not all; if it was just her physical beauty which attracted me, why not another woman more beautiful, or just as beautiful? It was an emotion stronger than any I had felt until then. I knew from the very beginning that she did not feel the same way about me. Why should she, I asked myself; there was nothing in me to make her feel about me the way I did about her. When I looked at myself in the mirror, I saw an ordinary man in an ordinary body. In any case, her feelings, or rather the difference in our feelings, changed nothing for me. It didn't matter—or so I told myself. Rashly, I convinced myself that I had enough love for both of us. All that I asked was that she allow me to love her; I was confident that my love would make up for all the deficiencies in her feelings.

I was hopelessly, completely naïve; I admit my stupidity now. Perfect love (one-sided though it may be), a happy marriage, a happy family—I saw these things as part of a chain, one inevitably following the other, all of them strung together and invariably linked. I have been reading RK's collection of the Victorians in these last few years. Reading Dickens, I thought of how the Victorians had perfected the idealization of love, marriage and family to a fine art, how they had raised it to a peak. And then, in *Bleak House*, I came upon words which belied everything that he said about marriage. 'Bone of his bone, flesh of his flesh, shadow of his shadow': his words for Mrs Snagsby, the suspicious wife silently trailing her husband, convinced she would catch him in some disloyalty. *Bone of his bone, flesh of his flesh, shadow of his shadow*. I could see the sneer behind the words, words that parodied the ideal of marriage, holding up the sham for exhibition. Telling me that he knew, yes, Dickens knew the truth, that even when he spoke of the ideal, he knew its falsity, its hollowness. Like movie makers who, knowing the untruth of the world they create, still continue to embellish it, decorating it even more to conceal the hollowness. He knew, yes, he knew the hidden rocks in the beautiful pool.

The first rock we hit, Vasu and I, one on which we could have floundered, was our differing ideas of passion. You can convince yourself that one can love enough for two, but what about passion? Can you supply the passion for the other person as well? Emotions can be faked, lips can speak untruths, but the body never lies. I found out on the very first night after our wedding that Vasu was incapable of responding to my passion. Which is why she found Jiji such a complete mystery when Jiji so desperately wanted Shyam. But *I* understood Jiji, oh yes, I did. As a father, I found it hard to be a witness to the raw sexuality of my daughter's feelings for a man, something Jiji almost flaunted. But as a man, I could understand her feelings only too well.

It took Vasu a very long time to let her body enter into our relationship. At first I thought she was too young, too ignorant. (Though I knew well enough that the body is the best teacher; you don't need to be told, you don't have to be taught.) I thought I needed to give her some time. Abysmal idiot that I was, I even tried, teacher-like, to tell her the facts about our bodies. I drew rough diagrams, I remember, to help her understand. She ran out on me in the midst of my precise, carefully impersonal talk, and I heard her retching in the bathroom. As the stalemate continued, my thoughts turned in a different direction. I became suspicious, I thought she loved someone else. If not, I said, speaking to her finally after a lot of consideration, knowing that my fears had to come out into the open—if not, I had to think that she found me repulsive, that she disliked me. I spoke out of frustration, from a sense of complete helplessness, driven to it by my inability to cope with the situation. Vasu was hurt, no, she was furious; she surprised me by her anger. Of course she didn't love someone else. Did I think she would have married me if she had loved another? And of course she didn't find me repulsive, either. Why was I imagining such terrible things? She liked me, yes, she did, truly, she found me pleasing.

'But ...?'

No answer.

'Why then ...?'

No answer.

She came to me that night on her own. She let me hold her, she permitted me to caress her, to kiss her gently on her cheeks, to touch her lips with mine. It was when I began to undress her that she went rigid, her body taut with fear. I could feel her heart fluttering wildly in her ribcage. I almost stopped at this point, but my body would not let me, I had gone too far to stop. And so my body took over from me and the thing was done. Our bodies met, they merged, our marriage was consummated, as they euphemistically, so delicately put it. She still had some defenses after that, but the main barricades were down. After this, she was always the one in control, she played the tune to which our sexual dance was performed.

No, not now, not today; I'm tired; it's too early; it's too late; some other time, tomorrow, don't ...

And always a 'no, no' when I tried to induce her to shed her clothing. So that each time my loving was hampered by her clothes, every time I had to work my way clumsily through them. Never the feel of bare skin, never that most exciting of all contacts, of skin against skin. And always, after it was over, the despair for me, the cold feeling of not being able to reach her, of never being able to let her feel my love the way I wanted to, never being able to feel her love for me through her body and mine. And yet the body, independent so often of the mind, has its own logistics. So suddenly one day it would be 'Yes, yes, yes now, now NOW'. Then, when it was done, she would turn away from me as if she was ashamed of herself, she would hide her face in her arms, her legs drawn up close to her chest and begin to cry. Silently, only her body's scarcely perceptible tremors telling me what was happening. But one night, after her body had met mine with a passion that almost equalled mine, I heard her sobbing, a heartbroken sobbing. I left her alone, I left her to it; I could not help her come to terms with the demands of her own body. How could I, when I found it hard to understand my own? It was only a little later, when I could distance myself from what had happened, that my doubts emerged: how could the body and the mind be so much at variance with each other, as if they were two separate entities, as if there was no link between them? Had I not seen for myself the exquisitely precise mechanism that linked the two, the finely tuned response of one to the commands of the other, the fine network of nerves that carried the commands everywhere?

And yet, this ... this beast inside me, grappling with my tenderness towards Vasu. Beast? Yes, that's how I began to think of it, a beast I wanted to control, but never could. Today, when I remember these things, I am full of sorrow, I grieve for both Vasu and me. I am grieved that I failed to convey to her the enormous tenderness I felt for her. That my passion, my urgent need of her body, erased all the other messages of love and tenderness. Why did I fail to make her understand that what I wanted was not to possess her body, or rather, not *only* to possess her body, but to feel myself complete by merging into her? I now know the entire truth of what I had heard my teacher say: if we humans are the greatest marvels in creation, we are also the greatest mysteries to ourselves. I continue to be amazed by the genius, the questioning nature, the ceaseless probing of humans to resolve the mysteries of the universe, the way in which, gradually but surely, so many mysteries have been resolved. Yet, the enigma of our own selves remains unfathomable. The ego, the libido, the unconscious—how little they explain! Such tiny dots on a vast uncharted map. The truth is that each one of us is a universe more complicated than the limitless universe we inhabit.

I woke up the morning after Vasu's death to a sense of emptiness, as if I was in an empty house. I woke up to a sense of a void which was *within* me. The house was neither empty nor silent, less so now, in fact, being inhabited by Jiji's and the children's voices. I could hear Gayatri's habitual coughing as she boiled the milk in the kitchen, I could hear Jiji's voice speaking softly to her child. But the sounds seemed distant; it was as if I was enclosed in a vacuum and nothing could reach me.

With Vasu dead, her body gone and even her charred and bleached bones vanished into the depths of the river, I was left with nothingness. As a scientist I rejected the idea. Matter does not cease to exist, it changes form. Something remains. Reading the Upanishads with Ramchandra Sir, I picked hopefully on the story of Svetaketu and his father. *Tat tvam asi Svetakatu.* I absorbed this idea of the body being only the outer covering, within it the essence, the unseen formless essence, from which the long infinite thread of life unwinds. But for humans who experience life, who get life through the senses, the not-seen, the not-felt is not much comfort.

I thought then of the idea of reincarnation, of the Christian idea of meeting in heaven. I realized that these ideas came out of an inability to accept the finality of death. Hoping, desperately grasping at the hope that somewhere, something continues. Hope overcoming reason. Yet, reason asks: how can we imagine that this self will go on without the body it was lodged in? How can we believe that a relationship will continue beyond this life when most don't last even this one?

Vasu's and mine didn't. Yet, without her I was incomplete. But this is not all, something worse happened to me then. If I have to give a diagnosis and name the disease, I will have to call it a 'crisis of faith'. It embarasses me to use such a clichéd phrase, but what else can I call it? For I did lose faith. And I know that faith is the adhesive that holds all the seemingly disparate bits of life together. Without faith, everything flies apart. For my part, I faced disintegration, chaos.

What had I believed in? The human body. Not in its perfection; I knew better than most people how vulnerable it is, and I saw, more than most, the imperfections in it, the aberrations. But I had believed in the body as a supreme assertion of creation, as the acme of creation. I believed, like the Buddha did, that the human body itself is a privilege. This pride in being human, so different from the arrogance of the ego, is in fact, close to what I imbibed from Dr Kapadia. But for it to end? To become nothing? All that enormous energy of creation, the miracle of life to end in nothingness? It made no sense. Even worse was the fact that Vasu had destroyed my theory that life matters above all, that survival is the first credo of humanity. I could understand that Vasu, suffering the way she was, did not want to survive, to live on as a cripple after the two amputations. *Enough*, she said after the second surgery. *Enough*, she said loudly and emphatically. Yes, I can understand that. No human wants to live with pain and suffering, to live dependent on others. (And yet I have seen patients wanting to live, struggling for life in spite of great suffering.) Now it is my turn, I am close to my end, and I know I would rather die than suffer the kind of pain that I know is waiting for me. But Vasu *invited* death even before her suffering began. She concealed her injury from us, she ignored all the symptoms which told her, which *must* have told her, that something was wrong. Not only was she a doctor's wife, she was also a diabetic's sister. I had told her, when Laxman's diabetes was confirmed, that the possibility of her having the disease was something we had always to bear in mind. But she said nothing. Her stoicism made me feel that she was cooperating with her illness. And when all her organs began to fail, I had a queer thought that she was responsible for this, that she was organizing a strike of her organs, willing them to stop working. A kind of perverse will in her stood apart from the rotting gangrenous body, away from the suffering person who moaned and cried in pain. Apart from these involuntary sounds, there was total silence.

Vasu had given up words even earlier. After Malu's death, she wrote nothing, not a word, she spoke very little and only when necessary. I thought that her silence would be broken when Jiji came. But as if to avoid this, she went into a coma before Jiji arrived. I had expected Jiji to be shattered by Vasu's death. Not only was this the mother she had once adored, and then been estranged from, it was a death that gave her no time for reconciliation. But Jiji was composed. Of course, she had the children to look after, it made a difference. But I also think that she had already done with grieving for her mother. I remember the terrible night after Shyam's death, when I heard Jiji sobbing in the next room. It was not so much a sobbing as a wailing, a terrible wailing that brought on an almost angina-like pain in me. She was crying out her mother's name—*Mai Mai Mai*. I thought it strange that she should cry out her mother's name in her grief, the same mother who had kept her apart from Shyam. Then I thought that it was an instinctive thing, that like all humans in times of distress and need, she was crying out to her mother.

Now I know that she was mourning not just Shyam, but her mother as well, the mother who she knew she would never have anything to do with again. Vasu was her mother, they had inhabited the same body for nine months. How could she cut off the roots of her own being without pain? The umbilical cord continues to exist, a phantom link, all our lives. We can never deny the ties of the body, we can never leave them behind us. The ties we forge through our bodies are the strongest, the hardest to sever. Look at the way we connect the organs of the body to emotions and feelings: we speak of blood, of the heart, the guts, the liver ...

As for me, what helped was just going through the motions. My own knowledge tells me that life is ceaseless, uninterrupted activity. The heart pumping, the lungs breathing air in and out, the digestive system working, the blood circulating, the constant movement of the eyelids—this is life. Nature does not believe in stasis; stasis is putrefaction, stasis is death. And so Gayatri and I had to move on, we had to keep going. Gayatri's goodness was part of the healing process for me. After she went, there was Raja. And now there is this writing. I can't explain how or why it happens, but when I write in this book, I go to bed feeling a little lighter, I get up in the morning with a kind of energy that I don't bring to my other tasks.

Raja tells me Jiji is coming. He wrote to her without telling me; he confessed this to me, a little nervous about my reaction. But I am glad she is coming. Even if we are no longer the Baba and Jiji we once were to each other, I am grateful that she will be with me till the last day, that I will not die alone. Raja is there, of course, but it is too big a burden for him to bear alone. And why should he? This is Jiji's duty. I was with my father in his last days, my daughter should be with me. It is a duty we owe our past; if we leave this undone, we can't move on, we will carry the burden of the past with us forever. I think it will help Jiji to be here with me, it may help her to lay the ghosts of the past.

*

Did Baba want me to read this? I'm beginning to think he didn't. Would he have written of his feelings for Mai, or of their sexual life, if he had thought that I would be reading this one day? Mai and he kept that part of their life secret. I can't say that they concealed it, because there was never a sense of anything being kept from us. The door of their room was always open. If I woke up at night, I knew I could go straight inside. Malu and I went into their room on Sunday mornings when they woke up late; we climbed on to the high bed, snuggling between our parents, kicking each other as we got under the covers. And when we'd found our places (mine next to Baba, Malu's next to Mai) and made ourselves comfortable, I would inhale with rapture what was to us a Baba-and-Mai smell, the smell of cosiness, of being loved and petted. The smell, indeed, of happiness itself. At times there was a faint whiff of another odour, which I realized much later, when I entered that world myself, was that of their mingled bodies, of sex.

And yet, who knows, possibly Baba did want me to read this. Perhaps he is giving me an explanation for something that has always puzzled me: the intensity of Mai's hostility when I threw myself so passionately into Shyam's arms. It explains something she'd said, words which I'd ignored then. If I'd thought of it at all, I'd imagined it was the kind of thing one parent says about another when they disagree with each other. Passing the buck, so to say. *Your son. Your daughter.* It's like they're saying: *I have nothing to do with their bad qualities, those come from you.*

'You're just like your father,' she said to me in the course of one of our many arguments.

Just like my father. Now I know what she meant. She was telling me my love for Shyam was nothing more than a physical passion. She was wrong, oh, yes, she was wrong, but it helps me to understand, it helps to know that Mai's steady hostility which had so baffled me, was part of her ongoing battle with Baba, it was part of her resistance to Baba's idea of the importance of the body.

But Baba gave up that obsession. He not only resigned from

his job in the hospital, he reneged on his feelings about the body as well; the passionate admirer turned sceptic. It began, I think, with Mai's death, no, even earlier, with the sight of Mai's body rotting while she was still alive. The sandalwood fragrant body he had loved, stinking so much that you had to cover your nose, to hold your breath when you went into the room. Is it surprising that it destroyed his faith in the body?

When I came here to be with Baba, when I saw him, gaunt and skeletal, my first thought was—why, he looks like Mr Bones! He had always been thin, but his disease had defleshed him totally. His emaciation was frightening, the skin stretched taut over the bones, accentuating the sharp edges, the ridges, the hollows. When I looked at his hands, I thought: if we play the game of my childhood now, if you ask me the questions you did then, I will be able to answer them by tracing the lines on your hand, the way we did on Mr Bones. I can say: this is the metacarpal, this is the phalanx, this is the … And I thought of how he had cut his nails, and ours too, painfully close to the skin, how his hair was always cut close to the scalp, the shape of his skull clearly apparent. I thought of him shaving himself with vigour, the scraping sound of the razor on the stubble setting my teeth on edge, making the hair stand up on my arms as I watched the red beads of blood springing up in the trail of the razor. As if, all his life, he had been preparing himself for this end when he would become, as he finally did, pared down to the bone.

I can see the same kind of cruelty to himself in his writing. Scourging himself, evading nothing, drawing a picture of himself in clear stark lines when he writes of his passion for Mai. An unrequited passion. Strange how it has made me see everything differently. Their bed, which had been a place of comfort and love, is suddenly the arena in which a man and woman fought their battles. He's drawn me into the most private world of humans, the most intimate and secret world of man and woman. I'm amazed that he could write of himself so clinically, so objectively. I see it as part of his plan to shed everything—his possessions, his flesh and now, even his past and his inner world.

Unburdening himself. There is a kind of naivety in Baba that fills me with compassion. He's like someone who's found a new occupation, a hobby which fills him with excitement and into which he plunges without thinking of what lies ahead. A bungee jumper ready to let go. Mai knew the dangers of this. Which is why she wrote the kind of stories she did, covering the bare bones with ornate clothes, with frills and brocades, with jewels which glittered so much that you noticed nothing else. Yes, Mai knew what writing could do: once you wrote a thing down, it became final, it was there forever, you could no longer ignore what had happened, you were pinned down to it, changed forever.

my mother was a writer

My mother was a writer, but for years we scarcely knew this fact. And even when we came to understand that she wrote, which we did very gradually, it didn't figure very significantly in our picture of her. To us, she was just Mai. *Aamchi Mai.* We never spoke of her without that possessive; she was *ours, our* mother, and we wanted to assert that all the time and to everyone. Mai was the centre of our universe, she was the sun around whom the three of us, Baba, Malu and I, revolved. On the few occasions when she went out by herself, generally to visit her mother, the house felt empty and the three of us seemed to be in a state of suspended living, our eyes on the clock, our ears cocked to catch the sound of her key in the door. And when we went out without her, Malu and I were eager to get back home, to tell her about what we'd done, calling out 'Mai, Mai' even as we were climbing the stairs, Baba hot on our heels, delayed only by pausing to take off his shoes, waiting impatiently for us to be done so that he could take over and give her *his* account of our outing. And when finally, reluctantly, we went to wash and change, we could hear them conversing, Baba speaking most of the time, Baba always more articulate, quicker to speak, to respond, to laugh, whereas Mai's words, her smiles and her laughter, were measured out with care and precision.

If anyone had told me then that Mai was not as happy to see us as we were to come back to her, I would not have believed it. And if I had been forced to believe it, I would have been heartbroken; to me, it would have been a betrayal. But today, when I remember the way she looked up when we entered, her eyes blank and unfocussed as if she did not see us, or, seeing us, failed to recognize us, when I think of the pause, a tiny moment before she spoke, it seems to me that we were not entirely welcome. I know now that in that small moment she made the journey from the world she was in to the world that contained us. When she had successfully negotiated that passage and got to us, she would smile, cap her pen, put it down carefully and say, 'So, you're back?' Even at that time, I noticed that pause, a miniscule moment when I had a feeling of Mai not seeing me. Of not existing, for if Mai did not see me, I did not exist. It frightened me. But I made the leap across the abyss with her and it was soon over. She was listening to us, holding Malu close, chiding me for shoving her in my excitement, for tugging at her sari. And the little blank spot between us was forgotten. But there was always this tiny mustard seed of suspicion in me; like a jealous, possessive lover I was always weighing things, wanting to be sure that I was loved, that she wanted to be with me, with us, that she did not want to be with anyone else, or anywhere else. Which is why when she said, 'Thank god only four days more before we're back home!' I was shocked. We were in Bangalore on our annual holiday and I was already mourning the impending end of it. She was combing my hair when she said this. I turned around sharply at that, so sharply that I whisked the hair she was plaiting out of her hands. I looked suspiciously, accusingly into her face and said, or rather charged her, 'You don't like it here? You don't want to be with us in Kaka and Gayatri's house?'

Without answering my question, my accusation rather, she gave me a sharp flick on my arm, one of Mai's *chatkas* as we called them, which could be very hurting, for her ring left a stinging pain behind. And then she said, 'Sit straight! And don't talk rubbish.' Holding me by my shoulders, she pushed me so that, pivoting on my bottom, I went back to my original position, my back to her, unable to see her face or her expression. But when she said '*Khulli*', I relaxed. If she called me 'silly', it meant she was not angry with me. Mai angry was Mai speechless, a silence that was truly terrifying, an ignoring that was like being thrown out of heaven. In my relief, I forgot that she had not denied my charge. The truth was that she *was* eager to get back home. We saw this clearly the moment we reached. 'It's so good to be home,' she said, even though her nose was wrinkling in distaste at the shit-smelling air that rushed in through the window.

Mai was a shy woman; her reserve and rather stern face concealed a shyness that made it hard for her to be among strangers. She did not encourage neighbours dropping in, nor did she visit anyone without a reason. She was happiest at home with her immediate family. In Bangalore too, it was family, yet in a way she was an outsider. Baba, Gayatri, RK and BK had known one another since they were children. And Kamala, the daughter of a cousin, had been part of their circle since she was a child. Mai may have felt a little alienated by their closeness. And by the language as well, for though all of them, except RK, knew Marathi well, when they were together they spoke Kannada which, though Mai could understand and speak a little, was still a strange language to her. There were also all those allusions and jokes that people who are knit together, not only by blood but by long association and friendship, bring into their conversation. I know that in Bangalore she seemed slightly diminished, a little faded, like an old photograph. So that I, who was entirely at home in Gayatri and RK's house and considered it as much mine as our home in Bombay, felt protective of her, as if I was the hostess and had to take care of her. I remember a time when I came upon RK's nephews, his sisters' sons, imitating Mai's singing. She'd been forced to sing the previous evening as part of a game of forfeits. To the boys, who'd never heard a Marathi song before, the song, the language and Mai's nasal singing must have seemed excruciatingly funny. When I took in what they were doing—they were making fun of Mai, making fun of *my mother!*—I pounced on them like a fury. I caught hold of one of them, grasping whatever I could get hold of, his hair, his shirt, his ears and pummelled him mercilessly, sobbing at the same time. Mai punished me for this, but I never told her why I had got into that fight, never revealed that I had been defending her. Even to speak of what they had been doing, to tell her that they were ridiculing her, was an affront to her dignity.

Whatever her feelings were, she came dutifully with us to Bangalore every year, becoming as much as she could, part of the family group. Nevertheless, she was enormously relieved to be back in her own home, the place where she was most herself. Plunging, thankfully I imagine, right away into her chores, getting us ready for a new year in school. Once this was done, she went back to her writing, which occupied her more during this period than any other time of the year. The months before Divali were the busiest for her; she worked hard to meet the demands of the magazines that needed stories for their special Divali issues. Mai never spoke of her own writing; she never, as far as I know, publicly proclaimed herself a writer. It was a kind of secret business, an activity she did in private, something no one in the family ever spoke of. RK was an exception; he was proud of her being a writer, even if he had never read her. He asked for her opinion during their discussions, he brought her into the conversation, he tried to make her talk. This was hard on her, since they had to speak in English, the only language they had in common. And Mai's English was not too good, she was never comfortable with it. This was another of those times when I felt very protective, looking around to see if anyone was smiling at her Marathi-accented, often wrong English, noting her little mistakes, loyally ready to take umbrage if anyone else did. But RK, whose own English was impeccable, never even smiled. To him she was that august being—A Writer.

Baba's profession was a loud fact in our lives, it was stamped on every aspect of our living; our very home, situated in a hospital campus, declared what he was. Inside the house too, his work proclaimed itself in the books and journals strewn around, the smell that he brought home with him, his white coat that hung in the hall next to Mr Bones, and indeed Mr Bones himself. But Mai's writing never intruded into our lives; she kept it to herself, away from all of us. The table in their room was littered with Baba's papers—the articles he was reading, the pages he was proofing for the journal that he edited. Mai's work was never visible. She worked at their table during the day and at night she sat at the dining table. She put her papers neatly away after she finished working, leaving nothing of her work about. I've begun to understand only now that Mai was scrupulous about giving Baba a paramount place in the house, giving him his due as head of the family, as the breadwinner. '*Annadata sukhi bhava*,' she muttered at the end of each meal, raising her food-soiled right hand, clenched into a fist, fingers turned inwards, to her forehead. Yes, Baba was the annadata, the breadwinner, a position she was careful about respecting.

And yet, she worked too. Since I began clearing up the house, I've realized the voluminous amount she wrote. The piles of magazines with her stories in them, and the published books, speak of hard work. She wrote steadily through the years except, I see from the dates on the magazines, for the gap of a few years, when she was busy being a mother. Years that wiped out the writer because she was wiping our noses, Malu's and mine, wiping our bottoms (with her face turned away!), feeding us, dressing us. She was popular in those days, something I learnt much later; she was not a great literary figure, no, never that, but her stories were popular and much read. She had a brief brush with fame too, after *Manasi* was filmed. But it was as a short-story writer that she was most known. Her name 'Vasu Narayan' figured in many magazines, women's magazines mainly, for it was of women she wrote and women who were her faithful readers.

It was the right time for the kind of writing she did. With no entertainment apart from the movies, there were many takers for these magazines, specially the growing number of working girls and women who had money to buy them and the time to read them on the local trains and buses as they travelled to and from work. Years later, when I was a working woman myself, I got a glimpse of Mai's readers, girls and women who, in the midst of the drudgery of their lives, both at home and in their working places, dreamt of love and of marriage to the right man. Women and girls who longed for a man to take them away from their dreary lives in which they were pawed, harassed and chivvied about, both at home and outside. Women who dreamt of families where they would be daughters-in-law and sisters-in-law, respected and loved, in positions of power. Seeing in Mai's stories the possibilities of this, imagining themselves living the kind of life she wrote about, which for them was a rainbow on the horizon.

I never read anything of Mai's when I was at home. For one thing, I did not read Marathi, I only spoke it. My first glimpse of her as a writer came when *Manasi* was being filmed. I had not read the novel, but I came to know the story through the movie. The family was there during the preview, but I was not with Baba, Mai and Malu; I was with Shyam, I watched it with his arms around me. The first story of Mai's that I read was after my marriage. By which time, I had reached the end of the story as Mai saw it, having got to the paradise of marriage she held out to her readers. I was living, like Mai's heroines almost always did, in the same house as my husband's family, but unlike them, living a separate existence. And, something that shocked even me, paying them rent for the single room we occupied. I could hear their voices, clear and loud, all day and though I could not understand what they were saying, since they spoke Sindhi, I knew they were bickering. They went on all day in varying combinations: father and daughter, sisters-in-law, mother and children, siblings. Shyam's brother was the only one out of it all, his voice never audible. Just a wall separated us, but I couldn't have felt more distant if we lived on separate continents. The hostility and bickering amazed me. Listening to Shyam's sister arguing with her father, I thought of our life at home, of Mai's voice which was never raised, of Baba's laughter, of Malu's 'Jiji, Jiji'. Used as I was to living in a family like ours, I couldn't understand how anybody could live the way these people did.

It was here, against the backdrop of these angry voices, that I read 'Annapoorna', Mai's story about a woman who marries a widower with a daughter. The man's child and mother are both hostile to her, but he tells her, 'Don't involve me in your problems, you've got to live with my mother and daughter.' I read of how Annapoorna patiently and quietly endured their hostility, of how she gradually won their love and trust and how she got her final reward—her husband's praise. Such a hopelessly sentimental and unreal picture, so unlike Mai's own uncompromising self. She's dishonest, I thought spitefully, fuelling my anger against her, against her refusal to understand my feelings for Shyam. And then, feeling a traitor to her, I sobbed, my homesickness and misery at our estrangement pouring out of my eyes.

Now, when I think of that story, it is not the story itself, or my response to it that comes to mind, but Mai's professionalism. She wrote the story in the midst of the chaos I'd brought into her life by my decision to marry Shyam, by my insistence on marrying him immediately. She completed the story even while all this was going on, she sent it to the magazine in time for the Divali issue. Yes, she was a professional, always meeting her commitments. She kept a meticulous account of her earnings; I remember her checking her passbook, toting up the figures, her fingers and lips moving while she did her sums. She didn't earn very much, not even from the film rights to *Manasi*. But she took us for a treat the evening she got her money. She was livelier than usual, flushed and smiling, while Baba joked and teased her about how she would be able to maintain us from now on and how he would give up his job and become the housekeeper while she wrote undisturbed. Mai was wearing a yellow and red silk, I remember, one of Gayatri's gifts to her, the bright colour giving her a vivacity which transformed her altogether.

Mai was a simple person and, unlike her two brothers' wives, not interested in saris and jewels. I remember the contempt with which she spoke of Mangal, Laxman's wife. Decking herself up like a bride at her age, she said. Her own wardrobe was piled high with saris gifted by her brothers and Gayatri, Laxman's gifts getting more flamboyant and gaudy each year, so that they remained unworn. No, these things didn't mean much to her. When I think of my mother now, I realize that what she valued most was freedom, freedom to be by herself, to be on her own, freedom from our constant demands on her, from our claims, from the need to be 'aamchi Mai'.

In the months since Baba's death, I've read almost everything she wrote. It's not just the volume of her writing that surprises me; it's the fact that she wrote at all. How did she, a shopkeeper's daughter who had not gone beyond school, begin to write? Where did it come from? I think of her dull and slow mother, her brother Laxman who, I guess, never read a word beyond what was absolutely necessary, of her brother Bharat, so prosaic and limited: this was where she came from. I have a very vague memory of the house she grew up in—just one room in a crowded chawl in Parel. A petty shopkeeper's daughter, she wrote of gracious old families. Living among women who had to be aggressive and strong to survive the endless drudgery and continuous lechery, she wrote of silent, sacrificing women. And she, who was always a little remote even when she was in the midst of her own family, wrote of family togetherness. An independent woman who hated being questioned, she wrote of women who found happiness in submission, not only to their husbands, but to their families as well.

I don't know much about writers, but I wonder: do they keep themselves carefully out of their writing? Do they *all* do this? Or was Mai specially cautious, guarding her real self from coming through in her writing? I remember how careful she was about not letting anyone, not even us, see her before she was properly dressed. Always presenting a self she wanted the world to see. I've begun to realize now that there was a maverick self hidden behind that decorous woman so conscious of the proprieties, a self that she was constantly battling against. Even today I cannot put a finger on what made her different; there was nothing to distinguish her from other women, at least not outwardly. It was something else, a remoteness, yes, that's the only word I can use, it's what comes to mind when I think of her in the midst of the family. As if she wasn't wholly present.

If there is nothing of herself in her stories, I can recognize some bits of her life, of our family life, in them. There's the quilt which she uses as a symbol of family togetherness in 'Annapoorna', the quilt that Annapoorna is making for her hostile step-daughter. I know where that comes from; Ajji, Mai's mother, had a lifelong obsession with making quilts. She made beautiful quilts which were presented to every person in the family, so that each one of us was a proud owner of Ajji's quilt though, living in Bombay, we never really had any need for them. She continued to make them even in her last years, but they were not the same. Senility changed Ajji from a silent, peaceful woman into a ceaselessly babbling one. And the quilts became a haphazard patching together of old rags, untidy stitches going every which way, large gaping holes showing where the stitches were too large. I remember Mai sobbing after Ajji's death over the last one, a pathetic, cobbled together, smelly collection of rags. Some time later she wrote 'Annapoorna', pouring her grief at the neglect of her mother and the ugliness of senility into the story, transforming the quilt, making it now a symbol of love and togetherness. Is this what writers do? Do they take everything that's unbearable in their lives and make it over into something entirely different?

I don't know. One thing is certain: Mai knew her writing self very well. If she recognized her own talent, she also knew her limitations, her ability to write only a particular kind of story. Which she did, ensuring herself a steady readership. She kept to the formula she had perfected, making a timid foray out of it only with *Manasi*. And then she wrote 'Blackout', in which she leapt over the boundaries, abandoning the saccharine sweetness of romance and family life and picking up the spiked burr of lust, cruelty and hatred. Such an astonishing story, that one. It makes me think: what would she have written after this? What path would she have taken?

But 'Blackout' was her final story. She wrote nothing after it, except, yes, one more story, truly the last one of her life, the most skilfully and carefully plotted story of them all. A story that remains in the darkness in which it was conceived, all the characters in it dead except one. I'm the only survivor, still living out her story, imprisoned within it, sometimes it seems to me, forever.

property matters

My yoga sessions generally leave me pleasantly tired, my body relaxed and at ease, as if the two hours of conscious movement have brought my body and myself together in a friendly companionship. But today I feel exhausted; it's like the earlier times when the pain in my back, which had driven me to yoga, seemed to be a resentful message from my body. A hot bath will help, I think, but it only enervates me more. I'm sitting half asleep, picking at my dinner in a desultory manner when the phone rings. I don't have the will or the desire to cross the room and pick it up, though the thought that it could be Anand or Sachi crosses my mind. They'll call back, I think, and allow it to ring until it stops. I'm preparing to get into bed when it rings again. This time I pick it up, expecting to hear Sachi's impatient 'Where were you?' or Anand's inquiring 'Ma?'. But before I can say 'Hello', a strange male voice asks, 'Why don't you pick up the phone?'

There is something peremptory about the tone, a rudeness that angers me. 'Who are you?'

The voice disregards my question and asks instead, 'Are you Badri Narayan's daughter?'

'Who are you?'

'Are you Badri Narayan's daughter?'

'What's that got to do with you? And *who* are you?'

'Never mind that. And *you* listen to us.' He uses the plural, I notice. Like the man who'd said he was from an estate agency. 'Are you selling the house? How much do you want for it?'

'Who are you?'

'Stop asking that question. Just tell us how much you want for the house.'

'I don't talk to people who don't tell me their names.'

'That has nothing to do with you. Just answer our question.'

'No, I'm not selling the house.'

'That's not a good decision. Think it over.'

'I don't need to think it over.'

'If you're wise, you'll sell it to us.'

I bang down the phone. My hands are trembling. It rings again. I pick it up and put it back in the cradle. It rings twice, then stops, as if the man is satisfied he's conveyed his message, he's made sure that I know he will not give up, that he will not leave me alone.

He? But he spoke in the plural. Does that mean there are more of them in it? Or is it the arrogance of someone used to being obeyed? Laxman began speaking of himself in the plural in the later years. 'He calls himself *aamhi*,' Baba had commented sarcastically. 'As if he's the Peshwa.'

Laxman? Is this someone like Laxman?

I lie in bed, staring into the darkness, puzzled, wondering what to do next. I won't be able to sleep, I think, but I do. And wake up, I don't know how much later, to an awareness of someone in the house. I am wide awake in an instant, my body frozen into stillness, my ears waiting for the sound that woke me to be repeated. No, there's nothing. No sounds. Just a feeling of another human in the house, a human smell, a sense of another person breathing. Or is it me? I stop breathing and then I hear it—a small scrape made by the slight movement of a chair. So tiny a sound, yet clear and distinct. Unable to bear the inactivity any more, I fling myself out of bed, throw away my blanket and am reaching for the switch of the bedside lamp when something comes at me. I can feel the impact of a body, of hands, hard rough hands pushing me, pushing me back against the wall. I am struggling now, kicking, trying to shout, when the hand comes over my mouth. I want to bite, but I can't open my mouth, the hand won't let me. I heave my body out of his grasp with a huge effort and begin to run when he grabs me again. I slip out of his hold once more and make for the door, but am pulled back yet again. It's like we're playing a deadly game in the dark. My breath is coming in gasps now, I am trying to shout, but no sound emerges. I make another wild rush for the door, but he gets hold of me firmly, by the shoulder this time, and throws me on the bed. I fall on my back, I can feel his knees on my body. Oh god, he's going to rape me. I thrust my body up against the pressure of his knees, my own knees come up in defence, but suddenly the pillow is jerked away from under my head. I feel a jarring pain at the back of my head. The pillow comes over my face. The fear of rape becomes the fear of death. I'm deprived of air, I'm going to be suffocated, I'm going to die. I kick out violently, my body flailing from side to side, I need air, I want air ...

Suddenly there is no more pressure. I lie still, then fearfully take the pillow off my face. I am afraid to stir; he must be waiting to get at me again, to hurl me back on the bed. The silence continues. I can feel the absence of any other person in the room, there is a sense of my occupying the space alone. Cautiously I get out of bed and move to the door, afraid to go out—*he's waiting there for me*. Afraid to shut the door and lock myself in—*what if he's hidden himself somewhere in the room?* I can hear my own breathing, loud and ragged, my chest is hurting. I pick up the phone, but I can't see anything, it's dark. And what number do I want? I am totally blank. I sit on the bed and stare at the phone for a moment. And then my fingers automatically stab at some numbers. I can hear the phone ringing at the other end, it goes on ringing for long. At last I hear a sleepy 'Huh? Who?'

'Raja ...' My voice comes out so reedy and thin I can't recognize it myself.

'Who?'

'Raja, come at once.'

'Jiji? What …?'

'There's someone in the house … a man …'

'I'll be there.'

I hear the sound of his car and wait for him to enter, until I realize I have to let him in. I nerve myself to cross the dark territory outside my room. Raja switches on the light the moment he enters and stares at me aghast.

'Jiji, what …?'

He goes in and returns with a sheet which he drapes around me.

'Sit down. What happened?'

'An intruder in the bedroom. He tried to kill me.'

'What!'

He begins moving through the house, switching on the lights in each of the rooms he passes through, turning the rooms from dark areas of terror to familiar places. Why didn't I switch on the lights myself? I follow him, holding the sheet tightly around me. When he comes to the bedroom, he stands looking at the chaos, the chair overturned, the bed lamp on the floor, the sheets and pillows strewn about.

'My god! My god!'

I stare at him dumbly. When he goes out, I rush to the bathroom, no longer able to control the fear-induced pressure on my bladder. I wash my face and look at myself in the mirror. Bruises on my forehead, around my mouth, scratches on my cheeks, one of them bleeding, my hair standing about my face. And my nightdress has a long tear down the front. I now understand why Raja covered me with a sheet. I brush my hair, change from my nightdress into a kaftan and go into the hall. Abhishek is there with Raja, the two of them conversing in low voices.

'Ma'am,' Abhishek says when he sees me, 'you should have called me. I was at home, I was right there.'

'I didn't … I couldn't … he was …'

There's something in my throat that won't let the words come through.

'Sit down, Jiji. And drink some water.'

'I'll get it.'

I drink the water, sipping it slowly. My throat hurts. Did he try to choke me?

'Can I make you some tea, ma'am?'

He's talking to me as if I'm sick, as if I'm a patient.

'I'm all right,' I say, but my teeth are chattering so much I think he doesn't understand what I'm saying.

'Yes, get her a cup, it will do her good.'

I hear Raja speaking on the phone to the police. My jaws are rigid with the effort to stop my teeth from chattering. I draw my legs under me as if I'm feeling cold.

'Here, ma'am, drink this.'

I am drinking the tea when the police arrive. The sounds of the car and their footsteps, loud and clear, seem to erase the surreptitious movements and the hushed sounds of the intruder. Raja lets them in and takes them around. They're at the back for a long time, their voices go on and on. When they return, they look at me for the first time. Obviously Raja has told them it's my house, that I was alone here at the time.

'What happened?' the policeman asks me.

I try to put things together, to get a clear picture of my ordeal. Some things emerge, but many links are missing. In any case, the man is not interested in getting too many details. For him, this is a small incident, just a break-in. Nothing has been taken, it's not a robbery, nor have I been seriously injured. He does make a perfunctory suggestion that I go to the hospital, which I quickly brush off. They go out, Raja and Abhishek following them.

'They've left a constable behind,' Raja says when he returns.

'Locking the stable ...'

'Well, they had to do something. He won't come back, you can be sure of that. But don't stay here alone, Jiji. Come home with me.'

'I'm all right, Raja. You said yourself that he won't return.'

'But look at you! And he's cut a grille out of the window at the back—that's how he entered. It's dangerous to be here.'

Abhishek adds his pleas to Raja's, but I refuse to go.

'I can't leave the house with that open window.'

'The constable will be around. And Abhishek says he'll sleep here tonight.'

Finally, seeing I won't give in, Raja decides to stay on himself, he tells me that both Abhishek and he will be with me. When I go to my room, I have an enormous distaste for getting into bed. I can feel the imprint of his hands, of his knees on the mattress where he knelt and grappled with me. I can't sleep on this bed, I just can't. Fiercely I pull the sheets off the bed, throw away the pillow and lie on the bare mattress, using a cushion from the chair as a pillow.

'Are you okay, Jiji?' Raja calls out, alerted by the sounds.

'I'm fine.'

'Go to bed. We have to go to the police station in the morning.'

They are both out of the house when I wake up. I make myself a cup of tea and wonder, as humans must have done through the ages, how the light of day can banish the terrors of the night and make them seem so distant. Almost illusory. But this was not an illusion. I can see the bruises on my face when I'm getting dressed, I see the window grille neatly cut. I think of the man patiently waiting for the night, soundlessly cutting the grille ... Suddenly I remember the other man who sat on the stairs and smoked a cigarette while he waited for me. Two different men? Or the same?

Raja comes, accompanied by a carpenter who will fix the window grille.

'The advantage of having an architect in the family,' I remark.

'What?' Raja seems preoccupied. 'Come, let's go. He'll do his work. We can leave him here, I know him.'

In the car Raja tells me he has rung up Venkat.

'You know Venkat,' he says in response to my blank look.

'Venkat?'

'*Our* Venkat.'

It takes me a moment to understand that he's speaking of Venkat, RK's sister's son. Raja's cousin. One of the boys I'd caught imitating Mai singing, the one who'd escaped my thrashing by running away.

'Don't you remember he got through the IPS? He's a DIG now. He's promised to ring up the local police station. It'll make all the difference, just you see.'

Raja looks pleased with himself and I laugh.

'What's funny?'

'Nothing. Just amazed by the contacts you always seem to have.'

'Contacts? Damn it, Venkat's family, he's not a contact. Why, he would have been sore if I hadn't told him about this.'

Raja reminds me that Venkat used to visit Baba, that he was there at the funeral; don't I remember seeing him? I don't. I remember nothing except Baba's wasted body and peaceful face. And Anand standing next to me, as if sheltering me from my own grief.

The inspector is not in; a man in civilian clothes, his secretary, perhaps, tells us so. But he'll be here soon, he assures us and asks us to wait. I can see he's been primed about us, he knows the Venkat connection. In fact, Venkat's name seems to hover about us, for I don't see anyone else getting the attention we do. Raja's mobile rings twice and I notice his surreptitious glances at his watch.

'You can go, Raja, I'm sure you have things to do. I'll manage this.'

'Don't be silly. It's only a client I was supposed to meet. He'll wait, it won't hurt him to wait for me.'

There's a kind of ripple, a stir that spreads around, which tells us the inspector has arrived. The woman at the telephone stands up, the two constables bending over some register straighten up to rigid attention like puppets whose strings have been pulled. The inspector goes past us with a quick glance that flickers over me and enters his room. We hear his secretary telling him something. After a few minutes the secretary puts his head round the swinging half-door and announces, 'Saheb says to come in.'

At first the inspector speaks only to Raja, until Raja disengages himself from it, telling him that it's my house. I give the man the details, clearer to me now than they were last night. He doesn't seem to be listening, but asks suddenly, 'Anything like this happened earlier?'

I tell him about the intruder I'd surprised the day I'd come home after getting my driving license. Raja gives me an odd look; he doesn't know this, I haven't told him about it. But it's a relief to speak of it now.

'Do you think it was the same man?'

'I'm not sure. I scarcely saw either of them, so I can't be sure. But I don't think so. Somehow the man last night seemed bigger.'

'Hmm. Any phone calls?'

I tell him about the calls, the earlier ones and the one last night. I have forgotten the name of the agency, but it comes to me as I speak. The Adarsh Agency.

'I'm sure there's no such agency. We'll check. Anyway, it's now clear it's a property matter. It's your own house, isn't it?'

While I hesitate, Raja butts in, telling him of RK—Venkat's uncle, he explains, who built the house. The inspector becomes a little less formal, a little more personal, he tells us he's heard of RK's reputation. He seems to recognize Raja's name too. We are constantly interrupted by phone calls which he deals with in a very businesslike manner. Finally Raja gets up, collecting me with a look. The man reassures us; we'll do our best, he says. And then confesses frankly, 'We can only do so much. You have to be more careful, specially because you live alone. You must arrange for security, sir,' he tells Raja. He gives us both his card. 'That's my mobile number, you can always get me on it. If you can't, call here, Nasir will know where I am most of the time. Get the complaint book, Nasir,' he says. When I sign, he looks with some curiosity at my name.

'Manjari Ahuja. This is your name, madam?'

'Yes.'

Raja drops me home, saying, 'Keep Ratna with you today. I'll come by in the evening.'

I expect an interrogation from him when he comes, he's going to ask me why I didn't tell him about the first intruder, about the phone calls. But to my surprise he says nothing. Instead he goes around, looking at the repaired window and at the back door which now has a crisscrossing of steel bars.

'Like a prison door,' I say wryly.

'It's for your safety.'

'I know, but it seems unfair that I should be the one behind bars.'

'Is Ratna sleeping here tonight?'

'Yes, she's coming. *And* her daughter. *And* Nirmala. Four females. More than a match for one male, don't you think?'

He doesn't respond, which tells me he's really anxious. 'I'll be all right, Raja,' I say seriously. 'Just don't worry.'

But he's at my doorstep early the next morning.

'Come to see if I'm still alive?'

'Jiji ...' he begins, ready, I know, to upbraid me for my levity, when I interrupt and ask fiercely, 'Do you want me to go back to the state I was in yesterday? I don't want to live with that kind of fear, Raja, I won't do it.'

He looks at me, nods and then goes on to practical matters. He's brought some more safety equipment for me. A mobile phone, in case my land line isn't working. (*Or if the wires are cut by the criminals*—I'm sure this thought flashes through his mind as it does through mine, but neither of us speaks of it.) He's asked an electrician to come and install a bell which will ring upstairs and warn Abhishek that I need him. Raja and I have a long discussion, an argument rather, about where the bell should be installed. In my bedroom? In the living room? The outside hall? Or discreetly concealed in the bathroom?

'Why not attach it to my body? That's the one thing that will always be with me.'

Raja glares at me, annoyed by what he thinks is a recurrence of frivolity. But I'm partly serious. It was my body that had felt threatened, it was the threat to my body that had frightened me the most.

With Raja gone, I think of the paraphernalia of security around me and I know I've crossed the invisible line that divides our sense of being safe from the danger zone. The idea of being in danger is like the idea of death: it can happen to others, it can never happen to you. Now I have to accept that it's happened to me, that perhaps I am now in the danger zone, though it still seems faintly unreal.

It becomes real enough when I have a flurry of visits from neighbours, the way I had after Baba's death. This time they have come not with condolences, but with horror stories of land sharks and criminals, of property grabbers and supari killings. They speak knowledgeably of these things, aware of the perils, yet comfortably distanced from them and assured of their own impregnability. They're safe, they're on the other side of the line. I hear, over and over again, the stories of how safe Bangalore once was—'we never had to lock our doors'—until the Bombay underworld descended on it. A woman who's never spoken to me till now, though we meet every day when she takes her dog for a walk, advises me to sell the house. 'Do it quickly,' she says. 'And quietly. You don't know how dangerous the underworld can be.'

I nod and agree and wonder how she would respond if I told her that the underworld is not as unknown to me as she imagines, that I was once connected to it, closely connected, in fact. What would she say if I told her that my uncle was part of it, one of the bosses in that murky world, that he lived a violent life and died a violent death? But the story is forgotten, no one knows of it, not even my children. There is no need for anyone to know it, no need for the story to intrude into my life here.

Venkat comes in the afternoon and I see him in all the glory of his position as a senior police officer. The car door is opened for him by a uniformed man who stands at the gate all the time Venkat is with me, springing to attention each time Venkat stirs, thinking he is ready to leave. Venkat seems a stranger, giving me no glimpse of the boy who had been one of my companions during our holidays. He does not refer to that time either. But he's friendly. We have coffee while he questions me about the incident and the phone calls.

'Do you suspect anyone?' he asks.

'No, I scarcely know anyone here.'

He asks what arrangements I've made for my security.

'Do you think they'll come back?'

'Probably. Not right now, they know we're here. But they're patient. They know we can't give you protection for ever. It's the house they want, you've realized that?'

'Yes, but if I don't want to sell, if I refuse to sell, what can they do?'

'Oh, plenty of things. Force you out by terrifying you and then occupy the house. They can get the records falsified. In fact, I think they may have been searching for the documents the first time.'

'But why, Venkat?'

'This is a corner plot and it's larger than most. It's very valuable. That's one of the reasons. And then you're a female, you live alone, there's no man around—all this makes you an easy victim.'

'Damn them, damn them!'

He smiles and as if my expletives have broken the ice, for the first time he speaks of the old house—for him too, as for Raja, the family home. He tells me how he'd felt when they sold it. And then he says, 'They needn't have sold it, that's what makes me feel so sorry.'

'But it was riddled with termites. They had to demolish it. What else could they have done?'

'Termites? What termites? It was wicked the way they were forced to sell it.'

My expression tells him I'm completely in the dark. And so he speaks of the strange inexplicable phenomenon that forced RK and Gayatri to sell the house. Stones of all shapes and sizes kept pelting the house, some hitting the walls and windows, some falling harmlessly in the yard.

'There was never anyone around, they kept a watch but they never caught anyone in the act of throwing the stones. It went on for months.'

I'm totally bewildered. 'I never knew, I thought it was the termites.'

'Termites?' he repeats yet again. 'Who told you that? No, it was this stone-throwing—some people called it witchcraft, they wanted them to do a puja, but you know how Ramumama was. He refused to do anything of the kind, he decided he'd rather sell the house. Now, of course, I know that it was a plot to force them to sell. I know the sort of things they do ...'

When he gets up to go, he says, 'Be sure that this time we won't allow anyone to force you out. I'm with you, remember that. On your part, just be careful, that's all.' And then he warns me not to open the door to anyone, not to do this, never to do that.

After he's gone, I think—is it worth it, living a fortified existence, living behind bars, as I'd joked to Raja? Is the house worth it?

Yes, I won't let them do this to me. My mind made up, my resolve has hardened: nobody is going to force me out of this house. I'm going to see that Sachi gets it. They meant it for Sachi, Baba and Gayatri and, who knows, maybe Mai as well. I'll hold on to it for her sake.

*

Property matters, the inspector said. I've taught history to children and I know it's true. Duryodhana's refusal to yield 'even a needle-point of land', Alexander's desire to conquer the world, Napoleon's grandiose plans and war-hunger, Hitler's excuse of Lebensraum, or even—let me come to something closer home— Laxman throwing people out of their homes: all these come out of greed for property. We can only do so much, the inspector admitted. He was being frank, but it frightens me, it angers me to think we can do nothing. This house was all RK had, or all he would have had if he had lived. RK reached the top of his profession, the civil service, he was chief secretary of the state for a brief while before he retired. But he was an honest man and an honest bureaucrat. I remember Gayatri expressing her anxiety to Baba about their future; the money from the old house, their share of it rather, would not be enough to get them a plot of land as well as build a house. For RK had decided that the money from the sale of the old house would be shared by all of them, the sisters as well as the brothers. This was unusual, but RK's sense of justice would not permit him to do anything other than an equitable distribution. Gayatri, while going along with this, managed to persuade RK to get a site through a government allotment, which would work out much cheaper than buying a plot of land from a private owner. And so he got this bit of land.

Prime property, the inspector called it. A large plot, with the main road on the right and a quiet, dead-end street in front. An open piece of ground beyond the main road, from where in the evenings I can hear the cries of children playing. Pleasing sounds. Otherwise it's quiet, sometimes so quiet that I can hear the sound of the clock ticking. Why have they zeroed in on this house? As Venkat said, it's the vulnerability of the house that marks it out and puts it in peril. A single woman living in it, with apparently no other family. No male heir.

When I came here to be with Baba, I was preoccupied by his illness. If I had thought then of the future, I would have presumed that the house would be mine after his death. And then I found that it was for Sachi. For a moment I felt cheated, betrayed, done out of something that was mine. Baba's gesture was like a slap on my face; not only was it a repudiation of me, it was directed specifically *against* me. He was telling me what he thought of me. Or so I thought at first. I've learnt to accept it since then, I've thought of many reasons for Baba doing what he did. But the sense of having been wronged remains. Having got the idea that it would be mine, it's hard to think that I have no right to it. Yes, it's greed. Desire for possession, for ownership. I think of Shyam's story of his grandfather who came to India after Partition, leaving his family home behind. And of how, so the family legend goes, unable to bear that loss, he just lay down and died. Yes, property matters.

But now, it seems to matter more that I don't let the house fall into the wrong hands. Whatever these criminals wanted to achieve, they've certainly made me align myself with Sachi. It's no longer Sachi's-house-not-mine, it's *our* house. Something I will not allow criminals to take away from us. I think of RK and his sense of absolute rectitude, of Baba's simplicity and his hard-earned money, of Gayatri's goodness, and I know I will be betraying them if I let the house fall into criminal hands. I will hold on to it. But I can't forget that someone wants this house so badly that they sent an intruder to hurt me, to scare me. Not to kill me—that is now clear. Getting past the confusion and the terror, I realize that at no time was the person seriously trying to injure me. Going through the whole game of hide-and-seek we played in the dark, disentangling the chaotic sequence of events, it becomes clear to me that he was trying to stop me from switching on the light, to prevent me from crying out loudly for help. Later, he was trying to defend himself from my fierce counter assault. And when he threw me on the bed, it was only to immobilize me long enough for him to get away.

Looking back, I also know that it was I who wanted to hurt him, that after a while, I was not just defending myself, but trying to inflict hurt. Rage, terror, pain—whatever it was that filled me, had let the adrenaline flow so that I could have killed him. There was a surge of pleasure each time I made contact with his body, satisfaction when I heard a sound that told me I had hurt him. I find myself thinking of what I will do if he comes back. This time I will be ready, I will have a weapon with me. I think of a variety of weapons and wonder which one is best—a stick, an iron rod, a plastic bag to suffocate him, a rope to throttle, a knife ...? Yes, a knife is the best; stabbing is the easiest and quickest way of killing. Bits of anatomical knowledge come back to me like remnants of a glorious past and I plan and calculate at which point of the body I will insert the knife.

I suddenly stop, horrified by my thoughts, by this self within me I've stumbled upon.

'You're hiding yourself,' Roshan said to me once, convinced that the flippant, refusing-to-think person I presented to her was not my real self. 'I know you're not really like this. You're hiding yourself.'

I denied it, but she was right. In fact, I myself was surprised by what I had become after Shyam's death. Hidden selves surface, our ideas about ourselves are constantly overturned—yes, we surprise our own selves. I thought Mai cruel, but what about me? Implacable, unyielding, refusing to accept anything from her, or from Baba, that would lessen their load of guilt. Turning my back even on Gayatri and her unquestioning, undemanding love. From where had this woman come? Had she been there all the while, concealed behind the so-eager-to-please-Jiji? And now this ready-for-violence-person ...

But will I really be able to kill? I don't know. No, I know that when the time comes my hand will falter, I will fail. But what if it is a matter of survival? What if it is my life or another's? I think of Laxman: did he too, the first time, pick up a knife to defend himself, to save his own life? Was that how the knife came into his hands? For long Laxman had been only an agent, a front for nameless men. When did he move on to becoming the boss himself? I don't know. I don't think anyone knows the whole truth of his career. I somehow think that overt violence was not part of his career profile—if I can call it that. But he supplied killers; isn't that the same thing? And what the hell am I doing? Am I trying to justify Laxman as Mai used to do? There was a time when it was hard for me to think of Laxman as a criminal. To Malu and me, he was our jovial uncle, the one who never came without his pockets full of treats for us, who met us with a big hug. Two selves: Baba saw a monster and Mai her brother, the one to whom she turned in her times of need. The brother who never failed her. Her respectable brother, Bharat, could never have done for Mai what Laxman did.

When we were children, if we woke up early enough, we would

hear Mai chanting her early morning shlokas, looking into her palms as she intoned the words, *'Karagré vasaté Lakshmi'*. Her face intent, making us feel that she could really see, as the shloka said, Lakshmi, Saraswati and Govinda in her palms. Malu and I learnt the shloka from her and for a while we recited it after her. One day Malu suddenly paused in the middle of the shloka and said, 'But Mai, I can't see any of them. Where's Lakshmi, where's Saraswati, where is Govinda …?'

'They're there, just keep looking and you'll see them one day.'

We stopped reciting the shloka at some point and it went into the store of forgotten things. But now I think of Mai's words and wonder—does the shloka mean that we can find glory, goodness and wisdom if we look deep into ourselves? Did Mai think this was possible for Laxman too, and was this why she didn't give up on him?

It was Laxman who came to tell me that Shyam was dead. Only his affection for me could have brought him, for by that time he had stopped going out; even surrounded as he was by his bodyguards, he didn't feel safe. But he came and stayed with me, uncaring of his own safety, until Baba's arrival. The moment Baba entered, he went away, knowing that I was no longer alone. I remember how they crossed each other, the two men who loved Mai, men so opposed to each other that each passed the other without a word, without a glance. I saw Laxman only once after that. I went to meet him after Mai's death; he sent word to me, the way he had done earlier, through devious channels. I thought he wanted to know the details of her death, to know how she died. But that was not it. The only questions he asked me about her death were: did I get there in time? And did she say anything to me? I told him she was already in a coma when I got there, that she died within an hour of my getting there. He left it at that; I realized he didn't want to know the details of her dying, not just because it would be too painful for him to hear, but also because it came too close to him. Being a diabetic himself, the fear of dying the way she had was added to his fear of a violent death, or so I guess.

And so we kept away from Mai's last moments. He spoke instead of Mai's early self, of the sister he had always admired. 'She was the cleverest of the three of us,' he said. 'Yes, she was cleverer than Bharat.' And then again, regretfully, 'She got married too early. She should have waited a little, gone to college, studied some more. She could have done much.' He spoke of *Manasi*; it was a bad film, he said. 'She deserved better than what that chap did. I'd have made a movie of her story, I told Vasutai that. But she said no and I left it alone. I would have done anything for her,' he added. 'Anything. But when she came and asked me for help, there was so little I could do. I couldn't help her, I could do nothing ...'

By this time he was crying, both of us were crying. He was sobbing like a child. He had put out his hand and was holding mine, clinging to it as if for survival. At that moment one of his men entered the room, he came in abruptly, hurriedly and said something to Laxman. Laxman jerked his hand out of mine, sat up and said, 'Who said you could come in? Get out. Get out.' The face so transformed that even I was frightened.

Hidden selves ...

the ampersand

There have been no more phone calls, no threats or scary incidents. Except for the mobile phone and my awareness of the switch for the new bell, discreetly hidden by my bed, it is as if the episode never happened. Fear recedes; it is impossible for anybody to live too long in any extreme state. But at night the terror returns. I have to nerve myself to get into bed, the bed which brings back memories of my struggle with the man. I find myself closing the windows, even at the cost of stuffiness, rechecking the bolts again and again. And then I lie awake, staring at the ceiling, my body tensed, ready to start up at a sound. I've thought of taking something to help me sleep, but the idea of being caught unawares, of being fast asleep when someone breaks in, is worse.

I'm alone in the house at night now. I told Ratna I didn't need her. It's not true, it's part of the front of bravado I'm putting up, but I don't want to become dependent, to get used to crutches. And now Abhishek has gone too. He left for Singapore last week. He told me he'd be back in three months, unless of course, he was sent to the States, in which case, he said, it would be four months, perhaps five. Amazing that this boy from a small town should be so blasé about globe trotting! I remember our excitement when we went to Pune to visit Bharat and Medha and the almost hysterical frenzy with which we began preparing for our annual trip to Bangalore, the preparations beginning at least a fortnight earlier, the suitcases dusted and kept in our room, Malu and I dropping into them the clothes we wanted to take. And the piles of luggage when we met at the station, Raja's family and ours, five children and two women with bags of all sizes and shapes around us—including a holdall that Kamala always brought along, swollen like a pregnant woman in the last trimester. It was stuffed with sheets, pillows and blankets for the journey, clothes for the children to change into at night and again before getting out, and all the things which couldn't be accommodated in the suitcases. And the food we carried with us was enough, Baba used to joke, to feed an army. The chaos, the mess we made in the compartment! I remember how two men peeped in once, ready to argue that one of the berths was theirs— which it was. Then, taking in the number of children and the confusion, they hastily moved to another compartment; we never saw them again.

And now Abhishek walks out with a suitcase as if he is leaving for an overnight stay.

'Abhishek's leaving?' Raja had exclaimed when I told him about it. I knew what he was thinking: I would now be alone in the house. But Abhishek had thought of it too. He'd suggested, a little hesitantly, that he could arrange for someone to stay in the rooms until he returned—if I agreed, of course.

'And you said yes? You've agreed to take an unknown person into the house? You need to get your head examined, Jiji.'

'But he's not unknown. I know him, Abhishek brought him to me himself. He's been helping me with the computer, you've heard me speak of my Computer Guru.'

'But you know how it is now ...'

'Exactly. Better to have someone than to be alone.'

'I told you we'll arrange for a watchman.'

'A doddering old man who'll sleep half the night. And whom I'll have to pay more than I can afford.'

'I said I'll pay.'

'No, thanks. And anyway, it's too late. I've already fixed it with Abhishek. The new chap is moving in tomorrow.'

Raja comes haring in now, to check up on me, as he says. To check on the new tenant is closer to the truth.

'What's his name, by the way?'

'Raman.'

'That's it?' Raja asks after a pause.

'Raman Joy Kumar.'

'That's his name? Sounds phoney. Like a film star ...' His voice trails away, remembering that his own name, Rajendra, came from a film star Kamala had admired at the time. It's something Raja is touchy about, a fact he doesn't like anyone to know.

'He was named Raman and then Joy to explain that.' When Raja stares at me in silence, I add, 'Abhishek told me this.'

'You mean,' Raja is intrigued, 'his parents put in an English translation of his name and made it a second name?'

'He doesn't have parents, he was brought up in an orphanage. It was a padre who named him.'

'He's an orphan?' Worse and worse, Raja's expression seems to say.

'What's wrong with being an orphan, Raja? I'm one myself, remember?'

'Don't be stupid. You had parents ...'

'I'm sure he had parents too. You can't not have parents.'

'... you knew who they were and ...' he goes on smoothly, ignoring my interruption, then sees my face and stops. 'You'll never take anything seriously, will you? What I am trying to say is, how do you know he isn't a criminal?'

My uncle was a criminal, I want to say. But this is not something Raja and I have ever spoken of.

'Abhishek knows him. He works for Abhishek's friend, the man who's assembling computers.'

I don't mention Abhishek's hint that Raman was likely to lose his job since his friend was not doing too well and would be cutting down on his staff. Instead I say, in what I think is a reasonable tone, 'Surely, Raja, we have to trust someone?'

'That's true, but I wish you hadn't done this. Anyway, is he at home?'

'Who?'

'Your bodyguard. If he's there, I'd better go and talk to him.'

'And don't forget to check the room, there could be guns hidden somewhere. Frisk him too, while you're at it.'

Raja goes up, ignoring my wisecracks and I wonder why I'm defending the man to Raja. I find him dull. I miss Abhishek, his quick steps on the stairs, his whistling, his cheerfulness which had become part of my life, the brief conversations we had each morning always enlivening me. And then there was his link with Baba. This man is shy, he ducks his head when he goes up, as if afraid of meeting my eyes. And he's humourless. I realized this when I was trying to learn the basics of the computer. He said 'Yes, ma'am' to any question I asked. I muttered 'Bring on the handcuffs' when the computer told me it had performed an 'illegal operation' and he looked at me with a deadpan face.

But it was his desperation for a place to stay which had got to me, that was really why I agreed to have him in the house. He'd been living with friends and friends of friends until now, Abhishek told me. Now, suddenly, he was without a place. And I thought, I know how that feels, I've been there myself. Though it had been worse for me, for I had two children, no job and no place to stay. It was a nightmare. Roshan had taken me in then, she had saved me. What would I have done if Roshan hadn't taken me in?

Raja comes back with an air of having done his job; I can almost see him dusting his hands. 'Be careful,' he cautions me, though I can see from his face that he has been reassured. He won't admit this, of course. 'Don't use the bell until we're sure of him,' he says. 'And don't let him into the house.'

'Yes, boss.'

When Venkat comes home, I know Raja has spoken to him about my new tenant. Venkat's is an unofficial visit this time.

'Just to make sure all's well,' he says. Also, I think, to send out the message that the police are still on the case.

'I believe your tenant has left?' he asks me.

'Raja's been speaking to you.'

He laughs. 'You know him.'

Nevertheless, he asks me about Raman. I have to admit that I know very little about him, except that he's from Mangalore and is working with Abhishek's friend, who has a small computer assembling company. 'They supplied me with a computer.' He asks me for the name of the company which, fortunately, I have. 'Abhishek has vouched for him,' I tell Venkat.

'And Abhishek?'

'He was with Baba for over a year. He was good to Baba. And Baba liked him too, they got along fine.'

Venkat says no more on the subject, except to repeat Raja's warning, 'Be careful. And,' he adds, 'keep in touch with the inspector.'

Before leaving, he invites me home for dinner. 'Raja's coming too,' he says, 'he'll bring you.'

I'm reluctant to go. I don't like these social occasions, but I know it would be ungracious to refuse. That's the problem with taking favours from someone, I think sourly; you find yourself trapped into doing things you don't want to do. But it turns out to be a surprisingly pleasant evening. Raja and I are the only guests and most of the conversation centres around our holidays in the old home. We bring up our corny childhood jokes, reminisce about events and people, specially the driver Venkoji who could transform himself in the wink of an eye from an entertaining clown to a straight-faced chauffeur.

Venkat's wife—what's her name? Venkat mumbled a name I didn't quite get. Was it Rohini? Or Mohini?—listens to us in silence. She seems friendly enough, but I can sense a slight suspicion of me, of my camaraderie and ease with the two men. I'm used to this, to the hostility that emanates from women when I'm with their husbands. Their hackles seem to rise when they see me, a single woman, being easy and friendly with men. I wish

I could tell her I'm no threat, that this is a continuation of our childhood when I was a kind of honorary boy.

'These stupid girls,' Raja would say scornfully of his sisters and Venkat's sisters. And I would heartily agree, forgetting that I was a girl myself. Since I wore shorts and a T-shirt all day and did all the things the boys did—except that I couldn't piss standing up—they looked upon me as one of them. The habit remained; I could never look at males as strange creatures. But it's different now, I have to admit. I can see it even in the way Venkat looks at me, a sudden glance that tells me he is aware of me as a woman. I'm used to this too, and can accept it with composure, but I know Venkat's wife is not comfortable with it. Venkat, in the way couples pick up each other's signals, seems to understand, for he turns to Raja and begins talking about people and things I know nothing of, leaving his wife and me to converse with each other.

'Come again,' his wife says when we're leaving, but I know I won't. I also know that Venkat will visit me on his own, that both he and I will be more comfortable that way. It's the past that links us and the past does not include his wife. Venkat comes out to see us off. The policeman on duty springs to attention at the sight of him.

'Does this go on all the time?'

Venkat shrugs and says, 'Part of the job.'

'Don't be taken in by that false modesty, Jiji. The chap enjoys it, he's got used to this durbar. I can't imagine what he'll do when he retires.'

'Plenty of time for that.'

I ask Venkat about his mother, RK's sister Saroja.

'She lives with me.'

'But my god, why didn't you tell me ...? And Raja, you—you never said ... I'd have liked to see her.'

Venkat hesitates, embarrassed and uncomfortable. 'Since my father died, she's become a little odd,' he says. 'Otherwise, I'd have ...'

I leave it at that, I don't want to probe. In any case, I'm sure

Raja will tell me the truth, whatever it is; he always has all the information about people. Sure enough, on our way back Raja speaks of Saroja. He tells me she has become senile; she's both aggressive and demented, turning all her hostility on Venkat and his wife, suspecting them of stealing her jewels, of manipulating her bank account.

'Poor Venkat,' Raja says.

Poor Saroja, I think, remembering her as she'd been, quick, energetic, always moving, leaving her voice trailing behind her. I think of her sitting in the back veranda with the other women, stringing beans, her hands quick and deft, impatiently slapping at her daughter, chiding her for clinging to her, saying, 'Go out and play, don't stick to me, go on now.' Saroja, who talked and laughed more than the other women, bossing the servants, as if declaring, 'This is my brother's house, I have every right to order people about.' And Gayatri, taking it in her stride, absorbing it, making nothing of it. Poor Saroja.

I am waiting for Raja to start the car but he, hand on the ignition key, is staring at me.

'You look different,' he says.

'I'm wearing a sari. I thought I'd dispense with my Chinese peasant outfit—that's what my kids call it—in honour of Venkat.'

'It's not that …'

He continues to look at me thoughtfully. I begin to feel uncomfortable, beset by a vague sense of wrongdoing. Now what have I done?

'It's Gayatri's sari,' I say, offering both an explanation and an excuse.

'No wonder you remind me of her.'

'Oh no, I can't! Gayatri was beautiful.'

'So are you.'

He starts the car, leaving me shaken. I don't know how to take this from Raja, I don't know this Raja.

'You're very quiet,' Raja says after a while.

'I was thinking of the old days.'

He says no more. I'm glad because I'm thinking of the

memories Venkat's words brought back, memories I don't want to talk about. 'It seems so strange to see you alone,' Venkat said. 'I can never imagine you without Malu. You were never Jiji, you were always Jiji-and-Malu.'

There are alliances in all families, alliances that shift and change in the course of the years. But ours, Malu's and mine, remained constant through all the years of our childhood. When the four of us were together, Baba and I formed one team, Malu and Mai the other. Baba and I were the protectors, the shepherds, the ones who went ahead and booked the tickets, secured the seats, made things comfortable. We were the pavers of the way, smoothers of the path, the Walter Raleighs to their Queen Elizabeth. But when Malu and I were on our own, it was another story; we lived in a close and impenetrable togetherness. Like most children, we had our own world with its secrets, its code words and symbols, its pleasures and fears, a world our parents knew nothing of and into which they were not allowed. I had the clue to Malu which even Baba and Mai didn't; her silences, her withdrawals, her fears were more explicable to me than to them. (It was only at the end, yes, only at the very end, that I failed to understand Malu, I failed her miserably.) The tie between us was much stronger than the casual link between siblings. Malu and I were never apart, she was always with me, behind me, holding my hand, holding on to my dress, so that a bit of it, close to the hem, was always crumpled. I was the one who spoke on her behalf; no, I spoke for both of us, because I knew what she wanted as clearly as I knew my own desires. Malu's statement, that the two of us would marry brothers and always live together, became a family joke brought up at every family gathering. But that was how Malu and I saw our lives, the way we imagined our futures: we would never be apart.

Of all the memories of us together, the one which haunts me the most is of Malu pestering Mai to let her have two plaits like I had. Mai reasoned with her, telling her that my thick unruly hair was best confined in plaits, while her soft fine hair was better left loose. But Malu was obdurate, insisting, 'I want to be like Jiji' until Mai, exasperated, gave in and stopped cutting Malu's hair. I can remember Malu's daily question, 'Is it long now? Is it long enough?' Until one day Mai, to put an end to this, coaxed Malu's still too-short hair into two tiny plaits. When this was done, Malu looked at herself in the mirror, her face framed between the two tiny plaits she held on either side of her face, smiling, beaming, triumphant, declaring her enormous joy at being 'like Jiji'. '*Jiji sarkhi*,' she said aloud. One of those moments of pure happiness never to be forgotten, which stays alive, enclosed within you until it springs out one day, like now, to hurt, as if embedded with sharp knives.

Ampersand: a word Baba discovered and, like he always did, shared with BK when they next met. 'What does it mean, Baba?' I asked, curious about their excitement over a word. Baba paused, looked around, saw Malu and me together and said, 'It means Malu.' When he saw my blank look, he added, 'And I. And I.' I didn't need to be told that he was imitating Malu's cry as she came after me, wanting to join me in whatever I was doing. The two men laughed and Malu and I looked at each other, wondering, as we often did, at the oddity of adults. What was funny about Malu wanting to be with me?

Years later, when this memory came back to me, I looked up 'ampersand' in the dictionary and discovered that it meant the sign '&', that it came out of a corruption of '& by itself is and'. And I thought then, maybe Baba was right, but which one of us was the ampersand? Was it Malu or was it I? Malu was younger, she came into the family after I did, she was the obvious add-on. But it was Malu who defined my role, Malu who made me Jiji. So that when she went away and I was left alone at home, I felt unreal, like a shadow, as if her hand in mine, her hand clutching at my dress, was what had given me substance all these years. All the drive and confidence in me was gone, as if, without her to be protected and looked after, there was no longer any need for these things. I would race down the stairs to the cry of 'Jiji' and look back automatically to see if Malu was following. Realizing she wasn't there, I would trail slowly down the stairs, running my hand along the railing, all the energy, the zing seeping out of me. Without Malu I was incomplete.

I'd gone through this earlier when Malu had decided to stop dancing. Mai was the one who had pushed us into joining a dancing class, encouraged by the fact that there was a teacher in the hospital campus. I'd been wildly enthusiastic too, as I invariably was when starting on anything new and Malu, as always, followed my lead. Plump and docile, I dutifully went through my lessons. We completed the alaripu and even, once or twice, happily thumped away on the stage in a public performance, mercifully as part of a large group. Malu was beside me, petrified, I knew, but holding on as long as I was with her. And then she rebelled, she refused to go on with the dancing lessons. She didn't say why, she never explained or justified her actions. Timid though she seemed to be, she could be wholly uncaring of others, oblivious of their responses, something which I, finely tuned as I was to Baba's and Mai's feelings, needing their approval and praise as I did, envied her for and disapproved of at the same time. Malu would not budge; not even Mai's disapproval and hurt could make her change her mind. Finally I had to go on my own, which I did for a while mainly to please Mai; or rather, so as not to displease her. It not only felt strange, it seemed pointless to dance without Malu to keep an eye on, to see that she was not lagging, that no one would say anything derogatory about her. Even the guru's praise, which I had lapped up so greedily earlier, meant nothing. When I announced my decision to give up dancing too, Mai was angry; more than that, she was deeply hurt by my betrayal, as she made it out to be. But even this could not make me do something which didn't include Malu.

And then Malu fell ill and everything changed. Things go on in the same way for years, then something happens and suddenly everything is different. Malu's illness—asthmatic attacks that came on suddenly, out of nowhere—threw our lives off their placid course. Baba and Mai were totally unprepared the first time it happened. I can remember them rushing her to the hospital in the middle of the night. I, left behind in a neighbour's house, certain that Malu was dead, howled for hours while they tried, vainly, to comfort me. My parents came back in the morning with Malu, recovered, but totally exhausted. And then it happened again. And again. And again. Life changed for all of us, it was never the same after that. Baba was right: Mr Bones is the most important person after all. It's the body that most often dictates events and changes in our lives.

When we went to Bharat and Medha's house in Pune for summer, it seemed like just another holiday visit. A change for Malu and a much more needed change for Mai who was exhausted, drained by Malu's illness. But it was the first summer in my memory that we didn't go to Bangalore. I was sore, but I was with Mai and Malu, so it was all right. Yet, it was strange too, because Malu was no longer with me as she had been until then; she was not allowed to run around any longer, she stayed at home, being petted by Mai and Medha. I was glad when it was time to go back home. I didn't understand till almost the last day that we were going back without Malu, that Malu would be staying on with Bharat and Medha. I couldn't believe it, I refused to go with Mai. If Malu wasn't coming, I wouldn't go either. I thought Malu would be with me in this act of rebellion, but she said nothing. She was quiet, the way she'd been since she got her first attack.

I went back with Mai; what choice did I have? I cried in the train, I cried until we got to Bombay. Mai was silent, she didn't even try to comfort me. It was Baba who told me that this was for Malu's sake. Hadn't I noticed how much better she was in Pune, how she hadn't had a single attack there? I had to accept that it was necessary for Malu's sake, Baba said. I did accept it finally, but I was never reconciled to it. 'You can meet in the holidays,' Baba told me. 'You can go to Pune or she can come here—let's see how it works out.'

But it was not the same. I saw the change in Malu the first

time she came home. She looked the same Malu, but she was not. She no longer followed me about, she seemed content to be by herself, or with Mai. She looked different too. Bharat and Medha, well-off and childless, had got her a whole new wardrobe, so that for the first time we didn't wear identical clothes, something we'd done with both pleasure and pride. She wore pyjamas when going to bed at night, this too something new, because we'd always gone to bed in our petticoats. And no more crawling into my bed at night, snuggling into my blanket and holding me tight so that I could feel her damp warm breath on the nape of my neck. Instead, she read in bed until she fell asleep.

The fact of our separateness was brought home to me even more when I went to Pune for my holidays. We'd always been fascinated by Medha's bedroom; she was the most sophisticated woman we knew. Her dressing table, with all the paraphernalia of women's cosmetics it paraded, enchanted us. We would go into her room when Mai and she had gone out, looking fearfully over our shoulders, afraid that someone would walk in on us. Once reassured we were safe, we would examine and touch all the things there—the lipsticks, the lotions, the perfumes. We spoke in whispers, we communicated through signs, making faces at each other as we probed these secrets, mysteries to us since Mai, a simple woman, never used anything except the sandalwood talc that Gayatri gave her. We rifled through Medha's drawers, tried on her lipstick—at least I did, licking my lips afterwards as I'd seen her doing—wore her high heels and walked up and down in the room. When I found a razor in her drawer, Malu raised her eyebrows at me inquiringly and I, raising my arm, mimicked shaving, the two of us stifling the laughter that threatened to burst out of us.

Yes, Malu and I had been on the same side, we'd been together. Now she was an insider, walking in and out of Medha's room without hesitation, no longer afraid, confident that she had the right to be there. Scarcely looking at the dressing table, as if all its secrets had been revealed to her and she was no more curious. Even saying once, blasphemy to me, 'Why doesn't Mai use lipstick? Why is Mai so old fashioned?' To which I'd angrily retorted, 'Mai is beautiful. She doesn't need to use lipstick.'

'Yes, but ...'

She sounded unsure, she didn't think Mai was beautiful! I was shocked. How could Malu ...! But Malu was no longer Malu; no, here she had become Malavika. That's what they called her, her friends, Pinky and Nita and Gracy. And I was not Jiji, but 'my sister'. I heard Malu speaking to her friends. 'Can my sister come? Please.' Pleading for me! *I*, who'd been the leader, *I*, who'd chosen her in my team!

But it was Sakubai, Medha's faithful retainer, who emphasized the gap between Malu and me, Sakubai who made me realize that Malu had crossed the line and moved from our family to theirs. Malu had entered the magic circle Sakubai drew around Bharat and Medha, calling them 'aamché Saheb', 'aamchya Tai', making them special, different from the rest of us, the common lot. Now Malu was 'aamchi Malu', her clothes were ironed and put away in the cupboard, while mine, most often unironed, were left on the dresser in the passage, marking my position as a mere visitor.

'You shouldn't have sent her away,' I charged Baba later, when Malu's problems had begun to show up. 'She would have been all right if she'd stayed at home.'

But I know how frightened Baba and Mai were by Malu's illness and how exhausted Mai was by those fearful episodes. And there were Bharat and Medha, ready, no, eager to have Malu, and Malu, happy, it seemed, to be with them, living a more affluent life than at home with Baba and Mai. Mai was the one who took the decision to let Malu be with her brother and Baba went along with it. What reason could he have given for opposing her anyway?

Our family would have disintegrated in any case; all families drift apart, people move away from one another. In time, we too would have learnt to recognize our separate selves, to live apart. But this happened too early, too soon, we were not ready for it. I think now of how different we were, Malu and I: I, exuberant, throwing myself at people, pushy, loud, clumsy, Mai's admonitions to slow down, be careful, be patient, following me all the time. '*Dum dhar,* Jiji,' Mai would say. (At which I, taking her literally, would hold my breath, angering her by what she thought was my sassiness!) And there was Malu, dainty, sure-footed, timid, deliberate in her actions and sparing with her words. It was as if together we were complete, together we formed a whole. Yes, without Malu, I was not complete.

I remember the year when, during our holidays in Bangalore, we were overtaken by the cycling craze. Not allowed to go out on the roads, we cycled in the yard, going round and round in endless circles, Raja, Premi, Pandu, Venkat, his brother Sheeni and I. Malu never learnt to cycle, she didn't need to, because I took her with me, she was always behind me, perched on the back seat. There was a day when she jumped off and I, not knowing she'd got off—she was so light I didn't feel the difference—went on speaking to her. When I got to the portico, there she was with the rest of them, all of them laughing at me for talking to myself, Malu too, grinning mischievously, pleased with herself for having tricked me. I was angry then, angry with all of them, ashamed of myself for having been tricked, but it blew over in a few minutes. Now it seems to me that I have been doing the same thing, doing it deliberately: I've been avoiding looking back, knowing that as long as I don't see the empty back seat, as long as I don't look ahead and see Malu's triumphant, grinning face, I can feel that Malu is still with me.

This is who we were. These are the things that happened to us. This is our history.

But I have erased all of it. There's nothing left and my children know Malu only as 'my sister who died young'. But in erasing her, I have deleted something of myself as well. A part of me died with her, the part she had defined was lost forever.

in control

I've been piecing together a picture of Gayatri's and Baba's life in this house after Mai's death—not consciously, no, but the pieces seem to keep falling into my hand, presenting me with a puzzle. I can see that the brother and sister led separate, self-contained lives, neither impinging on the other. They'd been closer than most brothers and sisters are, but after Mai's death, scarred perhaps by the manner of her dying, Baba withdrew from all companionship. In fact, even before this, Baba had turned away from everyone, including Mai herself. In his last years there were only two people in his life—Raja and the Sanskrit Master. When I think of this, I have to ask myself a question: here were two people, brother and sister, both of whom lost a beloved partner midstream. Why is it that Baba gave up so completely, while Gayatri managed to keep going? Actually, Gayatri's and RK's was a much longer partnership, for they got married when she was just seventeen. But more than this, theirs was an unusual companionship. I remember Baba and BK teasing her, pulling her leg about the way she and RK communicated, without words, or gestures, or even any kind of eye contact—like there was some telepathy between them. But devastated though she was by RK's sudden and unexpected death, Gayatri managed to come out of it. She remained herself, her light a little dimmer perhaps, but still burning. I can think of many explanations for this difference between them: for example, that Gayatri was stronger and more resilient. Or I could generalize and say that women are stronger and more resilient. I could also bring in Gayatri's goodness. All these things are true, but finally it comes down to this: Gayatri never let her connections to other humans die out, she kept them intact and alive. She continued to be there, not only for her family, but for many others as well. There's the vegetable vending couple whom Gayatri helped to buy a handcart; there's Ratna, so full of 'Gayatriamma'; and Nirmala, whose life changed, as she says so often, because of Gayatri. There are also the women I keep meeting, mothers of the children for whom Gayatri started a kind of library in her own garage—initially, just mats on the floor to sprawl on and all the books she could buy or collect, but soon, a place that became increasingly popular with the neighbourhood children. Gayatri died two years before Baba, but she continues to live on in these memories, whereas Baba is almost invisible.

After Gayatri's death, Baba found a companion in Raja. I don't think Raja took the place of the children Baba had lost; it was not that kind of a relationship. They were just two people who got on well together. It was as if Baba, having abdicated the paternal role, had no desire to take it on again. I sometimes wonder if BK resented Raja's attachment to Baba and whether this was the cause for the distance I sensed between them. I never heard Baba speak of BK in the months I was with him. I didn't dare to bring up the name either, afraid of scratching an old scar, of making it bleed. It saddened me, for it had seemed that nothing would ever divide them. Even BK's comparative affluence had not come between them. BK could do things for us, he could spend money on us, without acting like a patron, without giving Baba the feeling that he was being patronized. It was BK who gave Baba his old battered Fiat—our first and only car—when he bought himself an Ambassador because it was roomier.

'We need a larger car for our families,' BK had said.

'For our *growing* families,' Baba had corrected him, looking meaningfully at Premi and me, the two plump ones.

Raja enjoyed the joke tremendously, he exaggerated his enjoyment, doubling over with laughter, repeating 'growing families', making gestures that insultingly outlined Premi's and my shape in large circles.

I don't know what Baba paid BK for the Fiat, or whether he paid anything at all; if he did, I am sure it was a fleabite. I remember the day we brought the car home, BK driving, telling Baba about the quirks of the car, Raja, Malu and I in the back.

I remind Raja of this when we are taking my new car home. Raja's driver, Rashid, follows us in Raja's car.

'History repeating itself,' I say and add, 'your father was a generous man.'

'And I'm not?'

'Don't take things so personally. Actually, I wasn't thinking of you at all.'

'Thanks. I haven't given you my old car ...'

'And I wouldn't take it if you did. I don't want any favours from you.'

'... but if you think getting you a car that's both good and cheap is not a favour ...'

'Raja, I know very well it's I who've done you a favour by letting you choose a car for me. I know you love being a busybody on someone else's behalf.'

'There's gratitude for you!'

'I'll be properly grateful when I'm sure it runs well.'

'She's almost new, damn it! Look at the mileage.'

'But I wanted a *new* car!'

'Think of the money you've saved. And she's good. I can feel it.'

'If I were given a chance to drive, I'd be able to feel it myself.'

But he refuses to let me drive. I know his concern is not for me, but for the car. Raja is one of those men to whom a scratch on a car is a disaster, a dent a total tragedy.

'I'm going to take it out the moment you go,' I warn Raja. 'I have a licence, remember.'

'You're not doing any such thing. And if you're so keen on driving, you might as well do it with me in the car. I have half an hour to spare right now.'

When we get back home and Rashid is putting the car away, Raja warns me, 'Don't take the car out by yourself.'

'What do I do? Pick up passengers?'

He ignores that, but when he comes the next day, Rashid is with him. 'I'll be out the next four days, I'm visiting Pavan. Take Rashid with you whenever you want to drive.' He repeats the instruction to Rashid, 'Don't let Amma go out alone.'

'Don't worry, sir, I'll be with her, I'll take care of her.'

I conceal my irritation, I let them think I'm going along with them and put up with Rashid for two days. He's been with Raja for a long time and Raja lets him get away with much; theirs is, actually, a mutual admiration society. But he drives me crazy with his constant babbling of how successfully he has trained umpteen women to drive (yes, yet another man who thinks every woman driver is a moron!) and of how sure he is that I'll be able to drive at the end of two months—this qualified tribute not for me, but for his own abilities as an instructor. He is so sure I can't make even a simple left turn, that his hand is constantly moving to the steering wheel. And each time the engines dies because I've taken my foot off the clutch, he says in an agonized tone, 'Ca-lutch, Amma, ca-lutch.' I'm so exasperated by my failure to coordinate my feet that once I take my foot completely off the clutch and sit in silence, waiting for him to say it. He looks at me, his face stricken, knowing I'm annoyed, and I'm full of compunction. Why am I taking it out on the poor guy? It's not his fault, it's Raja's. His only fault is being scrupulous about obeying Raja, not understanding my need to be alone with the car, to get to know it in my own way, in my own time.

'Sorry, Amma,' he says.

When we get back home, I tell him I don't need him any more. He's upset. And scared of what Raja will say. 'Sir left me to take care of you,' he says. 'What will I say to him?'

I'm quite capable of looking after myself, I tell him. 'And I'll speak to Raja. I'll tell him this is my doing. I'll see you don't get blamed.'

He continues to argue, but I bear him down and finally he gives in. The next day I wake up early. I want to be on the road before the traffic builds up. Reversing out of the garage is tricky, but I manage it. And when I get on to the road, I'm filled with exhilaration. It's wonderful to be on my own, to have nothing between me and the car, to hear no sound but the gentle purr of the engine. Raja is right; it is a good car. I slowly get over my nervousness and begin to feel at one with the car, to enjoy the sensation of being in control. No more dual control, I think jubilantly, as I put the car away and imagine Raja's face when I drive up to his house on my own.

But the next day is a disaster. Raman has left his motorbike (Abhishek's really, which he's left for Raman to use) in the way, leaving me little room to manoeuvre the car out of the garage. The inevitable happens. I knock down the motorbike and it falls on its side with an alarming clatter. I rush out, thinking—have I dented the car? And then—*what will Raja say?* And almost instantly correct myself—*damn it, it's my car not Raja's!* Nevertheless, I am thankful there is no damage. I am getting back into the car when Raman comes running down the stairs, woken out of his sleep, obviously, by the sound. He begins to apologize for leaving the bike in the way even before I can apologize for knocking it down. He picks it up and puts it away, making room for me to reverse with ease.

'Shall I take it out for you, ma'am?' he asks.

'You drive?'

'Yes, ma'am, I learnt to drive a jeep. Can I …?'

'No, thanks, I'll manage.'

He waits by the gate to close it after me and when I thank him, he diffidently asks, 'Would you like me to come with you, ma'am?'

I hesitate, then say, 'Why not? Come along.'

'I'll be back in a minute.'

I don't know why I said yes, I curse myself for agreeing to

take him, but it's too late. He's back in a minute as he had promised. Thankfully he's quiet, he lets me go my way without offering any advice, or pointing out my mistakes—which are many. He is waiting for me the next day too, though I haven't asked him to come. I guess he's trying to show his gratitude to me for having let him stay here. In any case, he's so unobtrusive I forget he's there, though the fact of having someone with me does give me some more confidence. I'm surprised at how comfortable I am. I've quickly grasped the fact that driving requires two things: patience and an ability to judge distances. The second will come in time, I know, but the first? I find a different self sitting at the wheel, a self that looks upon everyone who comes in the way as a moron, a bloody fool, an idiot—all of which epithets I find myself muttering as I drive. I don't know what Raman thinks of me, for he says nothing. Perhaps he's cast me in the role of the eccentric landlady. The only time he reacts is when I ask him, at the end of a week, 'Do you think I can run this as a taxi?'

He seems startled. 'But why, ma'am ...?'

'Why? To earn some money, of course.'

'But you don't need to ...'

It's obvious he thinks I'm a rich woman. And why not? What with a house, which he thinks is mine, and now this car, I'm obviously quite comfortably off. Possibly, in his eyes, even affluent. But what difference does it make what he thinks? In any case, what I have is plenty as far as he's concerned. I think of Ratna's 'They have two hot meals a day, what more do they want?' when she speaks of people she considers well off. Two hot meals a day—yes, that's wealth to her.

'You're like Raja, are you? You think women shouldn't be taxi drivers.'

'No, ma'am, I mean, yes.'

When we get home, I tell him we can stop this exercise. It's a waste of petrol, I say. I can manage myself.

'Yes, ma'am.'

Don't be so scared of me, I want to say, I don't bite. But I know he will say 'Yes, ma'am' or 'No, ma'am' to this as well. It's like I am the dragon landlady. But I shouldn't complain; he has settled noiselessly into Abhishek's place, scrupulous about the conditions I'd laid down the day he moved in. No visitors, I'd said, so that the only friend who visits him stands on the road until Raman goes down to him. No late nights—this was Abhishek's condition. He should be around in case of need, he'd said. And so he's home early, never later than ten. No noise, I'd said, meaning no parties, no boozing. But he's taken it so seriously that he seems to tiptoe up and down the stairs and shuts off the motorbike even before he gets near the gate, wheeling it into place from outside. I was beginning to wonder whether power had gone to my head, but Raja approved, he thought my head was in the right place for once.

I've got used to Raman now, he's become part of my routine. And I feel safer, I must admit, because he's there. In any case, they, whoever they are, seem to have given up. I'm thankful that I never told Anand and Sachi anything. Why disturb them, I'd said to Raja, when swearing him to silence. It's over now.

That night it happens again. I wake up with a start, thinking I heard whispers. Soft whispers which make my body go cold. I spring out of bed, the fear of being pinioned to it, of being smothered by the pillow, rising so strongly in me that I just want to get away from the bed. I switch on the light and without knowing I'm doing it, I press the bell that rings upstairs. In a moment I hear Raman's voice at the door, asking, 'Ma'am, what is it, what's happened?'

'There's someone in the house.'

He comes in, switching on the lights like Raja had done the last time. The last time—how many times do I have to go through this? What's happening, for god's sake?

He comes back and says, 'Ma'am, it's all right, there's no one.'

'There is, I heard them.'

'I promise you, ma'am, I looked everywhere.'

I hear a voice outside. It's the constable who's supposed to be on the beat. Raman lets him in and tells him what happened. They go through the house and I join them this time to make sure. We go into the backyard as well, but there is no one, no sign of anyone having broken in. The doors, windows, bolts and bars are intact.

The two of them urge me to go back to bed, they wait outside until I've bolted the door. I keep the lights on in the hall and go to my room. But I can't sleep there. I lie down on the divan in the living room, putting a cushion under my head as a pillow. I'm shivering. I get myself a blanket, switch on the TV and, muting the sound, lie watching the screen blankly. When I wake up, it's still on and there's a saffron-clad swamiji with a holy expression saying something that, from his expression, is very profound. I switch off the TV and go out to see if the milkman has come. And there's Raman on the stairs, fast asleep, his head resting against the wall. I wake him up. He opens his eyes and looks at me. It's the first time I've seen his eyes, clear and unshaded. For a moment his eyes hold mine. Then he springs up, apologizing, it seems, for sleeping on the stairs. 'I thought it was better,' he explains, his voice trailing away as usual.

'Come in and have a cup of tea, I'm making some for myself.'

He demurs, but he's back by the time the tea is ready. He has washed and even shaved himself in a hurry. I notice the little bleeding nicks on his cheeks, a little bit of stubble he's passed over in his haste. I ring the inspector a little later, but he's not there. Nasir is not in, either. I'm reluctant to bring Venkat into it and it's a relief when his wife tells me he's out for the day. In the event, I'm glad I haven't spoken to anyone. How do I explain that what alerted me was something as intangible as a whisper, something less substantial than a shadow? They wouldn't believe me; they would say, like the constable did, like I could see Raman thinking, that I'd imagined it.

But I was right. I get a phone call in the afternoon. It's the same voice, again speaking Kannada, and yet again in a tone of calm reasonableness.

I should know by now, the voice tells me, that I can't live in peace. No police officer can give me that guarantee. So why don't I just sell the house and go away? And live in peace with whatever money I get? I'll get a fair sum, the voice says. I shouldn't expect too much, but it will be fair, he repeats. I'll get an offer one of these days, I should accept it without questions. And then the voice goes on to warn me. 'We don't want to hurt you, but ...' There's a pause before he adds, 'You're a woman, don't forget that.'

I realize this is a threat to my body. By pointing out my femaleness, they are warning me of my greater vulnerability. I think of them poring over Mr Bones like I had done, studying the chart, learning exactly where to strike so as to hurt most.

Now I have something concrete to tell Venkat. I ring him up the next day. He listens in silence and then says, 'Okay, now leave it to us.' He won't visit me, he says, but they'll be keeping watch. 'Are you scared?' he asks me.

'Yes.'

'Would you like to come here for a few days?'

'No, that's okay, I'll manage.'

And I won't ask Ratna this time, I decide. Whatever happens to me, I don't want her to be part of it. Brave words, but I find myself jumping up at every sound, quivering when the phone rings, fearful when I hear the doorbell. And then a huge anger fills me. This is what they want, they're trying to reduce me to this shivering cowardly mass of fear. I won't be scared. But I am, I am. I'm scared of violence, I'm scared of pain, I'm scared of death. Yes, hellishly scared, shit scared. I don't want to die. I think of that day after Shyam's death, the moment on the beach when I turned away from the sea, from thoughts of death to life. Yes, I want to live.

And then I think: is this nemesis catching up with me? Making me pay for what Laxman did? It comes back to me that this was exactly the way Laxman had worked, taking terror into the homes of his victims. Finally, the terror boomeranged, it came back to him so that he never moved without his bodyguards, Pawar and Bahadur. But they got him all the same.

Sometimes, thinking of Laxman, I wonder if there's any way you can chart the trajectory of a criminal's career. If the indications of success are moving from small peccadilloes to big crimes and having a large gang of underlings to do your dirty work, Laxman certainly qualified as a success. At the peak of his career he was a much-feared Don, a Bhai, or whatever they call them. His one failure was that he never became an international criminal—such a common figure today. Laxman's activities were confined to Bombay, though in his last years his influence did go beyond the city, after his help brought a political party to power. This gave him some control over the government, or so it was said.

I know these things now. But when we were children, he was only our uncle, Mai's favourite brother and far more popular with us than Bharat, who was a rather cold and reserved man. Laxman was genial, full of fun and jokes, and what mattered more to us, generous. Turning up with gifts, taking us for movies (he was crazy about Hema Malini, he said that he would marry a girl like Hema Malini), treating us to ice creams and popcorn in the interval. And then he stopped coming. His name too was never mentioned at home. After a few hiccups we learnt to accept his absence. We realized, the way children do, that we must neither ask questions nor speak of Laxman, for it was clearly a cause of tension between Baba and Mai. I heard them arguing once after she came back from visiting him. I heard her say, 'I go there to see my mother.' I remember her face set in an angry mask as she spoke, I remember her saying, 'He is my brother, I can't wipe that out.'

It was quite some time after this that I began to understand what Laxman was and why Baba was so set against him that he dissociated himself from him completely. And it was only after Laxman's death that I learnt, with a strange sense of shame and disloyalty, all the details of Laxman's career. His violent, dramatic death made him the focus of media attention for a while, all the secrecy in which he had shrouded himself and his activities for so many years suddenly ripped away. The media publicized his criminal career in gloating detail, beginning with the early, fairly innocent activities like getting together cricket or kabaddi teams and breaking matkas during Gokulashtami. This was the starting point, for this was where he collected the young men who later became the core group of his gang. More overtly political activities soon followed, like organizing street hawkers against the eviction order which was served on them as part of 'a cleaner Bombay' campaign. His success encouraged him to contest the corporation elections which he won. As a corporator, he sniffed the heady air of political power for the first time. After this, nothing could stop him from pursuing his destiny, which he did with single-mindedness and a fierce energy. But he never fought an election again. He became the X-factor behind others, the man who used his power to manipulate others, who made puppets of them. The more his power increased, the more invisible he became.

Laxman's success and swiftly growing affluence showed most clearly in his homes. The first family home, the one in which Mai had lived until she got married, was a single room in Maruti Chawl, a room in which the smell of unwashed vessels and wet clothes jostled for supremacy. After he was elected, he moved to Amba Sadan, where he occupied first one flat, then the entire floor, before taking over the whole building. Subsequently, he moved out of there as well and began living in a huge sea-facing flat in Worli, once again occupying the entire floor and once again, it was said, owning the whole building. By this time we had stopped visiting Laxman; I saw this home only when I went to see him after Mai's death.

It was a sad visit. Mai's death hung over us like a dark cloud and there were long silences between us, filled with so many of the unspeakables of our lives. Laxman had put on enormous weight, a corpulence that was perhaps the result of the unhealthy home-bound life he was forced to lead. Looking at the luxuriously furnished large room, with sofas such as I had seen only in movies, I thought of the long way he had travelled from Amba Sadan, which itself had been several steps above the squalor of Maruti Chawl. But there was something unreal about his luxurious home. What was real was his grief for Mai—and his fear, which seemed to fill the flamboyantly opulent room. After a lifetime of terrorizing others, he now lived with terror himself. The phone rang constantly all the time I was there and though there were instruments all over the place, he never answered it himself. A man sitting by a phone in the hall picked it up and spoke softly into it. Except for another man who brought us tea and a tray of things to eat, I saw no one else in the house. I asked him about Mangal and the children. He made a vague gesture, like a shrug, which seemed to convey either that it didn't matter or that he didn't care. And I thought of how he'd eloped with Mangal when he was twenty-two, how Mangal had turned against her own father, a respectable doctor, in the case he filed against Laxman after he had eloped with her. In time, Mangal became his public face, making herself increasingly visible while he retreated into the shadowy refuge of his home. She called herself a 'social worker', to balance, as Baba joked, her husband's unsocial work!

Baba's jibe was directed against Laxman, not against Mangal. Baba was cordial with Mangal; in fact, I think he rather enjoyed her loud boisterousness, the tactlessness that led her into making remarks which exhibited her outrageous ignorance. Like calling Baba and Gayatri Madrassis, like referring to Kannada as a Madrassi language. This didn't offend Baba, he even laughed good-humouredly at her.

'If you go about wearing all that stuff,' he told her once, when she came home loaded with jewellery, the way she invariably was, 'the Income Tax people will be after you.'

'Let's see their guts,' she flashed back at him. 'Let's see who has the courage to come after us!'

And Baba laughed at her, he laughed *with* her.

I think she enjoyed it too, sparring with Baba this way. 'Badrikaka, I know you are *leeg pooling*,' she would say to Baba, using the English term, almost converting it into a Marathi word with her strong accent.

Mangal, loud, bouncy and a bit of a joke was a great contrast to our other aunt, Medha. But like Baba, I preferred Mangal myself; a kind of balancing, perhaps, for Malu leaned towards Medha. There was something honest about Mangal, a kind of naivety, of which her ignorance and pretensions were actually a part. Yes, completely different women, our two aunts; yet, I now realize that they were strangely alike in the way they shaped themselves to their husband's needs. Mangal, even as a young woman, made herself into a mother figure, a façade that Laxman used for his own purposes, the way he used his own mother, converting the senile old woman into a saintly figure after her death, putting up her enlarged picture on the wall of his room, garlanding it with fragrant flowers every day. The poor demented woman became 'Aisaheb', just as Mangal was 'Taisaheb'. And Medha too, a small-town girl, quickly learnt the rules of the game and adapted herself to Bharat's needs, keeping pace with him, later taking the lead in their climb up the social ladder. There was always an undercurrent of hostility between the two women, Medha scarcely hiding her contempt for Mangal and Mangal, in turn, loudly making fun of Medha's pretensions. Their hostility was also an overflow of their husband's feelings. Bharat had washed his hands off Laxman when his elopement with Mangal became a scandal and the kidnapping case appeared in the papers. The breach between the brothers was complete; Mai was the only link between them. I also know that both her sisters-in-law were a little frightened of her, Mangal specially, who knew that to displease Mai was to anger her husband.

All three are dead now, the two brothers and the sister. Medha lives alone in Pune, but I have not heard of Mangal for years. I met Pushpa, Laxman's daughter, one of the twins, some years ago in Bombay at a bus stop. She had been staring at me for a while before she came up to me and asked—said, rather, 'You're Jiji.' And added, without waiting for my confirmation, 'I'm Pushpa, your mother's niece.' The silent wisp of a girl had become a sturdy woman, her square face framed by lank shoulder-length hair. We had never been close when we were children. Younger than me, than Malu even, she and her twin sister Suman had seemed to inhabit a world of their own. Which is why I was surprised when she asked me whether I had time to have a cup of tea with her.

We went to a nearby restaurant and after the initial awkwardness of meeting after years, compounded in our case by the fact that there was much we could not speak of—her parents, for example—she began to talk. I soon realized that her eagerness to speak to me had little to do with reviving old ties, for she volunteered no information about herself, except to dole out the fact that she was doing something in theatre and that she had been married but divorced soon after; she told me this bluntly, without any hesitation. And then she came to the point. She wanted to talk of Mai; Vasu-atya she called her, something I'd never heard her say when she was a child. She told me she had not known Mai was a writer, that she stumbled upon this only when she saw *Manasi* fairly recently. She hadn't liked the movie, she said, she'd hated it much more after she read the novel. They wasted a good novel, they didn't do it any justice, she said.

And then she told me she was thinking of doing something with a story of Mai's she'd come across a few months ago, a story that had obviously excited Pushpa greatly. Had I read the story? It was called 'Blackout' and in her opinion it was Mai's best; in fact, she went on, she thought it was one of the finest stories she'd ever read. She was thinking of making it a play, maybe even, if she could work it out, a movie. Would I give her permission? She would write to me, she said, and took my address before leaving.

She never did write. I hadn't read the story at the time. I thought her enthusiasm came out of her excitement at the discovery that there was a writer in the family—an enthusiasm which waned later, so that she dropped the idea. Now, having read the story, I see things differently. I understand her excitement; yes, it would make a marvellous play. But I also know why she never came back to me. Even at the time Mai wrote the story, it created some controversy. The story appeared, not in a magazine as most of Mai's stories did, but in the Sunday supplement of a newspaper. The phone rang constantly that day and for a few days after—all the calls were for Mai and all of them were about the story. Caught up in the routine of a new-born, distant from everything else, I did not pay much attention to what it was all about, but I could see that Mai was disturbed. She hated being the focus of attention.

But 'Blackout' couldn't be ignored. If, with *Manasi*, Mai had taken a timid step out of her usual writing self, with 'Blackout' she moved into another world altogether, a harsh world of cruelty, suppressed anger and violence. There is much that is unusual in the story, including the title itself. 'Blackout'—yes, she used the English word for her title—is the only one of her stories which does not have the name of the heroine for the title. In fact, the woman is nameless. And she's a Muslim, though that is never overtly stated.

The story begins with the woman switching on the light in her home, an innocent act which in Mai's other stories symbolizes the beginning of happiness. Here, it means something quite different, for this is a Muslim mohalla, and this is the year of the Bangladesh war, when a blackout was enforced throughout Bombay at night. Within moments of her switching on the light, there is a group knocking at the door. Self-appointed guardians, these, keeping a lookout for 'traitors' in this Muslim locality. And here, obviously, is a 'traitor'.

'Why haven't you observed the blackout?' they ask. 'Why have you switched on the light?'

The woman, her face hidden, says, 'I don't know.' And then she gives the standard answer of all illiterate and ignorant women, 'Ask my husband.'

'Where is he? Where is your husband?'

She points to the room inside. The group goes in and drags the struggling, protesting man out. The woman stands in the now-darkened room, listening to the sound of blows, the cries of pain, to the footsteps and the receding voices. There is a final long-drawn-out cry of pain which too dies away. And then there is silence. The woman closes the door, bolts it from the inside and goes into her bedroom. There, in the dark, she begins to undress, slowly, painfully pulling the clothes off her body, which is revealed to be battered and bruised. When all her clothes are off, she touches the multicoloured bruises, her fingers lingering over them. And then, with a sigh, she gets into bed, thinking, 'I can sleep tonight.'

Such a strange, such a wholly unMai-like story, this one. But my first thought when I finished reading it was—*now I know*! Suddenly I was able to connect the whispers and silences I had been conscious of as a child, and so many things which had been dark, unexplained puzzles became clear. The story illuminated in a flash a late night visit of Mangal's to our home, a distraught, sobbing Mangal who fell on Mai's shoulder with an anguished cry of 'Vasutai!' the moment the door opened. I'd gone out when the doorbell rang and stood watching the frightening spectacle until Baba saw me and said curtly, 'Go to bed.' Which I did, but not before I'd seen a huge bruise on one side of Mangal's face, a rent in her blouse, the sleeve almost completely torn off.

When I woke up, Mangal had left and neither Baba nor Mai referred to her visit. My one attempt to bring it up evoked blank looks which warned me not to go on; the incident was enclosed in silence. And then, much later, years later, Mai wrote this story, Mai, who had seemed to condone all that Laxman did, or, if not condone, at least ignore everything that she didn't want to hear about. She rarely spoke of him at home, knowing Baba's feelings about him, but we knew she visited him regularly. The one time Mai and Baba brought their disagreement into the open was when rumours linked Laxman to the communal riots which had just taken place, riots Laxman was supposed to have organized to suit a particular political party, unleashing goondas on a slum for a price. Mai tried to defend Laxman when Baba brought it up, she said they were only rumours, but Baba was, most unusually for him, in such a rage that Mai was finally silenced.

And then she wrote this story. The contempt in her story for the men who storm into the house looking for traitors comes through clearly. So too, the cruelty of the man towards his wife. No, there's no way Pushpa could have done anything with this story. The hawks on both sides would have pounced on it. Hindu fundamentalists would never stomach 'Hindu patriots' being shown as goondas. And would the Muslim fundamentalists have endured a story about a Muslim man's cruelty to his wife and her calculated revenge? Pushpa must have realized it was impossible to present this to the public.

And did Pushpa also connect the story to her father? Was that why it fascinated her and was it also why she dropped the idea? I don't know. Maybe I'm stretching things too much in linking Mai's story to her brother. Even now it is hard for me to reconcile the affectionate uncle I knew to the man who was supposed to have instigated violence, organized murders, taken over property and yes, was violent to his own wife—everything, except the last, done cold-bloodedly for his own gain. How could the man who rebuked Mai for scolding us, who then said, 'Come, Baby, come to Laxman-mama', how could he do these things? And yet, there were his children, the twins Pushpa and Suman, sealed into silence, with little of the exuberance or the joy of children in them, the daughters who escaped him as soon as they could. And Abhay, his son, clinging to his mother, whining and being carried about by her even when he was four or five years old; Abhay, who as far as I know, never completed his education, never had a job and, when I last heard of him, was unmarried and still living with his mother.

I was not in Bombay when Laxman died. He was shot the moment he stepped out of his house, his body riddled with bullets by two men who escaped and were never caught. I saw the pictures on TV, pictures of the 'spot', the blood spattered on the floor, sprayed on the walls. I saw these things, switched off the TV and sat for a long while watching the dark, empty screen, my body cold, my mind a blank. Thinking, thank god Mai is dead, thank god she is not here to see this. I was even more thankful when rumours linking Mangal to the killing began circulating, rumours which said that it was Mangal who had paid the killers, that she had been acting in concert with a rival who had become her lover. Eventually, the rumours died down and Laxman's death became just one more act in the unending drama of gang warfare. I had trouble believing that Mangal had anything to do with his death; I told myself it had to be part of the gang warfare, for his faithful bodyguard Pawar, the man who'd been with him since the earlier kabaddi and cricket days, had been killed just a month before Laxman was shot. But at times I have my doubts, because the rumour mills always have a grain of truth in them. And there's that late night visit of Mangal's, there's Mai's story. Had the story been a kind of foresight? Had she seen the possibility of Mangal taking revenge one day? Perhaps their imagination gives writers a kind of sixth sense, a Cassandra sense. Nemesis, indeed, if Mangal really had him killed. Live by violence, die by violence, some of the magazines said about Laxman after his death.

I cried for Laxman, I mourned the man I had known as a child. The truth is that Laxman would have died anyway, his body had already been invaded by the same silent killer which destroyed Mai. He was luckier than Mai, his was a more merciful death than Mai's was. The bullets were kinder than the gangrene which spread like wild fire in Mai's body, racing ahead of the surgeon's saw.

Mr Bones. Mai had always turned away from him, she had always ignored the body. In her stories too, except for references to liquid eyes, rose-petal-soft or milk-white skin and delicate features, the characteristics of beauty demanded of heroines which she dutifully bestowed on them, she had ignored the body. As if the parts, when lifted out of the body, were safer. Years later, when I watched a performance of *Twelfth Night* and heard the words: 'item, two lips indifferent red, item, gray eyes with lids to them' and so on, I thought of Mai. Exactly thus did she dispense the various accessories of physical beauty to her heroines—yes, and to her heroes as well. Now that I think of it, it was almost like the way Baba introduced his students to the human body, through the dismembered parts on the dissection table.

And then, in 'Blackout', the body came in with a vengeance— the man's body dragged out and beaten to a pulp, the woman's body covered with bruises. Mai writes about this in simple, stark words, without embellishment—so unlike her usual way of writing. And equally unusually, there is something sensuous in the way she speaks of the woman's hands lingering over her bruises; these are described almost as if Mai had imbibed Baba's knowledge, the colours differing according to the age of the bruise. As if she had been listening when Baba spoke of Mr Bones.

I sometimes wonder: what if Mai had been born a little later? Would she have written differently? Would she have been able to accost Mr Bones head on? You've got to do that some time. For her, it came too late, it came at a time when her writing was over.

love and marriage

My ad in the paper, offering to 'computer-type' a manuscript, has yielded a lone response. I call the number and speak to a woman who tells me I have to pick up the manuscript from their house. Her husband has a problem, she says vaguely, he can't go out, and she has a job. She gives me the address, adding a long list of directions, which I dutifully take down. And then, putting down the phone, I look at what I've got: 'Turn left at the bank, right at the bakery, go on until you come to a junction, go past the chemist ...' My god, this is impossible!

I ring up Raja who knows, or should know Bangalore much better than I do. It's a mistake. He asks me why I need to do it at all. 'Typing for others,' he says scornfully, 'like you're a typist or something.'

'So? What's wrong with that? I earned a fairly good amount once.'

'You don't need to do it now.'

'I have to do something, Raja. I can't make any plans until we decide what we're going to do with the house. And in the meantime, I'm getting bored.'

This is a mistake as well. I see him preparing to go back to the topic I want to avoid. Ever since he returned from his visit to

Pavan, he's gone back with vigour to his marriage proposals. My surmise, that he went to get Pavan's permission and returned successful, is almost confirmed when he adds the bait of giving 'poor Pavan' a mother.

'Raja, my own children tell me I'm a lousy mother.'

'That's nonsense,' he says sternly. 'They don't have the right to say that. You know, Jiji, you've given your children too many liberties ...'

' ... and they need a father. I get your point, Raja, but let's not go into that now. Tell me how to get to this place.'

Fending off his offers of taking me there himself or having Rashid drive me, I read out the directions to him.

'This is crazy,' he says. 'Let me see the address. Ulsoor...? Hmm, I think I know how to get there. Turn right after the Apsara theatre traffic light ...

'But she said to turn left.'

'She did? Let's see. Okay, turn left and then ...'

It's no use. I decide I'll find my way myself. More and more as I live, I realize that the belief that men know better, that they are better at practical details, is an illusion. I think of Gayatri, Kamala, Mai and all the women of their times deferring to male opinion in matters outside the home. Did they really believe that men knew better? Or did they, even after losing faith in the greater sagacity of men, go on pretending in the interests of domestic peace?

Speaking to Raja, I had insisted, rather childishly I admit, that I would drive myself. But I don't; I take a rickshaw. I know I can't cope with driving as well as searching for the house. Even the rickshaw driver goes round in circles for nearly ten minutes looking at the house numbers, while I watch the meter. My heart fails me at the amount I have to pay when we finally find the place. I can't afford this, the next time they're going to deliver the manuscript home. And then I wonder at my optimism, imagining that there will be more work coming my way.

'Did you find the place?' Raja asks me in the evening. 'How did you go? When did you get back?'

Really, I think, this is like being a kid again, accountable to your parents for all your movements. But let me not fool myself or wrong Raja; his is not a protective concern, or not *only* a protective concern. 'Something marked in his attentions.' The words come to my mind when I think of Raja's behaviour towards me, words which come enclosed within quotation marks, as if I've read them somewhere. Words that spell out, clearly, what's taking place between us.

Raja and I appear to be continuing our earlier relationship with all the freemasonry of two people who've grown up together. It is as if the intervening years, when we'd lost contact, have been completely erased. We have our spats, the way we did when we were kids; if it's a bad one, he disappears for a time. And then reappears just as suddenly in the morning, calling out my name. I join him, falling into step as if nothing has happened. Yes, it's just as it was when we were children. But there's something else now, a difference I can't ignore. Then we were on the same side, the two of us together looked after the others. But since Baba's death, things have changed. There's—yes, there's *something marked in his attentions*. An unusual (for Raja) awareness of my presence. A kind of 'pointed-ear'ness, something that I remember was part of Baba when Mai was around. And yet, sometimes Raja's persistence and doggedness remind me of a man set on doing his duty. As if Baba had said to him, 'Look after my daughter when I'm gone.'

I have to laugh at these thoughts. I can't imagine Baba saying such a thing. It's not only impossible, it's bizarre. And yet, the puzzle remains: why is Raja going on with this ... this ... what do I call it? I could have called it a courtship if it wasn't so shorn of all that is supposed to be part of a courtship. There are no lover-like attentions. On the contrary, he reminds me of the boy who, during our vacations, called me out with a hard-to-conceal excitement in the afternoons when we were supposed to be resting, strictly warned against going out in the hot sun. Raja would signal to me, saying 'come on' impatiently, enticing me out to do all the things we weren't supposed to do. Going up on the terrace. Climbing the huge tamarind tree. Going to the old woman's room which was supposed to be haunted by her ghost. Looking for the snake. Cycling on the roads. And I, finally succumbing, the Jiji who wanted to be good and obedient bowing out as she often did, making a rapid exit.

Now it's marriage that Raja is calling me out for. He's been quite open about his wish since the day he mooted the topic. At different times he has offered different reasons in favour of our marriage, most of them practical. After the latest incident of the intruder-who-never-was (as everyone, except me, thinks of it), he has begun to speak of my safety as a reason for marrying him.

'One doesn't marry for safety and security.'

'What for, then?'

For love?

I don't say it. Strange, that neither of us brings the word into our arguments. It's as if it has no place in our relationship, a relationship that can contain a great many things but not that word. For both of us, the word lies in the past, buried in our lives with Shyam and Rukku. It's like the measles: get it once and you acquire immunity. I've never seen Raja with Rukku, it's hard for me to imagine him as a lover. But clearly he married Rukku for love, because he married her despite his parents' opposition—Kamala's specially. In this our stories are alike: both of us went against our parents' wishes when we chose our partners. But there's a difference. Raja's parents got over their reluctance, they accepted Rukku, they even became fond of her. Whereas I ... Mai never forgave me. When I went home for Anand's birth, Mai did her duty scrupulously, meticulously, but Shyam was not part of it. As far as Mai was concerned, her duty was confined to me, her feelings were only for Anand, her grandchild.

Mai doesn't believe in love—the thought had come to me at the height of our fierce battle over my desire to marry Shyam. She writes stories which they call *prem katha*, but she doesn't believe in love. I remembered an incident which convinced me of this fact. It was the night the watchman at the hospital gate came to tell Baba that he had seen our car being driven out of the gate by an unknown couple. Baba had gone to the police station to register a complaint and returned to the parking lot with two policemen, waiting for the couple to bring back the car, as the police said they would. Mai and I, waiting anxiously for Baba to return, knew none of this. Baba came nearly three hours later, by which time I had fallen asleep in Mai's bed. I woke on hearing Baba's voice and heard him telling Mai that the couple had returned as expected, that they had been taken to the police station and charged. 'Poor things,' he said. 'They were only a pair of lovers who'd gone out for a joyride.' And then he added, 'It must be hard for them to find the time or place to be together.'

At which Mai had retorted, and I remembered this very distinctly, 'Love!' The word coming out of her with utter contempt. 'Love!'

No, she didn't believe in love.

As for me, I was ready, I was ripe for love when I met Shyam. I knew all about love, my knowledge coming from the books to which I had become addicted after Malu went to live with Medha and Bharat. Desolate, at a loss, not knowing what to do with myself without Malu, I attached myself to Sharmila, the anaesthetist's daughter. That was a kind of falling in love too. Like it does for any besotted lover, my day burst into light at the sight of her and like any ardent lover, I waited all day for a glimpse of her, often watching the window of her house, hoping to see her there. When she appeared and called out, 'Jiji, wait for me, I'm coming', I felt the way Romeo must have felt when he saw Juliet.

Wait! I would wait all my life. And when she came down and allowed me to walk with her, the two of us sedately going round the paths that circled the hospital, I was in a state of bliss. I scarcely listened to her unceasing (and I must admit now, foolish) chatter. I was in a daze with my beloved by my side. It didn't last long, of course. After this I discovered the books, booklets rather, with stories of sweet delicate girls and strong dark men who came together only after going through numerous trials and misunderstandings. I read these books at a stretch until I came to the end, with the man's strong arm going around the girl, his fingers gently but firmly lifting her chin so that he could see her face, though she kept her eyes shyly down. And when, at his insistence, she looked at him, her eyes (usually blue, only sometimes grey) shone with unshed tears. His lips came down hard on her soft sweet-tasting lips, his arms crushed her delicate slim body and she, nestling in them, felt his heart beating strong and steady against hers.

My own heart would be beating wildly by this time. How passionately I longed to feel a man's arm around me, to have a man hold me in a 'crushing grip', muttering, 'I will never let you go, my darling, never!'

Darling ... I heard Bharat say the word to Medha once and never forgot the thrill it gave me. Oh, to have a man call me darling!

Dreams. Only dreams. In real life I was, as Mai often told me, clumsy. Graceless. Awkward. *Vendhali, ghodi, gabali*: Mai's reproving words for me, all of them having something to do with my appearance. I was not neat and dainty like Mai and Malu. Mai never appeared, even before us, in anything but a neatly worn sari, the pleats hanging in straight lines, the pallu either tucked in at the waist or falling carefully over her shoulders. Whereas I was always running out without buttoning up my dress, my hair coming out of my plaits, the tying tape of my knickers trailing below my dress. My emotions were just as untidy and all over the place. I would throw myself at Mai, fiercely putting my arms about her, pulling her sari off her shoulder.

'Aga, aga, Jiji,' she would chide me, 'that's enough.' And when I reluctantly let her go, she would look sadly at me and say, 'How much will you love me, child!'

'So much.' I would throw my arms out wide. 'Soooo much. The whole-world much.'

I was the same with Shyam, throwing myself into the relationship with the same passion, the same fervour with which I'd hugged Mai. But Shyam didn't say, 'Aga, aga, Jiji', he didn't take my hands off him and put me gently away from him. On the contrary ...

It was hard for me to believe that Shyam's feelings for me were the same as mine for him. It felt odd. I was never the girl boys whispered endearments or wrote love letters to; I was the pal, the companion, at times the messenger, and once even, my most humiliating experience, the *kabab-mé-haddi*, sitting between two friends who made cryptic conversation like *'you don't understand'*, *'yes, I do'*, *'you don't care,'* *'yes, I do'* and exchanged glances over my bored and soon furious head. I was needed because she had said she was going out with me and she didn't want to tell a lie. Soon I was resigned to my fate: I would always be the good pal of boys, the *sakhi* of girls, I would always be the extra dancing in the background, the sidekick, never the heroine. How could any boy love me? My breasts were too small, my legs too hairy, my face too broad, my lips too thick, my nose too blunt: these were my preoccupations, these were my *fears* at that time.

And then I met Shyam. 'I can't believe you love me,' I said to him. 'I'm not beautiful, not like Mai and Malu.'

'Don't you ever look at yourself in the mirror?'

I didn't. I looked at Mai and Malu and found myself wanting.

'It's your innocence,' he said, 'that's what I love. The innocence of your being.'

I sometimes wonder if Shyam would have seen me differently if his first sight of me hadn't been through the lens of his camera.

I had come home from college to find Mai being photographed. Publicity pictures for *Manasi*. She'd told us in the morning that a photographer would be coming, but I'd forgotten. Now here she was, sitting regally in a chair while the photographer fiddled with his apparatus.

'My daughter,' Mai said, when I entered. 'Manjari.'

Manjari? Why was I suddenly Manjari instead of Jiji?

'Hello,' he said, still absorbed in his camera, giving me just one quick look.

I had a wash and came out to ask, 'Anyone wants tea? I'm making a cup for myself.'

'Yes. One spoon of sugar.'

I looked at Mai. She was staring at the man, a slight frown on her face. Was she displeased because of the casual way he'd spoken to me—instructed me, rather?

'And Mai, you?' I asked.

'Yes, get me a cup,' she said.

I was going past her when I tripped over her sari. 'Aga, Jiji …'

'Sorry, Mai, sorry.'

I knelt by her feet to set the edge of her sari right. I straightened her pleats and patted her feet, her tiny, beautifully arched feet that just about reached the ground, even sitting as she was, in the low chair.

'Now you're perfect,' I said.

And then he said—I'd almost forgotten him—'Look up'. I did and he clicked. I laughed and he clicked again. I rubbed my face against Mai's sari and he said, 'Hold that' and I did. He said, 'Sit down there.' So I squatted obediently at Mai's feet and he said 'That's good' and clicked. I did all that he asked me to, enjoying myself, knowing he was enjoying it too.

'One more?' I asked, when finally he paused.

'No,' he grinned. 'That's enough.'

I got up, went away and came back with tea for all of us. I remember how silent Mai was through it all, not a word from her while I posed and he clicked.

'I'll see you,' he said when leaving and I thought they were the usual words of farewell, that they meant nothing. But he returned to show Mai the pictures he had taken. He fanned them out as if they were a pack of cards and picking one out, gave it to me before giving the rest to Mai. It was the first picture he'd taken: I, kneeling at Mai's feet, looking up at him, my face startled, caught unawares.

'Your innocence,' he said. We were in bed when he said that, our legs entwined, his arms around me, our faces so close his breath entered my mouth. 'I saw it when I developed the picture. Your innocence. I fell in love with you at that moment.'

Yes, it's there in my face, unguarded and open. Vulnerable.

Mai didn't like the pictures he'd taken of her. She put them away without comment. I don't blame her, not really. Mai was not just tiny, she gave a feeling of being so light you could blow her away with a *POOF*. Her bones—her clavicles, her scapula, her cheekbones—had the flyaway lines of a bird's wings. But in Shyam's pictures she looked solid, earthbound, larger than her real self. One of those mysterious disparities between the reality and the image. More than that, in the pictures she looked not—as Baba said, trying to placate her—serious and dignified, but censorious and hard.

'My third eye,' Shyam called the camera. 'My eye which sees the truth.' In his pictures Shyam had captured the truth of Mai's feelings for us, for our relationship, he had foreseen, or rather his camera had, the way she would be with us. The intensity of her disapproval, the relentlessness of her opposition to our relationship surprised me. And angered me, driving me for the first time into opposing her. I came out of my room one day to find Shyam waiting for me. Mai had let him in but hadn't told me he was there, she'd let him wait. I knew she'd done it deliberately and so did Shyam, who sat placidly reading, waiting patiently for me to come out. Realizing what she'd done, I went to him and kissed him on the lips. A brazen declaration, not only of my love for Shyam, but of my defiance of Mai.

'Steady, steady,' Shyam said. 'Don't start something you can't control.'

I laughed and kissed him again. Glorying in my bravado. In the movies, love was always accompanied by soft, muted music. Mine came with the blare of trumpets, with the loud beating of drums. Declaring itself loudly to the world, to my parents, specially to Mai, who refused to acknowledge that I was serious.

But Baba opposed our relationship as well. 'You're too young,' he said.

'So was Mai when you married her,' I retorted.

'Marriage didn't interrupt her education. You've just got into medicine, this is something you've been preparing for since you were a child. Do you want to give it up? Wait until you graduate.'

Graduate? Four years more and then a year's internship—no, I could not wait that long. I could not make Shyam wait that long.

'If he won't wait for you, he's not the right man for you.'

'It's not Shyam, it's I who don't want to wait. I want him, right now.'

'You don't know what you want, you don't know what you're doing. It's only physical, don't you understand? Your body is confusing you,' Mai said to me.

She said it the same way she'd told me about growing up, her face showing her distaste for what she was saying, making it such a deep dark secret, something so dirty that it should never be spoken of.

'Your body is confusing you,' she said now with the same pinched, bad-smell look on her face.

But it was not. On the contrary, all the confusion had vanished. My body was clear now about what it wanted: it wanted Shyam. It wanted Shyam's love, it wanted his body. I had no doubts about it at all.

It was Shyam who pulled me out into the open and taught me to glory in my body, Shyam who showed me its beauty and made me rejoice in it. It was Mr Bones all over again and I, no longer tracing lines on a picture with a cane, but learning with my hands, my fingers, my lips. Shyam cupping my breasts, those protuberances Mai demanded we hide, and saying 'Look.' Asking me to admire them, forcing my reluctant gaze on them. And I, looking at them, at his hands holding them and stroking them, feeling my body respond to his touch, thinking yes, they are beautiful, yes, I am beautiful. It was Shyam too, who showed me the beauty of the male body. He took my hands, hesitant and unsure at first, on an exploratory tour of his body, tracing tantalizing paths, showing me the terrain that soon became more familiar to me than my own body.

'Mr Bones,' I said one day, tapping his ribs, and told him about my childhood lessons.

'Mr Bones, eh? Go on,' he said, 'tell me the names.'

I began, but I could not go on, my fingers lost their way as his living throbbing body enticed my hands into areas I was not supposed to have reached as yet according to my chart. We began to laugh then, laughter that he ended, his lips stopping my mouth, Shyam laughing even as he entered me.

She writes in clichés, I'd thought when I read Mai's love stories. But those little booklets which had so fascinated me—what were they if not cliché-ridden? How else, indeed, does one speak of love? What new words are there to describe love? Such few words really, the same ones over and over again, the words taking away the uniqueness of the emotions, making millions of love affairs seem exactly the same. Whereas my love for Shyam was such a complicated amalgam of ideas, emotions and responses coming from my mind, my body, from whatever it is we call the heart, from my breasts, my skin and from 'there' as Mai would say— all these together orchestrating a song whose tune it was impossible to confine within the few notes available.

Clichés again. Star-spangled costumes to hide the ordinariness, the shopworn tiredness of the words. *Baba was an ardent lover. Baba was a passionate lover*: I write these sentences and think of how little they say, how they convey nothing of his feelings for Mai, of the emotions that took over his life and shaped it for so many years. When I think of his feelings for Mai, I see the two of them in the bus, his arm around her, her head on his shoulder, his face, his eyes, inviting me to a conspiracy of silence, protecting her sleep.

'Why don't you ever speak of my father? Tell me about my father,' Sachi demanded at a time when her dead father suddenly became an important absence in her life.

Tell me about my father. I know so little about him myself.

Only my love for him, and his love for me and the way we were together. Our bodies knew each other much better. But I can't speak of these things to Sachi.

'He was a cinematographer,' I told her once.

She learnt to say the word, to pronounce it correctly. I heard her offering it to a friend, careful to say it right.

'My father was a cinematographer,' she said.

'What's that?'

'He was a cameraman.' And when the girl still looked blank, she added, 'He took pictures for movies.'

Yes, a photographer, but of the two of us together, incredibly, only one picture. Not even a wedding picture, just this snapshot taken by a child. I can remember his name, Ashok, I can hear his mother calling out to him, 'Ashok ...' I see him in a white shirt and grey shorts, the shirt a little too small for him, so that he kept tucking it into his shorts all the time. Proud of his first camera given to him as a gift by his father for doing well in his exams. It was the father who asked Shyam what the boy was too shy to ask, 'Can he take your picture?'

We went out then into the bright sunlight, Shyam carefully choosing the right spot, looking through the camera at me, then giving it to the boy, instructing him, his head bent over him, the boy listening carefully. Shyam running to me then, lifting his bare feet in small quick movements off the hot bare sand as he ran. Putting his arm around my shoulder and I suddenly saying 'Wait' and tidying my hair which was blowing all over my face. And Shyam pulling my hand away, blowing my hair off my face, his warm breath tickling me. And even as the boy clicked I began to laugh while his parents watched us from a distance. So here we are, the two of us, Shyam and I, his face turned to mine, his mouth pursed and I laughing. The two of us standing against the sea, our being together, it seemed at that moment, as permanent as the sea behind us. And yet, we were standing at almost exactly the same spot from where, a little later, Shyam went to his death, the spot where I stood and mourned Shyam.

I don't want to think of these things, I don't want to bring up these memories. I left them behind the day I turned away from the sea, turned away from death, back to life.

When we were children, we went to the beach every Sunday like so many families in Bombay did. It was a ritual, BK, Kamala and the children coming to pick us up and the four of us piling into the car with them (nine of us in that car!) and then going to the beach. Different places, different beaches every week—Shivaji Park, Chowpatty, Bandra, Juhu, Versova. Each time, however, it was the same routine. Baba and BK sat at a little distance from us, BK with his pipe, Baba abstractedly playing with the sand, letting it run through his fingers over and over again while he listened to BK, the two of them wholly engrossed in their conversation. Mai and Kamala were together too, but they rarely spoke. Kamala murmured to Hemi, occasionally she called out to us, but we never paid any attention to her. Mai, gazing at the sea, was always peaceful and relaxed. And Raja, Premi, Malu and I played the timeless games of children in the sand, digging, building castles, piling wet sand over our feet and pulling them out to leave a hollow, making tunnels and letting the sea come rushing into them, picking shells ...

The sea was there, but we scarcely looked at it, it was only the backdrop to our activities, its ceaseless rumble the background music to our weekly outing. At times we went wading into the shallows, we girls tucking our frocks into our knickers to keep them from getting wet, letting the waves climb over our feet and up our legs, shrieking with delight when the sea carried the sand away from under our feet, tickling us, vaguely aware of Kamala's voice calling out to us, warning us not to go too far, too deep ...

If I had looked across the limitless expanse of the sea then, I would have seen the place where Shyam and I stood to have our picture taken, the place where I experienced the greatest happiness of my life as well as its greatest sorrow. They were waiting there for the child who stood laughing in delight, her dress tucked into her knickers, her hair blowing all over her face. I had to cross that expanse to reach Shyam and all that was to happen to us, between us. Which I did, leaving Raja behind in that childhood playground of ours.

I can't come back to you, I want to tell Raja. I've gone too far away from you, there's no way I can go back to where you are.

PART 2

The ultimate meaning to which all stories refer has faces:
the continuty of life, the inevitability of death.

Italo Calvino,
If on a Winter's Night a Traveller

baba's diary

1 October 1997

I write the date—man of habit that I am, I cannot begin without it—and inevitably the thought comes to me: how much time do I have left? How many more months do I have? Like most doctors, I try to keep knowledge of my disease at bay, I try to face it as if I'm only a patient. Nevertheless, the white-coated man stands behind me, peering over my shoulder at the investigation results, watching the doctor's face, putting together my symptoms and the changes in my body ... And then—and then my medical self moves away and I am once again just a patient, hoping, fearing, having faith, disbelieving. I am beginning to understand why patients move from doctor to doctor: they hope to find someone who will tell them what they want to hear. Even when their bodies tell them the truth, they turn away from it. But as a doctor, this way is barred to me; I cannot ignore the truth. And it is this harsh truth that impels me into a summing up of my life. I find myself creating a balance sheet with two columns of credit and debit. There are some niggling doubts, but on the whole and *considering everything* (two words that contain all the uncertainties of life) I think that if I haven't done well, I haven't done too badly, either. Or so I tell myself.

But today this whole idea came crashing down. A few words I read in *Bleak House* destroyed my illusion. All day I have been haunted by them; I know they will run through my mind all night as well, that they won't let me sleep. 'He wos very good to me, he wos.' Simple words spoken by an unfortunate boy whose language did not extend beyond words of one syllable. Yet they came out of the page like bullets, they went straight to my heart, if I may use such a melodramatic phrase. 'He wos very good to me, he wos.' Jo's epitaph for a man who died nameless and alone. And I thought: will anyone say these words about me? What will my epitaph be? 'He did no one any good'?

These are morbid thoughts; I know they would never have occurred to me but for my illness. The other day, disposing of some old papers, I came across the reprints of a paper of mine. 'Some observations on applied anatomy of the skull base with reference to skull base surgery'. The title reminded me of how full of curiosity I had been about human bodies, how little thought I gave to the human mind. The skull interested me more than what was contained within it. I had always known, of course, from the little psychiatry I'd studied as an undergraduate, that there was a close link between the body and the mind; I'd learnt about psychosomatic illnesses. Nevertheless, it surprises me now that my physical condition should drive me to such a state of emotional weakness that a few words can create a turmoil. They seem to confront me with the futility of my entire life. Am I overreacting? Is it because I began reading late in life that I have succumbed so totally to the power of words, like a man falling in love for the first time in his old age? If I had been an avid reader from my early days, like Gayatri was, would I have acquired some immunity?

And yet, when we were young, it was I who had the reputation of being a great reader. Gayatri read only *stories* as they called fiction, the very word making the writing less serious, less significant. Whereas I read 'serious' books, which meant my texts in school and college and later, as a medical teacher, all the books and journals that were part of my profession. Beyond this, I read nothing. I remember with a tinge of shame that I actually boasted about the fact that I didn't read novels! I did read one though, after I graduated—*Final Diagnosis*, a book much read then and which became, in some way, almost compulsory reading for all medical students. It would have been difficult not to read it, for a copy was always lying around, left behind by those who'd brought it with them on night duty. I read it but it flew out of my head almost instantly, until years later when Vasu's surgery was going on. I remembered then, suddenly and vividly, the description of the girl's amputated stump and I wondered, very unusually for me, whether my reading of it had been an omen.

And then I married a writer of fiction. I did not know this, Vasu did not tell me that she had already had a story published by then. It was only some time after our marriage that she showed me the magazine in which her story had appeared. I was both surprised and pleased by the revelation. It showed me another facet to her, something apart from her beauty, which made her, to my mind, more interesting. I failed to understand that for her this was as intimate a moment as when she let me see her body. Looking back, I see myself as insensitive, poor in understanding. In any case, I never read what she wrote. I thought writing was only a pastime for her, a hobby which kept her occupied in her spare time. It was not like *my* professional writing, which was both serious and significant and took precedence, very naturally, over her writing. I took it for granted that the only writing table we had was for me to work at. I saw her clearing the dining table at night to work on and it seemed natural to me that she should work there, rather than disturb me. I also presumed that when I was writing I would be undisturbed, whereas I had, I remember now (with most uncomfortable feelings), no compunctions about disturbing her when *she* was working. I can see her raising her head and looking at me with eyes that seemed not to recognize my presence, and it disturbed me, that blank look of hers.

All these memories rushed back at me when, some time ago, I got a letter from a woman who called herself a feminist with a forthrightness which I thought unusual. This woman wrote that she was interested in Vasu's writing and that she would like to see me, to talk about her, look at her manuscripts, etc. I felt vaguely threatened by this. Apart from the fact that I had no desire to speak of Vasu, I did not want anyone (specially, remembering what had happened once, a feminist!) probing her work, which I knew would mean opening up her life. And so, coward-like, I used the excuse of my illness. I was not well, I wrote, and therefore I could not see her. Thankfully she left it at that. It has been on my conscience since then. I was an academic myself, I know I should have cooperated with the woman. But I console myself by thinking that if she had been serious, she would have persisted. I also think that some day she will come back with her request, hopefully at a time when Jiji will have to deal with her. There's also the thought that Vasu herself would not have liked such attention. I remember how acutely uncomfortable public attention made her and how uneasy she was when she had to deal with it for a brief while after *Manasi*. Being associated with a movie brought her into prominence, specially since the director, a brash and ambitious young man who went on after that to reach great heights, knew how to use the publicity machine for his purposes. She was interviewed a few times and even got invited to schools, colleges, women's clubs—things like that. She hated it; she was painfully shy, frightened of strangers and intimidated by crowds. I think she would have refused the invitations if I had not, rather strongly, urged her to go. I thought it would do her good to get out of the house rather than stay in and brood, for this was the time when Vasu was greatly troubled by Jiji's infatuation with Shyam. She went with reluctance and yet, sometimes when she returned, I could see that she was pleased with herself for having gone through with it; the faint flush in her cheeks, the glow in her eyes told me this.

She was beginning to enjoy the little bit of recognition when a writer, an important figure in the Marathi literary world, took her under his wing. I have no idea why he did this. He was known for enjoying the company of women and having many female admirers, some of whom, it was rumoured, were more than admirers. But Vasu was not that kind of a person; she was too dignified, too reserved. No man, certainly not one with so much experience of women, could be blind to this. So what was it that made him seek her out? I don't know; I only know that he took her up and tried to get her into the literary world, from which she had been very distant until then.

And then it came, a savage attack on Vasu's writing by a woman (how strange, I can even remember her name—Shalu Shinde), an attack that was based on a feminist view of Vasu's work. It appeared in the literary pages of a Sunday paper. I don't think I read the article, nor did Vasu and I speak of it at any time, but I gathered that the woman spoke with contempt of Vasu's stories. She called them reactionary and anti-women. Later we learnt that her ridicule of Vasu's writing was directed more against Vasu's patron than against her, that it was part of the politics of the literary world. But for Vasu, who was a total innocent in this world, it was terrible. She, who had been writing all these years almost in anonymity, was now dragged into full public view and ridiculed. She withdrew into a shell and as always happened when she was upset, she almost visibly shrank, her face taking on a pinched look, her eyes coming closer together, with the suggestion of a squint. Vasu's face, I think, more than most people's, showed the close connection between the emotions and physiognomy. I was torn by pity, I wanted to hold her close and comfort her, I wanted to take away that pinched look and bring back the composed, in-control-of-herself Vasu. But I could not help, for she would not admit her hurt to me. Perhaps the fact that our daughters were then following their own paths and were no longer part of our life, added to her unhappiness.

But her writer friend, her patron rather, took up her cause and became her champion. He defended Vasu publicly against the woman's attack during a literary conference. I don't remember the things he said; what mattered more was Vasu's reaction. To my surprise, his defence devastated Vasu more than the woman's criticism had done. Vasu was generally reticent about her feelings.

But I did realize, from something she once said, that she resented the condescending and patronizing tone that he used when he spoke of her writing. There was a huge ego inside that little body; I'd seen it within hours of our marriage. This was not all; his approval of her writing had shown her exactly the kind of writer she was. Vasu rarely cried—I remember the first time was when she discovered her mother's neglect by Mangal. She told me of the dirty tattered blanket she had found her mother using, something she had discovered only by chance. 'Ai is so innocent,' she said. 'Mangal should know it's like deceiving a child. If you had seen the way she clutched at the rag when I tried to take it from her! *It's so soft,* she said, *it's so soft …*' And Vasu began to sob, the painful sobs of one who does not cry easily. This time there were no tears. She gave up her association with her patron, she refused even to take his phone calls. I must admit that he behaved with dignity; he withdrew quietly from our lives, she never heard from him again. This was not the only association Vasu gave up; she never went out to any literary gathering after that, she froze into total seclusion. Soon after, she wrote 'Blackout'.

When I think of this story of Vasu's, I remember a singer who began her performance with a few words about her programme; she spoke in a soft, scarcely audible voice, her words faltering. However, when she began to sing, her voice emerged unrestrained, the power, the control and the volume contrasting strikingly with the earlier near-whispers; it was as if she had been deliberately guarding her voice earlier, carefully husbanding it, so to say. Vasu too, when she wrote 'Blackout', suddenly threw off her self-imposed restraint, she came out of the burkha she'd concealed herself in. I don't know whether, or how far she would have gone on this road, or where she would have reached. A question now of theoretical interest only, for very soon after, everything came to an end for her. They speak of 'writer's block'; Vasu blocked herself so effectively, so successfully, that it was a kind of literary suicide. She became wholly mute. I always thought this was the result of what happened to her daughters. Now I've begun to wonder whether the furore that followed 'Blackout' had some share in her decision as well, whether it brought home to her something which her creative excitement had blinded her to when she wrote the story. Curiously for a writer, Vasu was terrified of self-revelation, she was wary of attracting attention. I'm sure that when she wrote 'Blackout' she thought, if she thought of it at all, that it would get the same reception her other stories had: enjoyed by her few faithful women readers, ignored by others. Yet, clearly, she did have some idea that it was not like her usual stories. For why else did she send it to the Sunday section of a newspaper and not to the women's magazine which always published her? And yes, now I remember, it was the same paper that had published the attack on her. Was this her reply? Whatever her intentions, she was taken aback when the story became the centre of a controversy. She was disturbed, almost frightened at what she'd done.

Looking back, I have also to admit that I had looked at Vasu's writing in almost the same way the Great Author had done—with a kind of condescension. Not only did she write just fiction, no, *stories*, she wrote of women, she wrote about love, marriage and the home. And if that wasn't trivial, what was it? So I thought. Now I think I should have respected what Vasu was doing. She belonged to a profession which deserved much more than the condescension I granted it.

RK was the one person in the family who respected her as a writer. He was the first man I knew who actually *bought* books, books that were not necessary either for his studies or his profession. By the end of his life he had a huge collection. When I came to live here, the books were mine to read. I marvelled then at the range of the man's interests, at his delight in the books he read, the wealth of understanding he brought to them, as his scribbled notes on the pages revealed. I had always been in awe of him; he was not only my sister's husband, he was more than a decade older than me. But there came a time when I could converse with him on equal terms, when he spoke to BK and me of his ideas. I remember him speaking to us one day about Sanskrit drama, the careful balancing of the serious and the comic, of gravity and laughter in the plays. He spoke of two scenes in Kalidasa's *Shakuntala*: the heartbreaking scene of Shakuntala's rejection by the king, and the scene that comes immediately after, of the fisherman finding her ring. The down-to-earth quality of this scene, the language peppered with abuse, is such a total contrast to the elevated language, the pathos of the earlier scene, he said. Just the way life is.

He was wrong. There is never such a neat and tidy arrangement in life. It's always a jumble of happiness, sadness, boredom and a great many things mixed together. So many things happening, often almost at the same time. But for me it was, as RK said, like the Sanskrit plays; as if some dramatist had scripted my life, happiness alternated neatly with sorrow. The joy of my childhood days was followed by the sadness that came after my father's death. Then came the rapture of my life with my wife and children, a time when I seemed to have it all: work I enjoyed, a wife I loved, children I adored, a good friend, a sister … Oh, I had everything! The skein of my life had no place, it seemed, for sorrow—no, not even a strand of it. But it came finally, driving out all else. It is still with me, it will be with me until I die.

What am I doing? I seem to be making myself a tragic figure. I must remember Gayatri, who never gave the feeling of being a tragic figure, though for her everything ended with RK's death. Maybe that's because RK continued to be part of her life. Theirs was a companionship that could take in all the things that happened to them, even death. Unlike mine and Vasu's. All that had held us together came suddenly unravelled in one moment and there was nothing left between us. Even my initial anger was soon spent. Vasu was punishing herself enough and I could feel nothing but compassion for her suffering. No, there was no place for anger in our lives. There was just this—this *nothing*. We stopped communicating; in fact, there was nothing left for us to say to each other. Vasu never spoke much in any case; she was a strangely inarticulate person for a writer. And I—I did not know what to say. Silence was better than any words I could think of.

'Everything has two handles, one by which it may be borne, the other by which it may not.'

I came across this sentence, jotted down by RK in a book— how that man loved ideas and the words that expressed them— and I thought, yes, this is it, this is why: we chose silence as the only handle with which we could bear what had happened to us. We turned our backs on the past as the only way to survive. Jiji too joined in this conspiracy of silence, erasing her past so completely that the children know nothing of their own beginnings. It surprises me that she thinks she can continue to keep them in ignorance. Does she have no idea of the devouring thirst humans have for knowing their origins, does she not know how tireless we can be in searching them out? What is history, after all, but one facet of this search? In writing this, in going back to the past, am I not trying to understand what happened to us?

We've been talking about the Mahabharata, Ramchandra Sir and I. We've agreed that the whole of human existence lies within it *because* it is not a story written by one person; this is why it has something for everyone. One person's picture will always remain incomplete, always lacking. So will this account of mine be flawed. And yet, it helps. In searching for words, I find the clouds slowly dissolving. Things become visible, they become clearer, I see things I have not seen before. It is not always a comfortable revelation, for very often, too often, I see my faults, my mistakes. Like my attitude towards Vasu's writing. And towards Jiji. I remember how bewildered I was by the change in her after she met Shyam; I found it hard to imagine that a girl so intent on her career, so devoted to her parents, could turn overnight into a passionate, rebellious woman. Hormones, I told myself; it's the hormones raging in her body. Now I wonder: was it our fault? Was it our neglect of her that threw her into Shyam's arms? Yes, *neglect*; I have to use the word for what we did. In our absorption with Malu, panicking as we did after her recurrent attacks of what seemed, even to me, a medical man, life-threatening asthma, did we neglect Jiji? Terrified at the thought of losing Malu, did we lose sight of Jiji's need of us? We—no, let me speak for myself, for I don't know how Vasu saw it—I thought Jiji was tough, I saw her as someone who, in fact, was there to help us with Malu.

It's true that I don't know what Vasu felt about it, for though we spoke of Jiji and her infatuation, all that I saw in Vasu was anger. How *could* Jiji do this? Later, of course, we stopped sharing things; she did not share even her sorrow with me, as if she had forfeited the right to have any comfort when she lost her daughters. She contained everything within herself, even the seeds of her own death. It was Gayatri who told me that the injury on her heel would not heal, that it was getting worse. Do something, she said, her fear making her impatient with my inactivity. It was at that point that I thought of Laxman's diabetes and took her to the doctor. The tests revealed that her blood sugar was terrifyingly high.

'Why didn't she speak earlier?' Gayatri sobbed. 'Why didn't she tell us about it?'

Our rift saddened Gayatri, but she made no attempt to become a bridge between us. Yet, in creating a façade of a normal life, Gayatri actually began a slow healing process; normality itself is always healing. Again, when I look back, I think of how little I recognized the greatness of what she did. Jiji and Malu had been as much her children as they were ours. She had bathed them, fed them, put them to sleep, she had loved them almost the way we had done; it was a tragedy for her too. But she gave no indication of her suffering, she never spoke of her feelings. Gayatri was a good woman. It was not a saccharine goodness, though; she could be abrasive and her quick flashes of temper were famous, much dreaded by me as a child. Even RK was wary of them. But Gayatri knew how to love and even better, she knew how to express her love. I sometimes think I failed Vasu in this, that my love took too much the route of the body.

If there is a Gayatri, there is a Laxman. The balance, as RK said. Always an attempt at achieving some sort of harmony. But how can evil contribute towards any harmony? Does not harmony necessarily mean the absence of evil? Evil is disorder, it is chaos. Sometimes, when I think of why Laxman became what he did, I am forced to conclude that he was born evil, that he had no choice in what he did. A genetic flaw, a chromosomal defect, a numerical imbalance. I no longer believe that we start off pure and innocent and are gradually defiled. This idea of an initial perfection seems flawed to me, as flawed as thinking of 'progress' as a steady improvement since time, as we know it, began. It is only a myth that in our infancy we lived in a perfect, unsullied Garden of Eden and that we were cast out of it because of disobedience. To me, disobedience is not the original sin; in fact, I do not see it as a sin at all. It is a part of growing up, of moving on. Without the serpent we would have remained forever our child-selves, living in a state of innocence, nothing happening, our story stalled. We need the serpent to keep the story moving.

What am I saying? Am I saying that evil is necessary? That we need Laxman as well as Gayatri? Necessary, no; inevitable yes. You can't have one without the other. In any case, I don't believe in the biblical story of a serpent who lured us into sin and got us exiled forever from this primeval garden; not being a Christian, it is easier for me not to believe. I think the seeds of evil have been planted in some of us. It's possible, of course, that we were not meant to be evil, possible that there was a terrible mistake, a deadly error impossible to correct, for existence, once begun, has to run its course. Yes, it's better to think that evil is an aberration, for most of us are not made this way. Our moral nature is inherent in us, implanted for the sake of the preservation of the species; without it, we would have destroyed ourselves long ago.

Why am I spending my last days agonizing over things past and gone? I am almost sure now that the end cannot be too far away. I have sensed a new enemy within me these past few days. Enemy? Or should I call it a friend, this disturbance in the rhythm of my heartbeats? If it overtakes the other enemy, I know I will be spared much suffering. I do not plan to speak to anyone about this new pain, these irregular beats of my heart—not out of stoicism, nor martyrdom either, but because I know only too well what the doctor will say. 'Not significant,' he will say, rating it in terms of mortality. I know this myself, I know it is not significant, neither in terms of life and death, nor in terms of pain and suffering. Yet, it troubles me, because for the few moments when the heart beats erratically, my life moves outside the harmonious pattern of the universe, it goes against the clockwork rhythm of life. Not significant, maybe, but it threatens me, it brings on the fear of death. Let me be honest with myself: I may say dispassionately, 'the end is not far', I may speak as if I have lost my fear of death. Yet, the truth is that I am afraid of dying. All humans fear death. And to me, death has become even more unwelcome since Jiji arrived. I want more time with her, I want to break the barrier between us. It makes me sorry that we approach each other carefully, as if we are carrying water in our cupped palms and are afraid of spilling it. I think of all the time we have wasted; yes, so much time wasted. I am now full of regrets. I want to live some more time, I want to make up for lost time, I want to recover, for the last time, that old relationship between us.

'One day, when you have children of your own, you will know how children can break your heart. And then you will think of me, of what you are doing to me.'

Mai said this to me during one of our quarrels, one of those clinching arguments parents use—clinching, because there is no reply to it. How can you think of a time so far ahead, of being a parent, when you are still a child yourself? Mai, you were wrong—I didn't have to wait for my children to break my heart. You did it yourself, Mai, you broke my heart when you came back after Malu's death. Your face was like a howling wilderness; with Malu gone, there was nothing left but an empty shell. You broke my heart then. And when I came back to see you dying and looked at the empty space where your leg should have been, when I passed my hand over the white covers and felt the blankness, I remembered the day Shyam came to take your pictures and I, kneeling by your feet to arrange your sari, patted your tiny beautiful feet. I thought of that moment and my heart broke. You were wrong, Mai, parents can break their children's hearts too. You did it, and now Baba ...

new directions

Anand has suddenly turned up on the doorstep, explaining his presence with a brief 'It was a long weekend and I got a lift up to Belgaum. So ...'

He says no more. The nearly twenty-four-hour car and bus journey has taken its toll; he goes to bed after a bath and breakfast and wakes up only in the late afternoon to join me over a cup of tea. He tells me then that both Sachi and he were to come, but ...

'Sachi? You planned this visit? But you didn't say anything to me!'

'We were not sure. We didn't want to talk to you until we were sure. What if it didn't work out? Look how Sachi dropped out. But I thought I'd stick to my plan. I may not get time later.'

He leaves it at that. I sense something more, something unsaid, a purpose behind this visit, but I don't probe. Even if I did, I know Anand would not reveal anything. If he wants to speak to me about whatever it is that has brought him here so suddenly, he will. I guess that it has something to do with the intruder and the problems I have been having. I'm right. The next morning he asks me, 'Why didn't you let us know about what's been happening here, Ma?'

'Who told you?'

'You can't keep such things secret!'

'It was BK, wasn't it?'

He doesn't deny it, just brushes it aside and repeats his question. 'Why didn't you tell us about it?'

'What could you have done?'

'I'd have come.'

'And how long would you have stayed here?'

'Not too long, but ... Anyway, tell me about it now.'

I give him the story, editing out my terror, eliding the night when I grappled with the man in the dark. I tell him about Venkat and the special 'police protection' I'm getting because of him (an overweight, pot-bellied nearing-retirement constable!). I show him the safety devices Raja has installed: the bars, the bolts and the bell. After seeing these he looks even more disturbed, as if the things I'd hoped would reassure him have, on the contrary, brought home the threat to me, as if they've made the danger more real.

'Let's sell the house,' he says, breaking his silence.

'Sell it? To the crooks who are trying to drive me out?'

'No, Ma, to someone else.'

'And you think they'll let me do that? They'll scare away buyers, Venkat says that's the way they operate. I'll be forced to sell it to them. You want me to do that, Anand?'

'No, not that ... but if it's a choice between that and your safety, I prefer your safety. And you know Sachi wants to sell it, anyway.'

'Sachi!'

Sachi used to be furious with me when I changed jobs and homes, because each time it meant a change of school for her. 'You never ever want me to have friends,' she charged me once in the course of a foot-stamping tantrum. But Sachi, I remember, has always wanted me to be what I'm not, not to be what I am. 'Why can't you be like other mothers?' she'd asked me once.

I remind Anand of this. 'And now, when I want to stay put, she wants to heave me out of here. But I've decided I'm going to hold on.'

'But not at the cost of your safety, Ma,' Anand repeats.

I can see he's still troubled, but he doesn't have Sachi's habit of going on and on. So he stops arguing and settles down to make the best of the few days he has at home. Except for the evenings, when he goes out, he spends the day with me. I am pleasantly surprised by his behaviour, by his readiness to talk. When I peep in on him at night, sure he's gone to sleep with the light on as he usually does, I find him reading. On seeing me, he puts away his book and glasses and pats the bed, inviting me to sit by him and talk. This is so unusual that for a moment, I hesitate; he, however, is eager to talk and to my surprise, he speaks of Baba, who he says comes to mind every time he attends an anatomy lecture. He surprises me even more by asking, 'Do you know your old house has been demolished?'

'Our old house?' I've never spoken to him about it, I had no idea he knew we'd lived on the campus once. 'How did you know we lived there?'

'Baba told me. Why, was it supposed to be a secret?'

'Don't be silly. So, it's gone.'

'Yeah, a new Cardiac Centre is coming up. Sachi wanted to see the house before they demolished it, but she was too late.'

He speaks to me then of Sachi, of her latest interest. She wants to get into film-making, he says with a smile. It's because of a friend's sister who's doing a documentary, which Sachi is assisting her with. As always with Sachi, she's thrown herself into it with such enthusiasm that she has no time for anything else, even her studies.

'Write to her, Ma, it isn't right, the way she's neglecting her studies.'

'And you think she's going to listen to me! Leave her alone, she'll get over this in time as she's got over all her crazes.'

'I am not so sure, Ma. She seems serious this time.'

My father was a cinematographer. Does she remember that? Has she found it, the link she was looking for when she went blundering about like a bumble bee trying to find its way out, banging noisily against the window panes? She's had nothing but blankness until now, nobody behind her except me. And I, the person she never wanted to be, the person she did not want to model herself on. Have I done my children a favour by moving away from them, by leaving them alone so that they are free to find their own way?

Anand goes out the next day and brings home a scrabble board. Like old times, he says. When we played in the past, Anand always won, using words like zeugma, syzygy or zygort, words which gave him a whopping lead, Sachi and I left lagging so far behind that we could never catch up with him. Sachi often had tantrums, insisting there was no such word, until Anand showed her the word in the dictionary, confirming my suspicion that he carefully looked them up before playing. I remind him of that now and warn him, 'No dictionaries allowed.'

'I don't need it,' he says confidently and brings out medical terms which come to me like ghosts out of my past. I'm glad to be defeated and out of the game, surrendering my place to Mahesh, 'your little friend' as Ratna calls him, Mahesh, who lives in the new apartment block on our street. Once, finding him sitting forlornly on the steps of their apartment, waiting for his mother, I persuaded him to come home. He comes often now, staying on until his mother gets back from work. I notice how quickly he hears the sound of his mother's two-wheeler, as if his ears have been pricked to catch that sound. And then I think of Anand, of how his eyes had followed me about when I was getting ready to go to work and how, when I returned, they rested on me, as if they had found what they had been searching for all day. And when Mahesh's mother rushes in, panting, frantic almost, profusely apologizing for Mahesh's having imposed himself on me, I think, yes, I know how you feel, I know exactly how it is. I've been there too, I've known the gut-wrenching agony of leaving my child at home and going to work, of leaving him with strangers. It won't harm him to be with strangers, I want to tell her. I did it to my son and he's all right.

But Anand was only a baby then, he didn't understand anything. Does that make things better? At the time, however, to leave a baby of just over a year had been traumatic. I remember my hysteria if I missed a bus or train, fearful of I don't know what, of some catastrophe waiting for me at home, of an accident. I would think of Anand crawling, bare-bottomed, in the midst of the chaos in the small room where the two women cooked, of the knives and chopping boards lying about, the kerosene stove and the pots of boiling water. But when I got home, I'd see the women relaxing after a morning of hectic cooking with easier tasks like stringing beans or cleaning wheat, while a large picture—a poster, really—of a masked woman, a dashing figure in male costume, sword in hand, looked down on this cosy domestic scene. This incongruous witness was Zeenat, the stunt queen of early movies, Zeenat, so incredibly the mother of this domesticated woman, Ba, who almost never, it seemed, got out of the house. It was Ba who took charge of Anand, it was by her side that Anand slept in the afternoons. The moment I got home, she would hand him over to me with a smile, saying, 'Here's your Balkrishna.'

They were good to him, those two women, Ba and her daughter-in-law Neeraben; I was only a tenant but they loved Anand and treated him like their own. Once, coming home early, I found Anand sitting with a plate in front of him, Neeraben's little boy Ranjit by him. Anand was eating his phulkas like Ranjit, picking up a bit of vegetable with the phulka, the two women smiling with delight at the way he was aping the older child. Yes, they were good to him. And generous, refusing to take money from me for the child's food. 'My son will die of shame if he takes money to feed Shyambhai's son,' Ba said. I never spoke of it again. I paid them a small sum for the use of a room and how careful they were to let me have the room to myself, refusing my offer to have the children or Ba sleep in my room, though I knew what a crush it was for them, three adults and two children in one tiny room. And when I didn't have work, they let me help with the cooking, they let me pack the dabbas, though I was both clumsy and slow, unlike Neeraben, whose flashing fingers seemed to pick up four chapattis, the vegetables and pickles all in one go. But they let me think I was helping, so that I could feel I was not sponging on them.

Looking back, I think refusing Baba's help was the wisest thing I did. I would support myself, I said, and I did. The struggle to earn money, to survive, kept all thoughts away; I had no time to brood or grieve. It was down to the basics: work, eat, sleep, wake up, go back to work ... Yes, nothing but the body, only our bodies to look after, Anand's and mine. Getting my joy from seeing Anand's body put on weight, from seeing him grow. I survived and so did Anand. But guilt remains. For long, Anand's silences, his reserve, brought back the baby whose eyes followed me as I got ready for work in the morning, the baby whose eyes rested on me in the evening as if they had been carrying that image of me all day. For years, I thought that living among strangers, even those as kind as the women I left him with, had scarred him. I no longer think so; nevertheless, guilt remains. And who knows, maybe behind that dashing, masked stunt woman Zeenat there was a guilty woman too, for Ba told me how, unable to look after her baby, Zeenat had given her to her brother and his wife to bring up; only when Zeenat was ill and dying did Ba come to know that Zeenat was her mother. Yet, Ba came through it, a woman apparently without any grudges against anyone, able to love even me and my child, strangers suddenly pitchforked into her home.

And Anand ...? I look at him now playing with Mahesh, toning down his vocabulary, yet playing with him as with an equal and I think with a spurt of pleasure: he's a kind young man. Like Gayatri. Maybe kindness is passed on in the genes. Why not? If, as Baba says, criminality lies in the genes, why not goodness? Whatever it is, I enjoy my time with my son, pleased by his interest in my life. And enormously surprised by his excitement about the car. He wants to learn to drive, he says. Raja encourages him, he promises to send Rashid to help him.

'No worries about Anand damaging the car, I suppose?' I ask Raja sarcastically.

Raja, impervious to my sarcasm, says, 'Why should I worry?

Look at his hands. They spell confidence.'

'And my hands don't?'

'Your hands? Let's see.' He takes my hands in both of his, pretending to examine them carefully. 'Mmm ...'

I snatch my hands out of his abruptly, taken aback not so much by Raja's gesture as by the way his hands enclosed mine, purposefully, closely. Anand's smile and the way he watches us hint at a certain complicity and I wonder, another glancing thought, whether Raja has asked Anand's permission, or at least asked for his approval, as he did Pavan's. The last time Pavan came home, I could distinctly sense his approval of his father's plans, I could feel Raja constantly inviting me to see how well Pavan liked me, how comfortable he was with me. And now, it's Anand.

I get a very clear sense of this when Raja takes us both out for dinner the night before Anand leaves. He takes us to Koshys, a visit to which had been the highlight of our holidays. Raja and I, predictably, begin to reminisce, we laugh as we remember Premi's chagrin when only Raja was allowed to share the fish and chips with his father, her fury when Raja gave Malu and me some of his chips, the caramel custard which was to us forever *carmel cushta* because of the way the waiter pronounced it, our fascination with the beer that others were drinking ...

Aware of Anand's silence, I suddenly stop and notice him watching us with a look of tolerant composure, the way an adult looks at children. And so, uncomfortable somehow, I opt out of the conversation and sit back, listening to Raja and Anand conversing. Raja has got on to his pet peeve of the moment, Pavan's announcement of his ambition to become a professional tennis player. 'And only because he's the school champion this year.' Raja, though he would strenuously deny it, is the archetypal Brahmin, expecting his son to become a lawyer, a doctor, an accountant. Any of the intellectual professions. Putting the pressure of a long line of earnest scholars on his son, men who tied their topknot to a peg on the wall so that they would wake up if they nodded off. Is that why Pavan is veering off into something so unintellectual? In which case, my children are lucky, for they have never felt the weight of their ancestors. But what about Anand's desire, which he's had ever since I can remember, to be a doctor? What about his sudden interest in Baba, his urge to connect to him? Sachi, however, is free, she has never had to connect herself to the women in her background. Such different women, I think, with nothing in common except the fragrance of sandalwood, which came from the sandalwood soap, the talc and the sachets which Gayatri presented everyone with. None of them has anything to offer Sachi—so, at least, she will think, for they had nothing in their lives apart from their families. Except Mai, perhaps? No, not Mai either, for Mai struggled to keep her work out of sight, she tried hard to show the world that her family came first, that only her family mattered. Sachi will have no use for such stratagems. And I …? Rolling stone, Raja called me. I wonder what he will say if I tell him about all the jobs I've had—ayah in a school, salesgirl, typist, P.T. teacher, nurse almost to an old man who salivated over me … No, I know what he will say: 'But you didn't have to, you know your parents would have supported you, you know they would have looked after you.'

On our way back, sleepy and lethargic with the food, I wonder whether they're in it together, Raja and our children. Whether it's a conspiracy to bring us together, to make a family out of us. But no, Sachi can't be in it. I've seen how suspicious she is of anyone she thinks I am friendly with. I've suffered from her rudeness, her atrocious behaviour with any male who showed the slightest interest in me. Or has she decided that this is the best thing for me, that marriage to Raja is the best solution to the problem of my living alone? Do they think that if I marry Raja they will be free of their anxieties about me? Instead of me planning my children's future—which I have never done—are they now planning my future?

Marriage for security? I asked Raja. And why not? If it can keep my body safe … But the body craves not just safety, not only survival, there's more. I think of the way I felt when Raja took my hands and held them in both of his …

No, I don't even want to think of it. Never again, I'm never going to get into that situation again, staking everything, my life and my future, on one relationship, on one person. And then losing it all, like I did the last time. But the last time, I was only twenty-one. At my age now, I can't start all over again as I did then, picking up the pieces and remaking my life. It's impossible.

It's over, I had told Anand, you don't have to worry about me. But apparently it's not over, not as yet. There are two men at the door, asking for me. They came in a small Maruti, ordinary men, looking like 'one of us' as Medha used to say, meaning the right kind of people. It would seem that these people have nothing to do with the voice that has been intimidating me. They ask for 'Mrs Ahuja', stressing the 'Mrs', reading out the name from a piece of paper, making it clear that it has been given to them by someone. Somehow it makes them more respectable, less connected to the Voice.

Yes, I tell them, that's me. Can they come in for a moment, they ask. When I hesitate, they say they won't take more than a few minutes. I think for a second, then suddenly open the door. Why not? It's broad daylight, Ratna is in the backyard washing clothes, Mouna is working in the garden ... yes, why not? Why must I go on suspecting people?

Then they mention the house and instantly I realize I've made a mistake, I shouldn't have let them in. How could I have been so stupid?

'We've heard you're selling the house ...?'

'Who told you that?'

The man who'd asked the question smiles. A pleasant smile. 'Do you think such a thing can remain secret? Even if it's only a rumour, all the estate agents in town will know about it. Specially when it's a property like this.'

'But who told you?' I persist.

It was an estate agent; he divulges the information with some reluctance. And then the second man, who has been silent so far,

Moving On

comes into the conversation. It's he who wants the house, he says. Not for himself, oh no, he could never afford it, he's only a retired professor. It's for his daughter and son-in-law who are in the States right now. They're returning by the end of next year and they want a house in this area. 'When we heard about this place, we thought it was ideal.'

A retired professor. Plausible. His language, the way he calls me 'Amma' with a polite, almost courtly air. Yes, it is possible. And yet ...

'The price is no problem. They earn in dollars and you know how it is. No amount will seem too much to them.'

So far so good. I can believe what this man is saying, I can trust that these men are what they say they are, a retired professor and his friend. It's when they mention RK that I get a prickly sensation down my spine, a kind of invisible horripilation. Something seems not quite right, the story is too pat, too well put together.

It's the 'professor'—I think of him in inverted commas—who speaks of RK.

'This is his house, isn't it?' he asks and sensing my suspicion, quickly adds, 'I didn't know him, of course. But my uncle was his friend. You may have heard of my uncle, he was in the Forest Department. He was the chief conservator.'

He mentions a name which means nothing to me. But how would I know anyone? I was only a child in those days. And the name is so common, the place is teeming with Murthys.

'My uncle used to speak a great deal of Mr Ramakrishna. He admired him, he said he was one of the most honest men he'd ever met.'

Now I have to butt in, I have to tell them I have no intention of selling the house. My children are joint owners with me, I say. None of us wants to sell the house.

'But ...' the first man starts to speak. The 'professor' stops him with a scarcely visible gesture. I pretend I haven't seen it and go on speaking. 'My children want to live here—in fact, my son will be coming back soon. My brother is an architect, he's going to renovate the house for us. So it's out of the question. I'm sure you understand.'

They get up at that, they smile, they make polite remarks and go out with namastes and apologies for having taken up my time. I notice that the first man unobtrusively picks up the card they had given me. I wish I'd put it away, or at least kept it in my hand. Would they have asked for it back?

After they've gone I think: they could be perfectly genuine. How do I know they're not? Am I getting unduly suspicious? Am I going to be this way the rest of my life, seeing bogeymen everywhere? Like Laxman in his bullet-proof vest and bullet-proof car. But he was killed just the same, wasn't he? No, I can't get paranoid. Nevertheless, the story about the daughter was definitely a lie—a nice, plausible piece of fiction, but a lie all the same. They could be just builders, of course, who want to build an apartment block. Like the one Mahesh's family is living in, built after demolishing a house. But if they were builders they'd have taken me into their confidence. I'd have refused even then, of course. Why 'of course'? Because of Gayatri, RK and Baba? But do their feelings matter? I have to do the best for myself and my children; they would have wanted me to do just that. But what's the best? I have absolutely no idea. I only know that I will not be pushed into selling, I will not give up this house. What if they come back? Or, worse, send someone else instead? *'You'll get an offer, a fair offer …'* Suddenly the words come back to me. My god, of course, this was it, this was the offer I was not to refuse!

As night approaches, I become tense, I find myself waiting for the sound of Raman's bike. There's relief when I hear him coming, when I hear the sound of his steps going up the stairs. Yet, when the phone rings, I jump up, startled. It's a wrong number, which makes me even more jumpy. They're trying to see if I'm at home, I think. I check and recheck the doors and windows and get into bed quickly, leaving the light on. Damn, damn, damn—why don't I just sell and go away? Why do I have to go through all this? Sleep eludes me, fears hover around me like mosquitoes buzzing about my head. And anxiety too. I have to be up early tomorrow, Raja is picking me up at seven. I fall asleep finally. And when I wake up, I am convinced of the rightness of my decision, my determination not to give in is strengthened.

I tell Raja about my visitors when we're in the car. 'You shouldn't have let them in. You could have rung me up, I'd have come right away.'

'They looked so ordinary, Raja. How could I imagine ...'

'Whoever it is, you shouldn't talk to anyone alone.'

'No, I should loudly announce that I am a helpless female who can't take her own decisions.'

'Forget your feminism for a moment and face facts, Jiji. It helps to let people know you're not alone.'

'I did that. I spoke of my children, of my SON ...'

'The way you look, they'll think your son is just a kid.'

'Is that a compliment?' And if so, why is he so grumpy? 'Thanks, Raja. And I also told them about you. My brother, I said ...'

'Brother?'

'That's right, I said my brother is an architect, he's renovating the place for us ...'

'Brother! Don't fool yourself, Jiji. If they are what I think they are, they know everything about us, they know our exact relationship.'

I remember how they spoke of RK and I know Raja is right. But I don't tell him this. Raja is in a queer mood. Possibly it's the traffic. Already, so early in the morning, we're caught in a snarl of buses and trucks setting out from Bangalore. Raja, a careful driver, is concentrating on the road, waiting patiently for the right moment to overtake the over-loaded, road-hogging truck ahead of us.

'Have you got your certificates?' he asks after a few moments of silence.

'Yup.'

'Where do you get that "yup" from? You sound like a dog snapping its jaws.'

'Really, Raja, if this is how you're going to be, I'll keep my mouth shut. Or let me get out and we'll do this another day.'

I keep my word and my mouth shut. Finally, it's he who breaks the silence. He seems chastened by my reaction, or maybe he's just in a better mood now that we're out of the city and the traffic is easier. He speaks of the job. 'I know you think it's a long shot ...'

'Oh no, Raja, I'm sure I'll get it.'

'What made you change your mind? Yesterday you were sure it was no use even trying.'

'I read my forecast before we started. It says that since the Moon and Jupiter are both in my sign—or maybe some other planets, it doesn't matter—I'm sure to succeed in whatever I attempt today.'

'Don't tell me you believe in that stuff!'

'I do, when they say things like this. I don't, when they say nasty things.'

He laughs. 'That's a good state of mind to be in when going for an interview. But seriously, Jiji, I think you'll get the job.'

'Why? Because you're introducing me?'

'No, because there won't be too many takers for it. For one thing, not too many people will want to live on the premises.'

'But my qualifications, Raja. Or rather, my lack of qualifications,' I groan.

'You have a degree ...'

'What's a degree these days?'

'And you have the experience of working in a school, as the Principal's secretary. How long did you work there?'

'Five years.'

'See! That'll be your asset.'

I owe them to Roshan—my job, my degree. I think of her chivvying me into getting a degree so she could keep me on in the job. 'Get up, get up,' she said, 'what are you doing, wasting your life and time?'

'I'm waiting for a millionaire to come and marry me so that I never have to work again.'

'Stupid girl.' And the very next moment she said, making me laugh, 'You're a clever girl, what do you need a millionaire for?'

Stupid girl. It was like Mai's *chatka*, like Mai's word of rebuke—*khulli*. It was like being with Mai again. 'I told you, you could do it,' Roshan said when I got my degree. But it was not *my* success, it was Roshan's. It was she, my sharp-tongued saviour, who shook me out of my apathy and hopelessness. She not only pulled me out of my misery and torpor, she took my children in hand, she even made a human of Sachi—Sachi who had been like a little animal till then, refusing to do anything I told her to, responding to no one but Anand, clinging to him, avoiding me, driving me crazy.

I must have fallen asleep, hypnotized by the steady swish of the car. I wake out of my doze to find the car parked under a tree by the roadside.

'You were snoring,' Raja says.

I refute the charge vehemently.

'Why do women deny snoring? What's wrong with snoring? Rukku was the same.'

'I was not snoring!'

'I'll tape you the next time. Anyway … A tender coconut?' he asks.

I nod. He goes to the coconut seller by the road. I get out of the car and stamp my legs, trying to get the circulation going and think of his mentioning Rukku. Such a rare thing.

'Here!' he says, giving me a coconut. 'I chose this. I'm sure it's sweet.'

The liquid is sweet and satisfying. But his isn't, his face tells me that. I laugh.

'What?'

'If you could choose a good one for me, how come you couldn't do that for yourself?'

'These things happen,' he says with dignity.

I can see that Raja, for all his aplomb, is a bit nervous for me when we get to the school. Looking at the building and the large grounds, I am no longer nervous. I'm sure I won't get a job here;

if they have so much money, they'll hire the best, there's no reason why they will take me. The thought makes me more comfortable and I relax. And then, when I'm inside, it suddenly strikes me that Raja is the architect of this building, this beautiful place is his doing. Is that why he brought me here, to show me what he's done? Part of what I now think of as his campaign to make me his wife? But no, if he was truly such a clever, such a cunning wooer (and it's strange how dated, how old fashioned these pre-nuptial words are), would he have said, 'You snore'? Anything less romantic, more certain to put a woman off ...

Leaving me waiting, he goes in search of someone and returns with a man who I understand is secretary to the Board. Raja wants to leave us alone, but the man presses him to stay—'Unless you don't want him here?' he asks me with a smile.

'No problem,' I say. And once again I see a Raja I don't know. This is his professional milieu and in the next two hours, while we go round the school, I see a Raja who is much respected, yet easy and comfortable with everyone. He has none of BK's pompousness. In fact, Raja sometimes reminds me of his uncle, of RK, who could be naïve, a little uneasy in his personal life, not quite getting the right tone. And yet, in his professional life he was confident, assured, no hesitation in him at all. Raja is not naïve, he's ingenuous rather, but he too suddenly presents a different, a more sophisticated self in his professional life.

I lunch with Raja and two others. They call him Rajendra here, the name he's hated and concealed for years, as being the name of a movie star whom we'd considered something of a joke. He doesn't seem to mind it, though. After lunch Raja tells me he has some work, he may have to stay here overnight. Would I like to stay back? Or ...?

I decide to go back. Is there a bus ...?

'There's a train. I'll drive you to the station.'

On our way back, it suddenly turns dark and gloomy. By the time the train moves out of the station, it's begun to drizzle. I sit back and watch the landscape, glistening and wet now with the rain, flash past me. And then suddenly we're out of the rain and it's bright and sunny again. I think of the job—will I get it? If I do, I know it will not be because of my qualifications or experience, but because of Raja. Having seen him there, I know his word will count. In any case, it's not a teaching job, it's a secretarial job. But I will have to live there, it's not possible to commute. There was a time when I would have died for a job like this. It's different now, I can manage without a job; I have some money, a house to live in (do I?) and my children are on their own. What I really need to know is what I'm going to do with the rest of my life. I'm nearing forty now, which means, possibly, thirty years more. (If I don't get diabetes like Mai, that is. But I'm careful, I keep myself fit, that's why the yoga matters so much to me.) In any case, the idea of getting the job doesn't exactly thrill me. I remember how I'd felt when I got the job as secretary to Roshan. It was like being in paradise after the total despair of finding myself jobless, homeless and, above all, unable to cope with the memory of Mai's death. I suppose I'd thought that Mai and I had a lifetime before us to make up, to go back to being mother and daughter again. Instead, she had slipped away, leaving me full of sorrow and anger. Then I got the job and a house to live in. Just two tiny rooms, but for me it was home. And there was Roshan, such a stickler as a boss, so different at home. We became friends. Thirty years between us, but we were friends. It was she who brought grace and hope back into my life. And then she died. Must I go on losing people I love, I'd thought then. I don't want to go through this again, never again will I get close to anyone. But you can't escape, no, you never can escape. Raja doesn't understand ...

I come out of my thoughts to find the train slowly screeching to a stop. People mill about in the corridor, those getting out obstructing others boarding the train. Some of the men return with paper-wrapped parcels which they open as soon as the train begins to move. The odour of chutney and sagu fills the compartment. I'm not hungry, we had a late lunch, nevertheless the stimulation of my salivary glands by the aromas makes me buy a packet from a boy who's hawking them in the moving train. After debating with myself whether I should eat it or take it home and make it my dinner, I put it away and am resigning myself to enduring half an hour more of the journey, when I suddenly hear a voice say, 'It was only a voice, nothing more than a voice.'

I sit up and take notice of the group of men who are eating their dosas and vadas with the voracity of starving men.

'I was lucky,' the man goes on, 'the minute I saw the office, I knew what it was. I got out.'

I begin to garner the story, unravelling it with some difficulty because of the man's rapid, excited manner of talking and the way they cut into each other's speech with excited exclamations. I gather that most of them are small entrepreneurs and that the man is speaking of a time when he had a cash crunch and responded to an advertisement in the papers offering a 'loan on easy terms'. I listen to him describing the operation, the many calls, 'only a voice each time', and finally the appointment.

'At a five-star hotel. They made me wait a long time. Finally I got a phone, telling me to go home. This happened many times. I heard later that they look you over while you're waiting, they make sure you're okay. They investigate you, you know, making sure you're not connected to the police. It's surprising how much they know about you.'

It's clear now that he's talking of the underworld.

'I got out of it. I was lucky,' he says and speaks of another who wasn't so lucky. 'He died, it was called a suicide, but who knows? I have my doubts, I think he was not able to pay back the money.'

I'm openly listening to their conversation now. I'm watching them, surprised by the amount they eat, as if their appetites are sharpened by the dangers they speak of. At ease, because they know that these dangers are in the past, they're not for them. But the shadows of my own fears seem to be closing in on me. Suddenly I know why someone wants my house, I am beginning to understand the way the person operates. I wonder whether my being here and listening to these things is some kind of an omen, a premonition of my own future; the thought chills me. My fears accompany me home and when I get out of the rickshaw and find the house dark, I'm suddenly angry. I'd told Raman I was going out, I'd asked him to switch on the outside light. I open the door and get in quickly, bolting it behind me. I wash, change and decide to go to bed, my appetite having left me; the cold parcel no longer seems tempting. It's when I'm locking up that I see Raman's bike in its place. Is he home? How come I didn't hear him going up? I look up, but the place is dark. I can't sleep without making sure he's home. The man's story keeps swishing about in my mind. Damn him, why did he have to talk of such things, why did I have to listen? Finally I decide to go up and check on Raman. The door is open.

'Raman?' I call fearfully. There's some kind of a sound that tells me someone is inside. 'Raman?' I call out again. I hear a voice now, Raman's voice, but muffled. Is he ill? I go in, switching on the light in the room. He's sitting on the floor by the bed, his eyes startled, blinking at the light. He puts up his hand as if to ward off the light and I realize why when I see his face. He's been crying. 'No,' he says, distinctly this time, and I switch off the light but there is enough light coming in from the street for me to see his face.

'What is it? What's happened?'

He tries to recover himself, makes an attempt to get up, then falls back again. I go into the kitchen to get him some water. There's no stored water, only an empty Bisleri bottle. Obviously he drinks water straight from the tap. I fill a glass and take it back to him. He's sitting on the bed now.

'I'm sorry, ma'am, I'm sorry,' he bursts out when he sees me.

The sobs are torn out of him and I think how terrible it is to see a man cry. I force him to drink the water; his hands are trembling so much, he spills half the glass on himself.

'What is it, Raman?'

He doesn't have a family, what can be the cause of such grief?

Finally he manages to speak, he tells me that his friend, the man who used to call out to him from the road, is dead. Divakar, he calls him. It was an accident, he says. And over and over again he breaks into 'He was good to me, he was good to me.' I gather from his confused talk that he was his only friend, he was the one who helped him when he came here from Mangalore. 'I didn't know anyone. He gave me a place to stay, he helped me find a job.'

I let him go on, I say nothing until he tapers off. He stops and then he says again, 'I'm sorry, ma'am.'

I ask him if he has eaten, I offer him food. He shakes his head. He's been in the hospital all day, he says, they had to wait for the autopsy to be done. I don't insist. It's clear I can do no more. I get up. He looks up at me, seeming to take in my presence only now.

'And if you need anything ...' I say.

Such futile words, I've heard them often enough before. I know how little they mean, but what else is there?

'Yes, ma'am, I'm sorry, ma'am,' he says and tries to get up. I put my hand on his shoulder to push him down. 'Don't get up,' I urge him.

Suddenly he snatches at my hand, holds it in a convulsive grip and takes it to his face. I wrench it out of his grasp. He looks at me stricken, suddenly aware of what he's done.

'I'm sorry, ma'am, I'm sorry.'

I leave the room in silence.

He's at my doorstep the next morning. He hasn't slept, his face is puffy. He apologizes to me for last night, he does not say for what, but I know that it is his spontaneous, almost involuntary action, not his weeping or his distress he is apologizing for.

'It's okay,' I say, 'it's okay.'

But both of us know it is not and he goes away saying he will be out all day. I know it is his friend's funeral today, I know it will keep him away and I'm glad of it. I want to be alone, I want not to see him, not to remember what happened last night. It's not his action that has disturbed me as much as my own response, the way my body gave a startled leap in response to his touch. It's my body that frightens me, it's my body that is suddenly my enemy. I feel as if I have been invaded by a stranger, a stranger I'd kept out successfully for so long.

Raja calls up to ask whether I got back all right.

'Yes, comfortably. No problem.' There's a pause. He's waiting for me to say something. 'When did you return?'

'Just a while back. I thought I'd tell you that Bajaj seems to think there's a good chance you'll get the job. Of course, there will be an interview, but he will speak to the Board ...' He goes on for a while and then suddenly stops, sensing that I'm not listening. 'Jiji, are you there?'

'Yes, I'm here, I'm listening.'

'You don't seem interested.'

'It's not that. I'm ... I'm a little unwell.'

'What is it? Fever?'

'No, a severe headache.'

'Oh. Have you taken something?'

'Yes.'

'Right then, take it easy. I'll talk to you tomorrow. Okay? And Jiji, I'm glad about the job. It'll solve many of your problems.'

Will it?

'And remember it's confidential, this thing about the job. We can't be sure. Don't speak of it to anyone.'

I agree, but I know I have to tell Nirmala, I need to give her a hint. She depends on me, she thinks I will be with her in her plans for the yoga classes. And so when she comes home, I tell her about it, that I'd gone to see the place.

'Oh! How is it?'

'Posh. I'd never have imagined a school like that.'

I remember how impressed I'd been with Roshan's school in Panchgani, but that was nothing compared to this one.

'Everything is laid out in style. Huge playgrounds, a swimming pool. Well, I suppose, considering the amount the parents pay, it's right the kids should have it all.'

'You'll take the job if you get it?'

'I think so.'

'I'll miss you,' she says. 'I thought we would extend our classes, go on for longer hours in the vacations, you know, and start classes for women in the afternoons. There is enough demand, I'm sure of that. But of course, if you're not going to be here ...'

It's not just the yoga that makes her dislike the thought of my going away; she's a lonely woman. When I came here after Gayatri's death, her enormous grief had surprised me until I understood what Gayatri meant to her. Nirmala had given up her job to look after her paralytic mother. A terrible mistake, for the mother was demanding, impossible to please, tyrannical. Gayatri was Nirmala's only support, it was she who, when Nirmala was at the end of her tether, had taken her to a doctor— a psychiatrist, I guess, though this is never stated—and urged her to start yoga. I've been with Nirmala since I came here, first as a student, then as a helper.

'I can't pay you much,' she had said.

'I don't want anything, consider this my guru dakshina.'

'I haven't decided on anything yet,' I reassure Nirmala now. 'This was just an exploratory visit.'

Encouraged by this, she goes on with her ideas. 'I thought maybe I could roof in the terrace, that'll give us enough space. But I have to get my sister's permission before I do anything to the house. It's not easy. She's unpredictable. Unless I'm sure of you, I won't even talk to her about it.' Suddenly interrupting herself, Nirmala asks me like Raja had done, 'Are you all right?'

'I'm okay. Why?'

'You seem a little distracted.'

I've been wandering about, fidgeting with things, unable to sit in a place for long.

'Just restless. Why don't we go for a movie?'

'Today?'

'Now.'

'Which one?'

I say the first name that comes into my mind, a movie that's the rage of the moment.

'We won't get tickets at the last minute,' she says, but I persuade her. 'Who knows, we may be lucky.'

She's right, not only are there no tickets for that movie, we're turned away from another as well.

'Oh well, let's just go home,' I say.

I'm backing my car out of the parking lot when I hear a tiny sound. I look back and see a man on a scooter making faces, waving his hands. I stop and he comes to me. 'Don't you have eyes?' he asks rudely.

'Not at the back of my head. What's wrong with you? Where were your eyes? *You* should have seen me. I was reversing, how could I see you?'

'If you can't reverse, why do you drive a car? Stupid women!'

'Go home yourself, you can't even drive straight. Men! Ha!'

He rides off with a final swear word and I laugh, cheered by this exchange of childish insults. Nirmala laughs too. 'Your Kannada is improving,' she says.

'Isn't it? One or two more spats with autodrivers and I'll know enough abusive words to trade with these so and sos.'

'Let's have a dosa before going home,' Nirmala suggests.

She begins to talk over the dosas and coffee, speaking more positively of her plans now, as if I've given her some indication that I'll continue to be with her.

'I've been thinking—what if we get someone for aerobics? There's a lot of demand for that. And if you could begin the course for women by giving a small talk on the body—anatomy and all that, you know—I'm sure it would be a plus point. People are so ignorant about their own bodies!'

Mr Bones again! But who had told her about my medical background? We've had a comfortable working relationship, but so far we've been wary about intruding too much into each other's life. This information must have come from Gayatri. Who else?

'I think it will do well, I really do,' she says.

'Big business, eh?'

'Why not?' she grins. Then she suddenly gets serious and asks, 'Why don't we call it the Gayatri Physical Fitness Centre ...?'

She sees my face and says, 'No? Maybe not. But I owe her everything. If it hadn't been for her, I would have remained where I was, scared of everything.'

'You're lucky,' she says, 'to have had an aunt like Gayatri.'

Yes, I was lucky. I loved her and in an easier, more uncomplicated way than I loved Mai. Mai was jealous.

'Go to your atya, you have her, you don't need me.'

'No, Mai, I want you, I want to be with you,' I would cry, clinging to her, swearing my fealty, my love, my loyalty. Mai knew how to keep us, Baba, Malu and me, in her bonds all right. She knew I was her slave, she had no doubts about it; she just liked to feel her power, to flex her muscles, so to say. But I escaped finally, I escaped because I met Shyam, because I fell in love with Shyam. It was Shyam who broke the spell; he waved his wand, muttered 'abracadabra' and everything changed.

'Let's go,' I tell Nirmala. 'It looks like it's going to rain.'

It is suddenly dark and overcast. I'm almost sure we'll get caught, but we get to Nirmala's place before it begins.

'Come in for a while,' she says. 'Wait until it clears up.'

I don't want to wait, I'm sure I can get home before it begins. But I've scarcely got into the car when it starts pouring, the rain pelting down in an instant with a sound like a clap of thunder. Nirmala runs out and then dashes back in, gesticulating frantically, inviting me back into the house. I wave at her, it's meant to be a reassuring wave, but I don't think she can see me. The sheets of rain now enclose me and shut me off from all else. Everything looks wavy and blurred. It's a long time since I've seen this kind of rain. It's an incredible downpour; the gutters are flooded in a minute, the water flowing in a swift mad rush. I drive carefully, keeping to the centre of the road, for I can see little, I can hear nothing but the sound of the rain. I almost run into a car coming at me. Both of us stop, the water pouring down the windscreen making nonsense of the wipers' frantic screeching swipes. The other car, realizing I'm not going to move, backs a little and goes past me. I can see the driver's mouth open, as if he's saying something. I have to restart the car, but it won't start.

Frantically, I turn the ignition key over and over again. What shall I do if it doesn't start, please let it start, please …

To my relief the engine begins to throb and I move on. I don't want to stop now. Two more streets, just one more, yes, now I'm on our street, a few houses more … I've done it, thank god I've done it. I put my head down on the steering wheel, my whole body shuddering.

I hear a voice. It's Raman with an umbrella.

'Are you all right, ma'am?'

I look at him dumbly.

'I'll put the car in the garage, ma'am. You go in, I'll do it.'

He opens the door and gives me the umbrella; I take it from him mechanically, though I'm completely drenched. I unlock the door and watch him as he opens the gate and drives the car inside. I can hear the swoosh of the tyres over the water-logged driveway. The phone starts ringing. It's Nirmala.

'Jiji? You're home? Thank god, I was so worried. I was cursing myself, I shouldn't have …'

'I'm okay, Nirmala. I'll ring you later. I'm completely drenched, I must change.'

I put the phone down and stand shivering. I can hear the garage door being closed. I go out. He gives me the keys, his fingers are wet and cold. I close my fist over the keys.

He's going up when I call out. 'Your umbrella,' I say. 'Take your umbrella.'

He stands still for a while, staring at me, then comes down and takes the umbrella. And then he says hesitantly, 'I'm sorry, ma'am.'

'Sorry for what?'

He is silent. I don't say anything either. He is on the stairs when I suddenly call out his name. He turns around in slow motion. I look at him and go inside, leaving the door open. I know he will come in, I know he will …

After he has gone, I lie still in bed, wanting to have a bath, to feel the cold water run down my body. I want to pummel my body, to punish it with savage blows until it turns black and blue. I hate it, I want to disown it, I want to touch it, to let my hand move gently along accustomed routes, to feel its softness, its curves ...

Eventually I do nothing but pull the blanket over my face and lie still. There's nothing now but my body, the sound of my breathing, the beating of my heart. And a pain, a pain greater than what had been there the first time. For then I was young and ready and Shyam was ... Shyam was ...

The pain helps, it takes my mind off other things. Later, I realize something else has happened: the restlessness of my body has gone, something inside me has been stilled.

It's a grey morning, the sky full of drifting clouds that seem to be unable to make up their minds whether to stay or move away. There's a gentle wind that sets the coconut palm fronds moving, creating a sursurating murmur. The old man opposite briskly climbs the open stairs that lead to the terrace and peers into the tank to check the water level. Then, holding his dhoti in one hand, he descends at the same brisk pace. His wife comes out to meet him, I see her asking a question. He shakes his head and in a moment I hear the sound of their pump. The woman sees me and waves. I wave back. A daily happening this, a part of my routine now. Nothing has changed. A day like any other.

But Ratna notices the difference the moment she sees the sheets flapping on the line.

'Why did you wash the sheets today, Amma? Did you forget you washed them just two days ago? Or was it yesterday?'

No, I didn't forget, I know we washed them three days back, but the machine wasn't fully loaded, so I thought I'd get it over with.

She goes away satisfied and I think—I wish I could put my body in the machine and let it go through the cycles: wash, rinse, dry, wash, rinse, dry ...

And yet, I know that I feel full of energy, my body feels lighter. I'm aware of it from my fingertips to my toenails. I go for a walk in the evening, a brisk walk. I don't meet any of the morning walkers, this is a different set altogether. More women now, chattering women walking in rows, blocking the path. I come home, my body crying out in hunger. I haven't eaten all day, except for some toast at eleven. I make a proper meal now and am having my dinner when I hear the sound of the gate. And then a long pause. I hold my breath, my body taut with tension. I hear the steps resume, I hear them climbing the stairs, there's the sound of the door opening and banging shut. I relax and unclench my fist. And then think—I wanted him to come in, I was waiting for him to come. My god, what's happened to me, what have I done!

I go to bed quickly when I've finished dinner, checking the doors and windows, even looking under the bed—it has become a habit by now. I pick up the phone to see if it's working, then put it down again. Safeguarding myself against the intruder. But what about this stranger within me?

In the morning, on an impulse, I ring Anand. I tell the person who takes the phone that I want Anand Ahuja, that I'm Anand's mother. The voice becomes respectful, polite. Hold on, he says and putting the phone down, he goes away. I can hear him calling, 'Anyone seen Anand?' I hear a jumble of voices in the background and I think, yes, I've been there, I was there once, I was part of that.

'Ma?' Anand sounds breathless, as if he has hurried to the phone. And alarmed. 'What is it? Any problem?'

I should have known he'd imagine something dire had happened, I shouldn't have done this.

'No, nothing is wrong. I just thought I'd like to talk to you.'

And bring back the 'mother of Anand' self, wipe out the woman of last night, the woman with the body …

'You scared me. I was on my way to the lecture hall …'

'I'm sorry, Anand, I should have known this is not the right time. I'll call at night.'

'Sure, Ma, there's no problem?'

'No, I promise.'

Going for a lecture ... I remember rushing around in the morning, trying to get ready in time, convinced I would be late, though I didn't have to walk more than a few metres to get to the lecture hall. And I gave it up, I gave it up for Shyam.

'It's a mistake, you'll regret it,' Baba said to me. 'It's just your body, you'll get over it,' Mai warned me. Just my body. How crude she is, I'd thought. She talks as if what I feel for Shyam is only ... only lust.

'It's not that,' I retorted angrily.

'What is it then? Tell me, I want to know what it is.'

Tell me. But I didn't have the words, I didn't have the right words to express my feelings, to convince her. And what words could contain the expanse of my feelings for Shyam or his for me?

I tried to speak to Malu, I thought I could, I thought it was possible. I spoke to her when she came home to find Mai and me locked in this struggle.

'She doesn't understand my love for Shyam,' I said to Malu.

'Love!' Almost like Mai—but not quite. 'Love! And for that you're doing this to Mai and Baba? Hurting Mai so much. Can't you see you're hurting her?'

Malu was right. The word 'love' was too small to contain the emotion that made me defy Baba and Mai. Years later, I met a deaf and dumb woman who communicated skilfully, fluently, even elegantly with her fingers, her hands, her eyes, indeed, her whole body. I was enchanted. I thought—*this is it, this is direct, this is real.*

Shyam and I in the moonlight, his head on my lap, Shyam drawing me down to him until I am lying beside him, the two of us on our sides, face to face, our breath mingling, our bodies fusing with slow gentle movements into one. The moonlight moves slowly away, leaving us in partial darkness, the patches of dark framed by white edges of silvery light. When, finally, we move apart, there is complete darkness. We lie still, my arm across his body, his arm under mine. No words spoken between us all this while, not a word said through the long hours of that enchanted night.

Years later, I watched a couple making love in a movie. 'You are my country,' he murmured in her ears. And I suddenly remembered Shyam's words spoken on the night which I thought had been wordless. I thought I had forgotten nothing of that night, that every detail had been etched on my mind, but the words had been lost until they came back as I watched the movie. I went back then to the moment when our bodies came apart and, as if unwilling to let go, his arms tightened about me. Then he said it. 'Like dying,' he said, 'it's like dying.'

How little memory has to do with sexual experiences! Each time is different, each pleasure distinct and unmatched. And momentary. It dies in an instant, leaving nothing behind, not a trace, not a shadow, no echo, not even a whisper. And then these words. 'Like dying'. Post-coital euphoria-induced words. To think of them now is to invite pain, pain which collects like a clot in my bloodstream, damming the flow, making my heart throb wildly, fearful for its sustenance.

'You'll regret it,' Baba said. I never did, no, never. There's at least this left among the ruins: I never regretted anything.

baba's diary

14 December 1997

People are taking turns to haunt me. It is BK's turn now, BK's living ghost which has been with me the last few days. Thinking of him and our companionship, I've realized what tremendous good fortune it was for me that so early in life, when I was only a boy, I found a friend in BK. I have to give him the credit for initiating our friendship, for I was a little reserved, wary of strangers, unable to make friends as easily as Gayatri did. But with BK I was able to slip almost immediately into an easy intimacy, and then into a friendship that became important to both of us. Which is why I find it hard to believe that he and I are now so estranged from each other. Our alienation becomes even more mystifying when I consider that there never was any misunderstanding between us, nor did anything ever happen to make us part. There are moments when I have a great desire to see him again, to spend some time with him, but I know it won't be the same. It will be like a mockery of what there was between us. What happened to Vasu and me, what happened to our family, became a wall behind which Vasu and I retreated. We bricked ourselves into a small space and it was as impossible for us to get out as it was for others to get in. Vasu was more clear in her intention to seclude herself than I was; she did not want to meet anyone at all. In fact, there was no one she would miss; her mother was dead, Bharat had retreated into invalidism and Laxman had become unreachable. She knew it was wiser not to meet him.

For me, it was not so easy. BK had been a big part of my life; our friendship had survived a great deal. But looking back, I have begun to see that perhaps Kamala and Vasu didn't feel the way we did about our meetings. I now think that they may have resented our friendship, as being a part of our lives they could not enter. I'm wrong—Vasu was not resentful, she was indifferent. She often tried to get out of our joint evenings, many times she openly showed her boredom. Kamala's resentment was better concealed but it was greater, perhaps, for Kamala's world consisted only of her husband and children; clearly, she felt me an intruder in that world. Some of this suddenly surfaced when she turned on Gayatri and blamed her for alienating her son from her; this was after her conflict with Raja when he decided to marry Rukku. Kamala held Gayatri responsible for Raja's marriage, she charged Gayatri with taking her son away from her.

'She made me feel,' Gayatri said, showing me her deep hurt, 'that I was one of those childless women who crave others' children. I—I who never felt childless because I thought of your children, of her children, as my own!'

There was a strand of bewilderment in Gayatri's grief. How could Kamala—her own protégé, the soft-spoken, gentle girl she had brought into the family—say such things to Gayatri? How could Kamala, who had never argued with anyone, say such angry, spiteful things? One thing was clear: Gayatri knew that she could never have the same relationship with Kamala again. This became one more wall between BK and me. The distance between us grew. Yet, Raja continued to be with Gayatri and me, he's still here with me. In fact, I rarely think of Raja as BK's son now; to me, he's just Raja.

In my memory, our companionship—BK's and mine—

continues to remain fresh and alive. Those two brothers, BK and RK, brought something into my life that I valued very highly: an excitement about ideas, a passion for knowledge—and this knowledge an end in itself, not the means to any end. I had professional colleagues, of course, but few with whom I could discuss anything but medicine. There was never anyone like these two brothers, one an accountant, the other a civil servant and yet, both of them so much more than their professional selves. Their range of interests, the books they read, their ideas—all these fascinated me. When we were together, words and ideas flew about and the air seemed to be charged with excitement. Compared to them I was, I admit, ignorant; my knowledge, outside my own subject, was severely limited. BK never failed to pull my leg, to call me an 'ignorant doctor'—never unkindly, of course; it was always in fun, always a mark of our intimacy and friendship. I remember the time he asked me whether I knew what the names of the three buildings on the street where he lived meant: Santa Maria, Nina, Pinta. What were they? Names of saints? Of girls? The builder's daughters? BK feigned astonishment at my guesses, he hooted with laughter. Raja was panting to give me the right answer but BK allowed him to tell me that they were the names of Christopher Columbus's ships only after he had decided that I had been tantalized enough.

And there was the time when RK had just returned from Germany—East Germany in those days—which he'd visited as part of a government delegation. He spoke of a town they'd visited, a town called—now what was it? I can't remember the name, but it will come. Anyway, he told us about this palace called 'Sans Souci' (yes, suddenly the name comes back, it was Potsdam), which meant, he said, 'without grief'. Built by a rather melancholy king who'd had a sad life, the name, RK thought, was a form of wishful thinking. What intrigued him was that the name was written with a comma between Sans and Souci. 'Sans, Souci.' What does that mean, he asked the guide, but he didn't get a satisfactory answer. And so he laid it before us, letting us puzzle over it as he had done. Was it a mistake? If it was, surely they would have corrected it? If it was deliberate, what did it mean? In English, 'without' had once meant 'outside'; was it then 'Out grief!' as Shakespeare might have put it? Or was the comma a kind of pause, a superstitious pause, as if the king was afraid of spelling out his wish too clearly, scared of making his wishes so explicit? As if he believed that there was someone or something who would say, 'Aha! That's what *you* think. But I'll show you, I'll prove you wrong.'

This last argument was the contribution of BK, a man who dealt with cold precise figures in his work but who, when he got away from that accountant self, let his imagination run riot. And so we went on, from this to other things and then on to others and so on and on. All over now, all forgotten. RK dead, BK a sad and lonely man, the orderly tenor of his life, which he had taken for granted, completely disrupted. And I, alone, living in emptiness. Sans souci. Without grief. No, it is never possible. Grief moves with us, accompanying us like a shadow, waxing or waning according to the time of the day. Like a shadow, it gives us the illusion, for one brief moment, of having completely disappeared. And then it comes back, larger now, lengthening as the day nears its end. There was a time in my life when it seemed that grief had nothing to do with me. I was not foolish enough to imagine that my life would go on the same way forever. But I did think that my wife and I would be together, that my daughters would continue to love me, that they would be happy. When I look back to that time, I see a man who was convinced of the rightness of his life: I loved my children, I was a good father and a loving husband. When I saw how BK kept his children at a distance, letting Kamala take complete charge of their lives, and when I saw how critical he was of Raja, it was impossible for me not to think that I was doing things better. Doing them *right*. But what use was that? When it came to the crunch and we had problems with Jiji, it made no difference at all that I had loved my daughter uncritically until then. But, of course, I was not Jiji's only parent, there was Vasu ...

'Jiji didn't behave well today,' Vasu said to me the day Jiji and Shyam first met. And then she went on to use a Marathi word for Jiji, a word I'd never heard her use before. Her language was always sanitized, 'silly' and 'crazy' being the only abuses, if they can be called that, which she allowed herself to use. And now this word ... Though I was comfortable enough with Marathi, I had never had occasion to get familiar with words of abuse for women. Yet, even I knew what the word Vasu had used meant, I knew it was connected to wantonness, to brazenness. An ugly word. To hear Vasu use it astonished me, to hear her use it for our daughter, for *my* daughter, angered me. But I doused that anger. I knew it would serve no purpose for Vasu and me to enter into conflict. So I said nothing, though I knew Jiji didn't deserve it, though I knew she was innocent. Strangely, Vasu herself used the word 'innocent' for Jiji once. 'She doesn't understand what that man is doing to her,' she said. 'She's too innocent.'

But it was Vasu who didn't understand the power, the enormous potency of innocence. She thought Jiji's innocence made her vulnerable; on the contrary, it unleashed a power in her, a power that was greater because it was oblivious of all else, even of itself. Vasu had so many objections to Jiji's marrying Shyam, which she thought were irrefutable. Shyam was too old for Jiji, she said (forgetting, or managing to forget, that there were fewer years between them than there were between us). Jiji was too young to be married at all, she said; I agreed. Shyam was not 'one of us', she said and I had to remind her then that her family had said exactly the same thing about me.

'But that was different,' she said. I knew what she meant. I was a doctor. Mine was a respectable profession, unlike Shyam's, which was (in her eyes) not just disreputable, but worse, because there wasn't a steady income he could be sure of. Behind these objections lay the truth that Vasu didn't like Shyam. She said he was rude—which he was not, only brusque. But I knew what she meant; he did not give her the homage the girls and I did. I remember how displeased she was with the pictures he took of her. She put them away, scarcely looking at them. When we visited

Jiji after her marriage, a picture of hers and Jiji's, framed and enlarged, stared at us, Jiji at Vasu's feet, looking up and laughing. In this picture, Vasu's face revealed something she rarely showed in life. Vasu put the picture face down, an unconscious gesture which told me much about her feelings towards Shyam. Finally it was Jiji, our docile and eager-to-please daughter, who defeated Vasu; I never cease to marvel at that. Yes, Vasu had to give in, she had to admit defeat. But she did not do it well; much as I loved Vasu, I have to admit that she did not do it well. A little more grace, some more generosity—who knows, it might have changed our lives? But I have no right to judge Vasu. I didn't do too well by my daughters either. All my complacency about myself as a father, about how much better I was than BK, evaporates when I think of how I failed them. Not only did my love for Vasu and my loyalty to her keep me silent when I should have spoken, I made the mistake of trying to shape Jiji's life. I look back to the time when I tried to make her share my interests, to make my beliefs hers, a time when I tried to make her take on *my* ambitions and I am amazed. How could I have done it? *My* daughter, I thought, *my* child, I told myself. Did that give me the right to take over her life? We come to life as individuals; to be a parent is to be an instrument, the means of letting another human enter the world and have the experience of living—that's all. But I thought my daughter's life was mine to shape. In my worst moments, I think Jiji's actions were an act of rebellion against this, against me.

Bone of my bone, flesh of my flesh ...

Words so much more true of children than of a husband or a wife. Created out of our bodies, yes, but once again the mockery remains, the truth shines through. 'They are just like my children,' Gayatri said to me of BK's and my children. Yes, *just like*, but not her own. And therefore, perhaps, an easier relationship, more comfortable, less demanding. I think I realized the futility of saying 'my daughter' when I saw Jiji's passion for Shyam. This woman had nothing to do with the child I had loved and cared for, nothing to do with the girl I called 'my daughter'. 'Do something, say something to her,' Vasu kept urging me. But I could not. The Jiji who loved Shyam was a stranger. So did Vasu become a stranger to me later. I connected to her once again—later, much later— but it was through compassion, not love. Looking at her mottled thigh, the stump below it gangrenous and pus-filled, I could no longer be distant. It seems to me that finally, it is compassion we need more than love. I know it is compassion that has brought Jiji here and compassion that will keep her with me until my last moments. I am grateful for that.

I try not to think too much of my end; since Jiji came I have banished these thoughts. With her matter-of-factness and the way she ignores everything except the practicalities of life, she helps me to do that. But it is becoming increasingly difficult to ignore this shadowy companion of mine. I am given constant reminders. The pain and discomfort are hard to overlook; even to sit and write, as I am doing now, is becoming harder. Fatigue sets in far too soon. And there is my heart, beating suddenly, wildly, in my rib cage. Rib cage—yes, it is a cage out of which the heart, the life, the soul, or whatever you call it, is trying to get out. I'm reaching the point Vasu got to in her last days. I could not understand her then; how could I have? You have to get to the point of no return, which I am approaching, to know that death is indeed freedom. Release.

But I still long for life sometimes, when I am free of pain. I want some more time. I know that this desire has come to me with Anand's visit. To have Sachi and Anand here is perhaps the last bit of joy I will have in my life. It is strange that Jiji, my daughter, the child I brought up, seems a stranger to me; I scarcely know this composed woman. But the children, of whom I have seen so little, became at once familiar. I felt a closeness to them. To be with Anand and Sachi was a strange experience. Pleasure, regret, guilt—all these were part of it. Regret that I'd found this joy so late; why hadn't I insisted, why hadn't I asserted myself? And there was guilt too. When I remembered Vasu, Anand on her lap, the infinite tenderness on her face as she patted him to sleep, I was full of pity for her, and guilty that I was enjoying what she was never able to. But more than all these things, there was pleasure in the company of the young. *My* young. Yes, once again the possessive, but the line easy now, with a lot of slack, not so taut and, therefore, not so hurting. When I was with Anand, I understood for the first time why men want sons. I had been happy, more than happy with my daughters, but this was different. It was like seeing my own past, like seeing the possibility of a different future, it was like being given another chance.

I wish I could tell Jiji that I want to see them again. But I draw back. What right have you to enjoy my children? she will say. I brought them up all alone. What have you done? she will ask. And she will be right.

No, she won't say these things. It is my guilt that puts the words into her mouth. Nevertheless, I can't speak to Jiji. I lost contact with her after Shyam's death and there's no way we can go back to our old selves. *She* can't certainly. She recreated herself so completely, it was like a rebirth. And she was right; there was no other way she could go on. I remember how she looked after Shyam's death—hollow, as if her self had been scooped out of her. I remember that time so clearly. Ever since Jiji came here, it has been haunting me. I have never spoken of it to anyone, but I will write it down here, I will bring it out once and then perhaps be rid of it forever.

I went to Jiji when I got the news of Shyam's death. It was like meeting a stranger. I did not know what to say to her; worse, there was nothing to be done, either. I understood in the course of that long night why humans gather around their dead, why they set such store by elaborate rituals. Doing things helps, it takes the edge off grief. Here there was nothing, not even a body; just the two of us, with nothing to do, nothing to say. I asked her how Shyam had died. I had to. The man who had brought me the news, one of Laxman's men, had gone away without giving me a chance to question him. He drowned, Jiji said. That was all. In a while she told me to try and get some sleep. I went to bed, though I knew I could neither sleep nor rest. But she made it clear she needed to be alone. And so even when I heard her sobbing in the night, when I heard her cry out 'Mai, Mai', I stayed away, I left her alone.

The next morning she told me she wanted to go to Ocean Vista, the place where Shyam had drowned. She wanted to go alone, but I would not allow that; for once I was firm. When we got to the place, the caretaker couple came to us. The woman burst into wild sobbing at the sight of Jiji, but Jiji was tearless. A little later, the woman went in to make tea for us. Jiji wandered through the house, touching things like a blind person finding her way about through sensation, through touching familiar objects. Finally, she went out of the house. I did not want to follow her, but my uneasiness drove me out. I saw her walking on the sands towards the sea. I was frightened. What was she going to do? The woman came out and stood by me. 'Tai,' she said, making a darting movement, as if she would go after her. I held her back. Jiji had paused by a rock, she stood there for a long time. And then she moved on. She walked into the sea and for a moment it looked like she would keep going. It seemed to me that she was poised on the knife-edge between life and death. We were too far away to do anything now, too far even for our shouts to reach her. But once again she stopped, she stood there, the waves climbing up her legs. And I was no longer afraid, I knew she would come back. She did. She went past us as if she could not see us, as if she were indeed blind, her ravaged face the face of a stranger.

I stayed with her for a week. Before I left, I tried to persuade her to come back, to live with us. It's the best solution, I told her, it's the only solution.

I can't, she said. She never said 'I won't', it was always *I can't*. Sounding reasonable, never stubborn. But I was angry, I thought she was causing us a great deal of unnecessary suffering. 'You must forgive your mother,' I said.

'Who am I to forgive her?' she asked me. 'And this has nothing to do with forgiving or not forgiving.'

I went back without her; the days passed somehow, but the nights were full of dark agonized thoughts about Jiji. I could not get her out of my mind. And though we rarely spoke, I knew it was the same for Vasu too. As if I had a radar that could chart the course of her thoughts, I knew she was suffering the way I was. Looking back now, it seems to me Jiji did the right thing by rejecting our help. It enabled her to move on, to get beyond what happened.

A fortnight after I left her, Jiji walked out of that house. She told no one where she was going. When Vasu was dying, Raja traced her—I don't know how—and brought her home. And now she is with me. I know this is not the Jiji who was my daughter, but it does not matter. It is enough for me to know that she is here, enough to know that I will not die alone, that she will hold my hand when I'm going.

Recreate myself? No, Baba, it was not like that, it was not so easy. First I had to denude myself of all that I was. Cell by cell, I had to shed everything until I was sure I had destroyed myself. I thought I had done it. But Baba, you were right. The bones last, they remain, carrying traces of our old selves. So much has seeped into them that they are coloured by what we were. So that I suffered with you, Baba, I felt your pain, I died a little with you. With each pang, I recovered a few of those cells I had shed so painfully. But, recreate myself? No, Baba, I could never do that, it was impossible. The old Jiji wouldn't let go, she held on, clinging like an iguana to a rock. She will never let go, I know that now.

the dream

I am in a nightdress, a thin nightie with nothing underneath. I have nothing on my feet, either. I'm on a railway platform. I know this even though there are no trains, no crowds and no porters. Just a bare platform, with iron pillars at regular intervals holding up the high roof. I have to get out of this place, but I can't find my way out. The platform goes on and on, a long stretch that seems never ending. And then I see Abhishek. My body goes slack with relief. He will show me the way out, he will help me to get out of here. But when I ask him, he tells me there is no exit. Not here, he says. Where is it, then? Where is it? Even as I am asking these questions, I find he is no longer with me, he has disappeared. Thank god there's a staircase ahead of me. Not a proper staircase, but a ladder—a rope ladder at that, the kind trapeze artists in the circus use to go up to the swings. I begin to climb, my heart in my mouth, afraid I'll fall, but desperate, knowing there's no other way out. Strangely, the ladder is firm, it doesn't twist and turn the way rope ladders in circuses do. But the rungs are unevenly spaced, some so far apart that I have to cling to the ladder when I lift a foot to place it on the next rung. The ladder is as endless as the platform was. I'm getting frantic; it will never end, I will never get out of here. And I'm alone, there's no one around, not even a voice or a sound. Finally, I seem to have come to the end of the ladder. But there's still some considerable way to the top. How do I get there? I can't give up now, I have to make it. Scrabbling, clutching, panting, sobbing, I finally put my feet on the ground and find myself on a road—by the side of a road, rather. A road as broad as a highway, but deserted like the station was and just as dark. Perfect darkness, perfect stillness. At long last I hear a vehicle approaching. It looks like an autorickshaw, but when it comes close I see it has no seats for passengers; there's only a kind of crate behind the driver. The vehicle stops for me. Where do I want to go?

Dadar, I say.

The vehicle drives on, leaving me in the dark on the deserted road. Let me get out of here, let me get out of this, I tell myself, let this be a dream.

And I wake up. It was a dream, but it's still with me. The panic of being lost gradually subsides, my heartbeats slow to their normal rhythm. I begin to relax and then I remember. *Dadar*, I had said. I want to go to Dadar, I said.

Kamala was the dream person in the family. Dreams seemed to dictate many of the actions of her life.

'I dreamt of my grandfather,' she would say. 'He was angry with me. He asked me—why haven't you come home this year?'

So off she would go to Shimoga, taking Premi and Hemi with her, but leaving Raja behind. Raja refused to go, he refused to obey a dead grandfather who appeared in his mother's dream. After Raja's refusal, Kamala's dream would include the extra admonition, 'Why haven't you brought *all* the children?'

'Tell him I'm busy,' Raja would say rudely. Gayatri would reprimand him, but the quick look she and Mai exchanged told me that they didn't believe in Kamala's dream either. Later, listening to Gayatri and Mai talking about those times, I found to my surprise that the holidays which had seemed so wonderful to me, days of undiluted happiness, were not the same to Mai and Gayatri. There was an undercurrent of resentments and grudges of which we children were oblivious. Kamala's desire to spend more time with her family in Shimoga and less in Bangalore was one of them. Unable to withstand BK's authority, she invoked her dream.

If dreams signify nothing but our mental states, anxieties, wishes and deepest fears, why did I dream of a self that was trying so desperately to go to Dadar? That self which longed to be in Dadar is an almost forgotten one, those days far behind me—why has that wish come back to me in a dream? And why now, when the house has long since vanished, Mai, Baba and Malu all dead and I the only survivor? How impetuously I'd left that home, how easily I had brushed away all the arguments Baba and Mai had produced to dissuade me from going! What were all the arguments set against my desire to be with Shyam?

'Look at you, still wearing a skirt like a schoolgirl! And you want to get married!' Mai said.

'I'll wear saris. I'll wear a nine-yard sari like Ajji if you think that makes me fit for marriage.'

I was more astonished than angry at Baba's and Mai's attitude. How could they be so obtuse? How was it they could not understand me? And there were moments of intense grief too, at the slowly growing divide between us. Shyam was amused by the gusto with which I threw myself into the role of rebel, of misunderstood victim. I didn't need to spend so much energy fighting them, he said. 'Relax,' he said and holding my hands he kissed my fingers, one by one. 'Just relax. Don't get into a state. We'll get married, we *are* going to get married soon. Nothing can stop us. You're eighteen now, they can't stop us.'

I hadn't believed it would really happen, that Baba and Mai would give in, but Mai suddenly surrendered when, in total angry frustration I chopped off my hair one day, my long hair which Mai had been so proud of. I'd steeled myself to it, I'd turned my face resolutely away from the long twists of hair lying on the floor. Baba, recovering from his surprise first, began to laugh. Mai, unsmiling, said, 'Go and have a bath. And get it properly shaped, you look terrible.' And I knew it was over.

Malu was the most adamant and her hostility, so surprising and so unnecessary, was the hardest to break through. I remember trying to talk to her, to get her on my side. And she, scarcely bothering to look at me, concentrated on cutting her toenails, one foot on a chair, her thin body arched over it, the knobs of her spine, which showed through the thin stuff of her blouse, looking like tiny cacti. Malu was now taller than I was, but she was gaunt, her eyes too large for her narrow angular face.

'Do what you want, don't involve me,' she said. 'I don't want to hear of it, I don't want to talk of it.'

'But you'll come, you'll come for my wedding,' I said.

'I don't know, I'm busy. I have to prepare for my finals,' she said.

Malu, who had followed me about, Malu who had held my hand and clutched at my dress—she said she didn't care about what I was doing! She wouldn't come for my wedding!

'She says she won't come for our wedding,' I cried to Shyam in despair.

'Of course she'll come, of course they'll all come, this is not a Hindi movie. I promise you, Manju sweetheart, your family will be there.'

But he was wrong. Malu stayed away. I kept expecting her, but she didn't come. Medha and Bharat arrived a day before the wedding, but without Malu. 'Malu said she'll come later,' Medha told me, but she didn't. I had to go to the beauty parlour to have my hair done. I had thought I would take Malu with me, I knew how much more knowing she was about such things. I'd gone with her once to a parlour in Pune. 'A blunt cut,' she'd said confidently, already at ease, in the few months she'd lived with Medha, in that world which was still strange to me. I had thought she would be with me, but I went to the parlour with Medha instead. I didn't want her, but she insisted.

'You look chic,' Medha said, pronouncing the word with care, saying *sheek*, not *chick*. 'You look chic.'

What did I care for her praise? I wanted Malu and she wasn't with me. It eased the hurt though, that Gayatri came. Her presence, her enthusiasm for the wedding, her involvement in it made up for much. It was she who did what Mai should have done: she got me my wedding sari, the mangalsutra, the silver toe rings. BK and Kamala played hosts; the registration ceremony took place in their home. Mai was tight-lipped, a little aloof from everything, and Baba's face was sombre.

'Are you sure you want to give up medicine?' Baba had asked.

'Absolutely sure.'

'If it's a question of money, I'll pay your fees. I'd have done it anyway. Think of it as a loan.'

Partly it was the money, but more, it was a desire to give up everything for Shyam, to go to him clean and virginal.

When I got back with my college leaving certificate, Baba was sitting at his table, his face, resting on his hands, blank. It hit me hard. 'I'm sorry, Baba, I'm really sorry,' I said.

'No, no, don't be sorry, don't think of me. It's your life. You have to live it the way you want. As long as you're happy ...'

Happy? Of course I was. But later, after our married life began in a small room in Shyam's family home, there were moments of acute unhappiness, specially when I returned from the college I hated to the room that was no home at all. Waiting for Shyam to come back, I was overcome by a longing to be back home, to be with Baba and Mai again. But I wouldn't confess my longing to anyone, I wouldn't give them a chance to say anything, to ask questions, for I was afraid that they would be able to break through my defences. I knew they would, I'd never be able to hold anything back from them. And then I would have to admit how terrible it was living in that tiny room, how completely strange I found Shyam's family. And then they, no, *Mai* would say, 'We told you so!' She would say, 'We knew how it would be.'

Shyam had warned me that he didn't have a home for us to live in. Feroz, Shyam's mentor and boss, had given us his seaside house, Ocean Vista, for a week's honeymoon. After that we had no place to go to. Shyam said we would live with his family in

Thane for a while. Once Feroz signed his next film, Shyam would have enough money for us to get our own place. Right now, staying with his family was the cheapest option. We don't need to pay any deposit, he said, only the rent. I quaked when I thought of Mai hearing that Shyam's family was taking rent from him. 'Just like Sindhis' she would say contemptuously and I would never be able to convince her that it was Shyam's father who was that way. He drove everyone crazy, asking for an account of every paisa spent, grudging his family everything except the bare necessities. Which was one of the reasons Shyam had walked out. 'I refused to take his money, it was like becoming his slave,' he said. And yet he went back, and with a wife. I never knew how it happened, he didn't tell me, but I think it was because of his brother, the only person in the family with whom Shyam had some kind of a relationship. He kept scrupulously out of all family dissensions, Shyam told me, adding, 'Though how he manages to do it is beyond me!'

Hearing these things, I quailed at the thought of staying with them. But Shyam assured me, 'We don't need to have anything to do with them, you don't have to bother about them.' It sounded strange to me, but I soon realized that they didn't want to have much to do with me, either. If I kept aloof, so did they; I rarely met them. When I had to go to the bathroom, the corridor was empty, as if they knew I was coming and kept away. The only time we met was when I had a phone call. 'Manjari, phone for you,' someone would say. I had to pass through the dining room to get to the phone, past the table piled with used plates and uncovered vessels, the table that was never cleared because they ate at different times. I thought of home, of our conversation during meals, of Mai saying *'annadata sukhi bhava'* when we finished.

Despite this indifference and hostility, they were, at the same time, wholly involved with themselves. I've never seen a family so unaware of outsiders, so inward looking. And this, not out of affection, but out of hostility and suspicion. I heard the loud voices all day, voices that penetrated the walls, Shyam's sister's the loudest. She was, Shyam told me, the one who caused all the trouble in the family. The main aim of her life was to sow dissension between her father and her brothers, between her brother and his wife, between them and their children. Accustomed as I was to Baba's quiet voice, to Mai's soft tones, these voices were like an assault on my ears. Having to share the bathroom was another nightmare. Used to Mai's fastidious ways, I found myself holding my breath each time I went into the smelly, messy bathroom, the old man's urine spattered on the toilet seat and on the floor. I became adept at controlling myself, going to the bathroom as rarely as possible, fearfully remembering Baba's stricture when we were children, 'You'll get urinary infection if you don't empty your bladder.'

I was careful not to speak of these things to Shyam, afraid I would offend him if I was critical about his family. I soon learnt that he didn't care; his objectivity about his family amazed me as much as my adoration of my family amused him. 'You're like the kid in the ad who says "My daddy strongest, my mummy most beautiful,"' he once joked. He found my family claustrophobic, he said. I couldn't survive in that tightly shut room, he said. I didn't understand then what he meant. But I realized he didn't care much for my family. Which is why I never confessed my homesickness to him. I rang home when I felt really low, but the moment I heard Baba's 'Hello?' or Mai's 'Who is it?', I put the receiver down. After I'd done this a few times, Baba said, just when I was about to disconnect, 'Jiji, I know it's you. Don't disconnect. What's wrong? Is anything wrong?'

'Nothing, Baba, nothing is wrong. I'm fine. I just wanted to hear your voice.'

'Are you all right?'

'I'm good, Baba, very good,' I said, clenching my teeth to hold my jaw tight, to stop myself from bursting into tears. I wouldn't do that, I wouldn't give Mai a chance to be triumphant.

The truth was that I was not really unhappy. It was only that room, only Shyam's family and my new college, the subjects and studies which meant nothing to me, the boys and girls who were total strangers—these made me feel the way I did. For the first time in my life I had no friends; I avoided the other students, I kept aloof from them. For some reason, I didn't want anyone to know that I was married. And now, when I was disinterested, boys were interested in me, I found myself pursued by males. It made me uneasy, so I rushed back to the small room and waited for Shyam to come home. Long hours when I had nothing to do but stare at my books which seemed so unreal after my year of medical studies. Poetry, essays, novels—just words, I thought. No substance to anything, nothing like the reality of the human body. And after three years of focussed, intense work to get into medicine, after one year of hard work in medical college, I found it difficult to accept the lackadaisical attitude of the students in the arts course, the way they spoke, boastfully, about 'bunking classes'.

Baba came to see me a few days after our conversation on the phone. 'Your mother wants you to come home for Mangala Gauri,' he said.

She wants to show the world that everything is all right, I thought. She doesn't want people to talk about us, she doesn't want people to say that *she* hasn't done the things she should have done. It matters to her that nobody should criticize *her*.

'Just come, Jiji,' Baba said when I hesitated. 'Malu's coming for the weekend, she'll stay on until Tuesday if you come. And Gayatri wants to see you.'

'I'll ask Shyam.'

'Go if you want to,' Shyam said to me. 'What's your problem?'

I had yet to learn how much it irritated Shyam when I asked him to decide for me. 'Do what *you* want,' he always said.

That was the trouble. I didn't know what I wanted. I longed to be home, but I was afraid of meeting Mai, afraid I would give way and hold on to her and sob and she would think I was unhappy, that I was sorry I had married Shyam. She would never understand that I had no regrets at all about marrying him.

Finally, I went. When I got home, I could not believe that I had hesitated, that I had thought of not coming. Gayatri had come from Bangalore, she'd flown down, yes, she'd spent all that money just to meet me. And Kamala and Mangal were there too, enthusiastically helping Mai with the puja, Mangal throwing herself wholeheartedly into the all-night games and dancing. As for me, I inhaled the fragrance of Mai's presence with rapture, I gave myself up to the joy of being her Jiji once again. And yet ...

Yet, I was noticing things I'd never seen before; it was as if I was seeing my family through Shyam's eyes. I saw Baba's inability to assert himself with Mai, the steeliness that lay under the surface of Mai's gentleness, Malu's self-absorption and her refusal to take any interest in anyone but herself. They've changed, I thought. But Malu said the same thing to me. 'You've changed,' she said, something breaking through her I-don't-care attitude. 'Shyam Shyam all the time,' she said. And I thought perhaps she was right, for I was now seeing the world through Shyam's eyes, I was thinking his thoughts. Yes, I was completely under Shyam's influence, my mind lying under his, being penetrated and fertilized by his mind, the way my body was.

Mai did everything correctly, she did her duty as a mother as meticulously as she did everything else. But I was glad to go back even to the ugly room and the harsh voices; Shyam made up for everything. I was willing to put up even with the urine-stinking bathroom if I could be with him. As soon as I went back, Shyam told me that Feroz had offered him Ocean Vista for the next six months. We can live there if you think it's okay, he said.

Okay? I didn't have to think twice. It was the paradise I'd dreamt of so often, the paradise that seemed so distant from that dingy room.

'You'll have to give up college,' Shyam said. 'You can't travel all that way every day.'

I don't care, I said.

I won't be there all the time. When I'm working I'll have to stay on in Bombay. I'll come whenever I can, of course.

I was ready for everything. Yes, yes, yes, I said.

Baba thought the children should know about their beginnings, he thought I should tell them about it. But what can I tell them about Shyam's family when I know so little myself? I was with them for only a few days and what I saw of them, I didn't like. I never met any of them again, except Shyam's brother who came to see me twice after Shyam's death. None of the others did. I don't blame them. Why should they have concerned themselves with a strange woman? What did we have in common with Shyam gone, when there had been so little even when he was alive? But I have a few facts. I know Shyam's brother was a lawyer—not a very successful lawyer, but he worked hard and looked after his unpleasant father, he gave his difficult sister a home. I know that Shyam's father never got over the trauma of being left the sole breadwinner with three younger siblings to look after when he was barely sixteen. And I can tell the children that Shyam's grandmother, his father's mother, was a Muslim who was killed during the Partition, killed by her own people for having married a Hindu. And that Shyam's grandfather never recovered from this, that he died soon after they came to Bombay. This is all the information I have. For the rest I can only offer the chronology— that I was eighteen when I married Shyam; I was barely twenty-one when he died. That is all. How will this information help them?

the sea

I spring out of bed the moment the bell rings, getting caught in a tangle of sheets and clothes, tripping over them in my haste, sliding over my own slippers on the floor. After I've disentangled and stabilized myself, I hold on to the back of a chair and look at the time. It's nearly eleven. Who can it be? I won't open the door, I tell myself, I'll ignore the bell. But it rings again.

'Who is it?' I call out from the hall.

There is a knock this time. I hear his voice calling me softly, 'Ma'am.' Hesitantly, I open the door. He's holding a parcel in his hand.

'Ma'am, this came when you were out. A courier ... I took it and I thought ...'

'Why didn't you bring it to me earlier? Why did you have to wake me up at this time?'

He's surprised, no, more than surprised by my fierceness, by this savage assault. His face changes, the hurt springs out of his eyes.

'I'm sorry, ma'am, I'd gone out. When I came home, I saw your light on and I thought you're awake ...'

'All right, give it to me.'

'Ma'am ...'

What is he trying to say? Why won't he go?

'What is it?'

'Ma'am, I ...'

'Go away, just go away. And don't come here at this time, never again.'

I close the door, put the parcel on the table and go back to my room. I sit on the edge of the bed, my knees close together to stop my legs from trembling. What is happening? What have I done? What if he hadn't gone away? What if he had created a scene, barged into the house and ...?

For a long time I sit unmoving and blank. Then I think of his back when he turned away, of his hands when they gave me the parcel, of his face, his eyes ...

Finally, inevitably, I get out of bed and go to the back of the house. I climb the stairs, remove the heavy bars Raja had fixed to prevent intruders from entering. I unbolt the door, open it, close it gently behind me and cross the little patch of open yard swiftly. He's waiting for me, he's heard the sound of the door opening. He looks at me, but I don't want to see his face. I go into the room, slipping past him and say, 'Close the door. No, don't switch on the light.' He tries to speak, to say something, but I stop him abruptly, harshly. I don't want to hear his voice either. Only the body, his body, only my body, my starved body. No thoughts, no feelings, only sensations. The smell of sundried clothes, of sweat, the hardness, the pressure of his body, its weight on mine and my body responding, welcoming his. Yes, go on, go on, no stop, wait, wait for me, go on, go on, my god oh my god ...

Never again, never again, I tell myself when I'm back in my own bed, bathed and changed and yes, once again with my mind in a tumult but my body strangely at peace, strangely light. Never again. It's over.

But it's not the end, it's the beginning. It's something neither of us has any control over. Our bodies have taken charge; we're caught in the grip of something that won't let go. Nevertheless, I try to assert myself, I try to take charge. I lay down the ground rules once again as I'd done when he came to inhabit the room. New rules for this new territory. He can never come into my house, it is I who will go to him. He can never approach me, he can never ask me any questions. He has to wait for me to go to him, the decision will be mine, mine alone. He has to accept this.

In a while, new rules emerge, rules that I make up as I go along. There is to be no speaking, no words between us. He obeys this too, as he does my other injunctions. Yet, each time it bursts out of him in an explosion of ecstasy, 'Ma'am, ma'am, ma'am...' Only one word, the same word, but it says everything I've banned him from saying. No touching, I tell him. No, I say, each time his hands try to move over my body. No, I say when his lips come fearfully, eagerly, close to mine. The first time I stop him so harshly, so abruptly that he suddenly pauses, he withdraws. But in a moment his young body gets back into its rhythm. And then it's over.

I begin to sob.

'Ma'am, what is it, what have I done, have I hurt you?'

'Don't, don't speak, don't say anything.'

He soon learns what I want, he gives me just what I demand. No words, no touching. His body has none of the nervousness, none of the doubts he has, and it performs to perfection.

How swiftly he has learnt, how easily he has crossed the border and become familiar with this strange country, how well he has learnt its rules! Both of us have crossed the threshold and moved into a new area. We are rapidly learning its topography, its pleasures, its dangers. I'm playing the game as if I've done it before, as if I've been preparing myself for this. I'm careful, hiding all traces of our activity, letting nothing show. I'm proud of my own skill at concealment. Look, I find myself thinking, look how careful I am! As if I'm speaking to Raja, Raja who'd said to me, 'Are you crazy? Taking a strange man into your house! You need to get your head examined!' As if I'm trying to show Raja how careful I am. I have learnt to open the door at the top of the stairs noiselessly, without a sound, not even a faint clang, or a creak. I cross the yard swiftly—this is the only hazard, I can be seen by a neighbour at a window. But I'm across it in a second like a shadow, like a ghost. I never tell him when I'm coming, but he's always waiting, the door open, the lights off. He too has learnt to close the door without any sound, even though there's no one around who can hear. Everything in the dark, a darkness that is total. A blackout. There is no furniture to stumble over in the dark, only the bed and his body. No words, only our breathing. And my heart beating so loud—surely someone will hear it? When it's over, I walk away from him just as noiselessly, closing and bolting the door behind me just as soundlessly.

Who am I telling this to? To Raja? I think of Raja as a boy, curious about everything, wanting to see what is happening, butting at people with his round bullet head, saying, 'Let me see, let me see'. Weaving his way between people to get to the front. Is it Raja's curiosity I'm assuaging? Or is it Raja I'm most carefully concealing things from?

'You're putting on weight,' he says. When I deny this hotly, angrily, he says, 'Now, don't start dieting. What I meant was, you're looking good.'

Something about the way he looks at me makes me uncomfortable, as if my face, my body is showing him the very thing I'm trying to hide from him.

I look anxiously at my face in the mirror. Do I look different? Does anything show? No, it doesn't. But if the face knows how to deceive, the body can't lie. I can lie in words, I can make my face show what is not there, I can conceal what there is, but the body can't lie. The body is honest, yes, it told me its need and I've gone along with it, I've given it what it wants. I've done nothing wrong.

'Like drinking water,' Shyam said to me once.

'The same water, whoever the person is?' I teased him.

'No, not the same. You, my darling, are pure, clear, cold water. A mountain spring. I could drink forever. I never want to stop.'

Like drinking water when you're thirsty. Like a diabetic's craving for food. Nothing wrong with it. And yet, why do I bathe three times a day, why do I scrub myself when bathing as if I want to flay myself, why do I punish my body so angrily? The body and mind so much at variance with each other—Baba is right. Nature has done this badly. How can you want the act and hate the idea so much? Why am I ashamed of what I'm doing? Hiding all traces of it as if I've committed a crime, as if I've murdered someone. Like a criminal washing away the bloodstains. But traces always remain, the pink spots show.

'Why are you having so many baths, Amma? It's not so hot now.'

'You're eating well these days. I'd have got us one more dosa if I'd known you were going to be so greedy.'

'Ma,' Sachi cries over the phone, 'where were you last night? The phone kept ringing. Where did you go?'

And there's Raman himself. I am conscious of him watching Raja and me setting out for our morning walk. I don't look up, but I know he's at the window, watching us, following us with his eyes. My back is conscious of his gaze. I come home on Saturday night and find him on the stairs, waiting, it seems, for me to return. I see him when I'm unlocking the door. I stop suddenly and stare at him.

'What are you sitting here for? Don't ever do this,' I say. I open the door, go in and bolt it from inside with loud angry sounds. What if Raja had come in with me, what if he had seen him sitting there like a faithful dog?

I don't go up that night—or the next, or the next. I want to punish him. For what? For the possibility that Raja could have seen him, that he might have guessed? Why am I so scared of Raja?

I think of the book I read sometime back, a novel in which a woman academic has an affair with her young student. 'An arrangement' she calls it when she speaks of it to her friend. 'An arrangement that works well for both of us. He goes away in the morning and we don't speak of the night when we meet during the day.'

Arrangement—such a *sensible* word. Like 'single parent', which takes away the guilt of separation, the trauma of desertion, the ugliness of divorce, the tragedy of death. *Arrangement.* It erases the moral wrongdoing, the turpitude, it takes the guilt and ugliness out of the action. I think of myself telling Raja: 'I have an arrangement with the boy upstairs. It's doing me good, my body feels good. And it means nothing, it's not connected to any other part of my life. There's nothing more than this moment, nothing more than the here and now. I can walk away from him without looking back. He'll soon go away and it will be over. I will never think of it again.'

Who am I saying this to? Raja, again Raja. What do I owe him? This is my business, mine alone. I'm doing what I feel like doing and I can put a stop to it whenever I choose to do so. A click of a finger and it's over. I can end it this minute if I want to. But not yet, not as yet. It has to run its course. And then I will send him away and he'll go. He has to go. I owe him nothing either. Even less than nothing.

Since Shyam's death I've travelled alone. No one has any right over me, no one can tell me what I should do or not do. Even my parents forfeited their right to control my life. It was when I stood facing the sea after Shyam's death that it began, something that has grown over the years—a conviction that I would not let anyone into my life ever again. There were the children—I had to accept that—but apart from that I would not let anyone get close, become part of my life. No, I would not be hurt again if I could help it. Baba and Mai had so many reasons for me to not marry Shyam. But they left out the one reason that mattered: when you love someone, like I did Shyam, you become vulnerable. You shed your armour and there's nothing to protect you from getting hurt. Yes, Baba and Mai should have told me this. But would I have listened? I wanted nothing more than to be defenceless, to be fully open to Shyam, to have no cover, not even my skin. Offering myself to him the way I did when I stood in the moonlight, letting him look at me, allowing his eyes to travel all over me, not using my hands to shield myself, looking him straight in the eyes all the while. Offering him not just my body, but all of me, the entire expanse of me lying open before him like the sea.

I believe that the places we live in are not just shells we inhabit; they become part of us and influence not only our lives, but our natures too, making us act in certain ways. I have only to think of what I became in the three months we lived in Shyam's family home, living among people who were wholly indifferent to Shyam and me. I remember how I changed, even in that short while, from an open, friendly girl into a suspicious, unhappy one. So frightened of rejection that I was afraid to talk to my parents. Avoiding the overtures of the girls and boys in college, wanting only to get back to the room I hated, until Shyam came and transformed it. A dingy, mean little room which infected me with its qualities. On the other hand, there was Ocean Vista, the house by the sea, large and generous, the doors and windows open all day, letting in the light and the sea breeze, bringing in the fresh smell of the sea, an indescribable odour which haunted me for years. There were no walls, no gates, no fences; the sea, the sand and the house all merged into one another. Happiness, which I'd got in measly little doses in the room when Shyam came home, when he was not too tired, when he was not irritated by the voices beyond the wall—happiness now came in like the sea, huge bounding waves which swamped me.

I was alone a great deal of the time. Shyam was busy with a movie and came when he got the time. Yet, I was not lonely, no, never lonely. The caretaker couple Damu and Sheela and their boy Ashok had the two rooms behind the house and were around all day. There were the neighbours who walked past, morning and evening, with such regularity that I could almost set my watch by them, people who soon began to recognize my existence and waved and smiled when I waved at them. Above all, there was the sea which made loneliness impossible. Once Shyam left, I went out, I spent almost all my time on the beach. I took to running in the morning, enjoying the wet squishiness under my feet, relishing the ache in my calf muscles. I ran a long stretch until my heart was pounding in my chest and my legs were painful and tired with resisting the pull of the sand. Each day I ran a little more than the previous day, an exercise that was to stand me in good stead when the only job I could get was that of a games teacher in a school. Coming back, I would bathe and then devour the fresh loaves of pav left on the veranda in the meantime, pav which I ate dipped in tea. I was at peace, my body and I together. In the evenings I was again on the beach, dawdling this time. I was fascinated by the life teeming under the sand which seemed so dry and arid, enchanted by the wispy crabs, tiny feathery creatures who scuttled into their holes with an energy that belied their insubstantiality. I joined the group of children playing ball; we played until the sun set and twilight slowly descended upon the world. And there were times, the best times actually, when I did nothing but watch the sea. The sea cast a spell on me, I could never take it for granted. There was a pristine quality about it, as if it was still connected to its remote past, unlike the land which seemed to have given up the memory of its origins. As I sat there, hour after hour, I felt I was watching an unending drama—the waves coming in, dashing against the rocks, crawling, licking the beach and rolling back wearily, only to return once again with the same vigour. The tides became a part of my life, I grew adept at knowing the times, setting my clock by them. I watched the fishing boats waiting to set out fishing, a silent group slanted low against the sky, raring to go, their slanting silhouettes giving them a look of eagerness. And then, as if they had received some signal we could neither hear nor see, suddenly streaming out in a silent convoy. I thought it was the most beautiful sight I had seen and each time I saw it, my throat thickened with the sheer beauty of it. I watched them return in the mornings with their silvery haul, not triumphant, but with a look of weary satisfaction, of completion. Grateful to the sea for having let them return. And I thought, this is something that has happened for millions of years, ever since man dared to venture out to sea. Now, when I think of it, I realize that the sea took me away from the intense, self-contained world of Shyam and me, giving me glimpses of beauty that lay beyond our love.

This was also the place where I came to know Shyam. We had been married for nearly six months and we knew each other's bodies well enough. Now we sat together in long hours of silence while we watched the sea, his head on my lap, the smell of his body mingling with that of the sea and the fish. There were other times when we could not stop talking. Shyam told me things about himself, about his family and his work, facts which I heard and absorbed, making these things part of me in the same way that I accepted his body into mine. I learnt for the first time that he was a college dropout (and how thankful I was that I had not known this earlier, that I had not had to tell Mai about it). I heard about his fascination with the camera which began with a stranger, Jeremy Rodrigues, who initiated him into photography. But that was still photography, he said, and he wanted movement. 'Remember that song in *Sagar*, "O Maria"?' he asked me. The quicksilver flashing movements of the dancers drove him crazy, he said. 'I must have seen the movie—I don't know how many times, and only for that one dance.' And so he drifted into the movies. He joined Feroz as a lowly assistant, ready to do any work if only he could learn. Feroz was his guru; in fact, he called him 'Guru'. Feroz and the rest of them—Tarunbhai and Kantibhai and Suresh and Babu—became his family, the family 'I had never known until I met you,' he told me. I had wondered until then how he could live without a family. Now I knew: these people were his family. They became my family too, they were the people who helped me after Shyam's death. I could afford to refuse Baba's help because they were there for me.

For me Ocean Vista was a place of reconciliation as well. Baba came to visit me soon after we moved. I had not expected him; to see him walking in the narrow lane between the rows of tiny houses was like seeing a phantom. When I recognized him, for a moment I felt a jolt of fright. Why had he come? Then he smiled at me and it was all right. I thought I'd come and see you, he said. I was missing you. The words were like water to a parched throat. He stayed a whole day and night. When we went for a walk in the evening, he breathed in the sea air with gusto, with great enjoyment. Baba, who'd lived in Bombay all his life, had never seen such a sea; he was enchanted. He stayed out for a long time, he came in only when I announced dinner. For the first time, I played hostess and enjoyed it. I enjoyed looking after my father. I saw his surprise at my skill in cooking. I'd learnt it only since coming here, discovering in myself an ability to create which pleased me enormously. I could see that it pleased my father too. He went away in the morning—it was Monday morning, and he had to go—but I saw his reluctance. And I wondered how it would have been if Mai had been with him, whether we would have been so easy and comfortable with each other.

Mai came with Baba a few weeks later. 'Your parents are here,' Damu said. 'I saw them getting off the bus, I came to tell you.'

Yes, there they were, Mai, immaculate in spite of her bus journey, not a hair out of place, but looking older. And Baba too. Suddenly they were just any middle-aged couple. Then they came closer and they were Baba and Mai again. I could see that Mai was uncomfortable, as she was in any new place. And I—I was not sure how I should behave with Mai. Normally, I would have rushed to them, I would have thrown myself at her and hugged her, crying out her name. But now I stood where I was until they came to me. I took the bag out of Baba's hand, saying 'Come in', as if I'd been expecting them. Baba was more at home this time, not only because of the familiarity of his last visit, but in contrast to Mai who behaved like a guest, letting me wait on her. Baba helped me with my chores and it was like the old days when he and I did things together. We went out for a walk, the three of us, but Mai, never one for any physical activity, turned back in a while. Baba and I walked on in silence, I could feel his ease with me and I could see he had forgiven me. But Mai ...

And yet, when going, Mai, most unusually for her, passed her hand lightly over my cheek, then touched her own fingers to her lips. That rare and wonderfully tender gesture of love that was reserved for her softest moments. After they'd gone, I sobbed until it was time for Shyam to come home. I got up then and forced myself to stop crying. I washed and changed. After Shyam came, I told him about my parents' visit.

'I know,' he said. 'Damu told me. How was it?'

'Wonderful,' I said and burst out crying again. And he held me and comforted me. No touching of fingers to lips for us. But when I thought of that gesture of Mai's, I knew that she too had forgiven me. But not Shyam. She didn't speak of him, no, not once and she chose to go away just before she knew he was to return. Why couldn't she forgive him? And then I thought, angrily—what has he done to be forgiven? The regret was only momentary. It didn't darken my days with Shyam.

And then Malu came and the reconciliation was complete. Baba brought her, he left her with me and went back. How strange that he felt he had to accompany her, that he felt she could not travel even these few miles out of Bombay alone. For a while after Baba left, we were uneasy with each other, uncomfortable about being on our own in these strange new circumstances. And then she went in to wash and came out, her face soaped, her eyes screwed tightly shut, screaming 'Jiji ...' It was a cockroach. I killed it, threw it out and pushed her rigid figure back into the bathroom, saying, 'It's okay now, it's okay.' After that, it was all right. She had seemed so worldly and sophisticated to me after she went to Pune, alienated from me by her friends—Sophia and Ritu and Amy and Gulnaz—who were so different from the girls we'd known. But that was only a façade. Under it was the Malu I knew, innocent and spoilt. Once again admiring me, watching me in awe as I cooked. And I, showing off a little, working with more flourish to my movements than if I'd been alone. She followed me about as if memorizing my routine—though, truth to tell, I had none. In the evening we went to the beach and sat there until the boats were just tiny black dots on the horizon, the sound of the sea gradually becoming a whisper as it receded from us. She lay with her head on my lap, her skirt bunched between her thighs, her hands playing with the sand, sifting the fine particles through her fingers, throwing away what remained, then picking up another fistful and starting all over again. It was then that she asked me the question I have never been able to get out of my mind.

We had spoken of many things, but not of Shyam, as if Mai's taboo had pinned Malu down to silence. And then she asked the question, her face turned up to the slowly darkening sky.

'Jiji,' she began, then stopped. 'You ...' she made another abortive beginning. And then she rushed into speech. 'Jiji, what you do—is it dirty?'

I knew what she was asking me, I knew what she was speaking of. I have thought much of that moment since then, it has often come back to me, bringing with it the weight of Malu's head in my lap, the feathery fineness of her hair, the warm softness of her cheek under my hand and the subdued sursuration of the sea framing the silence of the evening. I have thought of the question and how I could have answered it. I could have said, 'Remember Mr Bones? Remember Baba telling us how everything in the body has a function, how every function is necessary for life? This is one of them. Needed for reproduction. Useful. Not dirty.'

Or I could have said, 'It's a way of connecting. So many ways in which we connect with others, in which we show our love for others. Remember how Mai touches our cheeks and then takes her fingers to her own lips? This is just another way.'

But I said none of these things. In any case, I didn't have the ideas then, at least not clearly enough to present them to anyone, least of all to Malu. Even if I had the ideas, I didn't have the words to convey them. I was only nineteen and enjoying physical love for the first time, experiencing the power and joy of it, caught up in its enthrallment; how could I look at it from a distance, how could I speak of it with a detachment which would give me the right words to answer Malu's question? I could only have said what I honestly thought: Dirty! My god, it's the most beautiful experience in life—if you love each other, that is.

Yes, this was how I felt when I thought of Shyam's body, his beautiful male body touching mine, entering me, his breath mingling with mine, his lips on my lips.

But I could not say this to anyone, least of all to Malu. Sometimes I wonder whether, if I had answered her differently, things would have been different, whether what happened later could have been avoided. I will never know the answer to that question. Yet, I am glad I had enough perspicacity to see that Malu felt a distance between us, that she felt I had crossed over to another place by marrying a man and living with him. For me it was important to bridge that gap, to make Malu understand that I was still the same person, still her Jiji. And so I said words that were no more than comforting, shushing sounds. Don't worry about it, I said. You'll find out what it is when the time comes. But don't think of these things now.

She left it there. She sprang up and began walking back to the house as if to prevent me from looking into her face, to avoid looking into mine. She walked slowly, picking up shells on the way. As I followed her, I thought of the shells we'd collected as children and how I'd done the same here at first, until Shyam had weaned me of the habit, saying, 'Let them be. They'll still be here when you come back tomorrow. Why take them home?'

I thought of saying this to Malu, but wisely refrained. Suddenly, as if the same thought had occurred to her, she shook out her skirt, let the shells drop and saying, 'Jiji, I'm hungry', she began to run, her longer legs and bigger strides giving her an advantage. But I'd learnt to run on the sand, my feet were more practised in coping with the pulling sand. I soon outstripped her and was waiting for her when she came to me and fell into my arms, laughing and panting.

I made omelettes for us, soft fluffy omelettes I'd grown skilled at making because Shyam loved them. Fat masala omelettes bulging with onions, chillies and coriander. Malu was so hungry she could not wait for the omelettes to be ready. She fell on the bread, she stuffed a loaf with blood-red garlic chutney and ate it. Quite unlike the usual fussy, finicky 'mustard-seed picking Malu', as Baba called her. During dinner we turned children again, giggling at things, not knowing why we were laughing, but unable to stop. Once even, with a delicious sense of disloyalty, bringing in Mai's awful cooking. 'This is better than Vasundharabai's food,' Malu said, imitating RK, dragging out the long name even more, so that it seemed funnier. We almost choked with laughter. We were back now in our childhood, the mealtimes when we'd kicked each other under the table and burst into laughter, holding our hands over our mouths to keep the food from spraying out. We remembered how we had laughed at Baba's assistant's name—Shende. It had seemed so exquisitely funny to us, we could not keep ourselves from exploding every time we heard Baba mention his name. Mai scolded us and Baba said, 'Go out and come back when you've stopped laughing.' We stood outside, doubled over with laughter, hysterical, trying to stop. But when we went back in, it started all over again. We didn't even have to hear the name or say it. Just to look at each other was to evoke it. Shende. And off we went again into hysterics. 'Now what shall we do with these girls!' Mai exclaimed. We knew it was mock exasperation, for she called us 'pori', which meant she was not really angry.

We remembered these things now. Then we washed up and made the bed together, fighting over the sheets and pillows. Playing games like children. Yes, like children. I was nineteen then and she was scarcely seventeen, both of us in our teens; I have to remember that. And I remember too, that in spite of the fun and games, I was a little tense about Malu, for I knew that if this was a good day, a bad one could follow. She was always balanced on a knife-sharp edge, she could so easily topple over into a different kind of mood, the gaiety vanishing as if it had never been. These mood changes of hers had never frightened me as they had Mai and Baba, but I had lost touch with her. And we were on our own after a long while. Yes, I was tense. But it was all right; Malu went away regretfully, reluctant to leave me, but she went away happy.

This was the last time we were together, the last time we bridged the gap. It never happened again. When I went home after Anand's birth, she was there too, having come back for good from Bharat and Medha's house. But this time, she had sealed herself against me. She seemed preoccupied with her studies and examinations, she made it clear that she found the baby's crying a disturbance. She was morose and bad-tempered and I, absorbed in Anand and his routine which dictated my day, my entire life, left her alone, refusing to be provoked even by her anger. And so we drifted apart.

After that, it was too late.

I learnt knitting from Gayatri and like it always was with me, it became an obsession for a while. I went about all day with the grimy ball of old wool Gayatri had given me to practise on, the needles projecting before me like weapons. At night too, I kept thinking: *knit purl knit purl*. I'm doing the same thing now, picking up a stitch on the needle, each stitch I pick up adding to the whole. 'My story'—how can there such be a thing as *my* story when other people's lives are so knitted into it? I cannot pick out one stitch and say, this story is mine, take another and say, this is Baba's story, then one more and say, this is Mai's ... All our lives so entwined, so knitted together that I will never be able to separate them.

revelations

I have a slight tremor of apprehension when I see the inspector
at the door. He smiles, making me easier in my mind, but when
he begins speaking my uneasiness returns. They've got their hands
on a small-time criminal, he tells me. They think—no, he corrects
himself, they're almost sure that he's the man who broke into
my house the last time. It would help, he says, if I could go down
to the station and identify him.

'Identify him? But I never saw him!'

'That night when he entered your room, you didn't get even a
small glimpse of him?'

'No! No, I didn't. It was dark and too—too ...' I grope for
the Kannada word and end up with the English—'confusing. It
was completely ...' Once again I settle for an English word—
'chaotic.'

'But, madam, you have some idea at least? What about that
first time when he came in the afternoon? You didn't see him
that time also? We think it was the same man both the times.'

I can see he's asking me to say, 'Yes, I saw him'. He wants me
to say that I can identify him. But I can't. In fact, I'm almost
certain they were two different men, though I have nothing to
support this, either. Just a glimpse of a blue shirt the first time,

the feel of a body that collided with mine the second time, of hands that grabbed and held—how can I be sure of anything at all? Put the man in a dark room with me, I want to say, and I'll be able to tell you if it is the same person. But I can imagine the inspector's response to this!

'No, I don't think they were the same. And I don't think I can identify either of them. I wish I could, but I can't.'

I can see he is disappointed. He expected some help from me, he expected more cooperation. For a moment he is on the brink of saying something. Then he pauses, thinking, I'm sure, of Venkat, of Venkat who is his 'Sahebru' and my 'cousin brother'. He goes on to tell me, instead, that he has been transferred to another area, another station. But I don't need to worry, he reassures me. His successor will be primed about me, he will contact me himself when he joins. 'Our Sahebru is very concerned about your safety,' he tells me.

He gets up to go, then suddenly seems to remember something else that he had wanted to say.

'The man who's living upstairs—what's his name?'

My heart jumps up and down in my chest. Irregular beats, like it's my heart that's startled and terrified.

'Raman Kumar.'

'Yes, Raman Kumar.'

He smiles faintly, as if he finds the name amusing, or doesn't quite believe in it.

'Raman Kumar,' he repeats, with a slight tinge of irony in his tone. 'How well ...' he corrects himself, 'I mean, what do you know of him, madam?'

Nothing except the feel of his body, its smell, its weight ...

'Very little. I think he's from Mangalore. And he told me he was a Christian.'

'*He* told you that?'

'Yes. Why? Isn't it true?'

'Who knows?'

'He said he was brought up in an orphanage—by the padres.'

'Hmm.'

He says this in such a doubting tone that my added statement, 'He wears a cross', comes out hesitant and tentative, more like a question.

He ignores my words and asks, 'Did you know him before he came here?'

'No. Abhishek is our tenant. This man is here only temporarily. Abhishek will be back in a month or two …'

'You know Abhishek?'

'Yes, he was with my father for more than a year.'

I tell him about Abhishek, his job, the company he is with and his relationship with Baba. All this, as if Abhishek's credentials will reflect on Raman. But the man brings me back to the point, he knows I'm trying to lead him away.

'Yes, yes,' he says impatiently, 'we know about *him*. It's this one we're interested in. Raman Kumar.' I don't like the way he says the name. 'Do you know where he's working now?'

'I think he's with a studio—a recording company.'

'Do you know the name?'

'No.'

'Hmm. Have you had any problems with him, madam?'

'No, none at all. He's very quiet. I scarcely see him.' And now at last my tongue forms the question: 'Why?'

He tells me it's because of a man who died. 'Someone knocked him down. It looked like an accident, but we don't think it was one, we think he was killed. We also know he was connected to a man in the extortion business—threatening people and getting money from them, you know. Just like these people who are trying to frighten you. Raman was the dead man's friend. He was there all day, waiting to claim the body.'

He sees the shock on my face and rushes on, 'We don't want to frighten you unnecessarily, madam, but I thought you should know. We could take him in for questioning, but the problem is that we have nothing, except that he was the dead man's friend. But if you know something, or if you have any doubts …?'

I remember how this same man had once very casually spoken of breaking a man's arms and legs. I think of all the things that

I've heard the police do when they're 'questioning' suspects …

'No, I've never had any problems with Raman. And he himself told me about his friend who died, he was quite open about his friendship.'

'Did he tell you what the friend's occupation was?'

'Why should he? Maybe he didn't know what his friend was doing.'

'Maybe.' The man's tone is doubtful. 'But I don't like his being here.'

'I feel safe because he's—because there's someone upstairs. And so far, I've had no problems at all.'

'All right. We'll be keeping an eye on him, he won't try anything as long as he knows we're around. In any case, madam, better ask him to leave. Yes, better do that. It's safer. You can always get someone else.'

He sat all night on the stairs guarding me. I should have told him that. But what about the whispers I heard that night, the night of the intruder-who-never-was? And how did he come down so quickly? What about that? Was he the one who was talking? And to whom?

No, I'm imagining things. The police routinely suspect everyone. We're all potential criminals to them. Nothing surprises them. But … no, he can't, it can't be all lies. The way he speaks Kannada, the pleasing sing-song tone, the words he uses—yes, he's from Mangalore. That at least is true. And his face looking at me, his voice as he says 'ma'am', the way his eyes looked straight into mine when I woke him up on the stairs that morning—how could anyone be so double-faced? But there was Laxman hugging Malu and me, saying 'my little beauties', and the other Laxman who did all those terrible things. And what about Shankar, his childhood friend and trusted lieutenant, Shankarmama to us in the days when we still visited Laxman? Yes, what about Shankar, burly amiable giant, the ardent Maruti bhakta who visited the Maruti temple on Saturday mornings and distributed prasad to everyone? Shankar, with his deep reverence for Ajji, whom he called Aisaheb, was a killer. He was finally decoyed out and stabbed to death, stabbed so many times that his body spouted blood like a fountain, killed with the same cruelty with which he had killed others.

Monsters, some people are born monsters. They can't help themselves.

Baba thought that Laxman was born with the genes that made him a flawed human. And that, therefore, he had no choice. But I think we have a choice, we always have a choice. This boy, so gentle, his eyes showing his vulnerability—could he be deceitful? And what about the cross which swings so lazily above me, teasingly touching my body, the cross that seems to venture where his hands and lips dare not go? Does the cross mean as little as Shankardada's puja and prasad did? He has never told me anything about himself. I only know his name, Raman Kumar. The way the inspector said it—is the name false too? Isn't it his real name? I know nothing, no, I know nothing about him. But I'm the one who wouldn't let him speak. No words, I warned him. Don't say anything. Only your body, I thought, only your body ...

Was all this planned? Impossible! How could he have known about me, about the hunger of my body, the response of my body? The body can't lie, the body never lies. Don't touch me, I warned him, but his feelings came to me through the pores of his skin, by a process of osmosis. His voice, his hands told me what he was feeling. Don't touch, I said, and he obeyed me, keeping his hands off my body. But he began caressing my feet one day. I drew back sharply. 'What are you doing?' I exclaimed. He looked at me, his eyes both fearful and pleading, his hands trembling, as if they longed to go back to their gentle caressing. But he said nothing, he was dumb. And I thought of how Malu and I had loved to massage Mai's feet, how we fought for the privilege of massaging them. Our love for her flowed out of us when we touched her feet. And this boy?

'Don't do that, stop it,' I said. But I'd seen his face when he caressed my feet. I understood the language of his eyes, of his body, which boldly, explicitly proclaimed his feelings for me.

His body, so finely tuned now to my needs, giving me just what I want.

I've told myself: I can stop it any time I want to. Enough, I will say and he'll be gone. Enough, I will tell my body and it will be quiet. Yet, each time after I've had this thought, I've told myself—but it must run its course, let it run its course. Maybe it is time to stop now, time to end it, maybe it has run its course.

I keep to myself for the next few days. It helps that I am busier than usual, typing a manuscript, the deadline for which is drawing near. It helps too, that Ratna asks whether she can sleep in my house for a few days. I'm used to this request of hers. It's part of a continuing battle with her husband, a battle that will never be resolved. The eternal conflict between man and woman, the man asserting his rights, claiming his right to her body, the female denying him. The problem is never spelt out so clearly, Ratna would be ashamed of herself if she said it in so many words; I deduce it from the way she speaks of the man. I've given him four children, she says, two living, two dead. I've given him a son. What more does he want? And again: his daughter is grown up. In a year or two we'll have to find her a husband, he'll have a son-in-law. Isn't he ashamed of himself?

She's tough, she fights back, but when it becomes too much for her, when his demands become too importunate, she escapes. Gayatri was her refuge. After Gayatri died, she had no one. Now she trusts me and comes to me. I'm glad of Ratna's presence. I know that her voice, the loud sound of the TV, with her favourite serials going on until late, will tell him I am not alone.

And then, having shown her power, having made it clear she will not give in to him, Ratna goes back home. The house seems abnormally silent that day. I become conscious of his presence, of his expectations. I must do something. I know what I have to do, I know I can't put it off any longer.

I call out to him when he is going up in the evening, studiously avoiding my eyes, pretending ignorance of my presence. He turns back at my call and stops.

'Just a minute, I want to talk to you.'

It takes me less than a minute to tell him I am planning to sell the house. His face changes in a moment from apprehension to shock. Then he says, 'I thought …'

'I've got a job in a residential school, I'll have to live on the campus. There's no point in keeping the house. You'll have to find yourself some other place.'

'But … ma'am …'

I'm getting irritated now. Why is he making it harder for me?

'I don't understand … why … what happened …?'

'What's there to understand? I'm selling the house. You have to find yourself another place. Raja has already found a buyer and I want to do it quickly.'

'But, ma'am, you can't …'

Will he never complete his sentences?

'I can't what? You knew that you would have to go when Abhishek returned. And I don't have to explain anything to you. I'll talk to Abhishek when he comes back.'

He doesn't move, he stands before me, almost looming over me. My heart is thudding in panic. What will he do? Why won't he go? Then he suddenly turns away and goes up the stairs. I am sweating with relief. It's over, I think.

But of course it's not over, it's impossible that he will go away so easily. He comes back the next morning. He looks wretched, as if he hasn't slept all night. I open the door and ask him to come in. He sits before me, dumb, looking at the floor between his knees. When the silence goes on, I speak.

'You knew,' I say gently, 'you knew you couldn't go on living here. You knew I was planning to sell the house.'

His throat works. The Adam's apple moves up and down. Suddenly he clutches at my hand. 'Ma'am, please don't send me away, please don't send me away from you.'

'What are you doing!' I try to snatch my hand out of his, but he won't let go.

'I promise I won't trouble you, I don't expect anything from you. Just let me stay here, don't send me away. I don't want anything, only to see you, only to look at you …'

What have I done, my god, what have I done!

'Please, ma'am, please ...' His grasp on my hand tightens.

'Let go my hand! You're hurting me.'

He lets it go abruptly and looks me in the face. They're wrong, he can't be what they think he is. He is suffering. This is real, this is no pretence.

'It's over, you have to understand. It's over.'

'I promise, ma'am, I won't ask for anything.'

'I'm sorry, Raman, it's over. It's my fault, I know it's my fault, but you have to go now.'

He gets up and walks out, dragging his feet a little. I keep seeing his face and eyes the whole night and think over and over again—what have I done, my god, what have I done? He will never forget this, he will never forget me. This experience will accompany him like a phantom all his life. I will be with him each time he sleeps with a woman. He will compare every woman with me, each experience with this one and he will find them always wanting. He will go on searching for me all his life, he will never forget, he will never let go. Like me. I had thought that with this man I would be able to let Shyam go, but it has not happened. Each time I have been with him, I have thought—*this is not Shyam*. Each time, I have hated him—and myself—because he is not Shyam.

In the morning, all other thoughts recede and fears begin. What if he won't go? What if he is what the inspector thinks he is? What if he threatens me? What if he blackmails me? How did I get into this, what was I thinking of? Sachi and Anand—what if they come to know? Will they be disgusted and turn their backs on me? Will I lose them? I think of Sachi's watchful gaze fixed on any man I speak to, of the way she plants her sturdy presence in our midst, making sure I am not betraying her. Why is it a betrayal of one to get close to another? Is that what Mai thought? Is that why she was hostile to Shyam, because she felt it threatened my feelings for her? Was it just jealousy after all?

What does it matter? It's all over. I've told Raman it's over. He has to accept it. But what if he doesn't? All day his eyes, suffering and anguished, haunt me. And I think—he can't be what they say he is, he will go.

Though I don't see him, though I never hear his steps on the stairs, I know he is there, I am conscious of his presence upstairs. I don't know what he is going to do. I wonder if I will have to speak to him again. And then I get a call. I'm no longer on my guard, I'm wholly unprepared for the voice that says abruptly the moment I lift the receiver, 'We warned you not to sell the house to anyone else. Remember our warning.'

Melodramatic, like the lines written by a script writer for the movies. But the menace is real. And telling me something I can no longer ignore: Raman must have told them. No one else knows I'm selling the house. It's not even true, it was only an excuse to send him away and yes, to test him. He's passed on the information. Only he could have done it, he has to be one of them.

The next day, I lie in wait for him and accost him when he's going out.

'I think you should go. Go quickly. You know what I mean.' He is silent. 'If you don't, I'll have to talk to the police. I think you should go before that. I don't want you to be hurt.'

He gets on his motorbike and drives away without a word, and I am left fearful, anxious, heavy-hearted. After a while recklessness takes over. What can they do to me? I don't mind dying. But I don't want Sachi and Anand to be ashamed of me. And Raja—for some reason, the thought of Raja knowing anything is unbearable.

I'm nervous when Raja comes the next day. But it's only to take me to his club. Venkat's wife has gone out of town with their kid. He's alone, let's spend an evening together, he says.

We sit on the lawn, voices drifting towards us, disjointed and wavering, like leaves coming down on a windless day. It's peaceful. I am silent, letting their conversation wash over me, when Venkat startles me by suddenly asking, 'And have you got rid of that tenant of yours, Jiji? Shivaprakash told me he spoke to you, he said he warned you about him.'

'What's this?' Raja looks suspiciously from his face to mine. 'Jiji, you never told me about this.'

For once I'm completely at a loss for words. Raja is about to speak, when Venkat tells him about their suspicions of Raman. Nothing concrete, he says, very vague really, and only because of his association with the man who died. 'But since Jiji is alone ...'

'I've told him to leave.'

'And he's going?'

'I think so.'

'You *think so*? Jiji, you're the limit. *You* tell her, Venkat, not to be so casual, she pays no attention to me at all.'

'Shall I ask Shivaprakash to take him in for questioning?'

'No!' It comes out of me so explosively that the two men look at me in astonishment. 'No,' I say, this time in a normal tone, hoping it will erase the earlier one. 'I mean, I'm sure he'll go. He told me he would go as soon as he found himself another place.'

'I'm not sure I like the idea of his disappearing, either. Maybe it's better that Shivaprakash talks to him. No, by the way, Shivaprakash is leaving, Rajshekhar is replacing him. I could ask Rajshekhar to talk to him.'

'No.' This time I try to tone down my response, I try to speak normally. But I'm not sure it comes off the way I intended.

'Why, Jiji, what's the problem?' Raja asks.

'I don't want to start things all over again. He's never been any trouble. Just let him go.'

And after he's gone, when I'm sure you can't get your hands on him, I'll tell you about the phone call. But not until then.

'All right,' Venkat says. 'Let's leave it for now. But I'm not comfortable with the connection. I'll ask Rajshekhar to see if they can get some more information about this guy.'

Raja is silent on our way back, a silence that is so unusual for him I know it means something. But he goes away without a word. He'll be back. I know he won't remain silent for long, he'll be back with whatever is on his mind.

I'm right. He comes the next day. I see him give a quick look up before he enters. No, he says, he won't sit down. He wants me to go with him for a drive. Something in his attitude tells me I can't refuse, that I will have to go with him. He knows, I think, he knows something. What is it? Has Venkat told him something about Raman, something he doesn't want to speak of here?

We drive to the park in silence. Raja parks the car on one of the quieter roads and switches off the engine. He makes no move to get out and now I know what's coming. He finds it hard to begin. I see him searching for words, the words to say what, to him, is unthinkable. He gets to it slowly, hesitantly. He tells me about the night Anand rang him up. He'd tried to reach me and when I didn't respond, he rang Raja, thinking I was with him. Raja, catching Anand's anxiety, decided he would check on me. And so he came home.

'I saw the light in your bedroom, so I knew you were at home. I rang the bell and waited a long time. When you didn't answer, I went around to the back, thinking that maybe you were in the kitchen. And then, for some reason, I don't know why, I looked up and saw you come out of his room. I thought—it can't be you, it must be someone else. But in a while I saw the light in your bedroom go off and I knew it had to be you.'

There is silence between us.

'At that time,' he goes on, 'I just thought it odd. I didn't think, I mean how could I, I just thought ... Oh, I don't know what. But I went away, because I didn't want to—maybe I didn't want to ask you about it. But yesterday, when you were so desperately trying to protect him, I remembered that night and I knew ...'

His voice tapers off. I'm still silent.

'Jiji ...?'

'You know it, why do you want me to say it?'

'So it's true.'

Again I say nothing, I hold on stubbornly to my silence. After a moment he bursts out, 'How could you, Jiji, how could you, your children ...'

'Don't bring my children into this. Say what you want to, but don't speak of the children.'

Suddenly he leans across me and opens the door. His hand is

trembling, there's something frightening about those involuntary tremors.

'Get out.'

I'm frozen into stillness, unable to accept this savagery.

'Get out.'

I get out of the car. He takes a U-turn, almost running over me, and drives away. I stand where I am for a few moments, then walk away to a bench and sit there blankly. In a while I realize it's getting dark. The park gates will soon close, I must get back home. I don't have any money, I didn't pick up my purse before leaving home, I'll have to walk back. I'm still in the park, nearing the gate, when the car stops by me.

'Get in,' he says.

I'm about to protest, but change my mind and get in wordlessly. I expect he will drop me and go away like he did last night, but he waits in the car until I unlock the door and then follows me in. He sits in the same chair and in almost the same way Raman had, his hands clasped, his face looking at the floor by his feet. It's like he can't bear to see my face, he can't bear to look at me. I sit opposite him, preparing myself to listen to what he has to say. But he does not speak. When the silence goes on, I say, 'Raja ...'

And then it bursts out of him. It's like a dam has burst. But strangely, he doesn't speak of Raman. Instead, he accuses me of almost every other thing he can think of. Of being insensitive, unfeeling, uncaring. He reminds me that I would not have come to my own mother's death bed if he hadn't brought me back. And after Gayatri's death, I could have lived with my father instead of letting him live alone. But, no, I wouldn't do anything as sensible, as human as that; I left him alone. Did I know how lonely he was? But I didn't care, I went back to that Parsi woman as if she meant more to me than he did. I had told them she was ill and I had to go. What about my father? Didn't he matter? I'm not normal, he says. Normal human feelings are outside my understanding. Did I know that my father asked him not to tell me about his illness?

'He must have thought you wouldn't come, so why trouble you? Your own father, damn it!'

'Raja, you don't know anything, you shouldn't say these things. You know nothing, nothing at all.'

'Oh yes, I know everything. I know you feel your life was tragic and you think you have to make others pay for your tragedy. You've enjoyed behaving like a tragic heroine, like a ... a Meena Kumari ...'

How strange that this, more than all his other charges, should rouse me to an intense anger! How could he say that I'd behaved like a tragic heroine? When did I ever do that? And to compare me to an overweight, over made-up actress with synthetic tears! I try to speak, I try to hit back, but he won't let me.

It seems that he's forgotten what this is really about; he's like Sachi, admitting at the end of a fierce quarrel with Anand, 'I don't know what for I was fighting.' We descend to the childish level of 'So!' 'So!', our nasty confrontational tones making up for the lack of real argument. Finally, when he seems to tire, I get my chance to fight back. I was twenty-one when Shyam died, I remind him. Twenty-one. Think of that. Did he expect me to live the life of a chaste widow the rest of my life? I remind him of his father's aunt, a child widow, and what that did to her. The way she interrupted RK and Gayatri when they were by themselves ...

His face changes. 'Don't bring them into this.'

'Why not? Why not?'

He won't answer, but I know what he means. 'You can say anything you like, but I can't. Is that it? Tell me Raja, have I asked you how you've coped since Rukku's death?'

'Now Rukku!' He speaks between clenched teeth. 'I said, don't bring others into this. Don't bring Rukku's name into your filthy argument.'

'Suddenly I'm filthy. Filthy!'

We've gone way past our original quarrel, we've almost forgotten Raman, until Raja brings him back saying, 'I never thought you would sink so low. With a chap like that.'

'Like what? Like what? Come on, explain that.'

'I don't want to say it, I don't want to say anything. It's too disgusting.'

'Disgusting.' I'm close to tears, but I won't give in, I have to go through with this. 'I'll tell you what's disgusting, Raja, I can tell you who's really disgusting.'

And I tell him about the man, a friend's husband, who thought he could induce me to become his mistress. Yes, a friend's husband. 'She will never know,' he said, as if that was all that mattered. I tell him about an employer, a man nearly Baba's age, who slobbered all over me and then fired me, saying I had a bad character. I tell him about the man who almost raped me in my own house, with my children sleeping inside. And he would have done it, yes, he would have if I hadn't fought back.

'Enough, enough,' Raja says, covering his ears with his palms.

What does he know, I rage at him, uncaring of his expostulations, what it is for a woman to live alone? I gave up wearing saris because I didn't want to look womanly, I cut my hair short like a man's, I wore my most forbidding expression. But it was of no use. They can smell it, yes, they can smell the woman in you. No matter how you dress, whether you shave your head or hide behind a burkha, they come at you, wanting your body, touching you, drooling over you, sniffing at you. Like dogs. Like dogs in heat.

'Jiji, stop it. Stop it.'

'Not nice, is it? Too disgusting for your clean middle-class Brahmin ears? I could tell you worse things. And if you listen to me, you'll know that this chap is decent compared to many others.'

'Jiji, don't defend him to me.'

'I'm not. The man means nothing to me, Raja. You don't understand anything.'

'Then why are you trying to whitewash him?'

'Because it wasn't all his fault. I was responsible too.'

'You—you ...'

'And for me it was just his body, nothing but his body.'

He gets up at that, so abruptly that I am startled, I am almost frightened when he looms over me, menacingly, it seems. I rise out of my chair too, an involuntary, defensive movement. He stands still for a moment, then goes to the door. And coming back immediately, pulls me close to him and kisses me on the lips, so hard that it hurts. I make an involuntary sound, my body shrinks from his. He lets me go, so abruptly I almost fall down. Then he walks out.

The phone rings after some time. It's Raja. 'I'm sorry about that,' he says.

'No problem, Raja, I'm used to it. Join the gang. This is open territory.'

He bangs the phone down and only then, finally, do I begin to cry. When I come to the end of my tears, I'm left with an empty feeling, like after a death, the peace and calmness that descends when it's all over, the struggle and suffering ended. In a while the pain of emptiness and loss will begin, but right now I'm too exhausted for anything, too spent.

I never imagined, I never thought Raja was serious about me. How could I have been so blind? 'Ghodi', Mai often called me as a child. Clumsy, she meant. And I was that: dropping things, spilling them, tripping over everything underfoot, banging into doors and walls. 'Aga, aga,' Mai would chide, 'slow down, child, slow down.' And then, when the disaster happened, as it inevitably did, she would say, 'Ghodi'. The first time I saw a horse, properly looked at it, that is, I wondered at Mai's choice of a word for clumsiness. Man and horse, the man leading it, the horse trotting on the sand in an easy rhythm, the muscles moving smoothly under the gleaming, burnished skin—it was a sight that made me exclaim to Shyam, 'Look!' We walked towards the horse then, we stood and watched as it ran around in circles, not at the man's bidding obviously, but for some obscure reason of its own, its legs sending up little puffs of sand with each step. Silent observers, both of us, of that scene of inexplicable beauty. And when it finally stopped, Shyam went to it and stroked it and I, looking at its marvellous elegance, at the perfection of its body, wondered once more at Mai's phrase. I told Shyam about it and he laughed and said, 'Of course she's right. You're as beautiful as a horse, you're as beautiful as this.'

Strange, but true: the clumsiness had gone. My movements were now deft and coordinated, they were confident and skilful, as if Shyam's eyes had made my body come together in a flawless perfection, the proportions suddenly just right. I knew it, for when I moved, I was conscious of the grace and suppleness of my body. But the clumsiness, I realize only now, had moved elsewhere, from my body to my behaviour. Earlier, I'd been finely tuned to others' feelings, to their responses. Suddenly, I seemed to have lost that faculty; I became dense, uncaring of others' feelings, of Baba's and Mai's pain, of Malu's hurt. And even with Shyam—I remember the day I saw him sitting on a rock looking towards the sea. I called out to him and he turned around, slowly and, it seemed, reluctantly. I felt a kind of chill, as if I was looking at a stranger. I felt an enormous distance between me and the man whose body had been part of mine just a little while ago. He made a gesture which said, 'I'll be with you in a moment, you go on.' I went in then and he came to me a little later, once again the Shyam I knew, not the strange man I'd glimpsed sitting alone on the rock. But I should have thought of it, I should have known there was another Shyam lurking behind this one. If I had, I would have been prepared for what happened, I would have dealt with it better. But I failed.

'Leave me alone,' he said to me one night, turning away from me. But I didn't. I thought I knew him, I thought I knew him through and through. I knew my power over him, I knew how he responded to me. But I didn't understand that there's some part of us that's always closed against others, a part that wants to live alone. It was the same with Malu. How could I have been so clumsy, so obtuse about her feelings, so insensitive to her moods? She had come home for good after Bharat's heart attack, Medha unable to cope, Sakubai too having left by then. It was like old times, I thought, the four of us together once again. But it was not the same, it was very clearly not the same. I was in the eighth month of my pregnancy, which made Baba and Mai more attentive to me and my needs, more caring of me. And there was Shyam who, when he came, wanted us to be by ourselves, even if my huge bulk made it impossible for us to do anything more than cuddle and kiss. Each time, Malu would bang on the door saying, 'Open the door.'

'I want to change,' she said once, and when I argued, 'You can change in Mai's room, Malu,' she retorted, 'I want to change in my own room. I don't like to be kept out of my room.'

'Don't close the door,' I told Shyam, but he laughed at me for being scared of my sister. 'She has to put up with it,' he said. Then there was a day, not long after Anand's birth, when we were alone in the house and Anand was sleeping. I was suddenly hungry for Shyam's body and pulled him on to me. I should have been more circumspect, but the pampering of my body, the massaging, oiling and fomenting it had been given after the delivery and the suckling, above all the baby's suckling, the tug at my nipples, had made my body come alive. How could I deny it what it wanted?

We came out a little later to find Malu at the dining table, a look of angry, stoical patience on her face. Shyam went out without a word and she said to me, abruptly, 'I know what you were doing.'

'We're married, Malu.'

'Not in my room, I swear, never in my room!'

And when she saw me feeding the baby, she said, 'Cover yourself. Aren't you ashamed?'

'Who's there to look?'

'I'm here. I don't like to see that.'

Why didn't I see? Why didn't I understand? It made matters worse that I never retorted, that I offered an adult, patient, putting-up-with-her-childishness response to her anger. Exasperation broke through sometimes, like the time I cried out to Shyam, sobbing that I wanted a home of our own. But most of the time I was an adult coping with an unreasonable, troublesome child who didn't know what she was saying. So blinded by the glory of motherhood that Malu became a remote figure, she receded to the periphery of my life. We all knew, we had known from her childhood, that Malu couldn't bear to be crossed. We had not forgotten those terrible times when Baba finally had to take her to a psychiatrist. But I ignored it all now, unaware of everything but Shyam and Anand.

If I thought of anything beyond Anand, it was of the joy of being reconciled to Mai, of being close to her. Mai and I were linked now by our feelings for Anand. Mai was besotted with him, unable to keep away from him, coming in even at night to look at him and touch him gently. We spoke in whispers, fearful of disturbing Anand, but Malu sleeping in the other bed would suddenly turn over and mutter so that we would guiltily shut up. And in the mornings, Baba, Mai and I would have tea together. Baba would make the tea and bring it to us, while Mai sat at her table, looking, even with her glasses on, ridiculously young to be a grandmother. The three of us would drink our tea, linked in a companionable silence; Malu, still sleeping, was outside the circle. Though I would never admit it, I knew even then that without Malu we were more comfortable, there was less tension. I was sure Baba and Mai thought of this as well, even if none of us ever said it. Why did I not see how it was for her, how could I have been so blind?

And Shyam too—engrossed in my baby, I shut myself out of his world, a world that I'd made so completely mine until then. 'When are you getting us a place?' I asked often. 'Have you found something?' I pestered him. 'Are you looking for a place at all?' I questioned him, suddenly suspicious at times. 'Wait,' he said, 'we have to wait. As soon as this film is over and I get my payment.' And then he stopped mentioning that movie and spoke instead of another one in which he would be on his own, Feroz having recommended him. This was his chance, he said, he was finally getting the opportunity to do the work he wanted to do, the kind of work only he could do. He told me the story of the film, he spoke of the new techniques he wanted to try out, of the pleasure of having a young director who was willing to give him the chance to do what he wanted. But what concerned me was that he had passed up the chance of another movie, a big movie. He would have been only an assistant, yes, but with guaranteed money. When I charged him with this, he tried to joke. He said, 'I must be the only Sindhi in the world to give up a chance to make money.' The excitement slowly faded as his 'great chance' seemed to become a distant dream, the director unable to get the money or the actors he wanted. Shyam did not tell me these things, but I glimpsed moments of depression, for which I thought the only answer was to have our own home. 'Once we're in our own home, once we're together ...' I said, thinking that once this happened, we would recreate the Ocean Vista magic once more.

Finally, worn out by my insistence, he got us a small room, for which he had to borrow money from Feroz. At first, there was only the joy of having my own home again. But it didn't last, it evaporated within a few hours. Sometimes I think misery was waiting for us in that room, it clutched at me the moment we entered it. Mai's face, when she saw the place, told me what she thought of it.

'It's only for a short while,' Shyam said. 'I'm hoping to get a big banner movie. I think this time it will work out. And then, the sky is the limit. We'll get a house wherever you want.' Once, trying to shake me out of my bad mood, he said, 'We have all our lives before us, Manju.' Yes, he said that—'We have all our lives before us.'

But everything went wrong for us in that room. Anand was never well and I blamed the room for it. The sink was so dirty I could never scrub it clean, the toilet stank and the bathroom seemed to have clammy fungal fingers growing all over it. All the accumulated misery of coping with a never-well baby in that small bleak room spilt over in the nights when Shyam came home. I knew our voices could be heard beyond the wall, as our landlady never failed to let me know in the mornings. A skinny woman bursting with an energy which she used to push furniture about all day, she never seemed to sleep. However late Shyam came home, she would announce the next day, 'I heard you quarrelling at night. We used to do the same thing, we used to quarrel the whole night.' She said it triumphantly, as if it was something to be proud of.

Anand was not well, he cried all night, which made Shyam irritable. 'I need my sleep,' he said. I was full of anger and bitterness. When I think of it now, I am surprised how little of it seeped into my baby, as if the sweetness of his conception allowed no room for ugliness. 'I need my sleep,' Shyam said, making it my fault, talking as if Anand was not his baby.

'Let's get out of here,' I urged him, blaming the room for everything.

'I don't have the money. The woman won't give us our deposit back until a year is over. I've signed the lease for a year.'

'You've changed,' he said once. 'I never knew you were so money-minded, I never thought you were such a bourgeois. You were not like this!'

'I didn't have a baby then. Don't you understand, I want nothing for me, it's for Anand.'

But he didn't understand, or rather, he refused to understand. He seemed to have closed himself against me. Though I didn't know it then, the film on which he had pinned his hopes had been finally abandoned, and the other one he had taken on had flopped. There was nothing else in the offing. He was doing some piecemeal work which kept him busy, but gave him no pleasure; in fact, it was the kind of work he hated. I knew none of this then. Closeted in one small room though we were, we seemed to be living on two different continents. In bed, we lay close, but without touching. It was like the game of pebbles I'd played as a girl, a game in which, if two pebbles touched, you were out. And so, you were given the grace of a tiny gap between pebbles, 'an ant's path' as we called it. Yes, Shyam and I too were given the grace of an 'ant's path'; nevertheless, our game was coming to an end.

For the first time, I saw Shyam's temper. I'd had a glimpse of it in Ocean Vista when he had had an altercation, a rather frightening one, with a man during a party. The man had been drunk, but Shyam was not, he rarely drank and never to excess. I knew the fight had been over me, that Shyam had reacted fiercely to something—fairly innocuous I thought, when I heard it—which the man had said about me. I'd been pleased then, proprietorial about his anger; the anger was for *me*, it was me he was protecting. Now the anger was turned *against* me. One night it suddenly flared into a frightening blaze, then died down just as quickly. He turned away from me, refusing to speak, refusing to respond to my words. 'Leave me alone,' he said, his voice exhausted. If I'd been older and wiser, I would have done just that. But I was not. Anand was having diarrhoea, he had been crying all day. And Shyam had just told me he had given up the work he hated. 'I can't do it,' he said. 'I'll get something else.' When I went on and on, he said, 'Leave me alone.' But I couldn't and he finally got up and walked out of the room.

He didn't return all night. I sat up, terrified for Anand who, I could see, was getting worse. The diarrhoea wouldn't stop, his face had fallen in and his skin was getting dry and parched, making him look like an old man. The moment I heard people stirring, I took a taxi and went home. We admitted Anand to Baba's hospital. I was still there, not having moved from Anand's side, when Shyam arrived. I didn't look at him and he didn't speak either. He stayed until Anand was better. I went back with Baba when Anand was discharged. I said nothing to Shyam, but I knew I was not going back to that room. Shyam too tacitly accepted it, for he didn't speak about my returning there, either. We stopped quarrelling after that, but there was a huge space between us. It was like I had gone back to being Baba and Mai's daughter. I had moved into Baba and Mai's room now, sharing it with Mai while Baba slept on the sofa and Malu slept by herself in her room. It was more peaceful. Anand was better, he was putting on weight. I was still frightened for him, but knowing now that he had a milk allergy, I was learning to cope. When Shyam came to see us, I no longer questioned him about getting a house for us. It was a temporary truce, the two of us behind our sandbags still, but with our weapons put away. In fact, we had achieved some kind of an equilibrium, balanced, if a little precariously—so precariously that, with just a little touch of a finger, everything came toppling down.

And I lost Shyam. He came more and more infrequently, he spoke less and less of the future, of *our* future, he said nothing about a search for a home. I didn't see, I didn't understand that he was trying to tell me that time was running out for us. I still remember the day he pulled me close in a desperate grip, his face devoid of love, affection, tenderness, even desire; nothing there, only desperation. 'Shyam,' I said and he let go of me, he stepped back and said, 'I'll ring you.' And he went away. And I saw nothing.

'Ghodi', Mai called me. Yes, I was like a horse with its blinkers on, an animal with a tunnel vision.

And I'm still the same. Blind to Raja, blind to his feelings. Unable to see the reality, the strength of his feelings for me. Taking him lightly, all that he said on the verge of being a joke, if not entirely one. I still saw him as my childhood companion. I thought he didn't care, not enough in any case, to be hurt by me. I thought we could go on as we'd done before, that our spats and disagreements would be as easily resolved as they had been when we were children. I thought Raja would bounce back easily, unhurt, unscathed. But I should have known that he could be pushed to a point and no further. Today I saw his anger and grief. The anger of the rejected male, the grief of the lover. And I saw the truth which came out into the open on my wedding day, the truth I was unable to see then, blinded as I was by my feelings for Shyam. Raja had been sent out by Gayatri to get the garlands which they had forgotten. He took a long time returning. Gayatri and Kamala, anxious that the auspicious time was running out, finally decided we would not wait any longer, that we would complete the formalities. Shyam and I had just signed the register when Gayatri exclaimed, 'Ah! There he is! You're just in time, Raja. Bring the garlands here.'

I looked up then and saw him in the doorway, the basket of garlands in his hand, his face blank and exhausted. Panic on it too, the look of a man who's just realized he's lost something. At that moment, I, who had just become Shyam's wife, who'd finally got there, where I wanted to be, saw nothing. But I can see it now, the anguish of loss in his eyes. It was there, the truth of his feelings which I saw again today, the same suffering, the same anguish. Raja is fine, Raja is invulnerable, I had thought. Always funning, never serious, not to be taken seriously. Blind, wholly blind. I've been like a tourist in a strange country, unable to read the signs because I don't know the language, unable to make sense of what I'm seeing, because I know nothing of how people behave in that place.

I ring Raja the next day. His voice is flat, incurious, unemotional. I've never heard this voice before, it's like listening to a stranger. It's Saturday tomorrow, I remind him. Can I come, or is he busy?

There is a pause. Then he says, 'I'm going out, actually.'

'That's okay,' I reply and put down the phone.

My heart is beating fast, my mind a whirling maelstrom of thoughts. It can't be forgotten, how did I expect he would forget? I made a mistake, I should have stayed away from Raja, I should never have got close to him. Take care, they say when parting. Take care. As if life is a perilous enterprise. But they're right, it is a perilous enterprise, this living. I learnt the truth of this when I lost Shyam. I knew then the dangers that lie in wait for us, I learnt that our very feelings can turn into lethal weapons that can hurt and make us bleed, sometimes even fatally. No more, I'd sworn that day on the beach, no more. But there were the children. And then Mai died. No, it never ends, you can never escape. Why did I not stay away from Raja? And Raja too—why didn't anyone tell him to take care?

The phone rings. I hesitate, then pick it up. It is Raja. He speaks as if I hadn't disconnected. 'I'm visiting a site tomorrow. I'll be staying with a friend. Would you like to come? We'll be back on Sunday evening.'

'I don't ...'

'Don't worry, it's not what you think. You'll be on your own. I'm going to be busy.'

'All right.'

'I'll pick you up at seven.'

'I'll be ready.'

Even as children, Raja and I came together after a quarrel as if nothing had happened; neither of us referred to our disagreement. Is that going to be possible now? No, too much has been said for that, we can't forget the things that have been said. Nevertheless, the invitation means something, I know that.

There are no sounds. Neither his footsteps on the stairs, nor any pacing above me. Yet, I know he is there. In the afternoon I hear the motorbike starting, but by the time I reach the door, he's gone. It's late when he returns. I'm waiting for him. He can't see me, I haven't switched on the outside light. So, when I call out his name, he's taken unawares. I see the startled movement of his body, then the sudden stillness.

'I'm going out of town,' I tell him. 'Just for a night. I'll be back on Sunday. I want you to go, I want you to be out of the house before I return.'

He does not move, does not even raise his head to look at me.

'It's for you,' I say gently. 'It's for your sake. You know what I mean, you know why I'm saying this.'

Now he looks at me, nods and goes up without a word.

'Raman,' I call out after him, 'Raman.'

But he does not respond. It was easy, yes, how easy it was! Like preparing to lift a heavy bucket and finding it empty, instead. All the preparatory effort of the body wasted. Nevertheless, I bolt the doors and windows carefully before going to bed.

He won't hurt me, he never will.

How do I know?

His face, his eyes, his voice ...

But he's conveyed to the Voice what I told him about selling the house. He's in it.

That could be a coincidence.

Coincidence? How absurd can you get? Why can't you accept

that he's a criminal, that he was here for a purpose?

But it's I who have hurt him, I who have used him.

Is that why he told them?

I don't know, I can't understand, I will never understand. I don't want to think of it, or of him any more. Fear and guilt chase each other in my mind for a long time. I'm just dropping off to sleep when the phone rings. I pick it up cautiously. It's Sachi.

'Call me back,' she says as usual and puts down the phone.

I dial her hostel number and she tells me she's coming home in about a fortnight. I hesitate. She zooms in on my hesitation with unerring accuracy and asks accusingly, 'Is it a problem? My coming, I mean.'

'Of course not.'

I hope Raman is out of the house by then, I hope there is no ugly aftermath. I don't want her to meet him. But I can't say these things to Sachi. I say, instead, that of course I want her to come. And then, before I put the phone down, I tell her I'm going out for the weekend. 'Tell Anand I won't be here. I don't want him to worry.'

'Where are you going?'

'I'm going with Raja to visit a friend of his.'

'Oh!' she says.

Such a doubtful 'Oh!' that I quickly add, 'It's a business trip. I'm just tagging along.'

Again she says, 'Oh.'

She's digesting the fact. Anand has told her something, he's made her promise to behave herself. He's the only one who can influence her; I never could. I didn't even try. Sometimes, remembering her difficult behaviour, I wonder whether she wanted me to impose my will on her, wanted me to behave like other mothers, something I found very hard to do.

'Have a good time,' she says finally, with such civility that I am tempted to congratulate her on her behaviour. But I shouldn't have told her about going out with Raja. Why did I?

Raja is at the gate exactly at seven and waits in the car for me.

I get in, conscious of Raman at the window watching us. I am sure Raja knows he is there too, but he starts the car without a word. This was how it always was; we never did greet each other, we moved into conversation easily without any introductory words. But this silence is different. Is it going to be like this from now on? I can't go on like this, it's impossible. I'm glad Sachi is coming. This can be our decision-taking time.

'Sachi is coming,' I tell Raja, determined to break the silence.

'Oh. When?'

'She's not very sure. In a week or two, she said.'

We don't speak after this. In any case, the grind and rumble of the trucks coming into the city makes conversation impossible. A little later we pass the newest and most garish temple in town, already a tourist spot in the few months since it's been built. I remember Raja speaking to me about it, telling me what an abomination it is. Now we go past it in silence. In a while we get off the highway and on to a mud road. I see newly planted saplings all along the road. Raja gives me no indication that we're nearing our destination, but suddenly there it is, a single low house set in the midst of nowhere, surrounded by knee-high saplings. In the background are the hills, with deep large gashes where the granite has been extracted. Raja introduces me to his friend Arun very briefly, saying 'Manjari'; nothing more, not 'cousin', nor 'friend' nor anything. The friend's casual acceptance makes me wonder whether Raja has spoken to him about me before. Arun takes me to a room and leaves me there. I wash and then lie on the bed, looking through the window at the low line of hills. I miss the sea, I think. I walked away from it after Shyam's death, but I miss it.

Coffee is waiting for me when I go out. The boy who brings it to me says the men have gone out, they'll be back in a while. I don't mind. I feel more peaceful on my own, without the tension of Raja's feelings to contend with. I wander through the house. There is a sense of familiarity about it and I realize it is because this house is Raja's creation; I can see Raja's creative mind in its simplicity and austerity. It reminds me somehow of Ocean Vista.

This house, without any wall or fence, merges into its surroundings the same way Ocean Vista became part of the sea and the beach. Raja never saw Ocean Vista, I remember now, he never visited me after my marriage. In fact, we scarcely met, except very rarely, in his parents' home. When we did, he seemed disinterested in me, full of his own affairs. And so casual that he seemed to have totally forgotten our childhood intimacy.

Arun and I carry on the conversation during lunch. He tells me something Raja himself has never mentioned to me, that Raja is going to build a house for himself here. 'I need a neighbour but I don't know when it will happen. Everything depends on Pavan,' Arun says, with a smile that tells me he knows of Raja's weakness for his son. If he's needling Raja, Raja takes no note of it. In fact, Raja has kept himself so completely out of the conversation, his face so morose and disinterested, that I have to wonder what Arun thinks of our relationship. Maybe Arun knows everything, maybe Raja has told him about me ... No, he couldn't have! But I am uneasily conscious of Raja's silence and then am angry with myself. Go to hell, I think, go to hell.

In the evening I sit in the garden where the boy gets me tea. I can see Raja and Arun at a distance. Arun turns around, sees me and waves. I wave back. Suddenly I am at peace. Perhaps this is Raja's gift to me, this peace, this tranquillity, his token of reconciliation. When they join me, we hear a sudden boom in the distance, an explosive sound. A quarry, I guess. I'm right. Arun tells me about his ongoing fight with the quarry owners, about the way they are destroying the forest and scaring wildlife away. He tells me about the brigand, the man who is really controlling the quarry owners. As long as they keep him happy, Arun says, they have nothing to worry about. If they don't pay him, anything can happen. Kidnapping, killing—anything! I'm reminded again of the thin veneer of civilization covering the murky world underneath. I think of Laxman and of the protection he had, of the protection he gave others.

We go indoors, driven in by the mosquitoes. Even inside we can hear insects banging against the mesh door and windows, vainly trying to get in. Arun gets us a drink. I move away from them and pick up a book of photographs of wildlife, some of the pictures taken by Arun, I notice. Raja never told me Arun was a photographer. Did he think it would bring back memories of Shyam? But does he remember what Shyam was? Did we speak about him at any time? I can't remember. I existed in a fugue in those days, Shyam and our love enveloping me in a nebulous mistiness. The reproductive instinct has a lot to answer for, I think. The things it makes us do, the way it makes us behave, turning us away from our usual selves. I wish Baba was here, we could have talked about this.

I go to bed early and fall asleep in an instant. And, inevitably, wake up too early. It's still dark, there's nothing I can do. I get a book from the book shelf in the room, I read for a while and fall asleep with the light on my face. And then I enter a dream, a watery dream. Strangely, it's not the sea, so much a part of my life, that I dream of, but a pool. Not a cheerful blue-tiled swimming pool, but a pool with dark unfathomable water and a rock jutting out in the middle. I'm sitting on the rock with someone, but I don't know who my companion is, not even whether it is a man or a woman; there is only a vague sense of someone with me. And then the person, whoever it is, slips silently into the pool. I can see the body enter the water, arrow straight, like a diver breaking the surface. But this body remains under water, completely submerged; there's no movement at all. I panic, I begin to cry out. I don't know what I'm saying, because no words emerge. Just the terrible thought: 'He's gone.' I wake up, thankful that it was only a dream, grateful to be out of that dark shadowy fear. But my face is wet with tears.

How long will I live this way? Making mistakes, hurting people. Making them suffer. How long will I go on this way? How long?

Light filters through the curtains, but the house is still and silent, heavy with the sleep of the two men. I long for a cup of tea, but I know that moving about in unfamiliar territory, I will blunder about and wake the sleepers. I get out of bed, wash, take a glass of water and go out. The breeze feels cool against my damp skin. The sunrise is on the other side of the house; here it is still shadowy, the sun completely blocked out. I sit sipping the water, listening to the birds. I have never heard so many birds before. It is like having a front seat at the opera, listening to various melodies, all of them merging into one harmonious song. I sit and think of Mai and of how she retreated into silence and how peaceful it must have been after all the noise and turmoil of the days before.

'Thank you, Raja,' I want to say when we're ready to leave. 'Thank you for giving me this.'

But he still finds it hard to look at me, he finds it difficult to speak to me. It is as if he can see the imprint of Raman's body on mine, as if he sees us together each time he looks at me. It's over, I want to say. It's over, Raja. 'Remember Mr Bones?' I want to ask him. That's all it was, nothing more. But Raja won't talk about it, I know. It's his problem, I tell myself, but I know it is not that simple. He drops me at the gate and, like before, stays in his seat while I collect my bag and get out. Then he drives off and I go into my empty, silent house.

Silent and empty—yes, the windows upstairs are closed, the motorbike parked in its place. The boy upstairs is not to be seen, Ratna says. She's concerned that I'm alone, she offers to stay the night. But I refuse. It is a bad night. I keep hearing footsteps, whispers and once, even Baba's voice. As if all the phantoms in my mind have come out to disturb me. What if someone breaks in, I think. I don't even have Raman to help. But it was he who … No, I don't believe that, I just don't. And then I think of Raja, of what has happened to us. Why does it hurt me so? For nearly two decades we had lost touch, we lived without being aware of each other. And now …

I get out of bed finally and sit reading Baba's book, *Bleak House*. It soothes me, my anxieties and fears recede. In a while I switch off the light and go back to bed.

I wait for two days before I go up and ring the bell. When no one answers—I hadn't expected anyone to—I let myself in with my duplicate key. There's a closed-in, musty smell inside. No sign that he has left. No sign, in fact, that he was here at all, except for a washed mug and a glass by the sink. Otherwise it is clean and bare, except for Abhishek's belongings. Even the bed has been stripped of its cover, the sheet folded and kept on the pillow. The silence is so complete, there's something eerie about it. There's no doubt about it—he's gone. I should ring up the inspector. But I'll wait for a week and then call. I will give him time.

In the event, the police come to me first. It's not Shivaprakash, but Rajshekhar, who's taken his place. He looks pleased with himself, he's brought me some good news, he says. They've arrested the Voice, he says, and goes on to tell me the man is wanted in a number of extortion cases. They didn't know he'd got into property deals as well, but now it seems he's involved in at least half a dozen cases of intimidation. They're sure he's the same man who was threatening me. This man, unlike Shivaprakash, is garrulous, happy to part with information; he even tells me that it was a tip-off that led them to their man.

And then I tell him about Raman, I tell him he's left. We'll get him, the man says, don't worry, we'll find him.

I hope you never do, I think. I hope you never get your hands on him.

baba's diary

21 Feb 1998

Last night, when I came to the end of *Bleak House*, I found myself strangely reluctant to put it away. Reading it for so long, I had become a part of that world, of the lives of the characters; it was hard to wrench myself away from them. I must say I've rarely had such pleasure from a book. Pleasure? No, that's not the right word. Satisfaction, then? Yes, that's it; it gave me great satisfaction, so much so that I've decided I will read no other book after this. I imagine it's the same feeling which made Jiji refuse to drink water after she'd eaten something she enjoyed hugely. 'I want to keep the taste of it in my mouth,' she would say. Yes, I want to keep the taste of this book in my mouth. No more books for me. There were times when I was afraid that I would not be able to complete the book. Yet, I never hurried. I am glad I didn't, that I read it at a leisurely pace. Each night, when I put the book away, a bookmark in place, I thought, 'I will go back to it tomorrow.' I think the anticipation gave me a kind of confidence that I would go on, that I would be alive to finish it. Now, when I have closed the book and put it away, Esther Summerson's words, about how time can suddenly shift into another scale, keep running in my mind. The words, so relevant to me at this moment, seem to echo my own thoughts: 'I had never known before how short life really is and into how small a space the mind could put it.'

This is exactly the way I feel when I look back; I have the same sense of compression, as if my entire life has been condensed into a small nugget. Then again, there is a feeling of distance which makes me think that all those things happened to someone else, a person as shadowy to me now as the presence of my dead mother was in my childhood years. Which is why I have often felt I was narrating things that happened to some other person, not to me. At the same time, the past seems more vivid and real than this present. Strangely contradictory things I can't put together, but that is how it is. And there is no one I can talk to of these things, no one with whom I can compare experiences. I often wish for BK's company, but would he enter into such a conversation? I've realized that humans don't want to talk of death. A kind of superstitious fear keeps us off the subject. In Vasu's last days, though we knew that the end was near, we scrupulously avoided the word 'death'. Even Vasu, who seemed to welcome death, said—and that too just once: 'My story is over.' A storyteller's way of describing death? Perhaps coming to the end of each story is like dying; in letting go of the world they have created, of the people who lived in it, storytellers do exactly what I'm doing now. But they have the chance of rebirth; to begin another story is to be reborn, to come back to another life, another world, different people. A rare chance, one given to few humans. For most of us, this chance never comes.

I am sitting in bed as I write this, putting off the moment when I have to declare that the day is over, that the night has begun. The nights are bad, I dread them. I've accepted the need for something to help me to sleep, but in spite of the sedation I wake up occasionally, my body arousing me with sharp nudges of pain. I woke up the other night to find Jiji by me, her face anxious, almost frightened, and I knew I must have cried out, the pain getting past my drug-induced sleep. The day will come when I will be forced to take morphine, but there is time for that; the pain is not yet unendurable. But I know it's not too far away, the time when the body will be only a source of pain and suffering. When that happens, I will be glad to be done with the body, to surrender it. 'A brief loan of the body'—where have I read the words? I can't remember. Memory has become unreliable; it frightens me the way things elude me, slipping away from me, preparing me, perhaps, for the final total blankness. I can't remember anything more than the words 'a brief loan'. How true they are! All my knowledge of the human body, of its capacities and functions, pales before this wisdom. Now that I've begun the process of repayment, I know how well the words fit. For I'm paying back, yes, I'm paying back through pain and suffering. *Enough!* Vasu said. Yes, enough. I'm eager to be free of this debt, eager to move on ... Move on? To what? I don't know, but surely things cannot end so completely? Does this mean that I believe in something after death? I don't know. But the cycle of living and dying seems so close to the cycle of sleeping and waking that it is impossible to imagine there will be no waking up after *this* sleep. And how odd it is that the closer I get to the final sleep, the more sleep evades me. When it does come, it is always disturbed, clotted with dreams.

I dreamt of my father last night. He was speaking to me, telling me something in his slow ponderous fashion while I, impatient, wanting to go elsewhere, chafed and longed for him to stop. The dream comes to me out of my past; I often felt this impatience when I was with him. It had troubled me after his death and I was full of guilt at not having spent enough time with him. But it passed. And now it returns when I am at the end of my life. I seem to have made no peace with my conscience. Was Vasu right? Do you have to atone through suffering? I find this hard to believe. I always thought that when the person you had wronged was dead, penitence, whatever form it took, was futile. Mere self-indulgence. Still, I have begun to see why people believe in God. We need to know that there is a power greater than us, which will set things right, give us forgiveness and grant us absolution.

Not to believe in God is to live in an orphaned universe. But it is impossible for me to have that faith, not even when I'm so close to death. I can't believe in Fate, either. Which leaves me with the hardest option: that there's no one but ourselves. We have to make the best of this life that has been given to us, we are our own creators. In which case, I have to admit that Vasu and I didn't manage well. We could have done better; the regret remains.

I don't want to torment myself with these thoughts now. Going through the day takes all my energy. Living has become a full-time occupation. My body is once again a major preoccupation. *A brief loan.* Why, of course, it was Dr Kapadia who had quoted these words in a lecture, words which, earnest student that I was, I had taken down and later used in my own lectures. Now, as if someone has switched on a light in my mind, I can see the page on which I'd written the words. I can read the words: 'A man possesses nothing certainly save a brief loan of his body. Yet the body of man is capable of much curious pleasure.'

Curious pleasure? Yes, indeed, such curious pleasures they seem to me now, when most of my life is over and behind me. Even a couple of years ago, the sight of a woman's body, of her hips, her breasts, could arouse me. There were times when I had flares of desire, flashes of pleasure from the beauty of a woman. Brief flares, sudden flashes, maybe, but they were there. Now there is nothing. No more curious pleasures. Only a longing for rest, to be in bed without pain, to have a good night's sleep, to wake up in the morning.

Yes, I have still not let go. I still look forward, when I go to bed, to waking up in the morning. Am I holding on because of Jiji, because of my concern for Jiji? It is true I worry about her, about the way she continues to wear blinkers. I hope that some day the pointlessness and emptiness of her life will force her into confronting her past. Only then will she be able to let go of it. Grief shackles you to the past, it pinions you to a moment of time, whereas happiness sets you free, it allows you to move on; Jiji has to learn to move on. It's so sentimental a thought that I'm ashamed to admit it even to myself, but I've begun to think of the possibility of her and Raja coming together. I am so accustomed to thinking of them as they were—boy and girl, companions, always together, brother and sister, almost—that the thought startled me when it first occurred to me. But I've seen Raja's eyes resting on her, I've seen his face when she comes into a room. Jiji is an attractive woman, though Raja's feelings, I can see, go beyond that. But Jiji is blind, she's caught up in the past, living in that time when she so briefly found happiness and so quickly lost it. I like to think that she will open her eyes and see what there is on Raja's face, that she will respond to him and …

Yes, I want a happy ending, like in Vasu's stories. I hope it will happen. Even now when there's nothing left for me, it amazes me that I still have hope.

'I like to think she will respond to him …'

Once again I have to think, to wonder: Baba, did you write these words knowing that I would read them? Hoping that after your death your words would matter to me, that they would take on a significance I could not ignore? Or were you merely thinking aloud?

Raja and I …? Childhood friends, yes, comrades yes. But Raja and I …? We don't agree on anything; we think differently about almost everything, we're always on opposite sides of the court, always in different camps. Yes, so many reasons for not marrying Raja. So many reasons for marrying him as well. But you don't marry someone *for* a reason, you marry because … because …? I married Shyam because he was Shyam. That's all.

Nevertheless, Raja and I …?

It's too late now, it's no use, it's all over. Raman has come between us. No, not Raman, it's my body which has played traitor. Raja will never forgive me, never.

good fairies—and bad

If Raja knows Raman has gone, he gives no sign of it. In fact, I've seen nothing of him since the day he dropped me home. I know it is not a closure of our relationship, I know that there is still a great deal of unfinished business between us which we will have to deal with some day. But this is not the time, nor can I take the initiative. In any case, I don't want to do anything. It feels good to be left alone, even if it's like being in limbo. There's nothing, no one in the world except me. Nothing to be afraid of, nothing to expect. Luckily, there is work. Raja's assistant, Mallika, has got me a manuscript for typing. A rush job, she says apologetically. It's a cookery book, a messy manuscript put together by amateurs, women who know nothing about writing and little about cooking. Such elaborate dishes! Why must they have so many ingredients, I mutter angrily to myself as I work. And such exotic ingredients at that! I think of Ba and Neeraben cooking the entire morning with ferocious concentration, knowing that the lunchboxes would be picked up on the dot of nine. I remember the perfect teamwork, the coordination between the two of them, the silence in which each performed her tasks. I remember how the women ate nothing until their work was done, just drank cups of tea to keep them going, tea which they allowed me to make when I was at home.

And now this—yes, this rich and idle women's pastime. I find the work tedious and boring. In any case, I don't want to do these things any more. Raja was right, this is not for me. I've accepted one more manuscript, a bureaucrat's biography, but after that, I swear to myself, no more. I can afford to choose my work. Shyam had called it a luxury. 'You can't afford to turn down any work,' I'd said to Shyam. 'Yes,' he'd retorted, 'I can't afford that luxury, but I'll still say no.'

'Bourgeois' he had called me, when I argued. 'Like your parents,' he said. 'Like your mother,' he had corrected himself. I had been angry, I'd thought him irresponsible, needlessly critical of my practical sense. But after he died, I understood what he had meant when I was looking after a paralytic woman whose husband drooled over me; I remembered his words 'like your parents' when I had to live in places Mai wouldn't have been seen dead in, did the kind of work that would have saddened Baba, who wanted the intellectual life for me. 'There!' I'd said to Shyam, as if I was continuing our argument after his death, 'there! I'm not a bourgeois any more.'

And now? I will do only what I'm comfortable with. Which is why I've decided that Raja's school is out. I haven't heard from them; if I do, if they offer me the job, I know I will refuse. Once having tasted freedom, I cannot get back into harness again. Yoga is the only activity that pleases me now. The harmony between mind and body, the sense of peace that I have after it—yes, it pleases me. But I need to learn more, I need to go to a proper yoga school for a while before I can work with Nirmala. She wants me to become a partner. 'I'll think about it,' I said. But I'm almost sure I'll agree.

And then Sachi arrives. I haven't heard from her since our last conversation. Now here she is, sitting on the doorstep when I return from the yoga class, her bag by her side. I am on the point of saying, 'Why didn't you tell me you were coming?' when she says, 'Hi.' Nothing more. Not even, as I'd expected, a complaint about having had to wait.

'You've lost weight.'

'I have?'

I couldn't have said anything to delight her more. She gets up and turns around, letting me glimpse her backside, compactly packed into her jeans. 'Everywhere?' she asks.

'Yes, everywhere.'

She follows me in, drops her bag and lets herself down into a chair with a loud sigh.

'I'm sorry, I'd gone for my yoga ...'

'I know. While I was waiting for you, *three* people told me that.' She emphasizes the number. 'No, four. There was a kid going to school ...'

'Mahesh.'

'You seem to have a lot of friends.'

I wonder whether I'm imagining the accusing undertone.

'I've been here for some time now.'

'You never made friends so easily.'

'These people knew Gayatri and Baba.'

She leaves it at that. I'm still a little wary, but she's surprisingly friendly after this. Anand has coached her, I think, Anand has told her to behave. I remember him saying to her after Baba's death, 'Stop harassing Ma. She's just lost her father.'

'So what! I lost my father too.'

'Years ago. And Ma doesn't have a mother either.'

'An orphan, huh!' Sachi had sneered, but she had softened. 'Poor orphan', I could see her thinking each time she was on the point of starting an argument. I wonder what the cause of her forbearance and compassion is this time. When she starts questioning me about the break-ins, I have my answer. It's over, I tell her. They've got the man who was behind it and the one who had broken in as well. I don't speak of Raman, it's she who brings him into the conversation. He's left, I tell her, there's no one living in the rooms right now.

I hadn't expected Sachi to take any interest in my life, but she is curious, peering into all my activities. I think of her as a child, strutting around, hands in pockets, curious, bold, wanting to know the 'why' and 'what' of everything, filling up perhaps, the huge empty space in her life with these useless bits of information. Now she reads the recipes and laughs with me over them. She comes with me for yoga, sits with the children at the back and chants '*Om sahanavavatu sahanoubhunaktu ...*' with them, mouthing the words as if she is familiar with them, winking at me when she sees me looking at her in amazement. She falls asleep during the *shavasana* and wakes up, startled, to the laughter of the children. Quite unabashed, she grins back at them, smoothing her rumpled mop of hair.

'Can I go up and have a look at the rooms?' she asks me now.

I am suddenly apprehensive. What if there's something that will give me away, what if I have left evidence of what happened there? But I can't tell her this; I can't evade her, either. She goes up with Ratna. I hear them opening doors and windows, I hear their voices, the two of them communicating in a queer jumble of languages, laughing at themselves. I think of her chatting with Nirmala, with Nirmala's niece, so easy with people. Like I used to be, once upon a time, making myself at home in the neighbours' houses in spite of Mai's disapproval. The house seems different, as if Sachi is an exorcist driving out the ghosts, banishing the devils. I suddenly think of her question, 'Why did Baba give the house to me?' And I think, whatever his motive was, he's done the right thing. He's made it possible for me, for us, to move on, to go beyond what happened.

Sachi comes down, her head full of ideas and plans. She's taking her ownership seriously, plunging into it with enthusiasm. I know what we'll do when Abhishek leaves, she says. We'll rent out the ground floor, we'll build an extra room, a kitchen and bathroom on the first floor and keep it for ourselves. Raja can do the construction for us. 'What do you think, Ma?'

This is not the first time she has mentioned Raja; he's come into her conversation often since she came. I'm certain Anand has spoken to her of Raja, of our companionship. Perhaps he's told her he approves and so should she. I have a feeling she's prepared herself not to be hostile, to try and be friendly. But

Raja has not turned up since she arrived, nor have I spoken of him. Her earlier wary references to Raja have given way to an open curiosity. Now, as if sensing that there is no danger, she is suddenly eager to see him. I've stalled her by saying that he's out of town, adding 'I think so' in the interests of truth. But the truth is, I don't know. Sachi, not satisfied with my vague replies, rings him herself, saying she wants to discuss the renovation with him.

'He's right here,' she announces triumphantly. He's coming in the evening, he's taking us out somewhere, she says. She doesn't understand why I am not getting ready, she gets agitated when it's past the time Raja had said he would come. I say nothing, but I am angry. He won't come, he never meant to come. How could he do this to her! He could have invited her home, he could have taken her out without me, he didn't have to deceive her like this! And then I get a call. It's from Mallika. Raja has had an accident. Nothing serious, she adds quickly. He was getting into the car and had one leg still outside, when Rashid started the car. His leg is fractured, he's in hospital. Venkat is with him, it was he who asked her to call me. Will I come?

Sachi takes charge of Kamala from the moment she comes, unconsciously doing Raja the best service she can by keeping Kamala away from him. BK would have done better to have come himself, but I imagine that Kamala's tears and her continual expression of fears and anxieties about Raja compelled him to let her go instead. She irritates Raja enormously. In fact, his normal good nature and tolerance seem to have vanished, leaving behind a fretful, irritable man. Even Pavan, who has rushed home, gets the rough edge of his tongue. Why did he have to come? What does he think he's doing, coming away just before his exams? He is not satisfied until Pavan leaves, which he does with reluctance, charging me to be with his father after Kamala goes, making me promise to call him if needed.

I stay away when Raja comes home from the hospital, giving the excuse of work. I visit him only the day before Kamala is to return home. She is tearful, insisting she can't leave Raja alone in the house. 'Why don't you stay with Raja until his father comes, Jiji?' she asks me.

'There's no need, Amma, I can manage. I have enough people around me all day. Too many, really.'

But it's family Kamala wants. 'Please, Jiji. Until his father comes,' she pleads. 'If Sachi and you are here, I can go with an easy mind.'

I know Raja does not want me, but there's no way he can oppose his mother, not unless he tells her the truth. And Sachi, unconscious of all the complicated feelings between Raja and me, blithely assures Kamala we'll be there. 'Don't worry, you just don't worry,' she says.

In the evening, when I watch Sachi teach Raja to play Scrabble, telling him the rules, seeing how much at home she's made herself here, I ask myself: has she changed, or is it I who have begun to see her as she really is? Remembering her comforting a guilty, inconsolable Rashid, thinking of how she took charge of Kamala, I wonder: what if I hadn't cut myself off from Baba and Mai? What if I had given her a family? But it's no use thinking of what could have happened. I decided to give up this kind of thinking long back. It's too full of torments. There's always a fork in a road, there's always a choice we have to make. It's no use going back, agonizing over the choice we made, imagining what would have happened if we'd taken the other road. It's like thinking: what if I'd defied Mai and gone back to Shyam? Would we have lived like other people, brought up our children, achieved happiness, success, whatever it is? But I never let the thought enter my mind. Now, looking at Sachi sitting cross-legged on the sofa, ensconced among the cushions like a kitten, playing with Raja, laughing at his mistakes, I think—she needs people, she likes to be of use, she wants to be needed. Perhaps I wronged Sachi, perhaps I wronged both my children by making myself invulnerable, by being self-sufficient. I should have shown them the chinks in my armour, I should have revealed my need for them.

If Sachi is comfortable here, I am not. Raja was right, he has enough people to manage, there's nothing for me to do. His cook, the Maami who's been with him for years, manages the kitchen with a kind of chaotic inefficiency; I know she will resent my interference. All I can do is to keep out of Raja's way as much as possible, leaving him to Sachi. And I go home every afternoon, to check the mail, see that the house is in order and give Ratna a chance to sweep and swab.

'Come back soon, Ma,' Sachi warns me the day she's going for a movie with Mallika. 'I've got to leave by four.'

'Take your time,' Raja tells me out of her hearing. 'I'm not going to drop dead if I'm alone for a few hours.'

I see an envelope in the mail box when I get home. A thick envelope, not addressed, no stamp, either. Delivered by hand, obviously. I open it curiously and a key ring with two keys falls out of it. I look at it blankly for a moment, then it hits me—these are the keys to the rooms upstairs. Raman's keys, which he had taken away when he left. So he was here! And he's all right, he's telling me he's all right. Thank god he's all right. It's over now, it's really over.

Over? No, it's not entirely over. It still lies between me and Raja, a ghost that will continue to haunt us all our lives. And having seen Sachi with Raja, I know I can't afford to let him go, I can't do this to Sachi. To myself, either. I can't go on shedding people, it's time to stop that. I must talk to Raja.

He's sleeping when I get back. Sachi has already left, so has Maami; there's no one in the house. I sit in Raja's room by the window which overlooks Rukku's walled garden. I can see the squirrels running up and down the branches of the pomegranate tree, baulked of their chance to get at the fruits which have been tied in plastic bags. There was a pond in the centre, Raja had told me once—Rukku's idea, I imagine—which he closed up, he said, because of the mosquitoes.

I hear Raja stirring. He looks at me and asks groggily, 'What's the time?'

'Just after four.'

'Sachi's gone?'

'Yes. Want some tea?'

'You didn't have to sit with me.'

'It's pleasant here. Cool. Want some tea?'

'Yes.'

When I get back, I notice that he's had a wash. He must have hoisted himself off the bed, on to his chair, to the bathroom and back. I don't rebuke him, I don't tell him he could have waited for me to help him. I give him his tea and we drink in silence. When I'm taking the cups away, he says, 'You can do what you want. I'm okay. Just give me that book. And the remote.'

I come back, nevertheless, after washing the cups and putting them away.

'I told you I'm okay,' he says, not taking his eyes off the screen. When I don't move, he exclaims irritably, 'Go, go, don't hover, I don't like it.' And then, 'I'm sorry, I don't like feeling dependent.'

'Raja ...'

'Okay, come and sit down, but don't hover like that.'

I sit on the chair by the bed. 'Putting up with my tantrums because I'm a sick man?' he asks. When I say nothing, he switches off the TV, sighs loudly and says, 'Right, Jiji, what is it? What do you want?'

'Nothing. Only to talk to you.'

'What's there to talk about?' I don't reply. He stares at me for a moment, then says, 'Come and lie down.'

I hesitate for a moment, then lie down by his side, the two of us as awkward as a newly married couple who've not met before this day. Our bodies are so close I can feel the warmth of his, I can smell its already familiar odour. I think of how Baba and I, votaries of the body, both of us, had eschewed touch so completely that even after Shyam's death, we had refrained from all those almost involuntary comforting gestures of hugging and holding. And of how Shyam and I had recklessly plundered the lavish riches of touching and caressing. Yet, at the end, when we lay together on a narrow bed, there seemed to be an immense distance between us. I think of Shyam getting up and walking away from me ...

Suddenly I sit up. Raja has a faint smile in his eyes, his lips twitch as if he's seeing the absurdity of the situation.

'Jiji, I think you'd better go home. It's no good your staying here. It's difficult for both of us.'

'I have to talk to you.'

'No, there's nothing to talk about. I don't want to hear anything.'

'It's not about Raman. That's over. I'm not going to talk about it. It's—it's about all those things you said to me. You have to listen to me.'

If I ever thought of speaking of the past, I thought I would be talking to Sachi. For some reason, I've had this feeling of owing Sachi something, of having to tell her about the things I've kept so carefully secreted within me. I've seen myself hacking my way through a forest, cutting down trees, clearing a path, finally getting to the point where I could stand and say, 'Look, there it is, there is your past.' But these journeys have always been imaginary. It's never been possible to speak, it's never been the right time. Now it is Raja I'm speaking to, and it should be easier. But it's not, it's just as difficult, there's the same sense of facing an exhausting ordeal. I thought the wound had healed, but each word I speak seems to pick at the scab, exposing some more of the raw, unhealed grey-white flesh; tiny drops of blood spring up even as I look. I feel myself drawing back from beginning, for to speak is to re-enter that world of grief and terror, to be back in those rooms in which the three of us, mother and daughters, had been closeted in a fearful, almost claustrophobic closeness, locked into a struggle that ended only with death. And when I begin to speak, I seem to be accompanied by sounds only I can hear: Malu's frightened cries, Malu mewing like a frightened animal, an animal in pain, Mai's soft murmurs going on and on, her shushing soothing words.

How much does Raja know of this story? I have never asked him, nor do I ask him now, for if I speak at all, I have to speak as if he knows nothing. And so I go back, beyond those terrible days, back to the time when Anand and I were in Baba and Mai's house. A time when I was content to be home, feeling secure, knowing that Anand would be all right as long as we were with Baba and Mai. I had stopped harassing Shyam for a home of our own. In fact, we had stopped speaking of it. So many things lay between us that we did not speak of. I knew he had to go out often on location, but I didn't ask him which film he was working on. There was plenty of time to talk, a whole future lay ahead, in which we would be together. So I thought.

But this is not my story, it is Malu's story I'm telling Raja. And so I speak of Malu and her increasingly odd behaviour. When she came back home for good, she was silent and uncommunicative. We thought she had to get adjusted to being home again. We tried to understand her sense of displacement. She had taken it for granted that she would be living with Bharat and Medha for as long as *she* wanted. And then she had to leave them, not because *she* wanted to, but because it was no longer convenient for Medha to have her there. Knowing Malu, I can imagine the hurt. Which is why we put up with her moodiness, her silences. After Anand's birth I had to cope with her hostility as well, a hostility that seemed inexplicable to me. 'It's her exams,' Mai tried to explain. 'You know how tense she is before her exams.'

It was not that; it was clear that she couldn't bear not being the focus of Mai's attention, clear too that she didn't like Shyam, that she couldn't bear to see us together. I'd never had such thoughts about Malu earlier, but her unreasonable hostility seemed to have released feelings I had not realized lay dormant within me. And I was right. When I came home after Anand's illness, the exams could no longer be an excuse, for they were over, but Malu had become increasingly odd. She burst into tears for no reason, sobbing as if she was bringing up her very soul. Crying jags that went on and on. Baba, knowing that this was something that had to be treated, suggested going to the same psychiatrist who had treated her earlier. But Malu rejected the idea of seeing a doctor with such frenzied desperation that Mai wouldn't let Baba even speak of it. For Mai, once again it was all Malu, she could see nothing but Malu. Anand, recovered now, had taken second place. She confessed her helplessness to me once, something she would never admit to Baba, for if she did, he would insist on her forcing Malu to see the doctor. I think of Mai, Anand in her lap, saying, 'I don't know what to do. I don't know what's wrong with her.'

It was I who guessed what the matter was. I had always been able to fathom Malu's feelings better than Baba or Mai, but this time her body was the problem and it was her body that gave me the clue. I had just had my periods and I remembered with idle amusement our code word for this which Malu and I used boldly in public, knowing no one would understand what we were saying: '*Rajasvala asmi*'. We got the phrase from Mai and Gayatri. I'd heard Gayatri telling Mai about one of her classmates who had been so stupid that when the phrase came up in their Sanskrit class, and the teacher hurried past it, she pestered him to tell her what it meant.

'Imagine asking a man that! We didn't know where to look.'

'But what does it mean?' I asked, butting into the conversation.

'Jiji! This is not for you,' Mai said sternly.

I got it out of Gayatri though, and when I heard it meant 'having my periods', I wondered why Mai couldn't have told me. What a fuss! I told Malu the phrase and from then on *rajasvala asmi* became a secret code by which we announced to each other what had happened. And then I thought of how we had stopped saying it to each other, of how we never communicated. And suddenly it struck me—Malu hadn't had her periods for the last … how many months? How could we have been so blind, how could I have been so stupid, I, who'd been *there*, who had been through it so recently. How was it I had missed the changes in Malu's body?

I told Mai my suspicions. Mai was angry, so angry that I thought she would strike me. Her lips became a thin straight line, her eyes were stony and glaring. She went into Malu's room, closing the door behind her. I could hear the murmur of their voices, Malu's rising, then trailing away into sobs. No, it was not Malu, it was Mai sobbing, such a strange sound, something I'd never heard before. She came out distraught, completely out of control. She took to her room and stayed in all evening, refusing to speak even to Baba. Baba and I found ourselves whispering fearfully in the hall, while the doors of the two rooms remained closed.

When Mai emerged from her room the next morning, she had erased all signs of weakness and grief. Bathed and dressed as usual, she had herself in control again. She was practical, having concocted a story which she must have plotted all night. She told us the roles we had to play in this script of hers. Her determination made it impossible for us to question her, to resist, or suggest any alternative plan. But before she set her plan in motion, she had to know who the man was. She had thought Malu would not reveal this, but she was mistaken. Malu confessed instantly, as if she had been waiting to be asked. Mai came out of the room within minutes, a dazed look on her face. 'Mai?' I asked timidly. And then she turned her anger on me. This was all my fault, I was the guilty person, I was the wrongdoer. I couldn't understand why she was blaming me until she told me what Malu had confessed. I don't know what I had expected. A boy in her class, or maybe a neighbour in Pune; after all, Medha had been so busy with Bharat after his heart attack, Malu could have done anything. But it was Shyam, Shyam who had made Malu pregnant. At first there was disbelief, then anger and finally humiliation. I felt betrayed, shamed. Nevertheless, I refused to believe the rest of what Malu had told Mai—that Shyam had raped her. I was steady in my disbelief; I did not believe it, I never would believe it, no, never.

I stop suddenly. It's hard to speak of these things even to Raja. But I nerve myself to go on; this is part of what I have to say to him, it's important that he knows the whole story.

Though I felt betrayed when I thought of Shyam and Malu together, I could not believe that he had forced himself on her, that he had slept with her against her will. I also knew why Malu had said it. I'd heard her give excuses when we were children, trying to deflect Mai's anger from herself, wanting to have Mai loving and cuddling her once again. It was the same thing now; I saw it so clearly, but Mai didn't. Perhaps it suited her not to see it. It suited her to make Shyam the villain.

I met Shyam a day or two later. I went out to meet him. Mai had warned me against his coming home. 'Khabardar,' she had said, using the word, the final ultimatum that had sent chills of fear up our spine when we were children. 'Khabardar if you bring him here.'

We met in a restaurant. I told him right away that Malu was pregnant. 'Christ,' he said. 'Jesus Christ!' His rare expletive, the one he'd picked up from Rodrigues. I knew then that I didn't have to ask him any more; it was a confession. I went on to Malu's charge that he had raped her.

'You believe that?'

'No.'

He tried to speak to me after that, he wanted to explain, but I didn't want to hear anything. To be with him, to listen to him, to understand him, to be reconciled to him, was to be a traitor to Mai and Malu. When I went back home, Mai told me she knew I'd gone to meet Shyam. Now she gave me the real ultimatum that invariably followed her 'khabardar'. I had the choice, she said. If I wanted Shyam, I was free to go back to him, but I would have to give up my family; they would cease to exist for me and I would cease to exist for them.

As if I need to absolve Mai, I break my narrative to tell Raja that I could have refused to make this choice. I could have gone back to Shyam and waited for time to heal the breach. But Shyam too had retreated from me. I didn't know where he was. He had moved out of the room we'd lived in; all that I had was a telephone number. I rang him over and over again from the Irani restaurant across the road, the same restaurant in which, many lifetimes ago, Baba and Mai had met before their marriage. The clatter in the restaurant, the cries of the waiters, the loud talk of the customers made it necessary for me to shout, to repeat Shyam's name desperately. 'He's not here,' the same voice said each time; a woman's voice. I had ugly, jealous thoughts about her, until one day she asked me who I was. In turn she told me that she was Shyam's friend Tarunbhai's wife, Neeraben. Yes, she said, Shyam was living with them, but he was out most of the time. Right now, he was on a shoot outside Bombay. I didn't believe her. I thought he was avoiding me, that he didn't want to have anything to do with me. I thought he had given me up. And there was Malu who was now beginning to show her pregnancy. So I went along with Mai, I became part of her plans which she put into effect right away. Laxman helped her; without his help Mai could never have managed. Laxman and Gayatri were the two people who were let into the secret. Such an unlikely pair of helpers, I say to Raja in wonder, two people I could never imagine together, but Mai needed them both. And they managed it between them, they did not let her down; they did not judge her, either, as I think Baba did. Sometimes, when I look back, I wonder why Mai was so frightened of people knowing. She had always been a loner, and yet she concocted this elaborate plan to keep people from knowing the truth.

Gayatri came and took Malu away when she left. People were told they had gone to Bangalore, when in reality they had moved to a flat in the suburbs—Laxman's flat, part of his illegally got property. Gayatri stayed with Malu until Mai and I could move in with her. Baba had applied for early retirement; the story was that he was building a house for us in Bangalore. I remember the farewell parties we had from neighbours and colleagues, I can still remember Mai's serenity as she went through the charade. I was amazed at the way in which she concealed her anxiety and fears. And then, leaving Baba to work out his notice, Mai and I left—I, to be with Shyam, Mai for Bangalore: so we said. Instead, we went to the flat where we would wait for Malu's baby to be born, the baby that would eventually become mine. Shyam's and mine. Yes, Mai's story needed Shyam too; he was one of the characters. And yet, she wanted him out of my life, she didn't want us to live together. I don't know how she could reconcile these things, I imagine she had not thought beyond the baby's birth. But the truth is, I have no idea how the story was supposed to go after the baby's birth. For things suddenly went out of control, the strings were jerked out of Mai's hands and the puppets began to dance to an unknown tune.

For a while after we began living together in that suburban flat, it was peaceful. Away from known people, from the need to pretend and lie, we felt easier. Yes, it was peaceful—but not normal. Malu would not talk to me. I tried to speak to her, but she would not let me. 'Go away,' she said to me. 'Go away.' Mai advised me to leave her alone. 'For some time,' she said. Mai was more gentle with me now, but she was with Malu all the time. We were like two separate units in one house: Anand and I, Mai and Malu. Shyam rang once, he must have got the number from Baba. I could not speak to him, I was conscious of Mai watching me, of Malu, hugely pregnant, in the other room. 'Afterwards,' I said. 'Afterwards.' And put down the phone, sobbing. Mai held me in a comforting hug, she sat with me until I was calmer. Shyam came to see me after that. He didn't say a word to Mai who opened the door, he came to me and said, 'I want to take Anand out.' He took him and left. I was frightened. What if he never brought him back? But he did. And when leaving, he said, 'It's up to you now, Manjari. (*Manjari*, not Jiji, not Manju. I was frightened.) I won't come here again. You have to come to me if you want me.' And he went away. I never heard from him after that, I never saw him again. But I asked Baba to let Shyam know when the baby was born. I guess he did that, I guess Shyam knew he had a daughter—a daughter in whose birth no one took any joy.

Once again I falter. These are things I've never brought up even in my own thoughts, these are memories I've refused to let emerge. Memories that have remained in images, memories I have no words for. When I try to speak, I have only the pictures: Malu holding out her hands, Malu screaming when I try to approach her, Malu snarling at me like a cornered animal, and Mai's face, pinched and suffering, Mai looking like the old woman she would one day become. And my one sight of the baby in the cradle, stolen when Malu was bathing, Mai having given me the signal. The baby, opening her eyes and smiling at me as if she was Malu herself. And then, Malu's body arched grotesquely, her face distorted ...

I banish the images and begin searching for words. Words are safer, words are easier, they don't hurt as badly as images do.

When Mai and Malu came back from the hospital with the baby, Malu went straight to her room. I wanted to see the baby, to hold her, but it soon became clear that Malu didn't want me to have anything to do with her. Mai was exhausted, but I could do nothing to help her; Malu would not let me near her or the baby. The one time I went into the room, she began to whimper like a frightened animal. When I tried to soothe her, saying, 'Malu, it's me, Jiji,' she began to scream, such loud uncontrollable screams that Mai ran in and pushed me out of the room saying, 'Go, go, don't come here, do you want to kill me, the two of you?' I sat outside, my head on my knees, my knees trembling, listening to Mai's soft voice, to Malu's cries, fainter now, to the baby's wails. I knew Mai's plan was going awry. 'One month,' Mai had said. In a month I was supposed to take the baby from Malu. Now Mai said, 'Maybe three months.' But I knew Malu would never let me have the baby, she would never give her up to me. Her scream of 'No, no' haunted me. Her face, her hands held out defensively against me, as if I was going to attack her, remained imprinted on my mind. No, Malu would never let me have her baby.

And then it happened. I was with Anand when I heard Malu call out for Mai. A moment later I heard my name. I could not believe it and stood still for a moment, until the cries became garbled, frightened sounds. I ran into Malu's room. She was sitting up and staring at the door, her eyes panic-stricken. 'Jiji,' she said, 'something is happening.' Her eyes were rolling, as if in search of something. 'Mai,' she screamed again, her hand gripping mine so hard that it hurt. And then her body became rigid, it began to arch, her back off the bed, her legs flailing, her face distorted into a scarcely human mask. 'Mai,' I screamed, 'Mai.' She came out of the bathroom in her petticoat, looked at Malu and went straight to the phone. Malu's body went on convulsing, writhing into such frightening contortions that I could not hold her down. By the time the ambulance came, Malu was unconscious. She died a few hours later in the hospital. Baba came and told me she was dead.

Raja, clearing his throat, speaks for the first time since I began. 'What happened?' When I don't reply, he goes on, 'We were told she died of meningitis.'

No, I said, that was part of Mai's story—Mai still going on with her story-telling, still weaving her intricate plot.

'What was it then?'

A post-natal complication, I tell him. A very rare complication.

Cerebral cortical venous thrombosis, Baba had said, giving me the full name as if I was a colleague, the doctor I should have been. And then he had turned away from me, confused.

Gayatri came to me after the funeral. She said I should keep the baby, that I should go back to Shyam. Mai had agreed to it, she said. I told her I had no contact with Shyam, I didn't know where he was. And in any case, I could not, I would not keep the baby. I knew I would always hear Malu's 'No, no', I would always see her frightened face, her hands held out, warding me off. Malu would always come between me and the baby. No, I could not keep her. They tried to persuade me. Even Mai came to me once, but she didn't stay long, we could scarcely look at each other. Finally Gayatri took the baby away. I stayed on in that flat because I didn't know what else to do. I didn't know what I wanted to do, where I would go. So we stayed among the ruins of Mai's plans, Anand and I, until Laxman came to me with the news of Shyam's death.

I stop here. The rest is not for Raja. But I have one more thing to say to him. I go back to his accusation that I did not want to see my dying mother. You are right, I tell him. I did not want to see Mai, the sandalwood fragrant mother I had loved so passionately as a child, the way he had told me she was, her leg amputated, her body stinking. For Raja, in his anger, had been brutal, sparing me nothing, giving me a graphic description of her suffering. But it was more than that: I did not want to see her because to see her was like going back to the scene of the crime, the crime both of us had committed. I often thought of us as murderers; I thought we had murdered both Malu and Shyam. Sometimes I thought of myself as the First Murderer and Mai as the Second Murderer, sometimes it was the other way round. No, I did not want to bring all that back. Yet, I knew I had to see her; it would be my atonement as well as my punishment. And so I went, not because Raja had shamed me into going, but because I knew I had to.

She was in a coma when I got to her. Gayatri spoke to her loudly, as if trying to reach Mai beyond that wall of unconsciousness. 'Vasu, Jiji has come. Vasu, Jiji is here. Vasu, wake up, Jiji is here.'

'Let her be,' I told Gayatri finally, unable to witness her desperation and distress, which no longer seemed to have anything to do with announcing my presence to Mai. It was like she was trying to bring Mai back from where she had gone, trying to make her retrace her steps and come back to us. Gayatri went away then, leaving me alone with Mai. I sat by her, I held her hand. I told her all the things I thought she wanted to hear from me, I made her the promise I knew she would have extracted from me. I told her I would take Sachi with me, that she would be my daughter and Anand's sister. I told her that she would never lack for love, that Shyam and Malu's daughter would have all the love that Malu herself had had. I spoke to her, too, about our estrangement and how I regretted it. I knew it was not possible that she could hear me. And yet, there was some hope that maybe she did; how do we know where a person is in that state of unconsciousness? Fanciful though the thought is, I think she heard me, for she let go almost immediately after that; she died within an hour of my reaching her bedside. I felt her hand become heavy and cold in mine, I saw her breath coming faster, grow more stertorous. At first I thought it was the sound of the fan, but the pauses between the breaths told me it was not the fan. Pauses that grew gradually longer, as if she was standing on the landing of a flight of stairs, deciding whether to go on. Each time the breathing seemed to stop, I thought of her words, 'dum dhar', her frequent reproof for me when I was impatient. Each time she paused, I found myself holding my breath, as if I was, once again, literally obeying that long-ago command of hers. And then a deep fluttering breath came out of her open mouth, a loud expulsion of air, a fluting sound, like air coming out of a glass pipe. Then, silence. Baba came in at that moment—or had he come earlier and I, travelling with my dying mother, had not noticed him? He held her wrist, felt her pulse and let the hand fall back heavily on the bed. 'She's gone,' he said loudly and angrily, 'she's gone.' He said the same thing to Gayatri, in exactly the same way, loudly and angrily.

I was the one who prepared her for her last journey. Gayatri tried to help me, but she couldn't, she turned away sobbing. I had no time for her, I told her to go away and went on with getting my mother ready. Someone came to help me—I don't know who. She came with a new sari Gayatri wanted us to wrap around Mai. We draped it around her tiny dismembered body. My heart felt heavy, like a rock in my chest, as we did these things. When we had done, when we put the flowers on her, I looked at her for the first time and saw how peaceful she looked. It was as if I'd brought peace back to her face.

'I gave up my anger then, Raja. You can't be angry with the dead, you know; you can't hate them, either. You can only grieve for them. But I could not do that, either. I had to give Baba and Gayatri time and space for grieving, I had to take care of the children.'

I have come to the end of my telling. There is no more to say to Raja; the rest is for Sachi. 'Tell her everything,' Raja had said to me—so long ago, it seems now. I don't know whether I will ever be able to speak to Sachi of these things; I don't know whether I need to tell her, either. But perhaps some day, some time, I will speak to her and Anand of Shyam. I've wronged them by not letting them know anything of him. Until now, it has not been possible for me to speak of him, but now that I've opened the book, now that I've revisited that time, I may be able to speak of him naturally and painlessly, the way a parent speaks to a child of a long-dead spouse—with affection and pride. But I can never talk of his death, I don't have the words for what happened then. When I go back to that time, there's just darkness and silence. And the rank smell of cigarettes. It was Laxman who sat smoking while he waited for Baba to come to me. Even after Baba cleared the overflowing ash tray and opened the windows, the smell lingered, it remained in the house all the days I stayed on there. The smell of cigarettes is still, for me, associated with death. To get a whiff of it is to go back to that time, to feel it again, that combination of despair and retching sickness.

No, I can't talk to my children about Shyam's death, but I can speak to them about him, about what he was, about our life together. And I can tell them about our family life: Baba, Mai, Malu and I. I can begin by saying, 'We were a happy family.' I want them to know that. But will Sachi listen? Stories of unclouded happiness are boring, they are dull. Happiness is a state of nothing happening. It's because of this that we have the wicked stepmother and the ogre, we have the bad fairy, the scorned uninvited guest gate-crashing the party with her lethal gift of curses. Only then does the story come alive, only then is there drama and suspense. We wait, our breath coming faster, our hearts beating a rapid tattoo, our hands clammy, thinking, 'What's going to happen now? What next?' This, in spite of the fact that we know that the wicked stepmother and the bad fairy won't have it all their own way. We know that there's still one good fairy to come—the damage control mechanism at work, goodness coming back into the arena to fight wickedness.

Sachi was the bad fairy in our story, bringing chaos and fear and finally death and disintegration into our lives; but wasn't she the good fairy as well? I think of her baby clothes which Gayatri packed for me when I was taking her away after Mai's death, clothes which Mai had stitched herself, Gayatri told me, the tears springing out of her eyes yet again. By hand, she added in awe. She didn't even use the machine, she said. I looked at the clothes when I went back. Tiny, exquisitely stitched, the stitches as even as Ajji's had been. Mai, who had never, as far as I could remember, held a needle and thread in her hand, Mai, who took even a button or hook to Ajji for stitching—she had done this. When I looked at the clothes, I thought, 'You were all right, Mai, yes, you came out of it.'

It was Sachi who helped her do that, Sachi who rolled back the darkness from Baba's and Mai's life and brought some kind of peace into their tortured lives. She changed our lives too, Anand's and mine, bursting into the small room we had closeted ourselves in, breaking into the intense closeness between us. With her loud angry cries for attention, with her clamour and her demands, she pulled Anand out of his silence, she made him talk, she made him laugh, she took away his frightening dependence on my moods. They became allies.

And I? I had entered a dark airless tunnel after Shyam's death, a space in which nothing could grow, nothing could survive. Worst of all was the feeling that I was set apart from humankind, that I no longer belonged to the world of ordinary people, ordinary living; each thing I did was a painful reminder of what had happened to us. I had lost the innocence which makes it possible to face each day with hope. Time is the greatest healer, they say. But for me, time was the enemy as well, taking me further and further away from Shyam, turning him into a memory, eventually making even the memories fade, so that finally I was left with nothing.

No, it was not time but Sachi who thrust me out of that dark tunnel into everyday, ordinary living. Back to normality. Not with angelic goodness, but with her noisy demands, her loud howls of protest, her cries of delight. Dealing with her, a child so unlike Anand, there was no way I could go back to that shadowy world I had inhabited after Shyam's death. Struggling with the small belligerent creature standing in front of me, legs apart, defying me, asking me a million questions, I was shaken out of deadness into arguments, impatience, exasperation, anger, often laughter. Sachi made these things possible; I can tell her this.

Suddenly I find the answer to her question, 'Why did Baba give me the house?' *This is why.* Not out of guilt, not as atonement, not as a statement against me, but because of what Sachi did for them. How strange that I never thought of this until now. Speaking to Raja, looking for the facts, for the words, I seem to have stumbled upon revelations. Yes, Baba, you were right. We need words; searching for words, I seem to have found a clue to Mai's anger, to Baba's silence. And yes, to Shyam's death as well. His suicide had seemed the final betrayal, his dying in the sea, the sea by which we had lived those days of perfect happiness, the worst treachery. But now I remember the night when he had walked out after one of our quarrels. When he came back, hours later, I asked him, 'Where did you go? How could you do this to me?' He said nothing. But later, when I stopped sobbing, he told me that he had walked the streets all those hours. 'I had to,' he said, 'I had to exhaust my body to control the devils in my mind.' I think it was the same thing that day. I think he went into the sea, not to kill himself, but to pit his strength against the sea, to exhaust himself, to control the devils in his mind. And then, he went too far in and had no strength to return, as the tide turned and carried him further and further away from land. I am sure this is what happened, I am sure he did not kill himself.

And there's Malu, Malu whose death left an aching emptiness inside me. Shyam's death devastated me, for Shyam was my lover, he was my companion. In losing him, I became a woman without a partner. But Malu was a part of me, she was connected to my very being, my soul. When she died, it was like losing something of my own self. I felt the way Mai must have done after they amputated her leg. Incomplete. Worse was the sense of betrayal, of having to live with her rejection, with her 'No, no' ringing in my ears. But now I see another Malu. In bringing back the past, I have gone back to the child, her soft fine hair confined in two tiny pigtails, her face gleeful and triumphant. Malu swinging her plaits, grinning at us, happy because she was now 'Jiji sarkhi'. Yes, that was all she wanted—to be like me. Jiji sarkhi.

the flowering

It's Sachi's last evening at home. She's ready to leave, her bags packed, the house already looking strange, denuded of her untidiness. We're going to Raja's house for dinner. It's BK's invitation rather than Raja's. BK has been a revelation to me; he seems to have recovered his old self in his son's house, the sad defeated man left behind in Bombay. Old self, yes, but with new and surprising manifestations—the way he's been able to relate to Sachi, for one thing. BK never had much to do with children, not even his own. Unlike Baba, he was uncomfortable and at his starchiest when he tried to communicate with us. He was not easy with women, either; I don't remember him ever speaking to Mai, except for an ocassional formal remark. And now Sachi and he have become friends. Yes, friends, I can't call it anything else. Sachi rarely has problems relating to people or drawing them out; what's surprising is that BK is just as easy with her as she is with him. Even more astonishing is the fact that BK—such a conservative man, the classic Brahmin (yes, in spite of his drinking and his meat-eating!) deeply imbued with the sanctity of education and degrees—supported her in her decision not to go on to college after completing her twelfth class exams. Wisely (or cunningly?), she sprang it on me in his presence. I guessed from his quick support of her that she had spoken to him earlier about it.

'I'm going into film making,' she announced. 'It makes sense to start as soon as I can.'

I tried to persuade her to complete her graduation. I was not very comfortable debating with her in BK's presence, BK who had been a witness to my own intractability when Baba had tried to argue me out of giving up my medical studies.

'Graduation? What for, Ma?' Sachi asked me bluntly.

Something to fall back on if things don't work out, I said, thinking of myself, of Sachi's own short-lived, fleeting obsessions. 'And that's a chancy world,' I added. 'You never know.'

'Not any more. There's TV—there are so many channels now, I can always find work. And if the worst comes to the worst, I'll find a rich man to support me.'

'Sachi!'

But BK laughed, saying, 'You can support a man any day, take it from me, you don't need to worry.'

I was so astonished by this that Sachi took advantage of my confusion to get me to agree.

'Let her go her way,' BK reassured me later. 'She knows what she's doing.'

BK's championship of Sachi and her pleasure in his company overcame all my niggling sense of uneasiness at what I'd committed myself to. But it's BK's relationship with Raja that pleases me the most. I remember the earlier acerbic, always critical BK, the sullen defiant Raja. Now the two men, father and son, are easier with each other, comfortable in each other's company. Remembering Baba's sadness at BK's problems with Raja, I find myself wishing that Baba could have seen this. Baba has been much in our thoughts and conversation since BK's arrival. BK visits me twice a day and sits with me for half an hour each time, timing himself to the second, almost; most of the conversation consists of his memories of Baba and their friendship. 'Badri and I' he begins and 'Badri and I' he goes on.

He's playing the host in his son's house today. He's planned this evening, he's been meticulous in his preparations, the table laid, the drinks ready. He takes me into the kitchen to show me what Maami has cooked for us. 'Is it okay?' he asks anxiously. 'Is it enough?' He won't let Sachi do anything. 'You're the chief guest,' he says. 'You just sit and relax.' He lets me help him serve the drinks, but even after we're settled, he keeps jumping up to make sure we have all we want. Sachi accepts his help with equanimity, but for me, to be waited on by BK is a strange and uncomfortable experience. BK is the one others waited on; what he wanted came to him without his asking for it. Finally—and only after Raja orders him to—he settles down, nursing his glass of whiskey the way I remembered him doing. He looks at me and smiles as if he's discerned my thoughts. 'This is better than what I could ever afford,' he says, raising his glass slightly. 'I don't get this pleasure very often.'

I wonder whether BK and Sachi have sensed that Raja and I prefer to avoid each other, whether they realize we are more comfortable being apart, for almost immediately we separate into two groups. Sachi begins a game of scrabble with Raja, her exclamations and Raja's comments forming the background to my conversation with BK.

'Alter ego,' Sachi calls out suddenly. 'Is that one word or two, Kaka?'

'Two.'

'There you are!'

'The oracle has spoken. If my father says two, two it is. I give up.'

'You knew it, you were just trying to pull a fast one.'

'But there's doppelgänger,' BK offers Raja, sorry perhaps that his verdict has gone against his son. 'That's one word.'

'It's not like that, Kaka,' Sachi explains kindly. 'We can only use the letters we have and there are only seven. So …'

'Can I try again, or have I lost my turn?' Raja asks.

'You're allowed to try again. But actually, you know, I like the word doppelgänger; it's such a nice word, isn't it? Sounds so round and happy and friendly. If I were to have another self, I'd like it to be a doppelgänger. Alter ego is thin and grim, it's a skeleton—like this.' She sucks in her cheeks and lets her arms drop stiffly by her sides.

'Mr Bones!' Raja and I exclaim simultaneously, and then look at each other, startled by our instant and simultaneous response.

'What?'

'Oh, that skeleton of Badri's,' BK says.

'But do you think,' Sachi goes on, addressing all of us, 'one can really have another self?'

Once again Raja and I give each other a quick glance, once again we're startled by the way we've responded together, as if we've rehearsed it. And then we look away, just as quickly. I hold on tightly to the arms of my chair as if I'm in danger of falling, warning myself, 'Take care, take care.'

The moment passes and they go back to the game. I go into the kitchen despite BK's protests—rather feeble now that he's comfortable with his drink—and begin heating up the food. Sachi joins me in a while.

'You're just like your mother,' BK calls out to Sachi when she's rushing in and out with plates and glasses.

I hold my breath. I'm aware of Raja's stillness.

'I am? How?'

'Rushing about. Jiji was exactly the same when she was a kid. Rushing about, banging into things …'

I'm ready to leave as soon as dinner is over but Sachi lingers, she seems reluctant to return home. I warn her that she has a journey ahead of her tomorrow.

'I can sleep in the train. Once the trains starts, I'll go to sleep on the top berth and wake up right in time for Bombay; I can always do that,' she boasts. I think of Malu who could sleep anywhere, any time, just like a kitten. I think of her sleeping even when the train was approaching Bangalore, all of us dressed and ready, only Malu still sleeping, her head on Mai's lap, clutching at her blanket, refusing to let Mai take it away from her.

BK seems just as unwilling to end the evening. After we've

cleared the table, he brings out a bottle of liqueur. 'I brought it for Raja,' he says. 'But let's all have it.'

He pours the rosy liquid carefully into tiny glasses, making a ritual of it. I think of him, connoisseur of good things, living the way he does now in his own home, and wonder why and how we lose control of our lives. Are we really so helpless? Even Baba seemed to concede human powerlessness. But I have to find my own answer.

'Can I give Sachi a tiny bit?' BK asks.

'Why not?'

'You don't have to ask my mother's permission,' Sachi protests. She takes a sip, coughs, splutters, makes a face and puts the glass down. 'Yuk, it's terrible. I can't drink this. Sorry, Kaka.'

I'm getting impatient. I can sense Raja's desire to have me leave—he has scarcely spoken a word to me the whole evening—but now it is Raja who delays us. We're at the door when he calls out to Sachi. Sachi goes in and screams, 'It's begun, come quick, it's begun.'

'It's the flower, it's started blooming,' Raja says when BK and I, puzzled and a little anxious, go into Raja's room from where Sachi had called out to us. It's thc Star of Bethlehem in Rukku's walled garden. The Brahma Kamal, BK calls it. Raja has been telling Sachi how close it was to its annual flowering, about the drama of the flowering. 'If you're lucky, you'll get to see it,' I had heard him telling her.

'Look,' she says now. 'I'm so lucky. I could have easily missed it.'

We look at the bud, one petal already a little uncurled. Yes, it's beginning. We can't go now until we've seen the flower bloom; even I know that. We sit in the narrow passage bordering the garden, Sachi and I on the ground, cushions under us, all of us intently watching the slow opening, the petals gradually unfolding, like the long slender fingers of a Bharat Natyam dancer doing a flower-opening mudra. A fragrance gently steals into the room, keeping pace with the unfolding. It's as if the flower, knowing how short its life is, needs to draw attention to itself and is nudging us. We watch the spectacle in utter silence, each one of us witnessing it separately in the secret spaces of our own minds. It's like we are unwilling to disturb the process, as if we're watching something as private and miraculous as the process of birth. The gradual unfolding seems to contain the drama of life itself. It's past midnight when the process is complete and the flower, both flamboyant and shy, it seems, of its new face, quivers a little.

'Look,' Raja whispers, 'look inside. There's the Cross.'

Sachi peers into the flower, draws in her breath, then claps her hands, a childlike gesture that releases the tension.

We part, knowing that we've shared an experience we will never forget. BK walks us back home. It is a dark night, but I have no fears. It's not just that BK and Sachi are with me, it's as if the terrors have gone back to where they belong, to their subterranean shelter. Before leaving, BK makes Sachi promise to visit him in Bombay. I hear the anxiety in his voice, I hear the warmth in hers when she says, 'Of course I will.' And I think, even if it's over between Raja and me, there's something salvaged from the ruins, something remains: Sachi has found a family.

baba's diary

Even if I didn't know it myself, I can guess from the faces around me that my end is near. I have not been able to get out of bed for nearly a week; I had to struggle to sit up in bed to write this. My body is giving up on me, but my mind is still clear, except that at times I have a sense of the world receding from me. Everything seems hazy and distant, days and nights get mixed up. When Jiji wakes me up in the morning, for a moment her face seems unfamiliar, like someone I knew once, long ago. Yes, it's not long now. I feel sorry for Jiji and Raja when they try to pretend that all is well, that I am all right. But I am also angry with them. Do they think I'm a fool, that I don't know what's happening? I'd always thought that when you come near the end, specially in an illness like mine, it would be easier to accept death, but I'm finding it harder. Anger surfaces more often. Why do I have to die, why must I leave this familiar world and go into the unknown? It's not that I want to live; certainly, I don't want to go on living the life I'm living now. I want to be done with it. And after seeing Anand and Sachi, I have the comfort of knowing that, even if *my* story is over, the story still goes on. Each life going back to its beginning, forming a loop, the loop snagging on to another loop, and so on and on in an endless chain. Yes, the story goes on.

What then? What am I afraid of? Death, of course. I'm afraid of the process of dying, of the moment of ceasing to be, I am anguished by the thought that I will no longer be a witness to the drama of life, torn away from all the things that I thought were *my* life. But we're all afraid of death, it's natural. What else is it then that troubles me? It's a sense of being incomplete, I think. So vague a feeling that I cannot understand it myself, yet it continues to nag at me. I spoke of this to Ramchandra Sir when he came to see me this morning. In response, he quoted a verse— a couplet from the *Isa Upanishad*:

Purnam adah, purnam idam, purnat purnam udachyate
Purnasya purnam aadaya purnam evavasisyate.

He explained the verse to me. It speaks of the wholeness of Brahman, he said, it asserts that creation cannot make a dent in that wholeness. Even while I listened to his patient exposition, my mind wandered. Words, only words, I thought. And then suddenly it occurred to me: why, *this* is God! We created God to embody the idea of a self that is complete in itself. This is the harmony that the astronomers of old dreamt of. To achieve this wholeness is the final stage of evolution, it is nirvana. But for us, who are only a part of that wholeness, it is unattainable. And yet, from the moment the umbilical cord is cut, we begin our search for the part of ourselves that will complete us, we look for that which will make us whole. It never happens, I know that now. The search is always doomed to failure. We are never complete, we will never be complete.

It makes no difference to me, anyway. I am at the end of everything. There is nothing left. Only to let go. That's all I have to do now—let go. Accept that it's over. No more ...

For the first time, Baba, man of habit as he called himself, didn't date his entry. I write a date now, the date of his death. He died on 30 March 1998. He died in his sleep. I am glad it was peaceful, glad that he let go without a struggle. He had hoped his cardiac problem would kill him before the cancer could get him. Perhaps it happened that way. We don't know. And it didn't matter. All I could think was: he is out of it, no more suffering, no more pain. And yet, the emptiness in my life at that moment when I found him dead ...

But Baba says the story goes on. An endless chain, he calls it. I hold on to the thought—it's not over, the story goes on ...

Eppur si muove ...

the right word

BK stayed until Raja's cast came off. It's been a fortnight since he left. I haven't heard from Raja after that. I'd promised BK I would keep in touch, but it isn't possible for me to go to his house, it's hard even to speak to him on the phone. Now, early in the morning, the phone rings, sending fears fluttering about me. Is it Sachi? Anand? Is something wrong? But it's Raja. Without addressing me, without even a 'hello', he says, 'Can you pick me up? I want to try out my leg in the park, but I'm not sure I can walk up to there.'

My first impulse is to crow, to say, 'You didn't want me to learn driving. And now, look!' But I crush the impulse in the very next second. We're no longer on terms which allow me to speak to him in this way.

'Sure. I'll be there in fifteen minutes.'

'Have Raja and you quarrelled?' BK had asked.

I'd hesitated and said, 'Yes, we have a problem.'

'You were such friends—always fighting, but always together. Now he's alone. I worry about him. I wish he hadn't sent Pavan away to boarding school.'

'It's good for Pavan. Raja spoils him abominably. He needs some discipline.'

'I know, but … I worry.'

'He's okay, Kaka, he has lots of friends.'

'Lots of friends, yes, but not one to whom he can open his heart. Like Badri and I—we were truly *jeevascha kanthascha* friends.' He brought out Gayatri's phrase for their friendship. 'Yes, we were lucky.'

'I know.'

'Has Raja said something to hurt you? He is rough sometimes, but you know him. He doesn't mean anything.'

'No, no, it's not that. I mean, I don't have any problem with him. It's he …' I pause and go on, 'He's not comfortable with what I am, or the way I live.'

'I see.'

BK is no fool, his swift look tells me he understands what I'm saying. 'Give him time, he'll learn to accept you as you are. You are family, after all; nothing can change that, neither of you can get away from that.'

Amazing that BK can say this despite what happened to his family, what happened to ours. But I guess you don't let go of an idea because it occasionally, or even often, fails.

Now I help Raja into the car and put his crutches in the back. We drive the short distance to the park in silence. When we get there, we go through the reverse process of getting him and his crutches out.

'You get on with your routine, I'll manage,' he says.

As I walk away, I hear voices greeting Raja, exclaiming over his crutches. When I return, he's sitting on a bench, so absorbed in his thoughts that he takes no notice of me. I let myself down by his side and sit in silence. There's a wintry feel to the morning, the air seemingly rarer, so that voices carry far. I can hear a group of men on a bench going on with their usual political arguments.

'It's nearly a year and a half since I came here,' I say.

Raja doesn't respond, he seems oblivious of my presence. Then he turns to me and speaks with a deliberateness which tells me that he's been thinking of how to say this.

'I'm going to Karwar next month.'

My silence is like a 'So?'

'I'm building a resort for a client. I'm going to see the site. It's by the sea.'

I'm still silent.

'Will you come with me?'

He looks me straight in the eyes, something he hasn't done for long. I see his anxiety give way to a twitch of amusement and it occurs to me that perhaps my astonishment makes me look comical. He goes on, 'Remember the last time I asked you to come with me to Arun's house? I said to you then—it's not what you think. This time I just want you to come with me.'

There's a flutter of panic within me. The sea—no, I can't go there!

'Well?' he asks, when I'm still silent.

'Give me some time,' I tell him, repeating BK's words.

'You've had enough time.' He speaks with asperity, with a touch of his old impatience. 'You said it yourself—it's been over a year.'

So he's crossed the hump, he's on the other side now. And I? I know we need to move on if we're not to stay mired in this impasse, this situation we've got ourselves into. As BK said, we *are* family, we can't get away from that, we will need to find some way to move on.

'Well?' Raja prods again.

'All right. But I'll pay for myself. I don't intend to be a Keep.'

'Right, we'll halve the petrol bills.' I look at him suspiciously. Is he treating this as a joke? No, his face is serious. 'I'm driving down,' he says, as if answering my doubts. 'And I believe the right word now is partner, not keep.' His face and voice are equally deadpan. 'But I don't like that word either. It's too temporary.'

'What's the right word then?'

'You tell me.'

Friend, family, comrade, partner, lover—I bring out all the words, consider the array and think: somewhere, between all these words, is the one that will define our relationship. (No, there's one word I've left out, the word that is Raja's choice— *husband*. But I can't think of it, no, not as yet.) The right word matters. I think of my grandfather speaking to Baba of his dead wife as 'your first mother'. Strange words to use for a wife. Yet, for him, perhaps, they were the right words. And for Raja and me? What is the right word for our relationship? And does a relationship have to be snagged on to a word? Raja would say it does. Yet, he has moved on—with an effort, I can imagine the effort—and gone past what happened between Raman and me.

'You know what I want?' Raja asks, after waiting in vain for my reply.

'Yes.'

Yes, if I'm undecided, Raja has made up his mind. And this time he has others on his side—his father, our sons. Whereas for me, there's only my reservation about Sachi, only the sense that she will not like it. And yes, the feeling inside me, the alarm that goes off, warning me, 'Take care, take care.' I remember my recklessness with Shyam and wonder—was there no warning then? What if I had listened to it? I would never have known Shyam, I would have missed the beauty and wonder of us together. It's different now. I'm twenty years older. And with two children, one of whom will—I can feel it in my bones— create trouble. I wonder whether I should warn him about my fear of disaster, of failure, of hurting each other.

As if he's read my mind, he adds quickly, 'I must warn you I believe in happy endings.'

'Like Mai's stories?'

'Did her stories end happily?'

'Yes, with people getting married and living happily ever after. As if!' The old childish negative slips out suddenly. 'As if!'

'You don't think marriage is a happy ending?'

'No!'

Knowing what happened to our parents' marriages, knowing how both ours ended so abruptly, leaving us bereft, how can you believe in a happy ending? How can you believe in the 'happily ever after' myth, I want to ask Raja. Perhaps his confidence comes out of the same thing that makes BK talk of families the way he does, the feeling that we've *got* to believe, that we can't let go of our faith. The same way we believed as children in the utter truth of good fairies, of valiant heroes and virtuous heroines. Faith. 'The adhesive,' Baba called it, 'that holds things together.'

I say none of these things. He waits a moment for me to go on, then says, 'Never mind.' And moves smoothly, with the ease and grace of a skater recovering his balance, into the details of the journey. Being Raja, he's planned it carefully. Two nights on the road, he says. We'll travel in easy stages. It's beautiful, specially through the ghats, he says. And when you come to the sea at the end of it—it's like magic!

Suddenly I feel the familiar choking excitement of starting on a journey. I remember our journeys to Bangalore. Raja and I sleeping on the upper berths, chatting across the aisle, the ghostliness of the dim blue night light. I remember Malu sharing my berth, fearfully reading the notice 'To stop train pull chain. Penalty for improper use Rs 50'. And Raja and I teasing her, threatening to pull the chain. But it was Malu who pulled the chain finally, Malu who got off the train. She paid the penalty; no, all of us did. Surely pay-off time should now be over?

I get out of the car when we reach his house, take his crutches out and open the door for him. He doesn't move, he seems to be wrapped in deep thought, the way he was earlier. Suddenly he asks me, 'Do you know why I married Rukku?'

'How would I know? I wasn't around then.'

'Exactly,' he says and taking the crutches from me, gets out of the car and walks towards the house.

I look at his receding back and even as I think that he's lost weight, the word 'alter ego' suddenly drops into my mind. Then I think of Sachi's words: 'doppelgänger is so round and happy and friendly'. Yes, doppelgänger is the right word for Raja, not 'alter ego'. Raja turns around when he gets to the door, sees me standing and waves impatiently, a backward flip of his hand, a gesture familiar to me from childhood which says, 'Go on, what are you waiting for?'

I laugh, start the car and wonder why the road looks hazy. It's me, my eyes are brimming over with sudden tears, like rain falling out of a cloudless sky, taking me by surprise. I wipe my eyes roughly and think: I was stupid! One word is not enough. No, there's no single word that will suffice.

'The search is doomed to failure.' Yes, Baba, you're right, we will never find what we are looking for, we will never get what we're seeking for in other humans. We will continue to be incomplete, ampersands all of us, each one of us. Yet, the search is what it's all about, don't you see, Baba, the search is the thing.